HOUSE OF DUSK

HOUSE OF DUSK

HOUSE
— OF —
DUSK

DEVA FAGAN

DAW BOOKS
New York

Copyright © 2025 by Deva Fagan

All rights reserved. Copying or digitizing this book for storage, display, or distribution in any other medium is strictly prohibited. For information about permission to reproduce selections from this book, please contact permissions@astrapublishinghouse.com.

This is a work of fiction. Names, characters, places, and incidents are products of the author's imagination or are used fictitiously. Any resemblance to actual events, locales, or persons, living or dead, is entirely coincidental.

Jacket illustration by Serena Malyon

Jacket design by Katie Anderson

Book design by Fine Design

DAW Book Collectors No. 1987

DAW Books
An imprint of Astra Publishing House
dawbooks.com
DAW Books and its logo are registered trademarks of Astra Publishing House

Printed in the United States of America

Library of Congress Cataloging-in-Publication Data

Names: Fagan, Deva author
Title: House of dusk / Deva Fagan.
Description: First edition. | New York : DAW Books, 2025. |
Series: DAW Books Collectors ; no. 1987 | Summary: "A romantic epic
fantasy featuring a fire-wielding nun grappling with her dark past and
a young spy caught between her mission and a growing attraction to
an enemy princess."-- Provided by publisher.
Identifiers: LCCN 2025012492 (print) | LCCN 2025012493 (ebook) |
ISBN 9780756420109 hardcover | ISBN 9780756420116 ebook
Subjects: LCGFT: Fantasy fiction | Romance fiction | Novels
Classification: LCC PS3606.A2646 H68 2025 (print) |
LCC PS3606.A2646 (ebook) | DDC 813/.6--dc23/eng/20250404
LC record available at https://lccn.loc.gov/2025012492
LC ebook record available at https://lccn.loc.gov/2025012493

First edition: August 2025
1 3 5 7 9 10 8 6 4 2

For Bob, always.

CHAPTER 1

SEPHRE

The new novice had been skulking at the edge of the garden for nearly a quarter hour. If he was trying to hide from her, he was doing a poor job of it. Sephre pretended not to notice, busying herself filling a basket with fresh, green leaves from the spindleroot bush. Brother Dolon had been having headaches again, and she was nearly out of his tincture. Then there were the yearly draughts of cold medicine still to brew. And the mint wanted thinning before it devoured the entire garden.

She watched the novice through a feathery screen of greenery as she worked. He seemed to be muttering something to himself. Stiffening his shoulders, he took one step out along the crushed-shell path. Only to catch himself, jumping back, as if he'd stepped on a scorpion. After the fifth time, she lost patience.

"If you stay there too long, the bees are going to fill your ears with honeycomb," she called out.

Not an idle threat. The novice did have quite large ears, jutting like the handles on a wine cup. He reminded Sephre of a sapling that had sprouted suddenly tall and skinny in a riot of new growth.

He gulped, darting forward, the short dark twists of his hair quivering. The braids were unusual, but perhaps he was Scarthian. Stara Bron might be located within the borders of Helisson, but it served all the lands of the Middle Sea. Then again, she'd always heard Scarthians were bold and reckless, and this boy was . . . not that.

Zander had been half Scarthian. The thought caught her, an

unexpected bolt, making her wince until she shoved it back into the past, where it belonged.

The novice apparently took this as a reaction to his own approach. "Sorry!" He made to retreat, not noticing the watering pail.

Sephre seized the boy's arm, catching him just before he toppled onto her carefully tended patch of gauzebloom. "Careful! No, don't run away, boy. I'm not angry at you. But I will be, if you squash my flowers."

He made his way gingerly and somewhat sheepishly out of the verge, taking refuge on the far side of the worktable. "Sorry, sister," he mumbled. Fates, what was the agia thinking, letting a quivering sprout like this into the temple?

Such arrogance, she chided herself, remembering her own floundering novitiate. She had come to it much older, of course, well into her thirties, with a lifetime behind her. A bloody, shameful lifetime that ill-suited her for this work. And yet she had done all that Agia Halimede asked of her. She had put in her time. Nine long years of service. Perhaps one day it would be enough.

Sephre directed her attention back to the novice, who seemed to be taking her silence as censure. "What's your name, lad?" She wasn't used to speaking gently. To speaking at all, really. It came out sharper than she intended, so she added a rusty smile.

"Timeus." He started to dip his head.

"I'm not the agia," she said, halting him. "You don't need to bow to me, Brother Timeus. Just tell me why you're here. Did Sister Obelia need more parsley for tonight's supper?"

"N-no." Timeus straightened, clearly making a valiant effort to gather his nerves. "Sibling Vasil sent me. They said you needed someone to help with the herbs and medicines. So that's me. I'm the helper. That is . . . if you're her. I mean, if you're Sister Sephre."

She smothered a sigh. This was the fifth "helper" Vasil had sent her in the past year. The last boy barely made it three days before displaying a potentially lethal inability to distinguish between oregano and deadly nightshade. Before that had been the promising girl who had fled her vows after reconciling with her spurned sweetheart. Or had it been the lad with the paralyzing fear of bees?

She considered simply sending the boy away, but that would only bring Vasil down on her. Or possibly the agia herself. And who knew, maybe Timeus would surprise her. She tried to recall whether she'd even seen him before. Last Sephre knew, there were five novices at Stara Bron, none of them a tall spindle with over-large ears. This boy must have only just arrived.

She really should stop calling him "boy." He must be at least seventeen. The same age she'd been when she enlisted.

Another dagger, catching her in the chest. Sephre breathed deep, filling her lungs with the spice of leaf and root, the sweetness of the honeysuckle that hung from the trellis behind her. Listened to the hum of the bees. One of them buzzed closer, circling Timeus's head. He didn't seem to mind. Well, that was something.

"Yes, I'm Sister Sephre," she admitted. "And I do need help." She held out the basket. "You can finish gathering the spindleroot. Be careful to pinch off just the newest. See how they're paler green? Those are the ones you want. Leave the others. And don't step on the roots."

Timeus took the basket reverently. Sephre returned to the work-table, watching from the corner of her eye. He wasn't as bumbling as she'd first taken him to be. Clearly mindful of her direction, he moved slowly around the bush, pausing before each step to check for the thin, tangled roots that gave the plant its name.

She felt him watching her, in turn. Slanting surreptitious glances when he thought she was busy with her mortar and pestle. She knew she ought to say something, but her conversation skills were as rusty as her smile. Maybe that was why Vasil kept sending her apprentices.

"Have you worked with plants before?" she asked. She had to make some effort, or Vasil would give her one of their disappointed looks next time she saw them, and probably try to talk to her about her feelings.

Timeus shook his head. "My parents are weavers. My eldest

brother, too. And Rhea—she's my twin—enlisted. She's going to serve in the third wing," he added, wistfully.

Sephre held her breath for a moment. Released it. Ridiculous. She could talk about such things. The war was over, and so was her part in it. She was an ashdancer now. Warmth flared in her palms, a reassuring heat, warning back the shadows of her past. "Was soldiering not for you?"

He bent his head, making a close study of the spindleroot. "They cast me out of training after the first week. They said I didn't have the talent for it. I suppose I don't have the talent for most things."

She wanted to box the ears of whoever had taught him this. "Talent is overrated. Skill is what matters. And that only comes with time and practice." And a willingness to make mistakes and learn from them. Something she herself should keep in mind. She nodded to the basket. "You're doing fine work with that."

His smile was fearsome. "Thank you, Captain! I mean—" He clapped a hand over his mouth. Unfortunately, it was the hand that had been holding the basket, which went tumbling to the ground, spilling a drift of leaves across the dark earth.

His brown eyes were wide. Aghast, but also appallingly curious.

She forced herself to take a breath before speaking. To make the words mild as milk, like a proper ashdancer, scrupulously paring away the ire, the pain, every baleful emotion. "*Sister*," she said. "Sister Sephre." Then she looked, very meaningfully, at the fallen basket.

Timeus crouched at once, retrieving it. "But you did fight in the Maiden's War, didn't you?"

This time it took three breaths to still herself. The heat in her palms flared.

"One of the other novices said you were in the seventh wing," Timeus went on, not waiting for her reply. Or perhaps she nodded. She wasn't sure. Her body seemed to belong to someone else. "Part of the final assault."

Smoke burns her nose, not quite masking the stench of decay.

HOUSE OF DUSK 5

The bodies lie crumpled, bloodless, in soft heaps like dirty washing. Her ears aren't used to the silence. No more clash of swords, no shouts and screams. Only the hum of the flies. And once, horribly, the wail of a baby. It stops before she can find it.

Done. Gone. Over.

Flames flared at her fingers, clear and bright and relentless, burning the memory back. She knew they must be snapping in her eyes as well, by the way he cowered before her. "I said I'm an ash-dancer now. But apparently minding your tongue is just one more thing you're bad at."

Timeus opened his mouth, then closed it, looking utterly aghast. Ducking his head, he began collecting the fallen leaves while making distressing snuffling noises that he was clearly trying to muffle in the sleeve of his new habit.

Furies' tits, she cursed silently. *Are you happy, now? You made him cry.* A few questions from an overly curious youth shouldn't shatter her like this. That life was over. She was Sister Sephre, who tended to herbs and brewed tinctures and would spend the rest of her life here at Stara Bron, where she could do no harm.

Aside from utterly destroying a perfectly fine batch of spindleroot with her self-indulgently dramatic gesture. She was staring mournfully at the contents of the mortar, burnt beyond any good use, when a woman came skimming into the workshop, the sleeves of her gray tunic embroidered with yellow flames, like Sephre's own.

"Sister Beroe," Sephre greeted her, relieved. "Have you come for Brother Timeus?" It would be just as well if the boy went elsewhere. One more failed apprentice. *Failed apprentice? Or failed master?*

"No, sister, for you." Beroe frowned at the still-smoking mortar. "The agia has need of you."

Sephre hastily dumped the burnt spindleroot into her compost pail. "Is it her chest again?"

The agia had been vigorous well into her seventies, even leading the procession of tombs the previous autumn. But lately she'd been bothered by pains in her chest, and a shortness of breath that troubled Sephre.

"No. They've found another body."

Another. Sephre counted back the days. That would be the third this month. Forty-seven in total. That they knew of.

"Like the others?"

She could feel Timeus watching. No doubt his overlarge ears were quivering. She remembered all too well how novices gossiped. Perhaps they'd already heard the rumors. A pattern of mysterious deaths scattered across all Helisson was ripe fodder for eager minds.

"Yes." Beroe's eyes were bright. Fates, she was practically quivering. "Snakebite."

Timeus gave a muted squeak. Sephre ground her teeth. "Timeus," she said. "Please go fetch a ewer of water from the well."

She waited until the boy departed, then cut her gaze back to Beroe. "If that boy has nightmares, it'll be your fault."

Beroe blew out an impatient breath. "That boy took the same vows as you and I. He knows it's our duty to guard the holy flame. To cleanse the dead. And to destroy any creature of the underworld that dares trespass in the mortal realm." She brandished the words like a banner.

Sephre swept the smooth wood of her worktable, catching up bits of leaf and stray twigs. She added them to the compost pile, then dusted her hands together. She had known people like Beroe. *Known them? You* were *them*, she chided herself. *So eager to fight for a cause that you didn't question it. Until it was too late.*

"What does Agia Halimede want me for?"

"She wishes for you to examine the body."

"The corpse is here?" Her voice crackled.

"Yes. The girl was from Tylos."

This was the first time it had struck so close. Stara Bron was the largest of the ashdancer temples, the oldest, its flame the most renowned, having been seared into the mountainside by the Phoenix herself. But there were others in bustling cities, in humble fishing villages, even in the windswept Scarthian plains and the shattered isles of the old empire. No doubt still others burned across the sea, though the Idrani kept their secrets too well for anyone to know for certain.

Centuries ago, there had been ashdancers guarding nearly all of them. But the cataclysm had changed much. There were barely fifty ashdancers at the temple, and only half that stationed outside Stara Bron now. It was from them that the earlier reports had come. Brother Itonus had sent the most recent firespeaking, from the shrine in the royal city, telling of a merchant found dead in his library. But Helissa was a five-day journey to the south.

Tylos was barely five *miles* from Stara Bron. Sephre remembered stopping there, nine years ago, dipping up cold water from the village well, wiping the dust from her face and hands, trying vainly to make herself presentable, clean and pure, the perfect postulant.

"Why me?" She gripped the edge of the worktable, her knuckles pale. "Any ashdancer can question the girl's spirit."

"There's no sign of a spirit," said Beroe.

Sephre's skin prickled. It didn't necessarily mean anything dire. Spirits were harder to reach the deeper they drifted into the Labyrinth of Souls. Even the agia's powers had their limits.

"Which means we have only the girl's body to give us answers. Agia Halimede believes that you might have some insights, given how much time you spend puttering around your tinctures and tonics." Beroe's lips pinched as she spoke. The woman had always been far more interested in spiritual dangers than in something as mundane as a fever or sniffle, and no doubt considered Sephre's work in the herbarium to be less meaningful than the prayers and invocations that filled her own days. Not that it had stopped her from coming straight to Sephre last spring when she broke her arm. Which was unfortunate, because try as she might, Sephre could not help but feel protective toward anyone she physicked. Even Beroe. Which meant she really had to do this, didn't she?

The day was apparently cursed. Or possibly this was an ordeal set by the Fates, a punishment for making Timeus weep.

Enough whining. She'd seen dead bodies before. She could handle this. And it would give her the chance to speak with Halimede. This foolishness with training an apprentice had gone on long enough. It was abundantly clear that she was a *terrible* role model. Timeus was a lily, too pure for her poisoned soil.

And if there was a chance that Beroe's suspicions were true, well, then Sephre could not shirk her duty. Not when the danger had come so close to Stara Bron, to this small corner of the world that had tangled itself into her weary heart.

"Right," she said. "Then you'd best take me to her."

CHAPTER 2

SEPHRE

She followed Beroe along the hallway, darkly wondering what state she'd find her workshop in when she returned. She'd left Timeus cleaning up the bed of kitchen herbs, which at the very least wouldn't poison the lad. She just hoped he didn't accidentally root out the carefully tended hibiscus she'd finally managed to shepherd through the cold, wet Helissoni winter.

"They've laid the corpse in the crypt," said Beroe, turning down a side passage that descended in a twist of narrow stone. She lifted one hand. A spark of yellow flame kindled in her palm, lighting their way.

"Where was she found?"

"Two shepherds spotted her body this morning, in one of the ravines along the southern road. She'd been missing for five days."

Well, *that* didn't bode well, though it could explain why they had been unable to reach the girl's spirit. Sephre drew in a bracing breath as they emerged from the stairs. She regretted it instantly. The air reeked of sweet smoke, nearly making her gag. And not just smoke, she realized. A fouler scent beneath it. Rot.

Four braziers had been set at the corners of the low, square chamber. Those must be the source of the incense-laden smoke. The other smell came from the stone plinth at the center of the room, where a linen-shrouded form lay still and silent.

Sephre's legs stopped moving, pinning her at the threshold, her mind lurching back again to the silent streets. The hum of flies. She curled her hands into fists, fingernails biting her palms, bringing her back to herself.

"Agia." She dipped her head to the woman standing beside the plinth, her tunic a white blaze in the gloom, the sleeves embroidered with blue flames that matched the sparks kindling in the depths of her dark eyes. Halimede was a small woman, and it seemed to Sephre that she shrank a little more with every passing year. As if the flame she carried was burning her away, bit by bit, until only skin and bones and holiness remained.

And yet being in her presence was like standing beside the sea. Or beneath an achingly clear sky full of stars. Something vast and timeless that made all your troubles seem small as ants.

"Thank you for coming, sister," said Halimede. "I'm sorry to ask this of you, but we must know if—" She paused, seeming to reconsider her words, "—what became of her."

"I thought it was a snakebite." Tragic, but not uncommon. And for all that Beroe might see some uncanny hand at work, Sephre did not think Halimede the sort to leap to conclusions. But the agia was clearly troubled by something.

"Perhaps," she said. "But I would still value your input."

Sephre swallowed. Her eyes avoided the plinth. "But she *was* bitten?"

It was Beroe who answered, moving to the corpse. "Yes. Here, on her arm."

The shroud was loose, the wrappings untied. The linen rested lightly, tracing the lines of the small body beneath. Only the girl's right arm was uncovered. Her skin was gray and mottled, but even so the punctures were clearly visible, raw and red.

Sephre took a step closer. If she focused on the bite, she wouldn't have to think about the fingernails, trimmed short and neat. Or wonder who had woven the beaded bracelet clasping the girl's wrist. None of that was her concern.

She measured the space between the punctures with a fingertip. "It wasn't large. Probably a brown viper. They're common enough in these hills." As a girl she'd learned to watch for them sunning themselves.

"And are they common enough in the middle of libraries in the heart of the royal city?" Beroe arched a brow.

Halimede made a quelling gesture. "Go on, Sister Sephre. Tell us what you see."

Right. No sense in dithering. She pulled back the shroud. Beroe made a small noise and retreated several paces. Sephre remained silent, but only because she'd been grinding her jaw tight in preparation.

Five days in the hills had not been kind to the girl. Sephre would have put the time at twice that, based on the state of the corpse. In a way, it was a relief. The bodies that haunted Sephre were fresh. Their eyes stared at her untouched. Even Zander's, startlingly blue, staring up into the night.

No. Not now. The blue eyes faded away, lost in the shimmer of yellow sparks. She forced herself to focus on small details. To think of the corpse as a stretch of soil she was working, one patch at a time. Eventually the job would be done, but she owed it to the girl to do it properly. The poor thing couldn't be more than fifteen. And here Sephre was, three times that and alive in spite of everything. The Fates had a bitter sense of humor.

"What was her name?" She should have asked the question sooner.

"Iola," said Halimede.

Time passed. Sephre's shoulders knotted, muscles in her back twitching. There were a few scrapes and bruises, nothing out of the ordinary for a hill girl. She'd broken her arm, but that was years ago, and mended well. "There's no sign of any other serious injury," she said wearily, as she worked her way down the girl—Iola's—left leg. "The snakebite must be what killed her." She hesitated. "Though by the state of her body I would've guessed she'd been dead far longer than five days."

Halimede's eyes sparked. "What could cause that? Venom?"

Sephre shook her head. "Some venom causes putrefaction, but not like this."

"What's that?" Beroe asked. "Just above her ankle."

A bruise? No, the dark mark was too regular, too precise. Sephre leaned closer, lifting the girl's foot gently as she called a spark of light to her free hand to illuminate the mottled flesh.

The shadows fled, revealing a sort of faceted ring. Seven points linked by seven lines. Her breath slid out uncertainly, not wanting to leap to conclusions.

Beroe had no such compunctions. She made a sound a charitable person might call outrage, but which sounded more like triumph to Sephre's admittedly biased ears. "The Serpent!"

"How is that the serpent?" It looked nothing like a snake to Sephre.

"It's a constellation," said Beroe, impatiently. "A star sign."

"I *know* what a constellation is."

"Then you know the Serpent's constellation is made up of seven stars. Just like this mark."

Sephre did not know that, but she wasn't about to admit it to Beroe. She had grown up in the mountains, taught by the slash of wind and demands of her father's sheep. She knew the Spear of Breseus that foretold the coming of winter. The bright eye of the Beetle that always hung constant in the north, guiding her home on late nights bringing in the flock.

And she remembered her father, one lean finger tracing lines across her freckled cheek. *The sign of the Archer. You must have been a great hero in some past life.* It was a common belief, that the Fates left such marks, hazy portents of what might be, if you could divine them from the freckles on your skin or the lines on your palm.

But the mark on Iola was something more than freckles. The lines were dark, as if drawn in ink. Sephre swallowed the tightness from her throat. She thought of Zander's arms, so beautifully banded from elbow to wrist with complex chevrons that entreated some Scarthian wind spirit to guard him. Was this mark a similar invocation? Meant to protect? If so, it had failed.

Beroe turned away. The corpse had served its purpose, and now her attention was on Halimede. "Agia, we can't ignore this. The signs are clear."

"What makes you think I'm ignoring this?"

The agia's arched brow would have sent Sephre to her knees in obeisance, but it only drew Beroe taller. "You haven't even informed King Hierax of these deaths."

"Because we still don't understand the nature of them. The girl's mark could be a coincidence."

"And forty-seven deaths by snakebite in a single year? Is that a coincidence? Even Sister Sephre admits that the body has been corrupted beyond what she'd expect. Beyond what is *natural*." Righteous sparks snapped in Beroe's eyes. "If the Serpent has returned, only the Ember King can banish him. And yet you refuse to recognize him."

"I recognize that Hierax rules Helisson." Halimede spoke softly, but with iron in her words. "But we belong to the Phoenix. Not to any mortal king, even if he is the Ember King reborn."

"Even *if*?" Beroe huffed. "Hierax brought the Faithful Maiden home to Helissa, just as the sibyl foretold. He cast down those who cursed and defiled her bones. He has proven beyond doubt that he is Heraklion reborn, the hero of all ages!"

Sephre could bite her tongue no longer. "He sat safe in his palace while thousands of soldiers died across the sea."

Beroe's mouth folded flat. "Died gloriously, to bring home his long-lost queen."

Sephre drew the shroud over the corpse in a single, sharp motion. Her words wouldn't sway Beroe, any more than her own father's warnings had swayed her. *I know it looks like freedom, lass. Coin, companions, a chance to leave this simple life. But you will be a tool. Are you so sure you trust the hand that wields you?*

At least he hadn't lived to see her shame. By the time she understood, by the time she returned home with laurels on her brow and blood on her hands, her father had been two years in his shroud. She'd visited the crypt, whispered to him that he was right. Some said that the spirits in the labyrinth could hear the prayers of the living. Maybe it had given him strength to find his way through the perilous land of the dead, to win rebirth. His body had fallen to ash soon after.

"Sister Sephre?" The note of warning in Halimede's words forced her back to herself. The yellow sparks she had kindled to drive back the shadows had become a handful of hungry flame. Hastily, she quenched the blaze, gripping her fists tight. "I'm fine."

Halimede looked unconvinced, but did not press the matter. "Very well. Then you and Sister Beroe can—"

"Agia, please, we must tell King Hierax," Beroe protested. "We must make preparations. At the very least, we should set watchers on the tombs. We all know the stories. The skotoi will rise with their master. They will seek entry to this world."

Now the woman was treading into pure fancy. There were no skotoi. Oh, Sephre had no doubt they had existed, long ago. It was one of the reasons the House of Dawn had been founded. The Phoenix granted her flame to the first ashdancers so they might keep the unholy creatures of the underworld at bay. Not content simply to feed on the spirits of the dead trapped within their endless labyrinth, the skotoi would sometimes claw their way into the mortal realm. And when they did, the ashdancers had been there to stop them.

Until the day three centuries ago when the god of death himself— the Serpent—broke free, wreaking devastation across the lands, releasing a scourge of demons and tearing open the earth itself. Sephre had seen the marks of it, sailing through the shattered islands that were all that remained of the old empire. She had stood on the shores of Bassara, looking up to the high curve of the cliffs that overshadowed the deeply cut harbor, where an ancient imperial palace lay sunken beneath the sea.

The same fate might have taken all the mortal lands, if the Ember King had not slain the Serpent. With their master gone, the demons of the labyrinth faded, their power diminished. They were nothing but stories now.

"If the skotoi return, we will meet them," said Halimede,

unruffled. "We will stand against them, as we swore in our vows, when the Phoenix first entrusted us with her flame. But for now, we have a more immediate calling." She nodded to the corpse. "Let Iola receive an invocation of the merciful flame."

"Are you sure that's wise?" asked Beroe. "We don't know for certain that she was innocent. The mark could be a sign of willing devotion."

"It makes no difference," said Halimede. "We pray for all the dead. Not only the innocent."

Beroe crimped her lips before replying, "Of course, Agia. Sister Sephre, perhaps you might care to—"

"I need to speak with the agia." Sephre forced her gaze away from the corpse, but it did no good. The images chased after her. Not just this body, but all the others, the silent staring eyes. Fates, she had to get out of here. And her unwanted bean sprout was as good an excuse as any other.

The agia's expression remained tranquil. But a tiny spark of blue flame lit her dark eyes. "Yes. I have a matter to discuss with you as well, sister. Come. We will speak in my office."

═══

When Sephre first came to Stara Bron, she had expected stillness and silence. That she would spend much of her time alone, surrounded by grim gray walls, slotted neatly into a bare sleeping cell or sterile shrine.

But while the ashdancers might be tasked with guarding and purifying the dead, their temple was no forbidding tomb. Emerging from the crypt, Sephre followed Halimede along a wide hallway striped with golden sunlight. The air smelled of pine and wild olive, blown in from the high rocky slopes, a breath of her own long-distant childhood. Through the arched windows, she glimpsed endless blue sky, a rumpled green valley far below. She filled her lungs with the sweet, chill air, letting it drive back the smell of death. She felt a twinge of guilt leaving Beroe with the corpse. But for all her flaws, Beroe was scrupulously devout, and highly capable. She would not stint in her prayers for the girl.

While you go and hide in your garden. But surely there was nothing to hide from, except her own memories. Like Halimede said, this could be simply coincidence. Still, her belly twisted. If this truly was some harbinger of the Serpent's return, what would become of Stara Bron? Soft, sweet-hearted Sister Obelia, who had spent half her nights last fall nursing three orphaned kittens back from the brink of death to flourishing sleekness? Would scholarly Brother Dolon truly have to put down his inks and brushes, and go forth to battle the demons of the underworld?

He would. They all would. She had lived with these people for nine years, listened to their small complaints and silly jokes, brewed them tonics, even—rarely—trusted them with her own secrets. They might live simple lives, but every one of them had taken the same vows. Every one of them carried the fire of the Phoenix, knowing that it was the one power that could banish any demon.

Her heart ached at the thought. Fates. And what about Timeus? Would his brown eyes haunt her some day, just like Zander's? No. Not if she could help it.

She followed Halimede into the shimmering brightness of the cloister. Like much of Stara Bron, the pillars that edged the four walkways were carved of morninglass, a soft, golden stone flecked with bits of mica that reflected even the frailest light of dawn into trembling sparks. Now, at noon, it made even the agia lift a hand to shield her gaze.

Time to strike. "Agia, Brother Timeus isn't going to work out."

A pause. Then Halimede flowed onward, her white robes swirling in her wake like smoke. "You ascertained so much in a single morning? What exactly did he do?"

"He . . ." *He called me captain. He thinks I'm a hero.* "He just . . . isn't suited to the work."

"Oh? It must be something truly dire, then. Did he put henbane in Brother Dolon's tonic instead of hollyhock?"

Was the agia teasing her? It had been an honest mistake, and Sephre had done her penance for it, weeding the overgrown nettles until her knuckles swelled to the size of lemons. "He's a good lad, but he'll better serve Stara Bron somewhere else."

Halimede's steps slowed. She halted between two of the golden pillars. The blue sparks in her eyes glinted as she fixed them on Sephre. "How many novices have you sent away now? Six?"

Sephre coughed. "Five. It wasn't my fault Sister Colocasia ran off to get married."

The agia waited. Holding her gaze was like trying to stare down the sea. Worse, Sephre could feel the woman's pity. Or maybe she meant it to be sympathy. Compassion. Whatever its name, Sephre did not want it. Did not deserve it.

"How is Sibling Abas doing?"

Sephre cursed herself. She ought to have expected the question. "They're doing well enough. The tremble hasn't gotten any better, but I think their mind is more clear." Her throat tightened, remembering her last visit to the infirmary. How frail her old mentor had become in just a few months. And the apoplexy had taken more than just Abas's flesh and physical strength. Abas had taught Sephre much, but there were so many things now lost within the fog of their wounded mind, no matter how hard they tried to fish them free. The sweet gum that worked so well to soothe menstrual cramps. The best way to propagate jewelvine.

"We're working on remembering the recipe for that azarine ink Brother Dolon is so desperate for." A feeble feint. Not enough to distract the agia. Sephre tried again. "I've been copying down everything I can. All the other recipes Abas taught me."

"A record is not the same as living knowledge," said Halimede. "Which is why it's vital to honor what we gain from experience."

"Not all experience is useful," Sephre bit back. Curse it. She'd let Halimede take control of the conversation. They were no longer talking about apprentices. This was an older argument. "Some things are better forgotten."

Or, better yet, burned away completely.

Halimede sighed. She cupped her hands before her, kindling a blue flame in her palms. The sight of it filled Sephre with an ache, her own flame leaping in kinship. "The flame does not make an ashdancer pure. An ashdancer makes *herself* pure. Which you have done, sister. The flame you carry is proof of that. If the Phoenix judges you a fit vessel, who are you to question it?"

"I'm not. I'm asking you to. It's been nine years, and it's still as bad as ever." People were always saying that time cured all ills, but Sephre doubted it was true. Not if the infection was deep enough, the poison strong enough. "You promised. You said that you would grant me the Embrace, if I truly needed it."

Halimede's lips pursed as she stared into the cupped fire between her fingers. "The Embrace is no small thing," she said at last. "The holy flame is still a flame. You cannot burn away only the memories you wish."

The tent is full of wounded soldiers, full of the stench of too many broken bodies, of sick and piss and blood and screams and moans. But Vyria needs her. Vyria is the only one left. A scream coils in her throat. She was supposed to keep them safe. And even now, she is failing. The healers cannot save the leg. The rot is spread too far, they say. All they can hope is to save her life. Vyria grips her hand with painful, desperate strength, as the man in the blood-stained smock draws out the saw.

She swallowed, hard. "I accept that. Whatever it takes. I could serve Stara Bron so much better if you'd just grant me this, Agia. Please."

"You'll forgive me if I trust my own judgment on that." Halimede's lips quirked. "I am the agia, after all. And I see a sister who has served well and faithfully, who has skills and strengths that none other has here."

"Making novices cry?" Sephre suggested. "Quarreling with Sister Beroe?"

"You are hardly the only one at Stara Bron with *that* skill," said Halimede, so drily that Sephre might have laughed if her throat weren't so tight. "Come. I will show you what I speak of."

Sephre ground her teeth, trotting after the agia as she continued across the cloister. The woman was impossible. It wasn't as if the Embrace was so unusual. Granted, it was generally bestowed on criminals, but it could be given as a mercy, too. She'd witnessed it herself, five years ago. A small boy had been brought to Stara Bron by his grandmother. Sephre didn't know what had happened to him, only that the hollowness in his eyes echoed against her own heart. He, too, had seen something terrible.

Something Halimede had burned away. When they departed the next day he had skipped beside his grandmother. Only the old woman wept, and her tears were joyful. Innocence had been restored.

Call it mercy, call it punishment. The end result would be the same. She would be free. If only Halimede would listen.

But clearly the agia had other things on her mind. She quickened her pace, leading Sephre up a seemingly endless set of steps cut from the stone of the mountain itself. Tradition placed the agia's chambers at the highest point of Stara Bron, just below the open ridge where the Holy Flame burned. The ascent left neither of them breath to spare. Halimede paused once, gripping the smooth curve of the balustrade, her fingers pale and thin against the golden stone. She kept her spine grimly erect, but the glimpse Sephre caught of her face—gray, tight-lipped—was troubling.

She continued on before Sephre could suggest a longer rest, pushing them both up the final flight to the arched doorway that led into the agia's office. Even Sephre was wheezing and puffing by then, and it took considerable effort not to simply collapse into the softly cushioned window seat that bowed out along one wall. Instead, she stood tall, sandals set against the smooth stone floor, relentless in her cause. "Agia, you promised to consider—"

"Look." Halimede touched a blue spark to the delicate copper lamp wrought in the form of a Phoenix that hung above her desk. "And tell me what you see."

I see an agia trying very hard to change the subject. But she was still too much a soldier for that sort of insubordination. Sephre joined the agia. The lamp revealed a broad oak table covered in papers. No, it was a single large sheet, marked with spiderwebs of ink and whorls of color. Rippling waves and sinuous rivers. She blinked, and for a brief, unsettling moment she was elsewhen, stepping into the general's tent, watching the Heron slide a single crimson stone past the inked walls. *It will end the war in a day.*

The map before her now did not show some distant island, marked with enemy fortifications and tactical positions. This was home. The entire sweep of the Helissoni peninsula. But there were markers, of a sort: round wooden chits scattered, seemingly at random. There were a dozen down along the southern coast, where the Hook curled out into the Middle Sea, trailing a chain of tiny islands. Then more spotting the midlands. A stack of five chits nearly covered Helissa City.

Scanning further north, Sephre found the sharp cut of the Veil, the line of mountains that severed the peninsula from the mainland almost completely. Only the Vigil Gap allowed clear passage into the northern steppes of Scarthia. A blue flame was inked onto the parchment just south of the Veil, above the words *Stara Bron*. Another wooden chit nestled close beside the temple. Squinting, Sephre noted the number painted onto it. 47.

"These are the deaths," she said, with a chill of understanding.

"Indeed." Halimede's brown eyes sparked blue. "And what else?"

Sephre scanned down to the southern coast, then north again. "The numbers. Those are . . . ?"

"The order in which the reports came in."

It wasn't a perfect pattern, but then, not all the bodies had been discovered quickly. "They're moving north. It's almost like . . . a trail." A trail of death.

Halimede nodded, looking grimly pleased.

Sephre gripped the edge of the table, doing rough calculations in her head. Whatever had done this was moving no faster than a traveler on foot.

"You think it's a person?" There were stories of mystics,

forbidden cults that still honored the Serpent. Sephre had never given them much heed. The evil she'd seen had no need to hide behind secret rites and masks. More often than not, it flaunted itself as righteousness.

"A pattern," admitted Halimede. "That suggests intent. There's more. Something that I haven't shared with the others."

A shiver rippled up Sephre's spine. "What?"

"Reports of a stranger," said Halimede, "seen in conjunction with at least half the deaths. A man with a shaved head, carrying a sword."

"There are plenty of bald men with swords in Helisson," said Sephre, warily. "Did anyone actually see him doing something? Attacking the victims?"

"No," admitted Halimede. "But they did make note of his eyes. Apparently they were a quite striking green."

Sephre clamped her jaw, considering this. Thinking of Brother Dolon's masterpiece-in-progress, how he had come to her to help compound a particularly vivid green ink for the eyes of the Serpent. "Then you think Beroe's right? That this is the Serpent's work?"

Halimede sniffed. "I think that if the god of death were traipsing about the countryside, it would be considerably more dramatic. But Beroe is correct about one thing: we cannot ignore this."

"So you're going to send word to the king?"

"If I did, how do you think he would respond?"

"I—I'm sure I don't know him well enough to say."

Halimede arched a brow. "You seemed happy to share your opinions earlier."

Sephre sucked in her cheeks, wishing heartily that she were back in her garden. "He would call it further proof that he's Heraklion reborn. Raise taxes, conscript troops, call anyone who denies him a traitor." Her thoughts drifted back to the earlier conversation. "Including us?"

Halimede nodded. "Indeed. Already he mistrusts us."

"Because you haven't publicly recognized him as the Ember King?" It seemed a small thing to Sephre. But then, she'd noticed that many powerful men seemed to find small insults more offensive to their pride than outright attacks.

"In part." The agia looked away. Clearly there was more to this than just the recognition of Hierax's claim to be Heraklion reborn. But whatever the secret, Halimede was not ready to reveal it. "But that isn't our primary concern. We are sworn to guard this mortal world from the demons of the underworld, whenever they rise again. If this is that time, then we all must be ready."

She lanced her gaze back to Sephre. "And that is why I need you, Sister Sephre. *All* of you. Who you were, and who you are. I need you to help me fight it."

CHAPTER 3

YENERIS

It was lucky for the princess that Yeneris had been hired to guard her life. Otherwise, Yeneris would almost certainly have murdered her by now.

Bad enough that she'd had to spend the majority of the past five days standing silently behind Sinoe for a mind-numbing succession of grooming rituals. The girl—Yeneris couldn't bring herself to think of Sinoe as a woman, even though at twenty-five Sinoe was five years her senior—spent fully two-thirds of her waking hours being primped and plucked. There were warm baths scented with rosewater to smooth her milky skin. Salted foot soaks to keep her ridiculously tiny feet soft. Rinsings with oakleaf to darken the russet hair she'd inherited from her Scarthian mother to a more acceptable deep brown.

All of that, Yeneris endured. Just as she endured the hours in the solarium, watching the patterns of sunlight creep across the walls painted with irritatingly twee songbirds and butterflies, while Sinoe hummed and sighed over books of love poetry.

By the end of her first week, Yeneris had begun to cherish the hope that someone would try to assassinate the girl, if only to break up the wretched tedium.

She should have known better than to tempt the Fates.

Now, on her seventh night in the king's service, Yeneris stood in Sinoe's bedchamber, staring down at three pillows that had been hidden beneath the silken coverlet, artfully plumped into the shape of a peacefully sleeping princess. She muttered a curse, one of the particularly foul ones she'd picked up from the soldiers in the refugee camp.

It wasn't a kidnapping. Yeneris could have held onto a few shreds of her pride if this was the work of Bassaran agents sent to steal away Hierax's daughter, in some vain attempt to force the return of the kore's reliquary. But Yeneris knew *quite* well it could be no such thing. She'd held out some hope that it was local criminals, seeking a fat ransom, until she saw the note.

A pretty little scroll of fine parchment, tucked between two of the pillows. Unfurling it, Yeneris found a single line of Helissoni script written in a surprisingly neat and careful hand.

I'll be back before dawn. Don't raise the alarm. Father will have your head.

Yeneris crumpled the paper in her fist. The girl was a blithering *fool*. A frivolous, self-interested ninny who seemed to think that a bodyguard was just another fancy trinket, like the amber earrings she'd lost five times in the past four days. On the most recent occasion, Yeneris had been forced to dig them out of a jar of Sinoe's favorite fermented fish sauce. Her fingers still smelled like rotting anchovies.

By rights, Yeneris *should* raise the alarm. Inform the royal guard, set a hundred soldiers out into the night to track the wayward princess.

Yeneris smoothed the paper, considering the warning. People said that Sinoe was touched by the Fates. The Sibyl of Tears. Her father certainly claimed as much, even when she was only a young girl. It was Sinoe's scryings that had sparked the war, after all.

Yeneris had seen no sign of such a gift thus far, but she couldn't discount it. King Hierax had been absent from the palace for the past week chasing rumors of serpent cultists in the western foothills. But he would return eventually, and he wouldn't be pleased if he learned that Yeneris had misplaced his daughter.

Her breath hissed out between her teeth. Fine. She would heed

Sinoe's words. But that didn't mean she was going to sit here all night twiddling her thumbs. She had a job to do. Two jobs, actually. The one she'd been hired for. And the other one, the secret one, that no one must suspect.

Both missions required Sinoe, however. Which meant ensuring that whatever ridiculous escapade had lured the girl from the palace did not end in injury, death, or disgrace. Yeneris ground her teeth in frustration. "Fool," she muttered, to herself as much as the princess.

A scornful chirrup sounded from the far corner of the lavish room, as if in agreement. Yeneris glanced toward the confection of intricate copper bars that was more miniature castle than cage. Within, the princess's ailouron was a blotch of darkness with baleful golden eyes. The creature chittered, clattering her sharp beak against the bars and half-extending gold-feathered wings, even as her feline hindquarters coiled to scratch yet another silken pillow to shreds. The Scarthian ambassador had gifted the beast to the princess only a few days earlier, and she'd already caused significant damage to Sinoe's bed linens and several ornamental plants, not to mention Yeneris's nerves. Even Sinoe had been forced to consent to caging the beast after Tami had scratched one of her handmaids.

If only the princess herself were so easy to keep safe.

Yeneris tossed the note into the nearby brazier, waiting just long enough to be certain it had caught fully, that there would be no scraps to betray her. Then she stalked over to the window.

An ancient wisteria clambered up from below, veiling the wide casement with frothy greenery. Leaning out, Yeneris surveyed the twisting vine. She doubted it would hold her own weight, but Sinoe seemed to be built of thistledown and sunlight.

There. Yeneris plucked something from the leaves below. A single thread of long, silky reddish-brown hair. Swiftly, silently, she slung herself over the casement, her fingers finding the ridges between the stone. A few moments later, she thumped onto the soft soil of the gardens. She dared not risk a lamp, but the frail silver light of the full moon was enough to reveal the imprint of sandals in the earth. Steps leading away, toward the far wall. Toward the city.

Where was the girl headed? Fates, please not a love-tryst. The girl was utterly obsessed with romantic poetry. No doubt she would think it thrilling to sneak out to meet some paramour, no matter the scandal.

It was almost enough to send Yeneris back up the wall. She didn't care one shred for Sinoe's reputation. If the girl were disgraced, it would hurt Hierax.

Remember the mission, she told herself. *Stick close to the sibyl. She is our path to recover the kore and hold the ancient vows.*

Yeneris gritted her teeth, biting down on the promise like a hound with a bone. She carried it with her as she set off across the dark garden, following the trail of the wayward princess.

====

It was *not* a romantic tryst. But it was still staggeringly outrageous. When Yeneris finally found Sinoe, an hour later, it was deep in the lower city, in the middle of a crowd gathered to watch a troupe of capering acrobats performing along the steps to the old necropolis.

Yeneris had to give the girl some credit. She'd *tried* to conceal her identity. Or at least, that was presumably the intention of the ragged shawl wrapped around Sinoe's head and shoulders. Unfortunately, it did little to disguise the fine gown underneath, six layers of linen so thin that you could read a scroll through each one. It was a small miracle no one had stolen the gold ring glittering on the girl's right thumb, clearly visible as she flung her thin arms into the air, cheering with abandon. Fates, where had she learned to whistle like a common sailor?

Yeneris halted on the outskirts of the crowd. Her uniform was meant to fade into the background: a simple red-brown tunic, a darker woolen over-cloak to keep back the evening chill and to hide the hilts of the twin short swords at her waist. She had five other blades hidden about her person. Even the Master of Guards hadn't found the smallest, when he searched her during her audition. Nor had she told him. It was one of her many secrets.

She had to be cautious. Not risk drawing any further attention than Sinoe—stupid, ridiculous girl—had already. If she thought she could get away with it, Yeneris might have knocked the princess over the head and carried her back to the palace. Instead, she was going to have to try to convince Sinoe to leave willingly. *Try* being the key word.

Yeneris drew a bracing breath, then began threading her way through the crowd, using her elbows as needed to clear the path.

Up on the morbid, makeshift stage, a very beautiful woman in a gauzy green tunic was now bending herself into shapes that made the crowd—and Yeneris—hiss with mixed fascination and horror.

Sinoe watched, her hands clasped together under her chin, lips parted. How could she still be such a child, after twenty-five years of life? Yeneris strained through her own memories. Had *she* ever looked at anything in the world with that sort of wide-eyed wonder? Maybe once, long ago. But Yeneris had been seven when the war began. The war that this foolish girl had started.

She shoved the thoughts away. It was the future she served. And she needed Sinoe to claim that future.

Yeneris spun a drunk woman gently to one side, slid past a man as he turned to shout something to a friend across the crowd, and suddenly there she was, beside Sinoe.

"Princess," Yeneris muttered, bending to ensure only Sinoe heard the word. "You shouldn't be here."

Sinoe turned abruptly, her eyes going even larger. Not with chagrin or fear or guilt, or even imperious condescension, which would have made sense. No, the princess turned those enormous brown eyes up to Yeneris with a look of absolute delight that made Yeneris's heart do something odd in her chest.

"Yeneris! You did follow me! Good. Look at her! Isn't she amazing?" Sinoe gestured, the gold ring winking provocatively, toward the acrobat, who had currently contorted herself into a shape that reminded Yeneris of an Idrani bread knot.

It *was* amazing. But it was also beside the point. Sinoe did not belong here, and it was Yeneris's job to get her back to the palace. Preferably without anyone realizing who she was.

"Princess," she tried again. "Your father forbids you to leave the palace without a suitable escort."

Sinoe waved a dismissive hand. "I have a suitable escort."

Yeneris frowned, scanning nearby. She saw no sign of any royal guard. Only a churning crowd of cityfolk, cheering and gasping and tossing back cups of wine from the nearby taverna. "Where?"

Sinoe laughed. It wasn't what Yeneris expected, not some insipid giggle, but a resonant chuckle that made something tickle in the back of her own throat. She swallowed. "What's so funny?"

"It's *you*," Sinoe said. "You're my escort."

Yeneris ground her teeth, trying a different tactic. "Then as your escort, princess, I must beg you to return to the palace. It's not safe here."

Sinoe arched a brow. "You don't think you can keep me safe?"

"Of course I can keep you safe," Yeneris blurted out, only to see Sinoe's eyes narrow in triumph. Fates, she'd walked right into that one.

"Good, then it's settled," said Sinoe. "So you might as well enjoy the show. I certainly am. Ooh, look, it's my favorite part! The fire spinners!" She gave a wistful sigh. "When I was a little girl, I wanted to grow up to be a fire spinner."

In spite of herself, Yeneris lifted her eyes to the front gate of the necropolis, where a pair of performers now stood. A young man and a young woman, both wearing so little that it made her cheeks flush.

"Just as well you're not," said Yeneris, stiffly. "Your father would never allow you to prance around like that, practically naked."

"Don't be a prude, Yen," said Sinoe. "It's for safety. Clothing might catch fire."

"Oh, right, I'm sure that's the only reason," said Yeneris, though part of her brain was still caught on *Yen*. She wasn't sure how she felt about the princess granting her a nickname. Was it a sign of companionship? Or did she think of Yeneris more like a pet hound?

"So you *do* have a sense of humor," said Sinoe. "I thought so."

The fire spinners began their performance, tossing torches between them in patterns that grew more and more complex. The streaks of brightness burned against Yeneris's eyelids, like the symbols of some strange alphabet she could not fathom.

Coins clinked onto the steps. Sinoe gave a small, breathless *oh* and began patting herself, finally pulling free a small purse that appeared to have been hidden in her cleavage. Yeneris flushed even more deeply. Then gave a yelp, as Sinoe heaved back her arm.

Yeneris snatched the purse before the girl could toss it at the steps. "Are you trying to draw every thief in the city?"

"They deserve it," Sinoe said, unrepentantly. "And what else do I have to spend it on? I already have everything I could ever dream of."

For the first time, there was an unhappy twist hidden in her smile. But the bitterness fled in a flash, in a wink, in an arch of her russet brow. "Aren't *you* enjoying the performance? You know, the Great Beetle crafted us these bodies as a gift. There's no reason not to enjoy a particularly fine specimen in action."

Yeneris tucked the purse into her own tunic for safekeeping. "Please, princess. Let me escort you back home."

Sinoe tilted her head. "Have I embarrassed you?"

Yeneris made an inarticulate noise.

"I'm sorry," said Sinoe. "I shouldn't tease you. You probably think it's not your place to tell me to shut up."

"It's not, my lady."

"Would it help if I gave you permission?"

Yeneris desperately wished that the princess would stop talking. Or at least, stop talking to *her*. The tedium of lurking in the background while Sinoe had her fingernails trimmed had never been so appealing.

Sinoe gave a reflective *hmm*. "I suppose not. It's just . . . sometimes I wish I could slip away somewhere that no one knows me. Be someone else altogether."

The irony nearly made Yeneris choke on her own secrets. A part of her twanged with pity for the girl, but that twang was drowned out by a deeper fear, that Sinoe might guess the truth.

"So that's why you came here?" Yeneris asked. "To play pretend?"

Sinoe's lips tightened. She looked hurt. "You think I'm silly."

Yeneris's mouth went dry. If Sinoe dismissed her, all the years of planning were for nothing. All the bribes that her superiors had paid to ensure she got this position. The agonizing hours of training. The years spent removing every trace of her accent. All utterly wasted.

"Come here," Sinoe said, abruptly tugging Yeneris along as she slid through the crowd, toward the base of the steps that led up to the makeshift stage. She didn't stop until they were pressed against an alcove along the side. It held an ancient statue of one of the godbeasts, so worn by rain and wind that Yeneris wasn't sure if it was meant to be the Sphinx or the Phoenix.

Halting beneath the towering, faded sculpture, Sinoe turned to face Yeneris, her expression tense. "You'll need your swords."

Yeneris put her hands on the hilts, warily. "Why?" She scanned the nearby crowds. What danger had she missed?

No one was paying them any heed. The fire spinners had reached the exciting climax of their performance, with the woman now perched on the shoulders of her partner, tossing the burning brands high, showing sparks across the dark night sky. Rapt with attention, the hundred-odd onlookers were cheering and whooping.

"Because of that," said Sinoe, pointing toward the performers. No, *past* them, to the dark gates of the necropolis itself.

Yeneris squinted into the shadows, barely making out the heavy wooden doors. As she stared at them, her heartbeat ratcheting, her skin prickling, the doors seemed to shift. To quiver.

Beneath the hum of the crowd, the whoops and hollers, Yeneris became aware of a slow beat. *Thud. Thud. Thud.* As if someone were banging at the doors from the other side.

Maybe it was a funerary priest who fell asleep on the job and got locked inside. Or a particularly incompetent grave robber. A pair of lovers with a fetish for the morbid? There were plenty of perfectly reasonable explanations for the thudding.

And her heart believed none of them. Yeneris moved to stand between Sinoe and the steps.

"What is it?" Yeneris demanded, glancing back. "Princess, what did you see?"

"Death." Sinoe's eyes were huge, and sorrowful.

A crack of splintering wood spun Yeneris back toward the gates, in time to see the doors finally give way, falling into splinters.

From the darkness, something slumped, staggering unsteadily. A human-shaped thing, with withered, skeletal arms and a body still trailing the gauzy tatters of a shroud. Pinpricks of bruised light burned in the wasted eye sockets, illuminating the leering skull as it paused on the threshold.

It gave a shattering, gargling cry, then attacked.

CHAPTER 4

YENERIS

The walking corpse tore into the fire spinners so fast they had no time to scream. It slammed into the man first, crumpling him. His partner toppled from his shoulders, her torches sputtering to the stones. A few cheers still punctuated the night. Some of the crowd must have thought this was part of the performance.

It wasn't. The creature hunched over the fallen fire spinner, making horrible wet slurping noises. The man's body twitched and flopped, then fell still. His partner scrambled to her feet and began to shriek.

The cheers vanished, replaced by unsettled mutterings. People began to pull back from the steps.

"Go on." Sinoe shoved Yeneris in the shoulder. "Stop it!"

Yeneris bared her teeth. "No. I need to get you out of here, princess."

"I'll be fine," she insisted. "But if you don't stop that thing, it's going to kill dozens. I've seen it."

Yeneris stared into Sinoe's wide brown eyes. They seemed suddenly very old, and very deep, the sort of eyes she could fall into and never escape.

Still, she tried. "Princess, my duty is—"

"*My* duty is to these people, Yen," snapped Sinoe. "I'm not leaving until they're safe. The skotoi have to be stopped."

Skotoi. It took her brain a heartbeat to translate the Helissoni word. *Enemy.* Any unclean, unnatural thing that had no place in this world.

Yeneris glanced back to the necropolis gates. The creature

appeared to have finished with its first victim. It stood, uncoiling with an uncanny smoothness, moving in a way that human joints and limbs should not allow. Gore spattered its dingy shroud, the wasted shreds of flesh and splinters of bone.

The glowing eyes fixed on the remaining fire spinner, who had retreated to the steps to seize one of her fallen torches. The creature gave a low, menacing hiss.

When she was a little girl, Yeneris had loved the story of mighty Akoret, who had pledged herself to the service of the Scarab, in the House of Midnight. Akoret defended her people against all manner of enemies: manticores, river-maugs, the last of the jeweled incarnals. And ghouls. Malevolent spirits that escaped the Labyrinth of Souls, using unclean corpses as doorways back into the mortal world.

But Akoret lived centuries ago. There were still stories of ghouls, sometimes. If a body was neglected. If the dead soul was particularly corrupt. That hardly seemed likely here. Surely all the dead within a necropolis in the heart of Helissa City had been properly interred, cleansed by the tomb keepers.

She could decide what to call it later. Sinoe was right. If the thing—ghoul, skotoi, monster—wasn't stopped, it was going to tear through this crowd as it had that poor fire spinner. Even now she saw the corpse cracking one arm back, lengthening the skeletal limb into a whippy length of bone, something more like a tentacle.

The bone whip lashed out, smacking the woman's hand, sending her torch flying to the side. Leaving her defenseless. The creature coiled itself to spring.

Yeneris moved. A fluid, precise movement, sweeping the hidden dagger from her thigh and sending it flying right into the monster's face.

By the time it struck, transfixing one burning black eye, she was halfway up the steps, swords drawn. "Go!" she shouted at the woman.

The fire spinner's gaze flicked just once to the crumpled body of her partner. Then she fled. And Yeneris turned her full attention to the enemy.

The dagger had done very little. It remained plunged into the skull of the ghoul, like some strange glittering ornament. The force of the blow had sent the corpse stumbling back. Given her time, but nothing else.

Well, at least she was no longer bored.

Grimly, Yeneris settled into a wary stance, her swords braced as she watched for an opening. She preferred an enemy she could sneak up on and take out cleanly, quickly, silently. Not this sort of raw, face-to-skull battle. At least there was only one of them. She could finish this quickly, and then get Sinoe away before anyone was the wiser.

Yeneris feinted and struck, slamming her short sword into the creature's left arm. Bone snapped, crunching. But the limb didn't fall. Some dark, slithery stuff boiled up at the shoulder, twining down to bridge the wound.

The ghoul slashed at her, finger bones sharpened to needlelike claws. Wonderful. Damaging it made it stronger. So much for her dreams of proving herself Akoret reborn.

Honestly, it was a bit embarrassing. That fire spinner had held the creature at bay for twice as long as this with only a torch.

The next slash of razor-sharp finger bones caught her sleeve, tearing a thin slice along her right arm, leaving a fine thread of pain. Yeneris bit down, regretting nearly all of her decisions that night.

Wait. She unwound her thoughts, back to the woman with the torch. The ghoul, cringing away from her. Not attacking until it knocked the burning brand aside. Fire. It feared fire. She sheathed her swords.

With an unholy gargling cry, the ghoul lunged. Yeneris danced to the side, not bothering to strike it. Instead, she dove for the fallen torch. It was still smoldering. She lifted it just as the ghoul swung round to face her.

The creature gave a low hiss, retreating a step.

"Don't like fire, do you?" She scanned the stones. A pile of spare torches lay over to one side of the tomb entrance, beside a clay jar and a bundle of clothing.

As her own brand began to sputter, Yeneris backed up, slowly. The ghoul followed. She caught up a second torch, lighting it from the one she carried. It blazed to life, weaving strange shadows against the stones of the tomb.

She tossed the first torch at the creature. Then lunged, slamming the fresher brand into the ghoul's torso as it tried to escape.

Whoosh!

The tattered shroud caught, flames spreading to withered flesh and the sad fringe of hair clinging to its skull. In a heartbeat the monster was wreathed in flame. The slithery darkness that animated the bones writhed and shuddered. A strange gray dust began to sift from it, clouding the air. Yeneris drew her sword again.

One swift slash, and the skull went rolling away. More greasy puffs of ash billowed from the thing. The body fell, consumed by fire. The dark gleam in the skull's remaining eye winked out.

She stalked over to it, tearing her dagger from its eye. Then she stomped down, hard. The old bone cracked, crumpled, fell to dust.

Finally, she drew a ragged breath. It was done.

Except that Sinoe was yelling something. Shouting at her, and pointing at the tomb. "Skotoi!"

That was when Yeneris realized her mistake. A stupid mistake that might very well mean her death. *Skotoi* was the plural, not the singular.

A dozen burning eyes filled the necropolis gates. A waft of cloying air struck her, sweet and dusty and terrible. The scent of a great many dead things. And something else, a strange, damp smell that made her skin crawl as if a thousand spiders were marching up her spine.

"Fire!" cried Sinoe. "I saw fire! You can stop them!"

This would have been reassuring, if Yeneris happened to have a bonfire handy. Or a firebomb. All she had were the last flickers of a dying torch. Unless . . .

Yeneris sprinted back to the pile of supplies abandoned along the steps. The spare torches, and that clay jar. Fates, let it be what she hoped it was!

She bent, sniffing the mouth of the jar. A noxious, sweet scent filled her nose. Naphtha, the same flammable stuff that the torches were soaked in.

Yeneris hefted the jar, spun, then threw it straight at the broken gates, into that terrible clutch of dark gleaming eyes. Then she tossed her lit brand after it.

Fwoom! Fire exploded from the mouth of the necropolis, and with it a high, wailing chorus. The wave of hot air sent her stumbling back. One foot slid off the topmost step. She toppled; stone slammed into her side as she rolled down to the square.

"Are you hurt?" A hand gripped her arm. Someone with the strength of a kitten was trying to heave her upright.

Yeneris groaned. The princess was beside her, brown eyes crinkled with concern.

"You tell me. You're the one with prophetic visions," Yeneris snapped. She felt like one enormous bruise.

The girl's mouth quirked. "I saw you stopping the skotoi. I didn't see you falling down the steps afterward."

"I'm fine," Yeneris said, uneasy with the way the girl was watching her. And with the weight of other eyes. Most of the audience had fled, but there was still enough of a crowd to cause them trouble, if anyone recognized Sinoe.

Yeneris clambered to her feet, scanning the tomb above. Smoke boiled from the entrance, but there were no more gleams in the darkness. No sign of any remaining ghouls.

Shouts echoed from the far side of the square. A quick tramp of booted feet, and a glitter of bronze helms. Soldiers, finally answering the alarm.

"We need to go, princess. Unless you want your father to learn what you've been about this evening."

For the first time that night, Yeneris saw actual fear—raw, self-preserving terror—flare in Sinoe's brown eyes. She gave a violent shake of her head.

"Then come," said Yeneris, gesturing to a smaller side alley. "Let's get you back to the palace."

======

"This would be *so* much easier if you'd just let me climb up the way I came down," said Sinoe, puffing out her cheeks in frustration. "We'd be back in my chambers by now, eating the milk candy I got last week from Ambassador Opotysi."

"That vine isn't strong enough, princess," said Yeneris, leaning out again to check the hallway. Empty. Finally. She crept out, waving for Sinoe to follow. "I'd be a poor bodyguard if I let you break your neck."

She tried not to wince at the irony of the statement. Yeneris knew quite well she *was* a poor bodyguard. And not only because she'd allowed her charge to cavort around the city alone for half the night. For now, her mission required Sinoe's health, but that might not always be the case.

"You needn't worry about my life," said Sinoe, her tone merry, spearing Yeneris's thoughts like a shaft of sunlight piercing a dark and shadowed room. "I already know how I'm going to die."

Yeneris halted abruptly. "What?"

Sinoe hooked a thumb at her chest. "Sibyl, remember?"

Yeneris's mouth went dry, her heartbeat quickening. She had a sudden urge to bundle Sinoe off across the sea, away from anything that might harm her.

Which was, again, ironic. Because at the current moment, it was Yeneris who probably posed the most immediate threat to Sinoe's life. Yeneris was the sheathed dagger, hidden in plain sight, waiting to be drawn.

Sinoe tilted her head, plainly watching Yeneris process this skein of emotions. "Oh, dear, and now I've upset you."

"I'm not upset, princess." Yeneris straightened, swallowing. "I only want to ensure I do my duty. How—" her voice stumbled—"how does it happen?"

Sinoe's eyes held her, deep with something like resignation, windows into some unfathomable future. One Yeneris did not want to face. Abruptly the princess shivered, and gave a brittle laugh. "It was a joke, Yen."

Was it? Or was Sinoe trying to protect her from something? Yeneris wasn't sure which possibility was worse. Only that the princess was a maddening, infuriating creature. "You really think this is a good time for jokes, princess? The dead are walking. And if your father learns you were out in the city, he'll probably take my head off."

"Oh, don't be a grump," said Sinoe. "You were splendid."

Even the rime of ice on Yeneris's spirits could not survive that smile, a glitter of teeth and dark eyes that rivaled the stars above.

"Not that I was surprised," she added. "You wouldn't be my bodyguard if you weren't the very best. Father would never risk anything happening to his pet prophet."

The starlight dimmed. Pet prophet, Yeneris noted. Not daughter. Was that how Sinoe saw herself?

"If you know how highly your father values you, why sneak out at all?" Yeneris found herself asking. "Why not tell him what you saw? Surely he could have sent his soldiers to stop those ghouls."

She winced, realizing her slip belatedly. But Sinoe didn't seem to have noticed the Bassaran word. The question had distracted her, and she was chewing her lip now, brow furrowed.

"It was one of the possibilities. But this one was better."

"A man died," Yeneris pointed out, though she regretted it when Sinoe's expression crumpled.

"I know." The princess swallowed, pressing herself back against one of the columns separating the walkway from the garden. She stared up into the sky. "I don't see a single future. That's not how it works. It's more like . . . a handful of threads. All of them slightly different colors. Different shades of possibility. But none of those threads ended with him living. Some things are fluid. Some things are . . . fixed."

They were nearly back to Sinoe's chambers. Just up the steps, along one hall. Yet she lingered, watching Sinoe stare into the night sky, her pale face reminding Yeneris of a moonflower, or some other bloom that opened only to the stars.

"I wish I could have saved him."

"You saved the others," Yeneris found herself saying. "You said more might have died if we hadn't been there."

Sinoe nodded slowly. Then she turned, abruptly transfixing Yeneris with those enormous eyes. "I owe you an apology. I used you. I knew the only way to get you to come with me was to sneak out. To force you to follow. I turned your duty against you. I made you my tool and I shouldn't have done that. I, of all people, should know better," she added, bitter with self-recrimination.

"You don't need to apologize to me," said Yeneris, brusquely. Heat flooded her cheeks. "Please. Let's just—"

She broke off at the sound of footsteps. Someone coming down the steps from the floor above. The floor that held Sinoe's chambers. Yeneris growled under her breath, starting to press Sinoe into the garden, out of sight.

Too late. A tall, slim figure hurtled down the staircase, bent with fierce intensity, as if he meant to slice his way through the world.

Sinoe slid from behind Yeneris with a happy cry and ran to intercept the living dagger. "Ichos!"

The young man halted, a look of relief flitting across his angular features. "There you are!"

Prince Ichos had the same proud bearing as his sister, but on him it seemed an attack, a dare to the world to strike him down. His hair, undyed, held richer glints of red, catching the light of the braziers like rubies. His eyes were not as clear as Sinoe's, more of a muddy hazel.

Ichos scanned his sister up and down, frowning at the dust clotting her gauzy skirts. Then he looked past her, to Yeneris. His gaze went instantly to the rag she'd bound around her arm, where the first ghoul had sliced her. It wasn't much of a wound, barely a scratch, but enough to need tending. And she'd given Sinoe her cloak, after noticing the girl shivering on their walk home.

"What happened?" He glanced to Sinoe, then back to Yeneris. His jaw tightened. "Was my sister in danger?"

Sinoe's laugh broke the silence, merry and tinkling, entirely unlike the low chuckle Yeneris had heard earlier. "Ichos, you know quite well I'm a danger to myself." She gave a dramatic sigh. "If you must know, I was out in the gardens earlier today and I lost an earring. I wouldn't have bothered, but it was one of the amber bees. You know, the ones Mother gave me?"

Ichos nodded, frowning.

"So I had to force poor Yen here to come with me to find it. And wouldn't you know, I'd lost it right in the middle of the rose bed. I would have gone in for it myself, but Yen insisted." Sinoe ended this speech with an elaborate shrug, the movement conveniently showing off the jewelry currently decorating her ears, gold settings shaped like honeybees clasping polished amber. "I'm hopeless."

It was a flawless performance. Yeneris was forced to revise her estimation of the princess yet again. If she could lie so easily to her own brother, she could certainly lie to Yeneris.

Ichos made a doubtful noise at the back of his throat. He was still glowering at Yeneris, as if this was somehow her fault. She fought to keep her own expression cool, impassive.

"Don't be sour," Sinoe told him. "I haven't eaten *all* the milk candies. I know they're your favorite. Come up. We'll have tea, and you can tell me all about that delicious poet you've been spending—"

"I didn't come for tea," said the prince.

Sinoe held her breath for a heartbeat. Going still, like a mouse that fears the hawk, spiraling above. "Why, then? What do you need?"

"Not me. Father." Ichos's mouth pinched. "He's returned. And he requires your services. Immediately."

CHAPTER 5

SEPHRE

In her old life, Sephre might have drowned her riled spirits at the taverna. Zander had always known where to find the best brews. Even during the worst privations of the siege, he'd managed—via bribes or threats or quite possibly sorcery—to obtain several bottles of Scarthian milk wine. *To celebrate our victories*, he'd told her, grinning. But the toasts she remembered were all in memory of the fallen.

There were no tavernas in Stara Bron, of course. But Sephre did keep a small supply of wine in her workshop, purely for medicinal application. After such a day as this, surely she might stretch the definition of "medicinal" and take a cup.

If only Brother Timeus hadn't taken her request to clean up the kitchen garden *quite* so literally. In his zeal he had weeded the herbs so carefully there was not a single errant sprout or fallen twig, then fallen upon the basket of neglected glassware she'd been meaning to wash and had left out hoping the rains would do the work for her. She'd returned from the agia's office to find the boy with his sleeves turned up, elbow-deep in a soapy pail, whistling cheerfully as he scrubbed his way through the mess. She hadn't had the heart to ask him to stop, even if it meant the loss of her usual refuge.

She could have gone to the dining hall instead, to join her fellow ashdancers in an hour of quiet companionship and spice tea before the evening meal. They were pleasant times, listening to Brother Dolon expound on some new scroll he'd discovered in the depths of the archives, or watching Brother Orrin try yet again to beat

Brother Petros—who cheated with more flair and aplomb than any of the professional dicers Sephre had known—at hopstones.

But the interview with Halimede had left Sephre too uneasy for that. And so she sought a more solitary relief. A different sort of drowning.

Sighing, she let her head tip back against the edge of the bathing pool, breathing in the hot steam as the warm waters did their best to unlock the tension from her limbs.

The baths had been an unexpected joy at Stara Bron. Fed by the hot blood of the earth itself, they were warmer than the finest steam rooms of Helissa. So old that the steps to enter the pool had been worn into curves by generations of ashdancers come to wash away the grime of a long and trying day.

If only she could so easily wash away Halimede's words. *I need you, Sister Sephre. All of you. Who you were, and who you are. I need you to help me fight it.*

Fight what, though? Rumors and speculation? The deaths were troubling, yes. But as yet there were no skotoi clawing their way out of the netherworld. No signs of imminent cataclysm, of the return of a long-dead god. The only devastation Sephre knew had been caused by a mortal man, in his quest for power, to prove himself the Ember King reborn. Maybe it was simply an excuse to justify denying Sephre the Embrace.

Oh, yes, she chided herself. *Because everything is all about you. Never mind the apocalypse.* The agia needed no justification for her decision. Even if it was the wrong one.

Sephre sighed, turning her attention to the more practical task of scrubbing herself clean. She had doused her hands in vinegar after tending to the corpse, but she could still smell the reek of death on her skin. She scoured the suds away, leaving bare a swath of clear olive skin, scattered with freckles. Gingerly, she traced a circle of seven. Then dug in her fingernail, a pinch of pain. No, it was ridiculous. Coincidence.

"Sister Sephre?"

She startled, sliding deeper, so that the foam covered her. Foolish, letting someone sneak up on her. *Especially* Beroe.

"You don't mind if I join you?" the woman asked, not waiting for Sephre's uncertain nod before sliding off her robe. She stood at the edge of the pool just long enough for Sephre to suspect it was for her benefit. Not an invitation, but a show of strength. A brandishing of supple limbs and creamy unmarked skin. A body in its prime, in comparison to one that had been harder used.

Sephre huffed, hunting for the soap. When she turned back, Beroe was safely submerged, but giving her a shrewd, calculating look. "I expected you to support me this morning," she said. "You're a woman of the world. Surely you see what we stand to lose in denying Hierax."

Sephre lavished her attention on soaping one callused foot. She did not want to have this conversation.

"Stara Bron is *dying*," persisted Beroe. "Two-thirds of the ashdancers are above fifty years. If the Serpent waits long enough, no one will be left to stop him."

The words itched with uncomfortable truth. Every night, Sephre climbed past a dozen empty rooms on the way to her own bedchamber. And on the weeks she couldn't wheedle her way out of the tedious summations meetings, she faced the rows of empty benches, enough to seat over a hundred, twice their current number. It disturbed her more than it should. The thought of this place she loved diminishing. Of her garden untended, falling to weeds when she was gone. Of the gentle murmur of prayer falling silent. But surely it wasn't so dire as Beroe made it.

"Brother Timeus is a promising lad," she countered.

"The stripling with the big ears?" Beroe scoffed. "His parents are weavers."

"And mine were shepherds. Do you think me lesser for it?"

It was not an uncommon view, especially among those born to power and wealth. To believe that they had earned such blessings through the deeds of past lives. That their current bounty was a sign of intrinsic worth. But Sephre had known plenty of powerful folk who were just as flawed as their so-called lessers.

Beroe met her challenging gaze without flinching. "I wouldn't be here if I did. I'm sure the boy will make a perfectly suitable ash-dancer. But he came here with three baskets and a bag of lentils. That's hardly the sort of offering that will allow us to prepare for what's to come. We need postulants with coin. Patrons with resources."

Sephre dug determinedly at the dirt crusting one of her toenails.

"But so long as Halimede refuses the Ember King, we'll see none of that. No one will dare risk his ire."

She let her foot fall back into the water. "What do you want, Beroe?"

"I want Stara Bron to survive. I want us to be strong. I want us to do our duty and guard this world against whatever evil comes to claim it."

Yellow flames flickered in Beroe's eyes as she spoke, waking an answering heat in Sephre. She sounded sincere. She probably *was* sincere, curse it. But that didn't mean she was right. And she hadn't answered Sephre's real question.

"What do you want *from me*?"

Beroe hesitated. Probably searching for the perfect twist of words. Sephre had no patience for subtlety. "Just say it."

"Very well. What did you and the agia discuss?" Beroe's lips pinched. "This is no time for secrets. And my flames are as yellow as yours."

Sephre scoffed. "You're jealous? Afraid I'll try to claim the white mantle when she's gone?"

Something sparked in Beroe's hazel eyes. A glint that was more than the holy flame. Oh, yes, she wanted it. No doubt about that.

Sephre shook her head, abruptly weary of it all. "Don't worry. That's the last thing I want. I'm not even sure—" She caught herself before she betrayed too much. "What I discussed with the agia was personal."

Beroe tilted her head, studying Sephre. When she spoke, her

voice was softer. Almost gentle. "It must have been a trying day for you, sister. To be reminded that there is such evil in the world."

"I don't need reminders. Some things you can't forget."

"No," said Beroe, carefully. "Some things can only be burned away, in the embrace of the holy flame."

The woman was too clever by far. Or maybe she'd heard something. It wasn't only the novices of Stara Bron who loved gossip. Sephre tried to recall if there had been anyone else in the cloister when she was pleading with Halimede. She ought to have been more cautious.

Though if she was so sure she wanted—deserved—the Embrace, why did it matter if Beroe knew?

"But the Embrace is a blessing only the agia can bestow. Or deny." Beroe watched Sephre closely.

That was why. Because knowing gave Beroe another tool to manipulate her.

"I've seen it, you know," said Beroe.

Sephre looked up from the milky waters, unable to help herself. She knew nothing of the specifics of the rite. "That little boy a few years ago?"

"No. Brother Dolon."

"Brother Dolon was Embraced?" That was a surprise. She had thought the man as much an institution at Stara Bron as Halimede. It was impossible to imagine the archives without his broad smile, his bushy brows arching with enthusiasm over even the smallest and humblest research request. A dozen questions crowded her tongue.

"It was well before the war," said Beroe. "You know I came very early to the temple, of course. I may be the youngest of the yellows, but I've carried the holy flame for nearly twenty years. I served my novitiate under the agia herself," she added, with a proprietary smirk.

Sephre considered privately that Halimede was fortunate that Beroe was a woman and not a hound, or she might well find herself pissed on. Claimed as territory.

"So what, then?" Sephre demanded. "You'll give me the Embrace if I help you become agia?"

A tinge of crimson colored Beroe's cheeks. "It's not about wanting to be agia. It's about what's best for Stara Bron. Can you honestly tell me you don't see the signs? That something terrible is coming? I'm asking you to help me *stop* it. To be the hero you say you are."

Cheers battering her ears. Her hands full of flowers. Someone slapping her on the shoulder. And inside, her soul screaming, her hands raw and rough from washing, and yet they never felt clean.

Before she knew it, Sephre was sloughing herself out of the water, shivering on the tiled floor, steam rising from her skin and her hair slithering around her shoulders. Her breath came too quick. She snatched a towel from the pile nearby, wrapping it round herself. "I never said I was a hero." She spun on her heel and quit the room.

===

When Sephre first arrived at Stara Bron, the slow, steady routine of prayer and chore had been a relief. She did what she was told. Chopped carrots. Lugged pails of water. Sang first rites every morning with the bright dawn stinging her eyes.

So when they sent her to the garden to dig out stones, she did that too. Dug deep, until her spade turned up a dark, rich loam. And then, for no reason at all, she sank to her knees in the soft earth, tears sliding down her cheeks and pattering the soil like rain.

She wept until her breaths softened to small gasps. And there was Sibling Abas kneeling beside her, holding a tiny horn cup to her lips, full of something sharp and pungent that unlocked the tightness in her chest. Teeth chattering, bones aching, she asked them what the draft was.

Come into the workshop. I'll teach you how to make it.

And that was that. Abas never asked why Sephre wept. Which

was good, because Sephre didn't know herself. Her body was an alien thing sometimes. An untamed beast that could turn wild at the smallest thing. The scent of burning cedar, a pool of rainwater if the light caught it at the wrong angle, even just the cold smoothness of a metal ladle against her palm.

Over time, she'd learned to quiet the beast. To creep past it, so it would not wake. She came to value the peace of the herbarium, the calm steady work of tending the plants, seeing that dark, deep soil birth new life.

Then came the morning just over a year ago, when Sephre found Abas slumped among the herbs, the scent of crushed mint and lemon balm stinging the air. Not dead, thank the Fates. But the elder ashdancer never fully recovered, developing a tremble in their legs and arms that made their old work impossible. They retired to the infirmary, and Sephre found herself responsible for the herbarium.

But that didn't mean Sibling Abas had lost interest in their former domain.

"Have you trimmed back the nettleswift?" they asked. "Ah, that's it. Thank you, child."

Sephre bent her head to hide her chagrin, scooping up another bit of ointment and rubbing it into the leathery sole of Abas's foot, feeling the tightness relax beneath her fingers. She hadn't been a child in over three decades, but she supposed someone nearly twice her age had the right to call her that. "Yes. And I put up the dartgloss. And I've got plenty of spindleroot ready for winter chilblains."

Abas snorted. "And you don't need some old goat telling you what to do anymore, I suppose?"

Sephre bit the inside of her lip. Abas looked more amused than insulted, but regret stung her. "That isn't . . . I just don't want you having to worry. Your garden is doing well."

"I'm more worried about my apprentice."

Abas had always seen her so clearly. "Your ankles feel a bit swollen," she said. "I'll bring some of the nettle tea next time."

"You think if you ignore me, I'll forget I asked?" asked Abas dryly. "My memory isn't *that* far gone. And I'll always have an ear for you."

Her love for the old ashdancer stabbed sharply. That had always been Abas's gift. Letting her be. Letting her speak, rather than telling her who she was and what she ought to be. A part of her wanted desperately to tell them about her day, but equally, she didn't want to burden them with her fears.

She cleared her throat, rubbing the last of the salve into Abas's instep. "It was just . . . a hard day."

"Because of the corpse?" At Sephre's startled look, Abas gave a grim smile. "I can listen to gossip as well as anyone. The kitchen novice who brought us dinner said that the woman died of snakebite, and that her body was half covered in scales."

Sephre snorted. "By tomorrow it will be five corpses with glowing eyes and fangs, dripping pools of poison." Ridiculous. And yet a lump caught her throat as she recalled the reality. The girl's thin wrist, the bracelet of carefully woven beads. Blue and green and white, forming the stylized eye of the Fates. Meant to guide the wearer home, if ever they were lost.

"Yes," she admitted. To Abas, she could say such things. "She was a child. Barely fifteen. Too young." She dragged in a shaky breath. "Beroe is convinced it's a sign that the Serpent is returning."

No doubt she was the source of the outlandish rumors. Did Beroe think that if she roused all Stara Bron to alarm, Halimede would be forced to act?

"What do you think?" asked Abas.

Sephre didn't *want* to think anything about it. She wanted it to be wiped away, gone. To have never happened. She sat back, tucking away the jar of ointment. "I think I've far too much work in the herbarium to have time for a second cataclysm."

The old ashdancer's laugh held the crackle of banked embers. Abas reached for her hand, fingers fumbling, then clasping tight. She felt the tremor, but also the strength.

"Child, did I ever tell you about turnsole?"

"It's a weed."

"*Weed* is a word for things ignorant people deem useless. But everything has some use."

Sephre eyed them suspiciously. "Is this some sort of inspiring metaphor to encourage me to believe in myself?"

Abas squeezed her hand again, then released it. A wry smile bent their thin lips. "I should know better, I suppose. You don't need me for that. What you *do* need is my recipe for azarine ink. Now stop goggling and get out your tablet."

Dutifully, Sephre tucked the ointment away, retrieving a small wax tablet and stylus from her satchel. Abas proceeded to dictate the instructions, then insisted that Sephre read it back to them three times to ensure she'd gotten all the details. She slid the tablet away, then went to fetch a cup of warm lemon-water. Talking had brought back Abas's cough.

When she returned, Abas was already drifting into sleep. She set the cup on the table beside their bed, moving softly. Watching the slow rise and fall of their chest, feeling a deep, bittersweet ache of gratitude and affection and wild fury that the old ashdancer could not live forever.

It was like watching a featherfrond, the bright golden petals fading, thinning, curling into themselves, seeming to wither to nothing. And yet the nothingness was a lie. Inside were a hundred silken strands, each tipped with a tiny seed, ready to burst out in one final, transitory puff that would carry life onward, to some new and unknown soil.

Soon, Abas would be gone. They knew it, but they didn't seem to fear it. Was it because they had done what Halimede said? Made themself pure? Or maybe they'd just been a better person to begin with.

You think no one else in the world has regrets? Sephre chided herself. *You're not so special as that.* She checked the brazier to make sure the coals would last through the night. At the infirmary door she paused, glancing back over the room, slumbering in the low golden light. Two of the five other beds were filled, both elders like Abas. A month ago there had been three, but ancient, owlish Sister Glauce had died a fortnight past.

Glauce, who had been the one to take Sephre aside when she was a miserable novice, and shared her trick for surviving Vasil's tedious serenity exercises—a layer of padded cloth secreted in her habit that she could use to protect her knees from the stone floor of the meditation hall. *Serenity is a lot easier to find when you're comfortable,* she'd said, with a warm, wicked smile.

If the Serpent waits long enough, no one will be left to stop him.

Sephre grimaced. The last thing she needed was Beroe stuck in her head. Her sandals scuffed lightly along the hallway, carrying her toward the garden. She had to get back to the workshop, to see what Brother Timeus had made of the blacksap she'd left him to boil down, and perhaps get a start on compounding the azarine ink. That was her job now. That was her role here at Stara Bron.

The scuff of her footsteps became a crunch as she emerged onto the gravel path. Sephre paused, breathing deep, drinking in the green, vivid scent of her domain, holding it deep to settle her.

Ssss.

Her hand went to her hip, muscles stubbornly reaching for the sword she had given up ten years ago. Apparently Timeus wasn't the only one who still thought of Sephre as a soldier. But she was an ashdancer now, she reminded herself.

Sparks flickered from her fingers, spilling golden light over the darkness, revealing the boxwood hedges and soft billows of flosscap. She squinted, searching for any hint of movement. Her heart thrummed briskly, but the old calm flowed through her, holding her tense and ready.

Nothing. She was an old fool, hearing things in the dark. It was probably one of the temple cats. This was Stara Bron, after all. Surely no creature of the Serpent would dare breach its walls, knowing it was full of ashdancers capable of burning them to a toasty crisp.

A pang of unease chased the thought. Not everyone in Stara

HOUSE OF DUSK 51

Bron was a full-fledged ashdancer. The lay-servants would have returned to their homes in the village by now. But not the novices. Not Timeus. Sephre cut abruptly through the bed of mint, arrowing toward the workshop. It was so quiet. What if—

She snipped the thought like a loose thread. Worry changed nothing. She squinted into the workshop. The large double doors were propped open, and by the glow of the cooking hearth she made out a lanky figure in gray slumped motionless across the table.

Panic surged up her throat.

Then the boy stirred. One hand brushed his cheek. He murmured something sleepily. A moment later she heard a faint snore. Lined up on the table before him were a dozen freshly sealed bottles.

Sephre sagged in relief. Only a cat, then. Or a breeze in the whispergrass. Or any number of things that were not dire minions of the underworld.

A movement stuttered in the shadows to her right. The stench hit her a heartbeat later, curdling her stomach, making her gag.

Two gleams of light winked in the darkness. Eyes that were dark as a bruise, yet somehow luminous, burning between the ragged strips of a tattered linen shroud. The same shroud she had seen hours earlier.

But this wasn't Iola. Not anymore.

CHAPTER 6

SEPHRE

The corpse stood lithe and sinuous, almost graceful. The shroud hung in ragged tatters, no longer concealing the dead flesh. Its bloated, purplish-gray feet were clotted with earth. The arms had an oily sheen, the fingers tipped with nails that were longer and sharper than they had been in the crypt. The little beaded bracelet was gone. At least she could not see the girl's face. Only those horrible, dark-gleaming eyes.

Eyes that watched her now, filled with a terrible hunger.

Skotos. She knew the word from stories, from her training, from her vows. But she had never thought to truly face one. For a heartbeat, she froze, panic stitching her tight, promising that if only she stayed still and silent, she would be safe.

Then something slid into place within her mind, a key unlocking a door long sealed. It swung open easily, and everything was right there, waiting. She unclenched her fists, brandishing the sparks of yellow flame. Too late to try to sneak up on the thing. Just as well. Sephre had always preferred a straight-on fight.

The skotos gave a low, mocking hiss. It turned toward the workshop. Toward Timeus, still sleeping, innocent and powerless, with no flame to guard him.

"You're not touching one hair on that boy's head." She moved to block its path, ignoring the snap and crunch of root and frond underfoot. She could plant more later. What mattered now was keeping this unholy thing away from her apprentice. Gold fire crackled in her hands. Cold fury burned in her heart. "You'll have to get past me first."

"*Yesss . . . you . . . the one . . . we seek.*"

The whispery words froze her. "Me?" she asked, stupidly, uselessly.

The skotos wove from side to side, like a snake preparing to strike. Linen still covered its mouth, but she saw the jaw working beneath. "*To stop . . . return.*"

"The return of what?" Not the Serpent. That would make no sense. Surely the skotos wouldn't wish to prevent that. Maybe it was afraid that she would stop it? Because she was an ashdancer?

One arm lifted, rippling with a boneless grace that made her stomach clench. A taloned finger jabbed at her. "*Destroy.*"

"Right, thanks for clearing that up." Enough. She wasn't going to get answers from this thing. "Time to burn you back to whatever pit you crawled out of."

The demon gave no sign of alarm. Only gave a low, slithering snicker. Its bruised eyes held her. "*You . . . also . . . burn . . . baleful one.*"

Sephre lunged, arms spread wide, flames licking from her palms. Bright gold, so pure it made her heart sing. She slammed into the skotos, grappling dead flesh and shadow. Cold tendrils slithered under her fingers, slick as oil. She gritted her teeth, willing herself not to let go.

Brightness spilled through her, no longer a gentle warmth to drive back the shadows. It raged, hungry and relentless, consuming all. *A silent street. A cut-off wail. Blue eyes, transfixing her with their desperate plea.* Yes. Burn it all away. For an endless moment she danced on the edge of the inferno, welcoming the coming immolation.

Timeus! Gasping, Sephre tore herself back from the brink. Not yet. Not until Timeus was safe. Not until the skotos was dust. She coiled the flames about her hands, then shoved outward, at the demon.

Engulfed in yellow fire, the corpse writhed. Its agonized shriek tore Sephre's soul. Monstrous, but with an echo of humanity. A girl pleading desperately to be saved, even as she fell apart.

A gasp. Then sudden darkness, and only a shadow of ash sifting to the earth. It was gone.

Just as Sephre allowed herself to sag in relief, she heard a grunt from the direction of the workshop, followed by a sharp gasp and a crash of shattering glass. Summoning another handful of golden fire, she charged across the garden. "Timeus?"

"Oh no no no no," he was saying, miserably, standing amid the ruin of a dozen cracked and shattered jars, and a spreading pool of dark, sweet-smelling tincture. "I'm sorry, sister! I was waiting for you, but I must have fallen asleep. I didn't mean to knock them over. I was having a dream . . ." His lips twisted, brow furrowing. "A nightmare. But that's no excuse," he finished, dipping his head wretchedly. "I'll get the broom."

"No," Sephre said, forcing calm into her voice. No need to panic the boy. "I've kept you up too late, brother. Go back to the dormitory. You need to sleep. And don't worry about the jars. I startled you awake. It was . . . my fault."

Thankfully, the boy still seemed to be half asleep. She held her tongue, held her swirling thoughts tight as she shepherded him out of the garden, through the halls, and safe inside the novices' dortoir.

Safe. Was he? Were any of them? Sephre swallowed. She was shivering now, her body reacting belatedly to the rush of battle, grappling with the fear she'd blocked away in order to fight the demon. She wanted to flee back to the herbarium, to sweep away the broken glass and set it to rights and pretend none of this had happened.

But it had. And she could not run from it.

She gave herself five long breaths to steady the trembling of her limbs. Then she turned toward the stairs that would take her to the agia's rooms.

━━━

Sephre kept her gaze fixed on the wall behind Halimede as she gave her report. She stared at painted flames as she recounted all that had happened in the garden, from the first whisper of alarm to the discovery of the skotos to its banishment. She did not spare herself or Halimede any details. Including the demon's whispers. *You . . . the one . . . we seek.* Partway through she realized she was standing at martial attention with her hands clasped behind her back, but she could not bring herself to shift position until she finished.

Silence slammed down. Then Halimede gestured to a chair beside the map table. "Sit."

Sephre sat. It felt good. Her legs were unsteady. Those damn stairs. She felt empty, now, having given her account. She was only dimly aware of Halimede moving softly about the room, a crackle of flame, the clink of pottery.

"Are you injured?" asked Halimede, now seated across from her. A cup of tea had appeared in Sephre's hands, the heat warming her palms, the steam sweet with honey and spices. Cardamom and clove.

"No." Sephre took a sip of the tea. Then another.

"And Brother Timeus?"

She shook her head. "He didn't even know it was there. He thought it was a nightmare."

"So you and I are the only ones who know of this."

She lifted her gaze. "Are you going to keep it secret?"

Halimede pressed her lips to a thoughtful line.

"What if it comes back?" Sephre prompted.

"A skotos can only remain in this world so long as it possesses some physical vehicle," said Halimede. "Usually a human corpse. Sometimes an animal, though those have lesser power, according to the teachings. In either case, if the material vessel is destroyed, the demon has no choice but to return to whence it came. Back to the Labyrinth of Souls."

Sephre sagged slightly. But it was only a sip of relief, and she was still thirsty. "What about Iola?"

Under normal circumstances, such a spirit would also return to the perilous land of the dead. The maze of sinuous and twisting passages was said to shift like the coils of the Serpent himself. Dank with pools of poison, twined with vines of perfumed dusk-bloom said to lure the dead astray, chasing phantasms of unrealized dreams. All to test each mortal spirit with the shames and sorrows they carried with them from this life. But Iola had been young. Surely she had no great shadow on her soul. Surely she would find her way through the labyrinth, casting off all the dross of this life so that she could be reborn anew.

But Halimede's expression turned grave. "For a skotos to claim a mortal body, it must first consume the spirit bound to it. That is how they gain entry to this world. I fear she is . . . gone."

Gone. Not just lost to this life, but utterly annihilated. Never even to be reborn. The teacup trembled in her hand. Sephre set it down with a clatter. "It's my fault."

"No," said Halimede, sternly. "The girl was lost long before you burned her body to ash. The demon took her. Not you."

"But it came for me. It said I was the one it was hunting. If I hadn't been here, maybe then—"

"Then the skotos might well have destroyed Brother Timeus. You cannot blame yourself."

Clearly the agia didn't know her very well.

"It's far more likely that the demon came for you because you're an ashdancer," continued Halimede. "It saw you as a threat. There may be no more reason than that."

"If it just wanted to kill ashdancers, there were half a dozen closer to the crypt than me. But none of them were attacked." She'd checked, tracing back the trail of gruesome ichorous spatters and tatters of fallen linen the thing had left in its wake. The path had led unerringly from the crypt to the garden. "It came for *me*."

Halimede held a question behind her teeth. Sephre could see her considering whether to release it. Finally, she spoke. "Iola bore a mark. Is it possible you bear the same?"

Grimly, she kilted up the hem of her habit. Dirt and bits of leaf clung to her ankles, but nothing more. Her sleeves next, quickly, before fear could sink its teeth.

Nothing but her own skin, marked only by the handful of familiar scars, testament to her days as a soldier. A scattering of freckles, but everyone had freckles. Sephre breathed out.

"There," said the agia. "No mark."

Not on her skin. But she had other wounds. *Baleful one*, the demon had called her. "The skotoi feed on evil."

"Suffering would be more accurate," said Halimede. "The skotoi feast on the pains and fears of the dead. As each spirit cleanses itself, it leaves behind such things. Some legends say the Serpent created the skotoi for that purpose, to keep his labyrinth from becoming choked with their poison."

"So if one of them managed to escape, they'd be hunting the same thing. Someone stuffed full of pain and shame." If so, best to remove the fatted pig from the table. "Agia, please, won't you—"

"Enough, sister." Halimede was starting to look irritated, but Sephre could not stop herself.

"You gave Brother Dolon the Embrace," she accused. "Why him, and not me?"

The agia regarded her coolly. "That is not your concern. And you should know better than to ask."

The reprimand stung. As it should. She was being mulish, childish.

"You swore to honor me as your agia," Halimede reminded her, not unkindly. "To follow the rules of this order."

True. All true. The more fool her for doing so. Had she learned nothing from the last time she made herself someone else's tool? Trusted someone else to command her?

But Halimede was not Hierax. Sephre drew a steadying breath. "I'm sorry, Agia. I was out of line." She bent her head, both in contrition, and to avoid the agia's piercing and far-too-sharp gaze.

"I accept your apology." Halimede sighed. "And I see your struggles, sister. I recognize the burden you carry."

But you will not let me set it down. Sephre caught the thought before it could show on her face. Instead she asked, wearily, "What now? Will you send word to the king?"

"No."

Given that she'd just been chastised for impertinence, Sephre ought to have held her tongue. "Why not? Why risk making Hierax our enemy? Wouldn't it be better to have him as an ally?" The king might be a vainglorious ass, but he did have a highly trained and competent army. If the skotoi truly had returned—and if there were worse to come—the ashdancers could only do so much. As Beroe said, there were simply not enough of them.

The agia folded her lips tight, her expression turned inward. Sephre tried again. "There's something else going on, isn't there? Some reason you don't trust Hierax."

"If only it were so simple as that." Halimede's shoulders drooped, making her seem suddenly small and tired and worn. There were dark blotches under her eyes. Why hadn't Sephre noticed them earlier? *Because you were too caught up in your own concerns, that's why.*

"Please, Agia," she said. "You said you needed me. If that was true, then tell me what I can do. Tell me what you're afraid of."

Halimede did not answer immediately. She stared into her cupped hands. A single spark of blue kindled there, unwavering. "I swore an oath to the agia before me, on the day he named me his heir. The same oath he swore to the agia before him, and she to her predecessor, and so on. Back to Cerydon."

Sephre shook her head, not recognizing the name.

"Cerydon was agia three centuries ago. They led Stara Bron through the terror and unrest of the cataclysm."

So they would have been alive at the same time as Heraklion. Maybe even known him. "What was the oath?"

The blue flame flickered. "To keep something safe. Something entrusted to Cerydon all those years ago."

"Safe from what?"

"From the Ember King. Lest we bring about a second cataclysm."

"But the Ember King was a hero," Sephre blurted out. "He *ended* the cataclysm."

Halimede lifted her gaze. "According to the official histories, yes."

Sephre opened her lips, but found she had no protest. The official histories called her a hero, too. She had ended a war, too.

"What's the truth, then?" she asked. "What really happened?"

"The truth." Halimede gave a wry snort. "Is there any truth, other than what we see, here, in the moment? The past burns to ash and the future is beyond our sight."

"Very poetic," said Sephre. "But it doesn't answer the question."

Halimede pursed her lips. "I've told you all I can. If there were more details, they did not survive the retellings."

"Do you know what it is? The thing we need to keep safe?"

Blue flames sparked in Halimede's eyes. "Yes. But *that* is something I swore not to speak of to anyone but the ashdancer who will be agia after me."

"That's fine," said Sephre hastily. "I don't need to know." She seized her teacup, as if it could shield her from the agia's expectant gaze. "Right now I'm more worried about the skotoi. The star sign. This isn't a coincidence."

Halimede stared at her a moment longer before nodding. "No. Cerydon warned that there would be signs. That there are those who carry the weight of the past, even if they do not know it. Many things may be reborn, not just the Ember King."

A flicker of ice licked up Sephre's spine. There was something strange in the way Halimede's eyes held her. But before she could name it, the woman looked away, saying, "We need more information."

"Somehow I doubt the Serpent is going to come knocking at our door, begging to explain his nefarious plans."

Halimede gave a grim smile. "No. But there is an opportunity to learn more. And perhaps it will soothe your fears that your presence here endangers Stara Bron." She gestured to the map sprawled across the nearby table. "I have a task that would take you from the temple for a time. It's not without risk, but it could gain us answers."

"What task?"

Halimede tapped a wrinkled finger to the northwest of Stara Bron. Another marker rested there, beside a dot labeled *Potedia*. A village some seven miles from the temple, with a populace that was more sheep than people. They tithed a small supply of woolen cloth each year. Sephre had traveled there once with Sibling Abas, years ago, to perform a cleansing of the tombs. They had stopped along the way to collect a particular species of creeping pergem that grew in the high meadows.

It took Sephre a moment longer to recollect the significance of the marker. Or rather, the number 48 painted onto the wood. She sucked in a breath.

"Another death?"

"The most recent yet. They found him yesterday eve."

"So you want me to go and examine the body? Check it for snakebite?"

"It *was* snakebite. The tomb keeper's death report said as much."

"And . . . did he have the same mark as the girl Iola?"

"He wouldn't know to look for it. Thus far we've only instructed the tomb keepers to report deaths by snakebite," said Halimede. "You will go and see for yourself. Check the body for the mark. Or any other worrying signs."

"Like if it gets up and tries to kill me?" Sephre offered wryly.

Halimede's lips crimped. "Indeed. Which leads to your second task. Even the invocation of the merciful flame could not guard Iola's soul. It seems we need a stronger deterrent. Once you have completed your examination, you will invoke the consuming flame. We must not allow another demon into this world."

Sephre's breath caught. The consuming flame was the most potent rite she knew, save for the Embrace itself. But rarely used, and for good reason. It utterly incinerated the corpse, removing any possibility of it being inhabited by a skotos. But in doing so, it deprived the soul of their connection to the mortal world, and the prayers and grave goods that might grant them strength during the trials of the netherworld.

HOUSE OF DUSK 61

Halimede arched a brow. "I realize you've spent much of your time in the herbarium these past years, but I trust you haven't forgotten your training?"

"No," Sephre found her voice again. "It's just . . ."

"It is better than the alternative," said Halimede. "The family will understand. It is our highest blessing, after all."

We'll see about that. But Sephre nodded, recognizing the logic. "Anything else?"

"Be wary," said Halimede. "And watchful. The demons have already come for you once. And they may have a mortal agent."

"The green-eyed stranger?" Sephre scoffed. "I'll be fine. I can take care of myself."

"I have no doubt of that. But you will not be traveling alone."

CHAPTER 7

YENERIS

Yeneris walked along the hallway, five precise steps behind Sinoe. Close enough that she could still serve her purpose. Not so close that she intruded on the royal presence.

She saw how Sinoe's shoulders hunched. The clench of her jaw that had been there ever since her brother delivered the summons.

But this was an opportunity. That's what mattered. A chance to finally see the fabled Sibyl of Tears at work. Better to focus on that. Not the way Sinoe's slender fingers clutched at the hem of her gown, picking and picking at the embroidery.

"He's a mystic," Ichos was saying. "A dedicate to the Serpent."

A small thread of relief unspooled. There had been a small chance it might have been another Bassaran agent. But this was nothing to do with her.

Still, she had to be cautious, if Lacheron was involved. It was the last warning Mikat had given her. *Above all, beware the king's heron. He is a master of rumor and secrets. His people are everywhere. You never know when you might fall under his shadow. His sharp beak waiting to plunge and tear you into the light.*

She'd asked Mikat why no one had been sent to simply kill the man, if he was such a danger to their cause. *They were. They failed. The man has an uncanny ability to survive.*

Yeneris halted behind Sinoe as they confronted a tall, arched door. Two soldiers flanked it, their bronze armor shimmering in the light of the brazier, their faces hidden beneath the ostentatious helms the Helissoni favored, scarlet crests like bloody wounds. As if they were proud of all the death they wrought.

Careful. She schooled her expression to calm indifference.

But her heart would not listen. It rattled in her chest. She stared up at the doors, heavy and glossy black, set with bright silver studs. She tried to count them, to steady herself. When they finally peeled open, she had reached eleven, the number of great deeds of Akoret. She tried to take courage in that, as she followed Sinoe and Ichos into the king's audience hall.

The chamber was large, the high ceiling domed, with an oculus at the center staring up into the night sky. It felt larger still, with so few people within. Braziers burned before each of the eighteen marble pillars bracing the curved walls. The flickering light caught in the carved stone of the capitals, so that the lions and stags seemed to leap and prowl, hunting and hunted.

On the far side stood an alabaster chair, flanked by two lions, though these were carved of red porphyry and decorated with golden collars. On the left, the sleeping lion, his ruddy mane curled like a magister's beard. On the right, the wakeful lioness, her eyes winking rubies, her jaws pulled back in a growl of warning, gold-tipped claws ready to pierce her stone pedestal. Between them sat the king.

Yeneris had prepared herself. She did not stumble. She had never seen Hierax before, except at a distance. But she knew all too well what he had wrought. The lives spent for his pride and ambition.

The hard part isn't remembering who you're supposed to be, Mikat had warned her. *It's forgetting who you truly are. The face you hide. The tears you cannot spill.*

She would never forget. She lowered her head, studying the man through the veil of her lashes. Heavy-lidded, heavy-lipped, heavy-browed. Everything about him was slightly overdone. Like the paintings in the oldest temples, the ones that had frightened her as a girl, because the people in them had looked so odd, their eyes enormous, devouring the rest of their faces. Her mother had told her it was because in the old times people had not yet learned that seeing too much could be as dangerous as seeing too little.

Hierax had those same eyes. They fixed on Sinoe.

The princess breathed in, a hitch in her step the only sign that she felt the weight of her father's gaze. Ichos quickened his pace, so that he was slightly in front of her.

The air pressed on Yeneris, a storm waiting to break. Was it only her thrumming heart that made the room feel so thick?

They were halfway across the hall before she noticed there was someone else beside the king. A spare man with a lean, ageless face that reminded her of an old statue, blurred by wind and water. His clothing was equally bland, a simple tunic that was neither gray nor brown, but the same indistinct color as the thin hair scoured back above his high forehead.

"Finally," rumbled Hierax, as Sinoe and Ichos halted before him. "If I'd known it would take you so long, Ichos, I would have sent one of the soldiers instead."

Yeneris had halted several paces back, making herself small and insignificant between two of the pillars. It meant that all she could see was the slight flutter of Sinoe's sleeve as the girl touched her brother's arm.

"It wasn't Ichos's fault, Father," she said. "I was in the garden. He had to come in search of me."

The king's jaw jutted. "I will assign blame as I see fit." He beckoned toward an annex along the side of the hall.

Two soldiers stepped forth, a man shuffling between them, wrists bound with thick rope. Behind them followed a pair of servants, one carrying a small brazier, the other a light wooden writing desk.

The servants moved with a practiced air, as if they'd done this many times. The one with the brazier set it down midway between Hierax and his children, the bronze feet precisely matching the lines of the marble floor. Then they drew back to stand beside the scribe, who knelt at the desk, waiting.

Hierax flicked his fingers. "Lacheron." The colorless man responded, pacing out a few steps.

Even now, with all their attention upon him, the man seemed

indistinct. Yeneris found her gaze slipping away from his face, to the gray-brown weave of his tunic, to the single bronze pin at his shoulder, to the pattern of his shadow on the wall behind him. She knew very little about Lacheron, other than that he'd served Hierax even before his rise to power. He struck her as one of those men who hitched their cart to the strongest ox, hoping it would pull them to greatness.

"We captured the man in the western foothills three days ago," said Lacheron, "where he had summoned a host of skotoi and sent them against his own kin."

The prisoner jerked his head up, eyes wide, protests rendered to gibberish by the cloth stuffed in his mouth.

"Remove it," said Lacheron.

One of the soldiers pulled the cloth free.

"I didn't!" the protest tore out of the man, ragged with outrage and pain. "I tried to stop them! But I couldn't . . . I couldn't . . ." He shuddered.

"Lies," said Lacheron, coolly. "We can see the truth, written on your own skin." He gestured to the prisoner's left arm, where his sleeve had been torn away. Beneath, Yeneris could see a ring etched onto the man's skin. "The Serpent's mark," said Lacheron. "The man is a mystic, a traitor to the Ember King and all he stands for."

The words skimmed past Yeneris like clouds across the sky. There was nothing she could catch hold of. Her training had focused on other things. How to kill a man without spilling blood. How to move silently. How to hold a perfect mental map of the palace in her mind. She wasn't like these Helissoni, obsessed with claiming old glories. Her duty was to the future.

"No!" the man protested. "I swear by the Fates! It's not true."

"You do not need to lie," Lacheron told the prisoner, his voice smooth as a pebble along the shore. "You cannot deceive the Sibyl of Tears. She hears the whispers of the Fates."

The prisoner was terrified. He shifted his feet. He wanted to run.

"You have a choice," Lacheron continued, still in that voice that should have been reading out shipping accounts. "You can tell us where to find the dagger now, of your own free will, and earn a quiet death. Or the sibyl will reveal your secrets, and you will die screaming."

The man slid a terrified look toward Sinoe. "I don't—I can't—Fates, they're all dead. I tried to stop them! Please believe me!"

Lacheron's lips pressed thin. He gestured for the soldiers to restore the gag. "Then we'll find our own truth." Lacheron turned to face Sinoe. For the first time, there was a spark to sharpen his features, giving Yeneris something to catch hold of. A brightness in his eyes, which now struck her as a clear gray.

"Sibyl," he said. "It's time."

The princess had gone very still. Like a small creature, sensing the circling eagle above.

"It's very late, Father," began Ichos. "Surely this can wait until—"

"You think the future of our realm can wait?" Hierax leaned forward, the long glimmering folds of his tunic catching the light. There was more gold at his throat. Glinting on his fingers as they gripped the head of the snarling lioness. "Lacheron has brought me rumors for months now. And tonight, a report of skotoi, spawned from our own necropolis."

She held her face still, watching Ichos stir at that. How he glanced to Sinoe. Then back over his shoulder, at Yeneris. She settled her vision in the middle distance, ignoring him.

"The Serpent nearly destroyed the world once before," said Lacheron. "And it was only the Ember King who saved us. Now, he must do so again. King Hierax must fulfill his destiny and reclaim the dagger Letheko. It is the only weapon that can slay the Serpent. Our only hope, if he returns."

Yeneris floundered in the sea of words, trying to stay afloat. It was jarring to hear the fabled Serpent-slaying weapon named *Letheko*, so close to her own people's word for "forgotten." But then, the Helissoni stories had always seemed so foolish to her. Why would one of the god-beasts grow jealous of the others? They were immortal creatures, vast and unknowable. Not like mortals, who loved and feared and hungered and hated. *Some people want their gods to be mirrors,* her mother had told her, once. *But the wise know that a true god is a doorway. And that we can never understand what is on the other side, until we step through.*

In the Bassaran legends it was mortals who brought pain and disaster to the world. Just as they still did, today. Easy, then, to believe this was just more Helissoni superstition. More of Hierax's myth. And yet . . .

She thought of the ghouls at the necropolis. How those uncanny shadows had slithered and coiled like serpents. No mortal had caused that, surely. Not unless they'd dabbled with the abyssal powers.

A sudden blaze of light dazzled her. Blinking, she saw that Lacheron now stood beside the brazier. She hadn't even noticed him light the coals, too lost in thought. Sloppy of her.

"Sibyl, you must seek visions in the smoke," he said. "Tell us where the dagger lies."

Sinoe did not move, except to shift her shoulders, as if she was bracing herself.

"It's a shame the Ember King reborn doesn't remember where he left Letheko," said Ichos, his wry tone scraping the silence. "He was the great hero who wielded it, after all."

The king moved so fast, Yeneris only had time to draw in a sharp breath. Then Ichos was coughing, sputtering, as Hierax's gold-banded fingers squeezed his throat. Standing, the king was tall. Taller than his son, now dangling in his grasp like a fish on a hook.

"I suffer no disloyal tongues," Hierax didn't shout, but somehow his voice still carried, resonant, implacable. "Not in my own house. Perhaps it is time to cut this one out."

The king held a sword. The blade pressed close to his son's cheek. Yeneris bit the inside of her cheek.

Ichos went suddenly limp. "No," he managed to gasp. "Please, Father. A joke."

"I did not laugh," said Hierax. The dagger trembled, the tip just beside Ichos's mouth now.

It was Sinoe who broke the moment, abruptly pacing forward to stand beside the brazier. "Father," she said. "Do you wish me to scry on my brother? Or on your prisoner?"

A strange question. But it had an instantaneous effect. The king released Ichos. The prince stumbled back a pace, turning to stare at the far wall, so that Yeneris couldn't make out his expression. Only the hard set of his shoulders.

Hierax rejoined Sinoe and Lacheron, his expression cool once more. Yeneris suspected he was the kind of man who packed every grudge and resentment away carefully, like fine jewels in a silken box, to take out later and admire.

"Let us begin," said the king.

Yeneris tensed, waiting. She had heard wild tales of Sinoe's powers. That the girl fell into fits and spoke in the language of the Fates, which could only be translated by mystics and sages. That when she was in the thrall of prophecy her tears became blood, spattering sigils on the stones that told the future. Yeneris had discarded most of what she heard as fancy. The Sibyl of Tears had never prophesied in public before, after all. Even the incident at the necropolis might be merely coincidence, a dream that happened to match reality.

Whether they were true or false made no difference. Hierax used them to gain and hold power. All that mattered now was to take what she could of this night and use it for her own purposes. And to ensure that nothing betrayed her.

But as Yeneris hunched back into the shadows, easing from one foot to the other, Sinoe suddenly turned to stare directly at her.

A thrum of panic. Was she discovered already?

But there was no accusation in the woman's gaze, only a sort of fine, firm resignation. "The pouch, Yeneris."

The pouch? Oh. The pouch. She'd almost forgotten the thing, a small silky bag that she'd been given on her first day of service, the one the master of chambers had made her swear to keep on her at all times. She'd looked inside, of course, and found only a tiny glass vial sealed with wax, containing what looked like honey. Medicine, she'd been told. In case the princess felt unwell. She must always have it ready, if Sinoe asked for it.

She drew the pouch from her tunic. "Bring it here," said Sinoe.

Yeneris approached, her steps clashing too loud against the polished marble. The king paid her no heed. She might have been an ant, crawling along the wall, so small to him. Lacheron did watch, but with half-lidded disinterest, his thoughts churning elsewhere.

Sinoe, though . . . Her attention was so fierce it nearly made Yeneris stumble. She was shamed to find her fingers trembling as she held out the pouch.

The princess nodded, but did not take it. "Keep it ready. Use it if there's blood."

Blood? A shiver rippled up her spine. She wanted to ask what it meant. If they'd been alone, she would have, but here, before the king and his heron, she felt her throat constrict. A wild fear clamped onto her, that if she spoke a single word, they would know what she was. They would hear it in her voice, in spite of all the years she'd spent filing off the edges.

So she nodded, stepping to the side. Sinoe's gaze held her for one heartbeat longer. She was frightened. That was clear as starlight. *And there's nothing you can do about it. Nothing you should do about it. Remember why you're here.*

"Let us begin." Sinoe's gaze released Yeneris, turning to the prisoner.

"Bring him," said Lacheron.

The man began to struggle again as the soldiers dragged him forward. To gasp and gargle against his gag. One of the soldiers cuffed him hard across the face.

"No, you fools," snapped Lacheron. "He must be conscious. The sibyl requires his pain if she is to see clearly."

Pain? Yeneris felt a queasy twist. That was how Sinoe's scrying worked? It was fed by pain?

The prisoner staggered, still awake, but clearly reeling. The soldiers wrestled him up to the brazier. One of them jerked the man's bound arms out, so that they were above the smoldering coals.

The other drew a small dagger from her belt, then looked to Lacheron.

"The hand," he said. "Only enough to bleed."

A slash, and the prisoner's palm was suddenly spurting blood, a red stream that spattered the coals.

As the prisoner's blood struck the flames, clouds of dark gray smoke boiled up. Hierax and Lacheron both stepped back, away from the heavy stuff. The soldiers retreated as well, dragging the prisoner with them. When she caught a whiff of the smoke, Yeneris understood why. It was foul, bitter as betrayal, making her eyes smart.

The princess stood alone, then, wreathed in gray veils. No cough shook her. How could she breathe in that smothering cloud? She stood straight, the thin linen of her layered tunic flaring and shifting, making her look as if she had become a part of the smoke itself.

Her round face no longer seemed childlike. She had become something ancient and terrible as the sea. Just watching her made Yeneris's belly swoop up and down, billowed by unseen waves. Sinoe's open eyes stared into the smoke. Gems glittered below her eyes. Tears, running down each smooth cheek.

Beside Yeneris, Ichos stood tense as a warhorse on the edge of battle. Lips crumpled, like a bit of cast-off rubbish. She thought he might be muttering something, very low.

Then Sinoe began to speak, and her voice devoured Yeneris's whole world.

Though it wasn't, truly, her voice. Not the low, musical tones she'd used to tease Yeneris. Not the firm, clean command that summoned breakfast. Not the light, silly sunshine that read aloud in the library, rapturous over some romantic trifle.

"Long has the old enemy watched and waited. Now he seeks to strike his second blow, and the world will not survive it."

This was the voice of a prophet. A voice that belonged to the sea, or a mountain, or a storm. Too large for a mortal. If Yeneris hadn't been watching Sinoe's lips, she never would have believed the words came from her.

"*The first light must reveal the weapon of unmaking.*" Sinoe writhed, her body a guttering flame. "*When it is found, when the Maiden steps forth from flame to take her rightful place, only then shall the old enemy fall.*"

Yeneris sucked in a sharp breath. Was she talking about the kore? Sinoe trembled and shook, no longer speaking. Only shaking out rough breaths as if she'd been running up the path of a thousand steps. Yeneris gripped the small vial. There was no blood, but how much more of this could the woman take?

Then suddenly the prince was striding forward, pulling his sister back from the brazier, tearing her free from the oily clouds of smoke. "Enough. You have your answers."

Sinoe shuddered, sagging into her brother's arms. Yeneris watched, feeling impotent and stupid. The girl's hair fell over her face, a sweep of darkness, gemmed with those stubborn crimson glints.

The servant who had brought the brazier leapt forward at a gesture from Lacheron, and began to smother the flames. Slowly, the smoke cleared. But the king's expression did not.

"So. It's true. The Serpent will return."

Lacheron was silent for several heartbeats, brow furrowed, a look of calculation. Then he nodded. "Indeed. And you must be prepared to meet him, my king. You must have the maiden reborn at your side."

Hierax glowered. "And yet Agia Halimede continues to refuse to restore her."

Yeneris held herself very still, but the words shook her deep inside. Restore the kore to life? Impossible. Unthinkable. How could such a thing even be possible?

"She cannot deny you now," said Lacheron. "Not with the word of the Fates on your side. And it seems she holds other secrets, as well."

He paced over to the scribe, who Yeneris now saw had been dutifully recording Sinoe's words. He bent over the tablet, a strange, quick energy seeming to spark in each movement. He was excited. Eager. On the hunt.

"*The first light must reveal the weapon of unmaking*," he read out, then turned to face the king. "And what is the first light?"

"Dawn," said the king.

"Indeed. The Sibyl of Tears has made our path clear. We will find answers in the House of Dawn. We must go to their temple. We must go to Stara Bron."

CHAPTER 8

YENERIS

"Good," said Hierax, with the fierce attention of a man biting into a bit of choice meat. "Lord Lacheron, you and Prince Ichos will see to it. It's time the fire witches made themselves useful." He swept his gaze back to Sinoe, still cradled in her brother's arms. "You've done well, daughter."

Sinoe's eyelids fluttered. She mumbled something.

"I'll take her back to her room," said Ichos, hefting her more tightly against his chest.

"No, Ichos," said Hierax. "You have other work." He nodded toward the prisoner, slumped in the grip of the two soldiers at the edge of the room. "I promised he would die screaming. You will keep that promise."

"But Sinoe—"

"The girl will tend to your sister."

It took Yeneris a moment to realize that she was "the girl." She tucked the golden potion away, then stalked over to Ichos. The prince had gone ashen, lips bloodless and tight. The look he gave Yeneris could have turned her to stone.

But he had little other option. Nor did she. Yeneris thrust out her arms, her throat dry.

"I expect you to take good care of my sister," said Ichos, his voice a threat and a promise.

"She'll be safe with me," said Yeneris. "I swear it by the Fates."

Something seemed to shiver in the air between them, over Sinoe's red-gleamed hair. Even Ichos appeared to feel it, lips parting slightly, as if breathing in the vow, tasting its truth. *You fool*, she told herself. *What was that?* She had no business making any such promise, especially binding it by the Fates. But the words were out now. Spoken. And they'd done their work. Ichos pressed Sinoe into her arms, a soft bundle smelling of smoke and honey and just slightly of fish sauce.

Yeneris clenched her jaw, keeping her expression stern, trying to ignore the tickle of Sinoe's hair as the woman nuzzled into her shoulder with a sigh. Ichos tucked a trailing fold of Sinoe's borrowed cloak more securely around her.

"I've given you a task, Ichos," said the king. "Don't keep me waiting."

The soldiers dragged the prisoner forward, into the center of the hall. Yeneris had one last glimpse of the prince's face before he turned away. Pale as ash, with a terrible resignation in his eyes.

Yeneris retreated for the door. The screams began just as she quit the room.

=====

Yeneris hovered outside Sinoe's bathing chamber, debating whether to knock again. The princess had awakened soon after Yeneris carried her over the threshold of the royal apartment, and had retreated at once to the bath. The last time she'd knocked, Sinoe had told her to go get some sleep, by the Fates, that she was perfectly fine.

That had been a quarter hour ago. Warily, Yeneris pressed her ear to the heavy mahogany, but heard only splashing within, punctuated by deep ragged breaths.

She'll be safe with me. I swear it by the Fates.

Stupid. Utterly stupid. Far worse than the legend of Khorven the Lovely, who had foolishly sworn to give his heart to a jeweled incarnal, who had unfortunately taken the promise quite literally. Vows were not something to toss away. Vows *meant* something.

Yeneris had sworn only one other vow in her life, on the night

Mikat had taken her, blindfolded, along a series of twisting alleyways so labyrinthine she thought they might have wandered into the netherworld. When Mikat had pulled the cloth from her eyes, there had been two other people waiting, faces lost in shadows, voices sharp and clear. *Do you commit yourself to our cause? Will you do whatever it takes to preserve a future for our people?*

There had been no hesitation then, either. Maybe that was the way of true vows. They sprang from your heart, from your lips, as easy as breath. *Let the Scarab herself bear witness: I swear I will set the kore free.*

Two vows. And for now, no conflict between them. Both served her mission. But what if that mission changed? Should she tell Mikat that she was compromised?

No. Because she wasn't compromised. If it came down to it, she would choose Bassara. She would choose her mission, and let the Fates curse her. She would pay that price if it meant ensuring a future for Bassara.

Resolutely, she turned away from the door.

A shriek came from the shadows near the window, followed by the rattle of claws on metal. Yeneris halted, scowling at the caged ailouron. The creature glowered back, her hawk eyes bright, her feline tail lashing. Golden wings mantled a challenge.

"What, do you think you can do better?" Yeneris growled.

Though honestly, if she weren't half convinced the ailouron would scratch her to shreds, she would have let it loose. The princess might welcome the bird-beast. In spite of its wild ways, the ailouron always gentled for her. Probably because Sinoe insisted on slipping it tidbits of every meal, doting on the creature, even naming it Tami—*honey*, in the Scarthian tongue—with not a whiff of irony.

Sinoe's heart was too soft for her own good.

Tami keened again. Her baleful stare seemed to flay Yeneris's skin.

She gave in, turning back, rapping again. "Princess Sinoe? Are you sure you're all right?"

A splash. A sigh. Then, "Go to sleep, Yen. I'm fine."

"I swore to your brother I'd see you safely to bed." Not entirely true, but close enough. Who knew what trouble a woman like Sinoe might get into, alone in a bathing chamber? She might over-heat the water and burn herself. Or slip on a tablet of soap. Really, there were endless possible dangers.

"I'm coming in, princess," she warned, before pushing the door inward.

Yeneris found Sinoe beside the bathing pool, clad only in her under-shift, a wan and tragic figure. She had a mass of pale, sopping wet fabric in her hands. Yeneris recognized the gown she'd been wearing earlier. It looked as if she'd been scrubbing at a blotch of bright crimson along the front. Blood.

"Princess!" Yeneris crossed the room in three quick paces, cursing herself. "Are you injured?"

"I'm fine. It's not my blood. It's his. The prisoner's." Sinoe batted her hands away, grimacing. But her eyes were rimmed in red as well. And there was a tremor in her voice, the rasp of unshed tears. "Don't look at me like that, Yen. I'm trying to hold it together. I can't afford any more tears just now. That's more than enough prophesying for one night, thank you very much."

Looking at her like what? Yeneris blinked, then jerked her gaze down to the tiled floor, just to be safe.

But she didn't leave. She collected the sodden gown, tossing it into the basket in the corner. "The laundry will handle that."

Sinoe huffed. "Yes. Of course. I should know better. Fates forbid I make myself useful in any other way than as my father's ferret." She crouched beside the pool, chafing her hands together. There were dark red clots under her fingernails.

Yeneris swallowed the tightness in her throat, then slid down to sit beside her. "I'll see to it, princess." She drew her smallest and most delicate blade, then took Sinoe's fingers in her own. She began to gently scrape the tip beneath her nails, one by one. It felt as if she were holding a songbird in her hands. She could feel Sinoe's pulse, thrumming beneath her wrist. It was not slowing. Yet she did seem to grow calmer, after a time.

When the blood was gone, Yeneris fetched a pot of scented oil, and rubbed it into Sinoe's fingers as well. And then, at last, the job was done. She released Sinoe's hands. "There," she said, busying herself tucking the dagger away again.

For a moment, she thought the princess was sniffling. But it was a soft giggle. "You really keep a dagger hidden *there*?"

Yeneris flushed. "It's not a spot most folk think to check," she said, stiffly.

"Where else do you hide your weapons?" Sinoe's lips quirked. "Any other interesting places?"

Well. Good. Obviously she was feeling better. Yeneris stood, retreating from the pool. "You should get some rest, princess. It's been a long night."

Sinoe's smile fractured, and Yeneris cursed herself for it. "Yes."

"Should I send for a tincture of dreamfast?" she asked.

"No. It won't help." Sinoe stifled a sigh, drawing herself up. "And I've kept you up far too late already." She glanced to the latticed window along one wall. The sky beyond showed definite signs of lightening.

"It's no trouble, princess," said Yeneris.

"Oh, I'm sure I'm a good deal of trouble," said Sinoe, merrily. And yet there was something bitter beneath it. A swallowed sigh. A wound untended.

Yeneris fumbled for something to say, but the princess was already breezing past her, out into the apartment. "Good night, Yen. I know it's your job, but you don't need worry about me. I'm stronger than I look."

Yeneris stood a moment longer, breathing in the sweet-scented steam of the bath, agonizingly aware that what she was feeling was most certainly *not* part of her job. Either job. And that she was most definitely going to worry. For Sinoe. And for herself.

Fool, she told herself, and went to bed.

Sinoe slept late the next day. Yeneris would have liked to do the same, but it was too good a chance to miss. She needed to see a familiar face. And even more, she needed to remember her true duty here. Not to stand for a full minute on the threshold of Sinoe's bedchamber, dithering over whether she might need to be woken from another nightmare.

Determinedly, she headed out from the apartment, taking a basket as her excuse. Two palace guards stood in the hall outside. They would keep Sinoe safe.

Yeneris continued down the hall, the spiral steps, and out past the pillared walkway, into the gardens. Dew still clung to the greenery, a glory of diamonds in the morning sunlight that was only just slanting in above the eastern wing.

She took her time, filling half her basket with rose petals and lavender for Sinoe's morning bath. She even hunted out a gold-eyed jasmine that was still blooming, knowing it was Sinoe's favorite. The heavy scent filled her nose, making her slightly dizzy. Or maybe it was the lack of sleep.

But all the while she watched. Such elaborate lushness didn't grow and maintain itself. She spotted a half-dozen gardeners clipping and digging and weeding. Then, at last, one particular gardener: an older woman, a blue scarf twisted round her gray-threaded hair, her light olive skin tanned by the sun. A woman who looked utterly harmless, moving slowly and deliberately about her simple work.

A woman who was neither simple nor harmless, as Yeneris well knew.

She paused on the opposite side of the rose trellis that Mikat was tending, making a show of searching for more blooms for her own basket.

"Progress?" That was Mikat. No pleasantries. Only business. Which was sensible, given the danger to them both in such meetings.

Even so, Yeneris felt a pang, wanting more. Wanting to unfold herself from the small, tight thing she had become.

Foolish. Mikat had never been that sort of mentor. And her harshness had kept Yeneris alive. Had rescued her from the churn and despair of the camp, giving her purpose again. *I am hard on you, I know,* she'd once said. *But a sharp blade requires a whetstone. And you wish to be my sharpest blade, don't you?*

"I haven't seen the reliquary," she said, reaching to pluck a perfect pink rose. "Sinoe hasn't even spoken of it. They keep the kore's bones sealed in the former queen's chambers. I could try to break in, but it would be risky."

Mikat considered a fading bloom, her expression hard, a pair of clippers ready in her hand.

"That might change now the king is back, though," Yeneris added quickly. "And I've other news."

"Go on." The clippers snipped, severing the faded bloom.

"I went with the princess into the city last night." She described what they'd encountered at the necropolis. The ghouls. And the scrying Sinoe had done, later, on the man with the serpent mark.

The clippers went silent. Mikat's jaw tightened. "What does it mean? They cannot hope to restore the kore to life. They have her bones, but they cannot touch her spirit."

"The king believes it," Yeneris said. "He's convinced that the agia of Stara Bron has that power. Do you . . . do you think that's possible?"

Mikat studied one of the faded roses. "I do not question the power of the Stara Bron. The Phoenix has been the enkindler of life since the dawn of this world. But I do question this so-called sibyl."

"There *were* ghouls at the necropolis," said Yeneris. "Just as she foresaw. I fought them. She has true power, for all that she's being misused horribly."

Mikat's gaze cut to her, sudden and sharp as a blade. "As horribly misused as our people, who died to slake her father's greed? Do not forget that the woman is our enemy, Yeneris. *Your* enemy."

"That isn't what I—" She stopped herself. Mikat cared about strategy, about useful information—"I only meant that there's an opportunity. A rift we could . . . exploit." The word was sticky on her tongue, but she spit it out, because it was what Mikat needed to hear. Yeneris couldn't afford to be doubted.

It worked. The older woman returned her attention to the rosebush. Yeneris plucked three more blooms. Her basket was overflowing. She needed to return.

"Yes," said Mikat, bending to collect her clippings. "A good thought. The more we divide the girl from her people, the more likely we can use her gifts for our own purposes. Does she trust you?"

Yeneris thought of Sinoe's hand in hers, the delicate scrape of her blade against the girl's nails. "Yes. Or . . . she's starting to."

"Then continue. Learn everything you can of these plans. If she trusts you, she will not suspect you when it's time to act."

She ought to have taken her orders and gone, but Yeneris lingered. "Act how?"

"True or false, her prophecies endanger the kore."

A chill curdled in her chest.

"Is that a problem?"

"No," she said, though her lips felt slightly numb. "I know my duty."

====

Yeneris paced along the hall as briskly as propriety allowed. It was not nearly fast enough to outrun her own misgivings.

She ought to trust Mikat. Mikat had saved her. Mikat had reached into the dusty ashes of her broken world, and kindled an ember of purpose. Yeneris owed her everything, not least of all her own life.

That was the punishment for thieving. She'd seen the bodies, hung from the old stone pillars at the edge of the camp, blood clotting their severed wrists in warning. One of them had been a boy her own age. Twelve, at most.

It hadn't stopped Yeneris. The sick ache in her belly was stronger than fear. And the Helissoni soldiers had tents full of supplies, just sitting there. She started small, learning to move slowly, silently. Snatching a single carrot here. A handful of barley there.

She grew more daring. A sack of lentils. An entire cabbage, stowed beneath her ragged tunic. Enough to not only dim her own hunger, but to share with a handful of others. The boy with the broken foot that hadn't mended. The little girl who never spoke, only made small whimpering sounds, like stifled screams. All orphans of the war, like her.

Then came the day she dared too much. One of the soldiers was roasting a chicken, and Yeneris hadn't tasted meat in months. She'd thought she had time when he stepped away to the latrine trench.

She was wrong.

His shout had frozen her, the bird clutched to her chest, the crisp, oily scent of it watering her mouth even as doom strode toward her.

Then, the miracle. An old woman, seemingly bent and harmless. A walking stick, thrust out at just the right moment. Yeneris was already running before the soldier hit the ground.

Mikat had found her later, smeared with grease, gnawing on the bones. *You're a clever girl. Quick and quiet. How would you like to steal something even better than chicken from our enemy?*

The approach of heavy footsteps broke Yeneris from her memories. Belatedly, she turned her attention outward again. She was just crossing the small courtyard that separated the eastern hall from the northern wing, where Sinoe's chambers lay. A plashy fountain spangled the air with mist. Four stone lions prowled at the corners. Azure tiles trailed a pattern of blue poppies across the floor.

Instinct drove her into the shadows behind the nearest of the lions. Her mind knew she looked a servant—dressed in the simple tunic of the household, her basket full of flowers for Sinoe's bath— but her body knew the truth: that she was something else, something sly and unwelcome.

A voice growled, deep and familiar, turning her body taut. The king! She ran one hand lightly over her thigh, taking comfort from the hard press of the dagger hidden there. She imagined drawing it. Lunging out. Stabbing it straight through one of those heavy-lidded eyes.

Not your mission. Be silent. Pay attention.

She pressed herself against the stone, breathing slowly.

"Better to send the entire third wing," he was saying. "Let them drag that fire-witch down from her sanctimonious mount and bring her here to account for herself."

A second voice, softer, calmer. "Your anger is understandable, my king. But we must be cautious. We need the agia of Stara Bron as a willing ally."

The Heron. Yeneris wished she could see the men. Voices could only convey so much. And Lacheron's was as colorless as the man himself. But she didn't dare move even the smallest bit.

"How, then?" demanded Hierax. His heavy footfalls stuttered to a stop. A faint flap of fabric suggested some imperious gesture.

"I will consult my records of Princess Sinoe's previous scryings," answered Lacheron. "Though it would be far better if—"

"No." The king spoke flatly. "My daughter stays here."

The faintest of sighs. "Sire, her visions are our best tool to reveal your enemies."

"You saw her last night." A slow step. Was the king pacing? "The toll it took on her. I . . . she is my daughter, Lacheron."

Yeneris chewed down a surge of bitterness. *I was someone's daughter, too.*

"Of course, sire. And I know it is the hardest thing in the world, to ask your child to risk herself like this. To watch her suffer, even knowing the cause is just, that it is all part of a greater purpose."

Interesting. That actually sounded like true emotion, for once. Was he speaking from experience? Mikat's people had found little information about the Heron's past. No family. Barely any records at all, prior to his first appearance as Hierax's advisor nearly two decades ago.

Whatever it was, he quenched it, continuing in his normal calm tone. "It would crush any man. But you are *not* a man. You are the Ember King reborn. The only one with the power and determination to destroy death itself. *That* is why the Fates granted their visions to your daughter. They know that you stand at the brink of a change that will reshape this world. To reject their gift would be . . . profane."

A clever bit of manipulation. Mikat was right to have warned Yeneris about the Heron.

"A new world awaits you, my king. But such things do not come without a cost, and I am sorry that your daughter must pay it. Perhaps I can find some means to help her control her gifts, once I return. I fear that she remains too free with them."

"Yes," agreed the king. "She is too free with many things. Which is why I will not risk her beyond these walls. You will find some other way to convince Agia Halimede to grant her blessing, Lacheron. And soon. My queen has waited long enough for her restoration."

Just try it. Yeneris trembled, tension and fury and cold fear mixing in her veins, as she listened to the two men's footsteps fade. *Just try it, and you'll find out soon enough that you are just a man. A man who can bleed and die like any other.*

CHAPTER 9

SEPHRE

"Gran never really liked honey cakes, but the tomb keeper told us that honey was best because bees are messengers from the spirit world," said Timeus, trotting up the trail with the boundless energy of a young goat.

Sephre squinted ahead, hoping to spot a twist of smoke. Something to indicate they were nearing the village. Her knees had begun to twinge unhappily with the seemingly endless ascent. If she hadn't been such a prideful fool, she might've put the cookpot in Timeus's pack.

She still didn't understand Halimede's decision to send the boy with her. Why not one of the initiates? Timeus had no flame. No way to guard himself, if another skotos came for her. It would be up to Sephre to keep him safe.

Maybe that was the point. Halimede wanted Sephre to know that she trusted her. That she was counting on her to bring the novice back to the temple unharmed.

"I must have mixed the batter wrong, though, because they just turned into sticky rocks," Timeus prattled on with the earnest enthusiasm of someone utterly convinced that he was speaking to a rapt audience. "Then I tried to hide them in the trash heap, but ants found them and the whole back wall of our apartment was black with them." He made a face.

So did Sephre, but that only seemed to encourage him to continue.

"Mother forbid me to make any more of the grave gifts, but she fell to ash the next day anyways. Mother said it was because Gran lived a virtuous life, but Rhea said it was because she didn't want to face any more of my baking." He gave a rueful laugh. "It's funny how it can take years for some spirits to be reborn, and others take only days. Mother said it took Granddad a full year because he was so sour over his brother stealing his recipe for goldenrod dye, and he refused to move on until Uncle Dymos burned ten bundles of his finest yellow cloth as a grave offering."

Sephre responded with a grunt, partly because she had no breath to spare, partly because she didn't really want to think about it. How long she herself might wander those gloomy pathways.

"I guess holding a grudge isn't that bad, though. I mean, compared to other things," Timeus went on. "It must be even harder when you've done really bad things. Do you think it's true? That—" He lowered his voice,"—that the skotoi can sense sinful spirits? That they hunt down all the murderers and traitors and . . . cowards?"

Sephre paused to catch her breath, and to fix the boy with a sharp look. The question had an edge of worry that was too personal. "We don't know anything for certain."

He continued to watch her hopefully. And she was his teacher, now, Fates help him. Fine. She remembered the lessons well enough. "The teachings say that you need to give up your burdens—your hates and regrets and fears—in order to find your way through and be reborn. But we can also set those burdens aside in this life." She ought to be ashamed of herself, giving the boy advice she herself followed so poorly. "And we can help others. Our holy flame can cleanse the spirits of the dead. Protect them from the skotoi."

Timeus bounded up a shelf of stone, then turned to offer Sephre his hand to tug her up. "Like that girl from Tylos?"

"What?" Sephre stumbled as she clambered up. "What about the girl from Tylos?"

Timeus flushed. "I know. I shouldn't listen to gossip. But the other novices were talking about it. How Sister Beroe gave her the invocation of merciful flame, and then the crypt was empty this morning. Her spirit has already been reborn!"

Sephre grunted, clamping down on a wriggle of guilt in her belly. She had told Halimede the truth. If the agia chose to let the rest of the temple believe a more pleasant lie, who was she to argue? She certainly didn't want to have to explain to the poor girl's family that her corpse had actually been stolen by a demon from the netherworld, her spirit annihilated. Even Beroe's invocation hadn't been enough to guard her from that fate.

The thought was a lance in her chest. She hoped they would find answers in Potedia. Something—someone—behind all this. Maybe Halimede's stranger with *striking* green eyes. She'd prefer an enemy she could fight straight on. There were too many secrets. Too much she didn't know. What was it that Halimede had sworn to protect from the Ember King? And why? *To prevent a second cataclysm.*

One had been bad enough. It had happened three centuries ago, but the signs of the upheaval were everywhere. As a girl, Sephre had loved to explore the tumbled ruins not far from her village, finding treasures there: shards of broken pottery glazed in crimson and black, etched with fanciful creatures. Glass beads. An arrowhead shaped like a hawk. She'd kept searching, until the day she found something smooth and gray, half buried in the ashy soil. When she uncovered it fully, the eye sockets stared up at her accusingly, as if the skull were offended by her living touch. And perhaps it was. It should have fallen to ash long ago. Unless the spirit bound to it was still within the labyrinth. Still wandering, unable to escape to be reborn. She'd shoved dirt back over the thing, and left it, and had nightmares for a month.

Sephre hastened after Timeus, whose long legs ate up the trail, making her feel like a beetle trundling after a grasshopper. At least he didn't seem to notice her silence, too busy spilling out his own thoughts.

"My mother says Helissoni spirits are always reborn in Helisson, but I don't know if that really makes sense. How would a spirit know? Especially if they forget everything from their previous life? And besides, it's the Fates who decide where to send them."

HOUSE OF DUSK   87

He halted, waiting for her to catch up. "Sister, do you ever wonder who you might have been? Before?"

She huffed. "No." A pale coil of smoke threaded the sky ahead. Finally. "There's the village," she said, before he could come up with any more questions. "Let's see if we can find someone to show us this body."

The village tomb keeper, Deucalion, was a surprisingly jolly man with a long, thin face and a round belly, giving the impression of a soup ladle. Sephre recalled him from her last visit, though she doubted he would remember her, given that she'd spent most of the time lurking in Abas's shadow. "Been a good seven years since we had an ashdancer come through," he said, as he led them up the stone steps to the mouth of the tomb. Like many of the hill villages, Potedia made use of natural caves to keep their dead. The entrances had been expanded, carved with decorative lintels bearing the images of the four children of Chaos, the first of the gods. Even the Serpent, Sephre noted, as they passed beneath the heavy stone and into the gloomy chamber within. The carvings must be very old, indeed.

"Sibling Abas, that was their name," Deucalion said, as he passed beneath the carved gods. "Good one, there, did right by us. Insisted on the fourfold blessing, even though it meant staying up until midnight and waking at dawn. Three of our corpses fell to ash not a week later. I hope the sibling is well?"

"Well enough," said Sephre. "They'll be pleased to hear that you remember them."

Deucalion frowned at her, then jabbed a finger. "You. You were their novice."

She could feel Timeus eyeing her curiously. She cleared her throat. "Yes. That was me. It was my first patrol."

"And now you're back with a novice of your own." Deucalion

smiled affably toward Timeus. "You can be sure we appreciate the honor of your visit."

She hoped he would still feel that way after they had completed their work.

"I was just about to move him into one of the deeper chambers. He's been washed and bound already, as you see."

He gestured to the plinth in the center of the dim room. It was late afternoon, but the bright golden sunlight hovered warily at the threshold, as if it knew it didn't belong in this place of death. "Just a moment," he said. "I'll light the torches."

"No need," Sephre said, cupping her palm, calling to the flame within her.

It surged up, bright and hungry, leaping tongues licking the stone ceiling.

"Whoa!" Deucalion retreated, shielding his eyes. Even Timeus took a step back.

What was that? Sephre frowned at the overeager sparks in her hand. Was it because they were in the tomb? Could the flames sense the presence of something baleful? She scanned the dark passages that led inward, deeper into the hillside.

"Are there many other corpses here?" she asked.

"Seven," said Deucalion, still giving her a wide berth as she moved to light the torches, filling the room with leaping golden light. "The oldest has been here twenty years. She was one of my first."

Twenty years. A long time to wander. But some souls carried greater burdens. And only when they had sloughed them off would they be free of the labyrinth. Only then would their bodies fall to ash, as the Phoenix carried their spirit into the world once more.

Unless something else found them first. Sephre swallowed hard. "So you've been the tomb keeper since then?"

He nodded. "Most folk don't care for handling the dead, but seems to me it's cleaner work than farming or fishing. Like Castor here. Barely a mark on him, aside from the bite."

Sephre turned back to the shrouded corpse, steeling herself, holding the flame close. "Your report said he died of a snakebite?"

"Yes. Definitely." Deucalion moved to the side of the plinth, gesturing to what Sephre took to be the legs. The linen was tightly wound round the body, and there was a sharpness in the air she thought might be rosemary oil. It wasn't enough to conceal the softer scent of rot beneath.

"They found him with his flock," the tomb keeper continued. "He was a shepherd, like his mother and grandmother before him. They're gone to ash now, but he has a sister in the village."

Sephre made a mental note to talk to the woman. But she had other work, first.

The holy flame gifted an ashdancer more than just the means to burn corruption. It could also reveal the unseen.

She sliced her hands through the air, two mirroring arcs, tracing streaks of flame to form the shape of an eye that remained even as she lowered her hands. Timeus gasped. "What is it?"

"An oculus. It lets an ashdancer see spirits." Sephre peered through the glimmering ring, searching the linen-wrapped corpse. But there was nothing, no hint of any uncanny gleam. "The spirit's gone." Which meant they could gain no answers from Castor himself. And that the corpse lay open for something else to claim it.

The back of her neck prickled, as if she was being watched. Sephre glanced uneasily toward the tunnels. She let the oculus die, but kept a handful of sparks ready in her palm.

"So you're done, then?" asked Deucalion. "If the spirit's passed into the labyrinth, you can't do anything more, surely."

If the spirit lingered, she might have offered it the touch of her flame, to cleanse and empower it, easing its passage through the netherworld. Hastening its rebirth. Even now, she could invoke the merciful flame to pray to the Phoenix for intercession. But there was only one way to absolutely ensure that the corpse could not serve as a doorway for something terrible.

She cleared her throat. She had other work first. "I need to examine the corpse."

Deucalion's brows arched. "He's already shrouded."

She hesitated. For some reason, it was hard to bring herself to ask the question. It would sound foolish. Or maybe she just didn't want to know the answer. "Did he have an inking on him?" she asked, measuring the size with her thumb and forefinger. "About this big, shaped like a ring?"

The tomb keeper frowned in thought. "I don't recall any inkings, but I wouldn't swear to it. Why does it matter?"

She gave a noncommittal shrug, aware that Timeus was also watching her, listening. "I'm sorry to undo your work," she said, moving to the plinth. "But this could be important."

She drew her belt knife, wincing at the flash of metal. Carefully, she sliced the blade through the linen shroud. A foul stench slammed into her nose as the cloth fell apart, revealing the mottled skin of the dead body. She bit down on a curse. Even Deucalion gave a startled, "Fates! He's gone fast."

Timeus surprised her by holding his ground, for all that his skin had a sickly gray cast. She gave him a small nod of approval before turning her attention to the corpse.

She made brisk work of it, searching the man from toe to crown. And found nothing, except for the bite itself. She wanted to feel relief, to cover him up and leave him in peace. *See? Just a coincidence.* But doubt chewed at her.

"Help me, please, Brother Timeus," she said. "I need to check his back."

To his credit, Timeus didn't hesitate, only gulped down another steadying breath, then moved to take hold of the corpse's left arm. Together, they rolled Castor to one side, exposing the broad expanse of his back. Muscles that would have hefted a young lamb easily, to bring it safely home through a storm. But now Castor was the one who was lost in the tempest, with no one to guide him. *We all walk the labyrinth alone.*

"Is that it?" asked Timeus, pointing to a shadow under the man's shoulder blade, partly hidden by the folds of the shroud.

Sephre squinted. Let out a long breath.

Seven dark lines, linking seven points into a ring. The Serpent's star sign. The same mark that she'd seen on Iola.

Prickles ghosted over her skin. She tensed, staring into the dark mouth of the nearest tunnel. *Just try it. I haven't forgotten how to fight.*

"Sister?"

She turned back to find Deucalion and Timeus looking at her the way two reasonable people might look at a person who was glaring dramatically into the darkness, holding a dagger as if it were a sword. She was breathing too fast, heart thumping, as if she were about to plunge into battle.

Carefully, she lowered her dagger, sliding it back into the sheath. It would be useless, in any case, meant for slicing cheese, not waging war against the unholy creatures of the netherworld.

Deucalion cleared his throat. "Does the mark mean something, sister?"

"Yes," said Sephre, wearily. "It means I need to invoke the consuming flame."

Deucalion rocked back on his heels, all jovial warmth gone. "You can't be serious." He stared at Sephre as if she had just declared herself high priestess of the abyss.

"I don't understand," Timeus said. "It's a blessing. Won't it help his spirit?"

"No," said Sephre. "The consuming flame destroys a corpse completely. To keep any skotos from using it to reach this world."

"But surely there's little chance of that," protested Deucalion. "Castor was a good man. Quiet, yes, but well loved. I doubt he ever had an unkind word for anyone. Would you deprive his family of the chance to pray for him? To leave offerings to strengthen his spirit?"

"I'm sorry." Sephre cupped one hand, summoning a hungry bloom of golden flames. "But if he is the man you believe him to be, then he'll find his way, with or without prayers and grave goods."

The flames leapt higher, dazzling her eyes. She could not see Deucalion's expression. Only heard his sigh. The scuff of his sandals as he stepped back from the plinth.

I'm sorry, Sephre repeated, silently, as she held out her hands to the still body of the shepherd. *Be strong, Castor. I hope you find your way quickly.*

The flames filled her vision then, leaping across the dry linen, licking across the oiled skin of the corpse, and rendering it to ash.

===

Sephre could feel Timeus watching her as they made their way back down toward the village. She owed him no explanations. He was a novice. Yet something compelled her to blurt out, "I had to do it."

"Of course, sister," he said, meekly. But she could still feel his big brown eyes staring into her shoulder blades.

A longer explanation hung from the tip of her tongue. Up until now, she'd kept the full details of their mission to herself, not wanting to alarm the boy if it all amounted to nothing. But it was clearly amounting to *something*. Something that made her skin crawl, sent her heart thumping at every dry whisper of grass, turned every innocent ripple of cloud shadow into a phantom serpent.

Fool woman, she told herself. *The skotos in your herb garden wasn't sign enough? He's not a child. Stop treating him like one.*

"You don't have to explain," said Timeus. "I'm only a novice. I don't need to understand."

She halted abruptly. "Yes. Yes, you do. Just because someone with a title tells you to do something doesn't mean it's right or noble or just."

"I'm sorry." He was shriveling like a spent bloom. Not looking at her.

Her irritation melted into regret. "No. I'm sorry. I shouldn't have snapped at you. You didn't do anything wrong."

He nodded, throat bobbing, eyes wide.

There. She'd apologized. But was it enough? Didn't he deserve more from her? "Listen, though," she said, before she could think better of it. "You *will* make mistakes. We all do. It's part of life. It doesn't mean you're cursed by the Fates. It just means you have something to learn. I'm not going to throw you out of my herb garden for an honest mistake. Believe me, I've made plenty. And not all of them honest, either."

She grimaced. "Maybe it was a mistake to call the consuming flame. Maybe I burned that man's corpse to ash and left his spirit unmoored in the labyrinth for nothing. Agia Halimede ordered it, but I did it. It was my choice. And now I'll live with it."

Timeus nodded. No longer cringing, but still cautious. "Why *did* the agia order it?"

Her throat closed, remembering the scent of rot. The thing inhabiting Iola's body, hissing at her. But Timeus had been asleep. He still believed the girl had been reborn. "Because dead bodies are how skotoi get into the mortal world."

"So you might just have saved this entire village from a rampaging skotos."

He was being far kinder to her than she deserved. She shrugged. "Only the Fates can know that," she said, as she continued down the trail.

It took a dozen more steps before he finally asked the question. "Do you really think the Serpent is coming back? Is there going to be a war?"

Zander's blue eyes blazed in her memory, his eager smile still so clear it could hollow out her heart. *What do you think, Seph? I hear it's only a matter of days. Hierax already banished the ambassador. Won't be long before the official declaration. I just hope there's still someone left to fight by the time we get there. Can't have the Second and Fifth getting all the glory!*

Sephre shook off the memory, but not the sting. And she gave Timeus her honest, heartfelt answer. "Fates, I hope not."

===

Castor's sister's name was Penthea. She welcomed them with brisk hospitality, shadowed by loss. Her clear brown eyes were red, and ash marked her cheeks, but clearly life hadn't ceased its demands for mourning. A handloom sat nearby, strung with grass-green yarn, and a little girl of about six was collecting tuffets of loose wool in a small basket.

"My brother would be honored by your visit." Penthea spoke the words by rote. Sephre remembered that numbness and disorientation, as if a great hand had plucked her up and set her back down at an angle from the rest of the world. She felt it still, when the memories surged up unexpectedly. "He was more religious than me," she added, a flicker of something sharper crossing her face. "He said when he was an old man he'd go on a pilgrimage. There's an old sky-temple path up on Mount Kronus. He meant to walk it, to purify his spirit." She drew in a shuddering breath, her gaze moving to Sephre, hopeful. "Folk say that ashdancers can speak with the spirits of the dead."

"We were too late to reach his spirit," Sephre admitted. "But we . . ." Fates, could she really tell this grieving woman she'd just burned her brother's corpse to ash? "We did what we could."

"Then . . . can I offer you a cup of wine?" Penthea offered, uncertainly.

"No, thank you. We just wanted to ask a few questions about your brother."

Penthea frowned. The little girl watched them wide-eyed from behind her mother, clearly finding the two visiting ashdancers far more interesting than her work.

"Castor? What do you want to know?"

"Anything you can tell us," said Sephre.

Penthea opened her hands, as if trying to shape something in the air. "He was kind. Gentle. I don't think I ever heard him speak harshly to anyone. When he was a boy, he insisted on looking after the orphaned lambs. He used to sing to them, and he'd stay up all night nursing them."

"He made me this," offered the little girl, tugging something from her basket, holding it up proudly. A small dog, felted of soft gray wool, cleverly embroidered with dark eyes and a playful expression. Clearly the girl treasured it.

Penthea reached out, drawing her daughter close. "He never married. I think there was someone, a boy from another village, but he went for a soldier and died across the sea. He was a good brother. A good son. A good uncle."

Sephre swallowed.

"So surely he won't wander the labyrinth long," Penthea went on. "And maybe he'll find love in his next life."

It was all Sephre could do to nod. Thankfully Timeus came to her rescue, offering a proper invocation. "May the gods guide him. It sounds to me as if he found plenty of love in this life."

Penthea nodded, actually smiled slightly. If nothing else, the visit seemed to have comforted her. But it hadn't given Sephre any answers.

"Did you . . . that is, do you know the meaning of his tattoo?"

"Tattoo?" Penthea looked puzzled.

Sephre cleared her throat. "The inking he had, on his back."

Penthea shook her head. "I had no idea. I've no notion where he could have gotten such a thing. I doubt he's ever been more than ten miles from the village." She frowned. "What was it?"

"A . . . star sign, we think."

"Maybe it was a tribute to the soldier he loved," offered Timeus. Sephre cut her eyes to him. The boy was either utterly naive, or far more clever than she'd given him credit for.

She plunged onward. "Was anything strange going on before he died?"

Penthea blinked. "Strange?"

Right. If there had been skotoi roaming about, someone would have raised an alarm long before this.

"There was a stranger in the village," piped the little girl.

Penthea shushed her. "I'm sure that's not what the sister means, Naida."

"But she asked about anything strange," Naida insisted. "A stranger *is* strange."

Sephre's skin prickled. "Do you get many travelers here?"

"No," said Penthea. "But it was probably just one of the merchants who come through every summer. Naida doesn't remember them, that's all."

"No," said the girl. "He wasn't a merchant. He had a sword."

"A sword?"

"He was very handsome, too, even though he didn't have any hair. I think maybe he was a hero in disguise, like in the shiny pig story."

"You mean Breseus and the Golden Boar?" asked Timeus, doubtfully.

Naida nodded. "You didn't see him, Mum, because you were busy at the dye pots. But he *was* a stranger, because he didn't even know how to get to Kessely. I told him," she continued, puffing up with pride, "and he gave me a gold coin to thank me!"

Penthea started. "A gold coin? Where is it?"

Naida hesitated, perhaps realizing she ought to have kept that part of the tale to herself. But she dug into one pocket, producing a small, glimmering disk.

Penthea murmured a prayer. Sephre leaned forward, squinting at the coin. "May I see that, Naida? I'll give it back," she added quickly.

The girl allowed her to take it, though her eyes remained fixed on the coin as Sephre turned it in her fingers.

It was old. The olive boughs marked it as Helissoni, but she didn't recognize the profile stamped into the metal. And no wonder. Helissoni history was crammed full of monarchs. Blood inheritance was rare. There were always plenty of claimants naming themselves this or that great hero reborn.

Some only ruled for a few months. Or, in the case of one very unlucky queen, nine days. Most of them had currency minted in their honor. Sephre turned the coin over. Her fingers froze.

HOUSE OF DUSK 97

The opposite side was stamped with another image. A ring. A serpent biting its own tail.

She offered the coin back to Naida. Clearing her throat, she asked, "Naida, do you remember what color the man's eyes were?"

Naida nodded, tucking the coin back into her basket. "I remember because they were the same color as the wool Mama was spinning that day." She pointed to the handloom in the corner. "Green."

CHAPTER 10

SEPHRE

It began to rain just before dusk. Sephre should have stopped earlier, but the hum in her bones pressed her to keep going, even when Timeus began to flag. He was a good lad, and didn't complain, but she saw how he lost the bouncy spring of his earlier energy the longer they trudged along the trail. More alarmingly, he'd gone silent, no longer asking if she thought that hills to the south looked like a sleeping lion, or whether she'd ever seen a camel, or what they were going to do if they actually caught up with the green-eyed stranger.

Sephre still didn't have a good answer for that one. Try to learn as much as she could. Try not to get killed. Try even harder not to get her novice killed. In the end, she'd told Timeus simply to keep his head down, follow her lead, and above all not say anything to incite a possible agent of the god of death to violence. Fates, she wished Halimede had not forced her to bring the boy.

Yet she didn't turn back, not even when the rain drummed down, soaking them both even through the thick cloaks they wore for travel. Timeus began to sniffle. She had to find them shelter. She wasn't going to get the boy sick on top of everything else.

The land was softer here, between the hills. Farmers had taken advantage of the terrain; they passed fields of barley and beans, even a few vineyards. Through the blur of the rain, she spotted a distant villa, the dark spears of a line of cypress leading to the gates. They could throw themselves upon the mercy of the land-owner to escape the rain, but it would take them out of their way, and likely involve far more conversation and explanations than she was prepared for.

A better option was the small barn ahead, just off the road. They could take shelter, maybe even find some hay to pillow their heads. Sephre pointed to it. "There. We'll stop for the night. Continue in the morning."

Timeus's expression bloomed with relief, giving her another pinch of guilt. "Do you think we can start a fire?" he asked, as they approached the low stone building. "We could toast our bread and cheese, and dry—oh. Hello!"

He had halted, just ahead of her, in the open door of the barn. Between the fog of the rain and Timeus's collection of lanky limbs blocking her way, it took Sephre a moment to see who he was talking to.

Her breath caught. Another traveler had taken shelter here already. A man. He had his cloak drawn about him, so she couldn't see much. But still, it was enough.

A close-shorn scalp, shadowed with dark stubble. Handsome, but with a sort of predatory leanness that unnerved her. And bright, leaf-green eyes.

For a moment, Sephre considered turning round, walking back out into the torrent of rain. But then what? They'd come looking for this very stranger. And here he was, offered up to them by the Fates like a festival cake on a platter.

A cake that might be full of venomous serpents.

A cake that *definitely* had a sword, tucked against his side, the hilt just visible beneath his cloak.

Sephre caught Timeus by the shoulder before he could say anything rash. "Let me do the talking," she whispered, holding him there until he nodded. Then she slid past him, into the barn.

It was small and low and smelled of hay. Several bales of dry grass were heaped against the stone walls. Not a good place for a fight, Sephre's old instincts warned. Too crowded, too close. Not to mention that wielding her flames in such a combustible place seemed . . . unwise.

But there was no reason to expect violence. The man hadn't leapt to his feet and challenged them. On the contrary, he'd remained exactly where he was, settled comfortably against a loose heap of hay. She wondered if he'd found it that way, or if he'd cut open one of the bales to make himself a bed.

She felt his green eyes moving over her. "Fates keep you, stranger," she said. "I see we're not the first to look for shelter here. You won't mind if we share with you?"

He could hardly refuse, unless he was the landowner himself, which she doubted. His clothing was of good quality, but worn. There were patches, neatly mended, on the cloak, and he wore simple sandals like her own, with no ornament.

He gave a shrug. "The shelter isn't mine to offer."

It wasn't really an answer, but she advanced into the barn anyway, gesturing for Timeus to set down his pack in the corner, as far away from the stranger as she could manage, and near to the door. Sephre positioned herself between them, casually laying her pack so that it would trip the stranger if he tried to come at them.

Fates, her heart was thrumming. Sephre missed her sword. Missed the heft of it, the power it gave her. But that power was tainted. It had never been just, never holy.

She curled her palm, calling to the holy spark within her. A yellow flame licked up from her skin, spearing brilliance across the dim barn.

"My name is Sister Sephre," she said, "and this is my novice, Timeus. We come from Stara Bron."

"Nilos." His eyes seemed even brighter in the light of her flame, and one corner of his mouth was quirked with either humor or irritation.

Sephre hesitated, then spoke again. "The Fates be kind to you, Nilos. We have bread and cheese to share, if you'd like to join us."

It was a risk. If he accepted, they would be bound by the ancient rites of hospitality. The Furies would not be kind to Nilos if he broke them. Like, say, by shoving his sword into her gut. Sephre would be bound, too. But she hadn't come seeking violence. She was here to learn, to gather information, that was all.

"Thank you." He reached for something beside him. Sephre tensed, but it was only a travel sack, very much like her own. "I'm not empty-handed, myself. I've wine and fresh figs to share."

Nilos drew the parcels from his pack. She tried to glimpse what else might be inside, but he flipped the leather flap closed before she could see. He unrolled a cloth between them, then tipped a hefty sack, tumbling dark purple figs into a juicy, tempting pile.

"Oh, I love figs," exclaimed Timeus. Ignoring—or more likely oblivious to—Sephre's warning glance, he abandoned his safe corner to bring forth their own provisions. "It's like a picnic," he said, cheerily adding the bread and cheese to the spread.

He was about to reach for one of the figs when Sephre caught his wrist. "You're too hasty, brother," she said, fighting to keep her voice calm. "I should ask the Phoenix for her blessing first."

Timeus curled back on himself, looking chagrined. "I'm sorry, sister. I—I forgot. I'm sorry."

He hadn't forgotten. There was no such thing. If any of the gods were going to bless a meal, it would be the Beetle. But hopefully Nilos wouldn't know any better. Sephre trusted the Furies to take vengeance against the man if he violated the bonds of hospitality, but better not to get poisoned in the first place. And he looked like the sort of man who might well risk the anger of the Furies to get what he wanted.

"God of Flame and Spirit, bless this meal." Sephre swept her hands over the food, letting the flame lick between her fingers. If there was baleful poison in any of it, the flames would find it, as they found all that was corrupt and impure.

Nothing. She stifled a sigh. It would be easier to have some clear sign that Nilos was the enemy they sought.

"Here," said Nilos. "You might as well *bless* the wine, too." He held out a clay jar, one corner of his thin lips quirked. He was laughing at her. Because he found her supposed piety amusing? Or because he knew it was a pretense?

Fine, then. She took the jar. Her fingers brushed his as she did, and for a brief moment she thought she saw something shift in his expression. Pain? Concern? Surprise?

It was gone before she could name it. All she could do was uncork the jar, and foolishly wave her flickering fingers over the mouth of it.

The wine, like the figs, was untainted. And by the scent of it—sweet and earthy, with a faint hint of some warm spice—very good. Grudgingly, Sephre took a small sip. Then another. It was, in fact, *very* good wine.

She would have returned the jar, but Nilos was busy slicing a bit of the cheese for himself. She passed it to Timeus instead. "Not too much. We need to stay clear-headed."

They ate in silence for a time. She needed to learn more, but what to ask? How much to give away?

"Where are you traveling?" she asked, watching Nilos twist one of the figs between his slender fingers. He hadn't eaten much. Neither had she. Timeus, with the appetite of youth, had been the one to heroically polish off the majority of the meal.

"South, to Amoura," said Nilos. "To meet a friend. I came by way of Potedia," he added. "And yourselves?"

"We were in Potedia as well," she answered, deciding to stick as close to the truth as she could. She'd never been a good liar. *Avoid fighting with a weapon you don't know how to use,* her first captain had said. "On temple business. A man from the village died of snakebite, but we were too late to cleanse his spirit."

Nilos frowned at his fig. "A shame. And where do you travel now?"

"Kessely."

"Did someone die there, too?" he asked, so smoothly she almost missed his brief squint of irritation. *Amoura, my ass.* He was definitely hiding something.

"Not that we know of. We trust the Fates to guide us where we are needed."

"Needed for what?" He used a small knife to slice off a bite of the fig, eating with a clean precision, no dribbles to turn his chin sticky, like hers. "Forgive me, I've never been particularly devout. What is it that ashdancers do, exactly?"

Sephre swabbed a damp sleeve over her mouth. She still tasted the fig, even sweeter than the wine.

"We seek out evil and destroy it," answered Timeus, proudly. "So that the spirits of the dead can be reborn."

"Ah." Nilos tilted his head. He drew something from beneath his cloak, making her tense. But it was only a lump of wood. He began to scrape at it with his short dagger, paring away curls of wood. "And how do you know these evils?" he asked. "It would be a handy trick, to be able to spot it so clearly, like a bit of dung on the road."

"Oh, that's easy," said Timeus. "Skotoi are terrible monsters of shadow and blight. They smell of death and have horrible uncanny eyes, and if they touch you, they can consume your spirit!" He spoke with the relish of someone who had never actually seen a skotos. Perhaps realizing this, he turned to Sephre. "Sister Sephre would know better than I, though. I'm only a novice."

Sephre gritted her teeth. She did not care about impressing this man.

"Was that always your calling in this life, Sister Sephre?" Nilos asked, his green eyes fixed on her. "To destroy evil?"

Sephre had kept her handful of flames kindled, to provide light within the barn. It was dark outside, well past sundown, and the rain still drizzled down, veiling moon and stars. Now the sparks flared with her irritation. Why had he asked? What did he care?

"No," she answered, truthfully. "Or maybe yes. I don't know. And you?" She was here to find out this man's secrets, not to share her own. "You carry a sword."

"Yes."

"Are you a soldier?"

"No."

She hadn't thought so. "So what, then?" She nodded to the carving, to his blade slicing away shards of wood, revealing some sort of four-legged beast. "A wood carver?"

He leaned back, his eyes half-lidded, still watching her. "I gather stories."

She snorted. "A bard who carries a sword instead of a lyre?"

"Not a bard. I collect stories. I don't share them. Most of the time."

What did that mean? She was tired of his tricksy answers. Maybe it would be best to speak plainly. *Did you murder Iola? Do you know what happened to Castor?*

And then it happened. So fast she had barely time to gasp. Nilos, shoving himself forward, one arm lashing out toward her. A flash of his dagger, reflecting her flames.

Even in the prime of her training, Sephre doubted she could have moved so quickly. Like a crack of lightning across the sky. One moment, lounging back against the straw. The next moment there beside her, so close she could feel the heat of his arm, as he drew it from the shadows. A dead serpent hung limp from the tip of his blade.

The sight of it made her belly flip. Not just dead. *Rotted.* Slippery white bones showing through between tattered scales. A waft of fetid air nearly made her gag. Timeus pressed a gray sleeve to his nose, coughing.

"Here, sister," said Nilos. "Something more for you to *bless.*"

The flames between her fingers had gone hot and hungry, burning away her initial shock. She held them out. Nilos shook the uncanny thing gingerly into her burning hands, where it flared once, then fell to ash.

Timeus gave a choked gasp. "Look!"

For a heartbeat, a ribbon of something darker seemed to hang in the air, where the serpent had been. Two slitted glints of purple flared. Then it was gone, and the flames in Sephre's palms subsided.

"What was that?" croaked Timeus. "That wasn't a normal snake!"

Nilos had returned to lounging against his hay bale, looking completely unruffled, as if deadly demon snakes invaded his picnics every day. "You should know. If all that was true, about the ashdancers fighting evil demons from the underworld."

"Is that what it was?" Timeus looked even more alarmed. "A skotos?"

"How did you know it was there?" Sephre demanded, glowering at Nilos.

He shrugged, tucking the carving and dagger away. "I've had a lot of practice."

"A lot of practice fighting demons that no one has seen in centuries?"

"Would you rather I'd let it attack?"

She'd rather he jump into the abyss. It was obvious he knew more than he was telling her. But he had—possibly—saved her life. "No," she said, sourly. "Thank you."

"You owe me nothing." The words felt heavy, resonant. Nilos settled himself deeper into the hay, tugging his cloak tighter. He leaned his head back, eyes already closed. "Good night, Sister Sephre. Brother Timeus."

Good night? That was it? He was just going to go to sleep?

"What if there are more skotoi?" asked Timeus, and for once she was glad of his questions.

"There aren't," said Nilos, eyes still closed.

Timeus goggled at him. "How do you know?"

The only answer was a faint snore. Sephre gritted her teeth. It would serve the man right if she grabbed his sword and took him prisoner. Except that she doubted she was capable. He had moved so fast. If he'd wished her ill, he could've simply let the skotos bite her. She could guess, now, what had happened to Castor, Iola, all the others. But why? Had they simply had the bad luck to stumble on one of these serpent-skotoi? Or had the creatures hunted them?

And she herself had nearly been one of them. Another marker on Halimede's map. But instead Nilos had saved her.

She sat in silence, yellow flames flickering and snapping in her hand. It was the same sort of frustration she'd felt when she used to play pebbles with Zander. No matter how she tried to capture his pieces, he always managed to slip out of her grasp. But Zander had been her friend, her trusted companion, a fellow soldier who had been at her side through the very worst of times. Nilos was none of those things.

She did not trust him.

"Sleep, Brother Timeus," she told the boy.

He glanced toward Nilos. "Are you sure?"

She nodded, and he dutifully curled himself into his corner. Trusting her.

Sephre propped herself upright with a sigh. She'd spent plenty of sleepless nights. Not just during the war, but at Stara Bron, when she had bubbling tinctures to oversee, and nightmares to avoid.

She cupped her hand, willing the flames to subside, drawing the darkness in.

═══

Her first sluggish thought was that the captain was going to murder her for falling asleep on watch. Then she remembered that, no, she was the captain now, so she would have to murder herself. Sephre blinked, groggily, and saw the dim outlines of a stone structure, smelled straw and a faint whiff of something sweet. Figs.

Then, finally, she remembered herself fully, and shoved herself upright. Her muscles protested, weary from a day of travel and unused to sleeping on the ground. But it was nothing to the pounding in her skull. Furies' tits, she hadn't drunk *that* much.

Her mouth tasted like old cheese. And now her heart was

galloping too, because the gray morning light made plain that something was missing from the barn.

Nilos. The man was gone.

Timeus lay curled in his bed of straw. She watched him for a moment, until she caught the rise and fall of his shoulder. Sleeping. Safe. A tiny knot of tension in her released.

Wincing, she ran her tongue over her teeth, tasting the lingering sweetness of the wine. How much had she drunk? Surely not enough to knock her senseless.

But there was something else. A sharp herbal note clinging to the back of her tongue. Not mint. Not chamomile.

She swore as it came to her, finally. *Dreamfast.* Fates, she was a fool. She'd doled it out often enough to others at the temple, if they were having trouble sleeping. She'd trusted the holy flame to purify the wine, but dreamfast was no poison. An infusion of the leaves was, however, more than enough to ensure a heavy slumber. Especially combined with wine. And the weariness of a long day.

"Timeus," she called. "Time to get up."

A muffled groan came from the novice. "Is it time for morning devotions already?"

"No," she said. "It's time to chase down some answers."

"But *why* would he do it?" asked Timeus. "He didn't take any of our things. Not that we have much, of course, but if he were a thief he might've taken our cloaks. And if he meant worse, he could've slit our throats while we slept."

Yes, and it galled her to admit it. "You don't drug someone out of kindness and good intent," she said, quickening her pace. They were nearly to Kessely. She could see the outline of structures above. Several small, blocky houses clung to the rough ridge, bare to the bright blue sky that had swept in to clear the last shreds of the storm. Like many of the villages in these parts, the folk of Kessely had built their homes in the heights, in memory of a more violent age, when Helisson had been a fractured land of city-states, and no peace had held back the Scarthian war bands.

She led the way up the last of the switchbacks. In the village, they were greeted by a man hoisting water from a well.

"A stranger? Yes, I spoke with him, an hour past or so," he said. "Said he was looking for friends, had come with a gift for their newborn babe. I sent him up the old hunter's path." The man pointed to a trail that wound away into a bit of scrubby wilderness, still higher up the hillside. "Charis birthed her first last month. Fine, healthy child."

Sephre thanked him, then tugged Timeus after her, jogging now. "What does he want with a baby?"

"He didn't seem like a bad person," said Timeus.

Sephre gritted her teeth. The boy was *impossibly* naive. "You mean he didn't have glowing eyes and smell like death and cackle at us with malevolent glee?"

Silence then. When she glanced back, the novice had his head down, focusing on the narrow, rough trail.

Well, he had to face the truths of the world someday. Life wasn't a story like the Golden Boar, full of handsome heroes and loathsome villains. They called her a hero, and look what she had done.

"There's a house," panted Timeus.

Sephre surged onward, ignoring the tearing of her quick breath, the heat that burned in her chest. Inside, she found a woman, curled on the floor as if asleep.

And she was, in fact, asleep. Not dead, thank the Fates. There was another woman a few feet away. A heavy staff, the sort used by shepherds in these parts, lay tumbled beside her, as if she'd been holding it.

Fighting back, against a green-eyed stranger who came for her child?

But there was no sign of the baby. Or Nilos. A fist of panic clenched Sephre's chest.

"Listen!" said Timeus suddenly, turning toward the door. "Do you hear that?"

HOUSE OF DUSK 109

In the distance, a thin wail.

Sephre dashed back outside, following the cry. The trail that had led them to the house continued higher, winding past a stand of ancient olives. She pelted past the trees, around a sharp turn of stone, climbing higher and higher, until finally she came out to a wide, flat shelf of stone, the blue sky a bright bowl above.

And halted.

Nilos stood before her, a wriggling bundle in his arms. He regarded her with annoyance over the soft curls of the baby's head. "This would have been so much easier if you'd just drunk all the wine."

CHAPTER 11

YENERIS

Yeneris knew the city of Helissa was large and sprawling, but even so, she was taken aback by the view from the tower. The palace itself was vast, a green sea of terraced gardens and pools, punctuated by the crimson roofs of long buildings hedged by striped blue and green pillars. Gold glimmered from the rows of statues along the sloping paths and wide white stairs, each of them a testament to some ancient monarch or hero of legend. Helisson had no need of new heroes, it seemed. Or new kings.

During her training, Mikat had told her a story of two Helissoni men, both powerful already, one the owner of a large tin mine, the other a merchant with a lucrative trade in spices from across the Middle Sea. Both had claimed to be Breseus reborn, one on the word of a soothsayer, the other based on a pattern of freckles on his cheek that resembled the star sign of the boar-slayer. It seemed ridiculous to Yeneris, but she had been curious enough to ask, *How did they decide?*

They went into the wilds to hunt a particularly savage boar, said Mikat. *They agreed that whichever of them slew the beast could claim the title. But the boar was crafty and slew them both. They might have mastered it, had they worked together, but they cared more for individual glory. Like all Helissoni.*

Yeneris wondered, now, if the story was true, or just another way for Mikat to remind her that she was a part of something larger than herself. She and Mikat and a dozen others, all of them working together to regain what was lost.

In spite of herself, Yeneris turned to the south. She couldn't see the ocean from here, only the silver snake of the river. One week's sail to the Middle Sea, then another to the isles, if the weather was fair. Or so she'd been told. She had never made the voyage in that direction. Only the opposite, when she was just a girl, and that had taken far longer.

Sinoe leaned from the parapet, her fingers tightening on the stone balustrade. Tami clung to her shoulder, wings half-spread for balance, velvety tail swishing down the princess's spine. The ailouron was behaving surprisingly well, though she had cast her scat perilously close to Yeneris's feet earlier.

"I see them. That is them, isn't it? There?"

Yeneris moved closer, squinting at the tiny figures down at the main gates, a pair of enormous bronze doors set into the outer wall that surrounded the palace, separating it from rest of the city.

"Yes," she said, recognizing the prince's glittering helm and the crimson spatters of the soldiers. And the spot of gray that trailed after Ichos like a blurry shadow. The Heron.

Yeneris gave Sinoe a sidelong glance. The girl's expression was remote, but she could see the signs of worry, the tightness where she must be chewing the inside of her cheek. Tami ducked her head, crooning softly as she groomed the few loose curls that clustered at Sinoe's temple. Yeneris's belly clenched, seeing that sharply hooked beak so close to the princess's lustrous eyes, but Sinoe had no fear. She stroked the ailouron's crest. "You should fly. Enjoy your freedom while you can."

Tami keened again, her feline hindquarters tensing, muscles rippling beneath charcoal fur. In one smooth leap, she flung herself into the sky. Yeneris's breath caught at the sight. She hadn't realized the ailouron's wings were so large. For a heartbeat, they eclipsed the sun, and Yeneris dreamed of what it might feel like to rise above this world.

Sinoe was watching too, her face a study in glory and desolation. *If she trusts you, she will not suspect you when it's time to act.*

"Your brother seems very capable," said Yeneris. Which was

only partly a lie. She'd seen the prince sparring. He could handle a blade, even if he couldn't hold his tongue around his father. "I'm sure he'll return safely."

Sinoe cast a wry look at Yeneris. "So you're the sibyl now, Yen?"

"No, princess. I didn't mean it like that. Only—"

"It's fine. I know what you meant. And yes, my brother is capable of a great many things. I'm certain he'll find answers at Stara Bron. Especially with that man to help him sniff them out." Her lips pinched briefly. "I just . . . I've been here before. I'm always here, watching people leave. Because of my visions."

Likely she was talking about her mother, the former queen, Kizare, whom Hierax had divorced and then sent back home to her people soon after he declared himself the Ember King reborn. Because of Sinoe's prophecy.

"How old were you when your mother left?"

"Nine."

Yeneris's throat clenched. She'd been ten when her mother died.

"And you haven't seen her since?"

Sinoe huffed. "Father won't allow her to visit."

"You could go to her, surely?"

That got her an arched brow. "My father barely allows me to leave the palace. He's hardly going to send me into the hands of his enemies."

A screech rang out, drawing both of them to turn their faces skyward. Tami had apparently taken insult from the pennant snapping at the crest of the tower above. She dove, but the wind flicked the cloth from her grasping talons at the last moment.

Undaunted, the ailouron beat her golden wings, climbing again, her cries growing more and more outraged as the banner defied her. When she finally managed to tear loose a strip of the crimson cloth, her shriek was as triumphant as if she'd bested a manticore.

Sinoe laughed, and it was her true laugh again, the bewitching tumble of merriment that plucked at Yeneris's throat. Almost, she let the conversation die. But she was here to learn, not to laugh.

"I thought there was a peace treaty with Scarthia." She'd seen the ambassador at a lily-gazing party Sinoe had attended earlier that week: a tall, imposing woman who looked as if she could run twenty miles, wrestle a lion, and then compose an epic poem about it. Yeneris had approved. Even more so when she saw the woman thank the servant who brought her wine. It was Ambassador Opotysi who had gifted Sinoe the ailouron. A significant gift, from what Yeneris knew of Scarthians. The creatures were much prized in the north, treasured and loyal companions generally kept only by those who shared blood with their chieftains. Kizare was sister to the leader of one of the largest clans.

"Treaties can be broken. And my father is not a trusting man." Sinoe looked back toward the gates. The figures were gone now, on their way north to the temple of the House of Dawn to claim a mythic blade to slay an ancient evil.

Prickles fluttered over her skin as Yeneris remembered Sinoe's voice—the voice of the Fates—intoning the words that had sent Ichos and Lacheron on that mission.

Long has the old enemy watched and waited. Now he seeks to strike his second blow, and the world will not survive it. The first light must reveal the weapon of unmaking. When it is found, when the Maiden steps forth from flame to take her rightful place, only then shall the old enemy fall.

But the kore was not meant for flame. She had given herself to the earth. She had bound her spirit deep in the bones of the earth, a sacrifice to save her people.

Yeneris thought of what her mother had told her on the day the crimson sails had appeared on the horizon. *They've come because of a lie. Their king believes the kore belongs to him.*

We should tell them the truth, then, Yeneris had said. So young, so naive.

They don't believe us. They have their own stories. And it is very, very hard to make someone believe a new story about themselves.

Hierax gripped his own supposed destiny with an iron fist. He would never willingly release it. Yeneris would have to take it.

Return the kore to her rightful home before the Helissoni could undo her sacrifice. With Ichos and the Heron gone, there would be fewer watchful eyes. Perhaps she should try to break into the queen's chambers tonight. Steal away the kore's bones and be done with crushing herself into this other world.

Steps sounded on the stairs. Yeneris shifted smoothly, setting herself between Sinoe and the door. A moment later a man in the pale blue of a palace attendant appeared. He dipped a low bow to Sinoe, who waved for Yeneris to step aside.

"Bright One, the king sends his blessings and wishes you to share your noon meal with him."

"Very well." Sinoe's voice was perfectly calm, but Yeneris caught a flicker of tension in her jaw. She whistled, a single sweet note. Tami spiraled down to land heavily on Sinoe's shoulder. Her golden eyes fixed on the servant, who took a step back, warily eyeing the bit of crimson cloth trailing from the ailouron's claws. It looked distressingly like blood against Sinoe's pale gown.

The princess reached up, soothing the bird-beast with her touch, and seeming to draw strength from Tami in return. "Will anyone else be joining us?"

"No, my lady. Your father requested a f-family meal."

Why had the attendant stammered over the word *family*? Was it some slight to the absent prince?

Sinoe's fingers froze for a long moment, buried in the thick golden feathers of Tami's ruff. "Very well. Come, Yeneris. Best not to keep them waiting."

===

Them. Yeneris considered the word as she followed Sinoe down the spiral of pearly marble steps. So far as she knew, Sinoe had no close relations besides her father and brother, at least not here in the city. Hierax had no siblings, only a scattering of distant cousins.

They crossed the myrtle courtyard, cool and plashy with

fountains, then into the southern section of the palace. A thrill of alarm and expectation shivered through Yeneris. The queen's wing.

But why? Sinoe took most of her meals in her own chambers, which were in the north wing, or in the solar, with a small company of ladies of the court. There was a grander feasting hall, of course, its walls painted with scenes of a royal hunt, and couches for a hundred guests. But that was in the western wing. No doubt Hierax had a private dining chamber, but his suite was in the eastern wing.

She had to ask. Had to prepare herself. This could be an opportunity. "Princess, where are we going?"

Sinoe halted so abruptly Yeneris had to catch herself to keep from smacking into the woman. Tami hissed at her from the princess's shoulder, snapping her hooked beak until Yeneris drew back, tucking her hands behind her. "It would be helpful to know. So I can ensure your safety."

A man from the palace guard had given Yeneris a tour before she began her service. Important to know the exits, the routes she might need to take to get Sinoe to safety, in the case of any threat. But the tour had not included the south wing. *No one goes there now*, the guard told her. *The king keeps it sealed.*

It was only from the gossip of servants that Yeneris learned it was where Hierax had secured the reliquary. She supposed it made sense, if the man believed that the kore was his fated bride.

"We'll be dining in my—in the queen's salon." Sinoe bit the inside of her cheek. "You don't have to come. You can wait outside. Tami can stay with you. It might be for the best."

Yeneris arched a dubious brow at the ailouron, just as the bird-beast gave a scornful shriek. Apparently neither of them liked that plan.

"I'll be safe," said Sinoe. "These are the most secure rooms of the palace."

Yeneris had noticed. She'd counted eight guards so far, mostly in pairs, several in stationary positions, others patrolling. All well-armed, in spite of their tasseled ceremonial armor and gilded helms.

"But you don't *feel* safe," said Yeneris. She couldn't risk being left behind now, even if the comment verged on inappropriate. "I'm not leaving."

Sinoe gave her a wan smile. "You may regret that." Then she led the way onward, to a heavy wooden door inlaid with a geometric pattern of black and white tile, guarded by two more soldiers. The princess took a bracing breath. "Be good," she whispered, presumably to Tami, as the guards opened the door for her. Yeneris followed, her skin humming, nerves on fire.

The reliquary was here, somewhere. Little chance of recovering it right now, but she might be able to make plans for a future attempt. She just needed to figure out where Hierax had it hidden.

The room was nearly a perfect, windowless cube, as tall as it was broad, the walls painted with false columns, so it seemed as if they were entering a marble pavilion looking out over a starlit meadow. The dozens of tiny oil lamps scattered about the room added to this effect, providing a shimmering quivery light that made it hard for Yeneris's eyes to focus.

She blinked, thinking that was the reason she saw double. Two people, seated at the head of that long, imposing table, rather than the one she had expected.

But it wasn't a trick of her eyes. There was Hierax, with his overlarge eyes and gold-ringed fingers and heavy lips pursed in expectation. And beside him, a veiled figure, her brow clasped by a circlet of beaten gold leaves and crimson gems. Bony wrists jutted from the sleeves of her gown, stiff with gilt embroidery and precious stones. A sash clasped her impossibly narrow waist.

"Hello, Father." Sinoe dipped her head, her voice tight. Tami gave a tiny hiss.

Hierax's brow furrowed. "That beast should be in its cage."

For a moment she thought Sinoe might protest. But she only swallowed, nodding. She turned to Yeneris, her face strained and pale. "Take her, please."

Impossible to argue, not here, in front of the king. Even Tami seemed to sense the weight of Hierax's displeasure, and consented to be coaxed from Sinoe's shoulder onto Yeneris's arm. Her talons pricked painfully. She gave a low, mournful keen as the princess turned away.

Hierax cleared his throat significantly as Sinoe moved to take her seat at the table. "You haven't greeted your mother, Sinoe."

Mother? Yeneris gaped, trying to fathom the words. Queen Kizare was gone, exiled back to her people in Scarthia.

There was a beat of silence. Then Sinoe dipped another bow, this time to the veiled woman. "Hello, Mother."

There was no response, not even the slightest stir of the gauzy linen veil. Hierax gave a rumble of approval, and Sinoe finally took her seat. She was pale, except for two spots of brightness high in her cheeks.

"There," said Hierax, leaning back, more relaxed now, almost jovial. "See how happy it makes her, to have you here with us?"

A pit had opened inside Yeneris, and all her sensible thoughts were spinning into it, sucked down by a realization that was too horrible for her to accept. She stared at the veiled woman. Unmoving. Skeletally thin. She could just barely make out a shadowy face through the veil: the pale, sharply cut features, the empty dark eyes, the hint of a leering grimace.

It took all Yeneris's control to hold herself back behind Sinoe's chair. A wild laugh snagged in her throat. So much for her fears that she might not discover where the reliquary was hidden. She had found it. Or rather, she had found the sacred bones, the last mortal remains of the revered kore of Bassara.

Here they were, right in front of her.

It wasn't enough that Hierax had stolen the bones. That he'd slaughtered an entire city to claim them. But to *pervert* them? To dress the kore like a child's doll, propped at his dinner table?

She bit her tongue, feeling Sinoe's eyes. Had she made a sound? Thankfully Tami's bulk hid her face somewhat. She struggled to regain her composure. *Listen, watch, learn.* Later, she could be horrified.

And so she catalogued all that was before her. The table, set with a dozen silver platters. Dishes of roasted quail and cheese-filled pastries. Rabbit stewed with prune. Jeweled heaps of pomegranate and fig and ripe apricots.

Hierax made a show of slicing the choicest cuts and setting them on the plate before the kore. "Only the best for you, my love."

Sinoe took a sizable sip of her wine, then set the cup down with a clink that was just slightly too loud. "Did you hunt the rabbit yourself, Father?" Her voice was a cracked jug trying desperately not to spill.

And there was nothing Yeneris could do to help. *You can do your job,* she chided herself. *The real one.*

The king had accepted Sinoe's conversational gambit, and was now expounding on different techniques for hunting rabbit. Yeneris let the words fade to a hum as she absorbed the layout of the room, fixing the details in her mind.

She doubted that this was where the kore was kept normally. The way Hierax had spoken, the way he acted even now, told her this was no farce. He truly believed that the kore was his beloved, his bride. His queen.

Queens did not sleep in dining rooms.

There were two other doors, aside from the one by which she and Sinoe had entered. One of them must lead to the queen's bedchamber. Was that where the kore lay during the night? Her bones tucked into a silken sleeping gown, a scarf tied round her poor bare skull?

Did the king—

Raised voices interrupted her thoughts, which was probably all for the best.

"The ambassador meant no insult, Father," Sinoe was saying.

"What did she mean, then?" The king tore at a leg of quail, fingers digging into the oily flesh.

Sinoe gave one of her light, tinkling laughs. "Tami's an ailouron, not a marriage contract. You should be happy about it, Father. It shows how greatly the Scarthians esteem us."

"It shows how shamelessly they try to manipulate you," scoffed Hierax. "That woman thinks she can win you over with amber baubles and ill-bred pets."

"Tami isn't ill-bred," protested Sinoe, her expression hardening. For the first time, Yeneris saw the resemblance between father and daughter, as they glowered at one another. "The gift of an ailouron is a great honor. A sign of respect for me, as Kizare's daughter."

Crack!

The king's fist struck the table so hard it made the wine slosh from Sinoe's goblet. "Enough. I will not have you insult my true queen. You will return that beast, or we'll be feasting on ailouron flesh next time we dine together. Now. Apologize."

Sinoe's lips trembled. Yeneris winced as Tami's talons clutched at her, and she could hear the low growl beginning to boil in the creature's chest. *I know. I want to tear his throat out too.* But that would only make things worse.

Gingerly, she lifted a hand to stroke the ailouron, the way she'd seen Sinoe soothe Tami earlier. Surprisingly—but gratifyingly—Tami did not snap her fingers off. The feathers around her neck calmed somewhat, though she continued to rumble unhappily.

"I'm sorry, Father," said Sinoe at last, though there was little repentance in her tone.

Hierax stared back, still thunderous. "I'm not the one you insulted."

Sinoe's shoulders hunched. She looked ill. But she turned toward the silent, veiled figure. Her voice was almost a whisper, hoarse with unhappiness. "I'm sorry. Mother."

They finished the meal in silence.

CHAPTER 12

YENERIS

Yeneris snuck out two nights later. She waited until Sinoe was asleep, then another hour to be safe. When she moved to the window, Tami creeled faintly from the cage, but a handful of her favorite dried lamb quieted her.

Sinoe had said nothing of returning the ailouron to the Scarthians. If anything, she lavished more attention on the creature than ever, feeding her choice treats, grooming her feathers to a mirror gloss. She'd shocked Yeneris by waking at dawn that morning in order to take Tami to the gardens. They'd watched the ailouron fly, her wild swoops making both of them laugh. But there had been a ghost of sorrow in the princess's eyes.

Yeneris shoved all thought of Sinoe's eyes aside. Tonight, she belonged to Bassara. Tonight, she was herself again. Holding that thought close, she slipped out into the night.

She still didn't trust the wisteria to hold her, but that was all right, because she was going up, not down. She gripped the ornate casement and pulled herself up. This was one of the advantages to the excessive ornamentation the Helissoni favored. It made scaling the palace exterior *much* easier.

A few minutes later she was on the roof, padding lightly across the crimson tiles. She'd scouted the route during her first week, when she first heard the rumor that the reliquary was in the south wing. Too risky to do more at the time. But now that she'd seen the interior, she at least had some better sense of where to go.

Still a risk. Maybe she was being a fool. But the memory of the kore dressed as a puppet queen haunted her. And it wasn't as if she were planning to take on all eight guards single-handedly—though she had to admit a part of her brain was playing out that exact scenario, and even insisting on including Sinoe as an admiring observer, which was ridiculous, since if the princess had known what she was up to she'd be anything but admiring.

No, she would play this smart. From what Yeneris had seen, the south wing was laid out in almost a mirror to the north. Which meant that there was a good chance that it would have the same air shafts in the ceiling. If she could make it onto the roof undetected, that might give her a way inside.

Harder to get back out again, of course. She'd need rope, which might be tricky.

Everything was going just fine until she reached the southwest tower. There were four of these tall spires, one at each corner of the palace. Yeneris had bypassed the northwest tower easily enough, spidering her way around just beneath the circular balcony—the same balcony from which she and Sinoe had watched the prince depart.

It should have been easy enough to do the same at the southwest tower. Except for the foxwings that had decided to build a nest right between what would have been her third and fourth handholds.

She heard the warning chitter just in time to snatch back her hand, narrowly avoiding the stab of sharp teeth. Cursing silently, she tried to work her way back. Maybe she could get around the other side?

The foxwing gave another warning chitter, louder this time.

"Shh!" Yeneris hissed. "I'm not trying to steal your babies."

Voices rumbled above, and she smothered another curse. So much for her cunning plan. All she could do now was try to get back to the roof as fast as possible, hoping that her plain dark clothing would hide her, or at least obscure her identity for long enough to escape.

But there would be a cost. If the guards saw an intruder, they would increase patrols, maybe even set soldiers on the rooftops. There would be no second chance.

This was what she got for being rash. She should have waited to contact Mikat before acting. She'd let her emotions rule her, and now she was on the brink of utter failure.

"Excuse me." A familiar voice drifted from above, sweet and innocent as a daggerdove. "Sergeant Ophus?"

"Princess? What are you—"

"I'm here on the business of the Fates, of course. I have a message for you."

"A m-message?" The man sounded terrified.

"Your wife has just started her labors. I believe it will be your firstborn child?"

"What? Now? But the physician said it wouldn't be for another two weeks."

"Do you think the physician knows better than the Fates?" Sinoe demanded. "Go on, then. You should be with her."

"But I can't—"

"I've informed the watch commander. Someone else will be along shortly to take your post. Go on. Say hello to your daughter from me."

"A girl? She's a girl?"

There was the faintest suggestion of a sigh. Then a hasty, "Of course, Bright One. Thank you. Thank you for letting me know." Then the quick thud of feet, retreating down the steps.

Yeneris had frozen at the first sound of Sinoe's voice. There was still a very slim chance that the princess didn't know she was here.

"Are you coming up from there or not?" called Sinoe. "Believe me, I'm nothing compared to a foxwing defending her nest."

Yeneris grimaced, and began hoisting herself up. She disagreed. Princess Sinoe was a threat *far* greater than any foxwing.

"Well?" Sinoe prompted, after Yeneris slung herself over the ledge and onto the balcony.

Yeneris straightened. "Well, what, princess?"

Sinoe rolled her eyes. "Are you going to tell me what you're doing gallivanting around the palace rooftops at midnight?"

"I thought I heard an intruder." She kept her features calm, her voice even.

"And you didn't alert the guard?"

"I didn't want to cause a panic. If I was wrong. Which I was. It was only the foxwing."

"Mmm. I see."

Yeneris followed Sinoe to the stairs, trying not to feel chastened. The princess did not speak again until they were crossing the myrtle courtyard. She halted beside the central pool, kneeling to dabble her fingers in the water. Sleek silver fish rose to the surface, burbling eagerly. Sinoe pulled a crust of bread from her sleeve and began breaking it into crumbs over the water. "I know you're Bassaran."

Surprisingly, Yeneris didn't freeze. Her heart continued to thump steadily. In a way, it was a relief. Except for the part where she might need to flee for her life.

"Or you have Bassaran ancestors."

"You scried it." Of course she had. Foolish to think she could deceive a woman who heard the whispers of the Fates.

Sinoe scoffed. "I'm actually capable of figuring some things out on my own, you know. The Fates didn't tell me that man's daughter was being born. I overheard his watch commander. I have eyes. And ears. And I know that the Bassarans don't call skotoi by that name. They call them ghouls. Yes?"

Yeneris nodded. Pointless to lie now. But Sinoe might not know all of it. There were plenty of Helissoni with Bassaran heritage. Trade had brought some, and others had fled north after the cataclysm shattered the isles. She could still salvage this.

"And then there's Ambassador Opotysi's son Hura. His father is Bassaran. He's the one who told me about the salt."

"Salt?"

"How Bassarans always take salt from the cellar with their left hand. Something to do with the queen who founded the city holding an olive bough in one hand and salt in the other? Is that right?"

Ah. If she survived, she'd have to let Mikat know. Such small things to betray her. A pinch of salt. A single word.

Sinoe tossed another handful of crumbs, then held out the rest to Yeneris. "Here, try it. It's very soothing. Just watch out for that big orange one, he's always trying to steal everyone else's supper."

Yeneris took the crust. It was good to have something to busy her hands.

"I don't blame you for keeping it quiet," said Sinoe. "I haven't told anyone. You've done your job. And you've kept my secrets. It's only fair I keep yours."

"You're not worried I might mean you harm?"

Sinoe's eyes were dark pools, drinking her in. "No. I don't believe you will."

"Because of a vision?"

"Because you like me, even if I infuriate you sometimes." She cocked her head. "Are you *trying* to do an impression of the carp? If so, I think you need to open your lips just a bit wider."

Yeneris slammed her mouth closed. What should she say now? How much more did Sinoe know? Clearly she didn't believe Yeneris's story of chasing a phantom intruder. Maybe she ought to speak bluntly, as the princess did.

"You still haven't told me what you were really doing," Sinoe said. "Was it the Faithful Maiden?"

"Yes," admitted Yeneris. "I wanted to see her." The truth, but not the whole truth.

"I understand she's a holy figure to your people as well as mine," said Sinoe. "But you call her something else, don't you?"

Carefully now. Sinoe was too confident; it made it too easy to believe there was trust between them. "The Bassarans call her *kore*."

"Will you tell me more?" Sinoe asked. "We can talk here. No one will hear you over the fountains."

How had Sinoe had learned that trick? Who else had she needed to whisper secrets with? Yeneris's stomach tightened. Could she do this? Should she?

She thought of her younger self, asking her mother why they couldn't just tell Hierax the true story. She took a breath, and began. "They say that she was a priestess of the House of Midnight. Dedicated to the Scarab, with the dark earth in her bones. Flowers bloomed from her footsteps and her breath was sweet as wine."

Yeneris tore her crust of bread, scattering the last crumbs to the fish. "The world loved her, and she loved the world, and all its creatures. But others were not accepting. One day a man—a king, in fact—was traveling through her forest, and came across a serpent in his path. Fearing the creature, he slew it. But the serpent was no ordinary beast. It was one of the children of Chaos, the first and greatest of the gods, and in slaying such a great and holy creature, the king unleashed the cataclysm. As the mountains smoked and the islands broke, the kore begged the great Scarab to heal the world. The god-beast of the earth answered her call, and told her what she must do. And so the kore gave herself to the mountain, body and soul, and only then did the destruction cease."

"Is that why her bones haven't fallen to ash?" asked Sinoe. "Because her spirit is trapped in this world?"

"Not trapped. It was her choice to bind herself to the earth."

"So if she *were* reborn, it would be a bad thing."

"A very bad thing. And . . ."

She bit the inside of her lip. Sinoe waited.

"Bassarans don't actually believe our spirits *are* reborn, not the way you do. We're all part of something greater. When we die, when we walk the labyrinth, we leave behind the things that separate us from others. Hatreds and fears. When we're able, we rejoin the . . . we call it kos, the world soul. The kos births new souls and sends them back to the world. So they do carry the past within them, but . . . in smaller fragments, mixed together . . ." Yeneris stumbled. Why couldn't she find the right words? But Sinoe was nodding.

"Like compost."

Yeneris laughed. "Yes. I suppose."

"It's so different from the Ember King's story," said Sinoe. "But also the same. There's a cataclysm, and a blade, and a king, and a serpent, and a maid. But there's nothing in your version that talks about the Serpent's return?"

"No."

"Mmm." Sinoe frowned into the pool. "Do you think the skotoi are coming because we stole the kore's bones?"

Stole. A surprisingly honest word.

"I don't know. The ghouls in our stories aren't connected to the cataclysm. They're just demons from the underworld that like to eat mortal souls. Did *your* prophecy say anything about it?"

Sinoe's lips quirked bitterly. "The prophecy that caused the war, you mean?"

"Your father caused the war." Had she really said that? It was this place, this courtyard with silver fish and Sinoe looking like a slender moonbeam with huge, dark eyes.

"I don't remember," Sinoe admitted. "I can control the visions better, now, but back then I would get . . . completely lost. I was a ewer trying to pour out an ocean. And I was . . . angry." She gave Yeneris a sheepish look. "I cursed the Fates every night for months." Her shoulders hunched. "I even left a rotten fish on their shrine. I thought if I offended them they'd take it back. Everyone said it was a gift. But it's not."

Her sigh filled the silence. Yeneris thought of the conversation she'd overheard. Lacheron, telling the king that it was all for his glory.

"Then what?" she asked, finally. "What purpose do the visions serve? What do the Fates want?"

"I wish I knew. I've read a hundred different legends. In one, the Fates help Breseus defeat the golden boar, but in another they doom him to be drowned in the abyss. The best answer I found is from this one scholar—her name was Kalanthe, she was amazing, she even created a pair of wings that she used to fly across the Bleeding Sands to the City of Abandoned Tears, remind me to tell you that one, it's not nearly as depressing as it sounds—" Sinoe gave Yeneris a single heart-stabbing grin—"Anyways, Kalanthe hypothesized that the Fates were a balancing force to Chaos. That ultimately their purpose is to find and reveal patterns. Cause and effect. They want the world to make sense."

"They should speak more clearly, then," Yeneris huffed. "Er. No offense."

Sinoe laughed. "Believe me, I would be much happier if my prophecies were more clear. Last year I had a vision that I was going to be stung by a bee, and I spent the entire summer avoiding the garden only to end up stabbing myself in the backside sitting on one of my earrings."

Yeneris snickered. She couldn't help it. Sinoe's smile curved, bright as the crescent moon above. The darkness seemed to be pressing Yeneris toward the princess, like a moth to a flame.

She took a deliberate step back, dusting the crumbs from her hands. The fish continued to burble at the surface of the pool, insatiable. Wanting more.

"There are records, though," said Sinoe. "Lacheron keeps them. A transcription of every one of my prophecies. All my doom-sayings."

"Not *all* of them," said Yeneris, thinking of the necropolis. "How many do you keep to yourself?"

"Only a handful. Most are small things. A stray kitten and a lonely clerk who can give it a home. A rumpled rug that needs smoothing, to save a servant from smashing a platter and getting punished."

"How do you conjure them?" Yeneris asked. "With smoke? Like you did for your father?"

Sinoe grimaced. "I don't need the smoke. All I need is an emotional focus. And tears."

Yeneris hesitated. There was a wound here, and she didn't want to poke it unnecessarily. But she needed to understand. Sinoe's visions were at the heart of everything that was happening. They had brought her father to power, led him to steal the kore's bones.

Now they might lead to an even greater desecration. To disaster. Sinoe had opened this door. Best to get a look inside before it slammed shut again.

"Do you actually . . . see things? Or is it only the words, speaking through you?"

"Sometimes I see images. I saw the skotoi at the necropolis, and the fire. And you." A brief smile touched her lips. "But it's more like what I said before. Like I'm pouring something out of me. I'm just the vessel. I don't choose the words."

"So you can't be sure exactly what they mean."

Sinoe frowned into the pool. "No. But Lord Lacheron seems very certain, doesn't he?"

Was there an edge to her voice? A crack. "You don't agree with his interpretations?"

Sinoe wrinkled her nose. "Who am I to know? He's a scholar. An alchemist. He's one of the wisest men in the world and I'm just a girl."

Yeneris would have bet her favorite dagger those were someone else's words. Hierax's, probably. "Wise men who are truly wise don't need to lord it over others. You're the Sibyl of Tears. They're *your* prophecies."

Sinoe shook her head. "No. They aren't mine either. They belong to the Fates. Or to the world. At least, they should."

Every conversation builds a bridge. It was something Mikat had told her, during her training. *Some you can collapse when you've no more need of them. Others will bind you forever. Be certain you know which sort you're building.*

This was not the sort of bridge she could collapse. She'd already cast out boulders. But so had Sinoe.

"So you're taking them back. Saving kittens and sending me to slay skotoi."

Sinoe nodded.

"And what about the ones Lord Lacheron interprets? Do you think they're being misused? That they might mean something different?" That was as far as Yeneris dared go. She tensed, as if she truly stood at the end of some fragile span of stone, waiting to see if it would carry her.

"Yes. And I think I have a way to prove it." The princess fixed her with a look that was half wary, half challenge. "But I need your help."

Was this blackmail? Sinoe had said she would keep Yeneris's secrets if Yeneris kept hers. "What sort of help?" she asked, warily.

Sinoe's crescent grin flashed. "You'll see. And I promise we don't need to climb out the window this time."

CHAPTER 13

SEPHRE

"Let that baby go," Sephre ordered. She was deeply aware that she had no weapon, but then, Nilos had not drawn his sword either, his hands being full of squirming infant.

"What, just drop the little one onto the cruel earth?" He tsked her. "I'm not going to harm them. Quite the opposite. So long as you don't interrupt."

"Put them down on the ground. *Carefully.*" She brandished one hand, kindling the holy flame. "Then back away."

"I can't do that," said Nilos, far too calmly. "Not if you want the baby to live."

Timeus joined her, breathing hard but wearing a determined expression. Good lad. He had even thought to grab the oil lamp from the cottage. The tiny flame wouldn't do much, but it was better than nothing. "Be ready to take the baby," she told him. "Leave Nilos to me."

"Indeed," said Nilos. "We do have unfinished business, you and I. But this is more important."

He glanced down at the baby, who had stopped wailing, and was actually smiling up at the man. And was that a *gurgle*? Sephre huffed.

"On your left," said Nilos, suddenly.

She barely had time to register the rush of movement, the sudden stink of decay, the burning eyes, before the skotos was in her face. Not a dead snake this time, but some other animal. Maybe it had been a deer once? A goat? Now, it was a stomach-churning slither of bones and weeping flesh, hide mottled with rot. It had too many limbs. Four of pale bone, four more of slithering darkness. The black tentacles reached for her.

Sephre flung her handful of flame, but the movement was stilted. She'd been too focused on Nilos. The golden fire spattered across the stones in front of the skotos, merely an inconvenience. It leapt to one side, coiling down. The long jaws split, lined with needle-fine teeth. Her own death waited there. Desperately, Sephre clawed her hands. Only flame could save her.

Crack! Something smashed into the dark maw. And suddenly the skotos was ablaze, flames boiling from its mouth. Shards of pottery fell to the ground. Dimly, Sephre recognized them as a broken oil lamp.

She lanced her own golden flames at the monster, but it was already crumpling, bone turning gray. As it fell to ash, she glanced to Timeus. "Well done."

For a moment she was afraid he might faint. His skin had gone gray, his eyes enormous. But her words seemed to free him. He gulped, then managed a wan smile.

"Yes," said Nilos. "You have my thanks as well."

Sephre whirled back to face the insufferable man. "What is this?" she demanded. No more games. No more lies. Only answers, even if she had to rip them out of him word by word. "Why are there skotoi everywhere you go?"

"Because they seek the same thing I do."

"Speak plainly," she snapped. The flames coiled around her fingers, and a brighter flame filled her chest.

"Easier to show you." He spared a moment to tickle the baby's belly, loosening the swaddling, revealing a plump brown shoulder dusted with darker freckles. Then he traced one hand lightly over the skin.

Sephre gasped. It was as if Nilos had dipped his finger in ink. The lines bloomed beneath his touch, one by one, until they formed a faceted ring. The same mark she had seen on Iola, on Castor.

Nilos made a face at the baby, who began to gurgle in delight.

"What are you—?" Sephre broke off, casting a hand over her face against a sudden burst of light. Lines of brilliance blazed against her eyelids, as if she were staring up into the stars themselves.

"There. That's better, isn't it?"

Sephre swore, blinking to clear the dazzle from her eyes. At first she thought nothing had changed. Then she saw it. Or rather, she realized what she was no longer seeing. The mark had vanished, as if it had never been.

"What did you do?" she demanded.

"Saved a life. Possibly more." Nilos gave her a feral grin. "What have *you* done?"

Bodies heaped like trash. The clatter of blades, beating against shields in triumph. Blue eyes, begging her. Help me, Seph.

Sephre wrenched her thoughts back to the present. To Nilos, looking at her as if he could somehow see her thoughts, a trace of something like pity in his eyes.

"You don't remember, do you?" he asked, still with that infuriating note of sympathy.

No. She *did* remember. That was the problem. She remembered all of it. Even after nine years hiding away from the world, losing herself in prayer, in silence, in her garden. Oh, how she remembered.

"Catch," said Nilos, then tossed the baby at her.

She lunged, arms outstretched, barely managing to quench her flaming palms before a bundle of wriggling, squishy baby smacked into them. Fates! Was he mad?

She shoved the baby at Timeus. "Go. Get away! Keep the baby safe!"

The novice fled, gray tunic flapping, his long legs eating up the earth. In a moment he was gone down the trail.

Sephre spun back to Nilos, who had taken her distraction as an opportunity to retreat toward the far side of the clearing, where the trail continued. "Oh no you don't!" she snarled, flinging a handful of flame.

The yellow sparks burst against the stones just in front of the man. "That's far enough, baby-tosser."

He faced her again, folding his arms over his chest. "You have the child back. What more do you want?"

"I want some answers." And Fates help her, she was tempted to burn them out of him. "What did you just do? Why did you put that mark on that baby?"

"I didn't. I removed it."

"Where did it come from, then? The Serpent is dead."

Nilos's dark brows arched. She could see him better now, in the warm sunlight. He held himself still, but it was the sort of stillness that promised violence. She thought he must be closer to forty than thirty. Or even older. He knew his own power. Confident, but not arrogant.

"And what does a sister of Stara Bron know of the Serpent?" Nilos made a tsking noise. "I thought he was your enemy. Aren't you afraid of corruption?"

"Knowledge isn't corruption," she said.

He arched a dubious brow. "No? Well, then I'll answer what I can. The Serpent is dead, yes. But not gone completely. His power was shattered into fragments, scattered throughout the labyrinth of the dead. Like seeds in a fallow field, waiting to sprout."

She didn't like where this was going. "Sprout how, exactly?"

"By binding to one of the spirits that passes through the labyrinth. And being reborn, with them, into the mortal world."

"So you're saying that baby was carrying a piece of the Serpent's power?"

"They were. I merely awakened it. Made it visible, so that I could claim it."

"Why?" she demanded. "What are you?"

"I told you what I am."

She scoffed, "A story collector? And I'm the Winged Architect." She licked her lips, felt the comforting flare of the flames in her palms. Flames that could burn away all that was corrupt. "You're trying to bring back the Serpent."

"Yes." He said it simply, without pride or shame. He might've been telling her he was going to buy fish at the market.

"Why?"

Sephre hadn't planned to ask that. The reason shouldn't matter. The Serpent had nearly destroyed the world, once. There was no answer Nilos could give that would sway her. But apparently she was too curious for her own good.

"The world needs the Serpent," said Nilos. "The same way it needs the moon, and the sun, and the sea. Things are unbalanced. Tilting into chaos. You can't just remove one of the first gods and not expect something else to try to take its place."

"And that's your excuse? For murder?"

"I didn't kill that shepherd," he said. "Like you, I was too late. Someone else found him first. A power that doesn't want the Serpent to return."

"He died of snakebite," she protested.

"No," he said. "He was killed by a skotos in the guise of a serpent. Because someone wants you—and your order—to believe that the Serpent is behind this evil."

She didn't want to believe him. But unlike the baby, the corpses still had their marks. So perhaps he wasn't to blame, not for that. And then there were the words of the skotos that had attacked her. *To stop return.* It made no sense to her then. It made no sense now.

"I don't trust you," she said.

He smiled then, a slice of white teeth. "Nor should you. My goals are not yours. But even so, you'd do well to listen to my warning. The skotoi hunt those who are marked. Their master does not want the Serpent to return."

"Their master *is* the Serpent."

"Not any longer. They've found a new lord. And he will do anything it takes to prevent me from claiming the fragments. As you've seen. They would have killed the child. And . . ." He watched her closely, letting the words hang between them.

She found herself brushing a hand over her arm, tracing the

freckles that spattered her skin. She didn't feel as if she had a fragment of a broken god of death inside her, but then, how would she know? The skotos at Stara Bron had hunted her. As had that skotos-serpent, in the shelter last night.

"They can sense it, just as I do," said Nilos. "I could awaken it now. Claim it. Set you free."

For a moment it sent her heart leaping. It was this alien thing, this taint that had corrupted her. Lured her into enlisting. Led her to that island. Made her a part of that horror. It wasn't her fault.

But that was too easy an answer. Like excusing a man who beat his child because he was drunk. She'd made her choices freely.

And there was no way she was letting this man put his hands on her. Even if she believed that he wasn't to blame for the deaths, that didn't mean she was going to help him restore an ancient death god that had been destroyed for very good reasons.

"No." The flames snapped from her palms, a warning.

But he only nodded, as if he'd been expecting the answer. "Very well. But know that it makes you a target. They will come for you, Sephre."

She bared her teeth, the fire coiling so bright it was nearly white. "I should burn you to ash."

"No," he said, with infuriating calm. "You're going to let me go. Because you know I'm not your enemy."

"You drugged me!"

"You needed the sleep," he replied, glibly. "And I saved your life. You owe me."

She bit down, stifling a growl. He had begun to back away from her, slowly, pace by pace. "Wait," she called. "Come back with me to Stara Bron. If this is true, the agia needs to know."

This could have something to do with Halimede's oath. With the whatever-it-was that Halimede had sworn to keep hidden, to prevent a second cataclysm. With her suggestion that the Ember King's true story was not the one scribed so neatly in ink.

"Alas, I must decline," said Nilos. "I'd prefer to avoid being roasted like a spitted hare. Besides, I'm not the one with the answers you need." Another step. He was nearly to the edge of the hilltop. "You need to find the Faithless Maiden."

Faith*less*? Sephre knew of the Faith*ful* Maiden, of course. She'd gone to war for her, after all. Was he speaking of the same woman? "That's it?" she demanded. "Riddles and nonsense? That's all you can give me?"

He winked. "Sorry. No time for anything more just now."

Insufferable man. She lifted her hands, yellow flames snapping from her fingers. "Who is the Faithless Maiden?"

"*You* should know better than I," he answered, with a strange twist to his lips.

"What does that mean?" Her brain stumbled. "Why me?" She was suddenly deeply afraid of what he might say next. It was the same icy flicker of fear she'd felt when Halimede had spoken of Agia Cerydon's warning. *There are those who carry the weight of the past, even if they do not know it. Many things may be reborn, not just the Ember King.*

Nilos cocked his head, letting the possibilities gnaw at her for another heartbeat before answering. "She ended her days in your temple. But then, the secrets of the Embraced are always held close."

"The Embraced?" Sephre repeated, stupidly, thinking she must have misheard.

A few more paces and he would be beyond her sight. Probably beyond her reach. She remembered how fast he'd moved, back in the barn.

When he'd saved her life.

"Don't worry," he said, almost cheerfully. "We'll meet again. You have something I need. And one day you'll ask me to claim it."

Enough. She flung a fistful of flames straight at him.

He leapt easily aside. She had one last glimpse of his grass-green eyes, a slice of a grin, and then he was gone, down the far side of the hilltop.

The baby's parents insisted that Sephre and Timeus join their evening meal and stay the night. And it was hard to find a good reason to refuse, given that the likely alternative would be spending the night in the same barn they had sheltered in the previous evening, eating the last stale crusts of their travel rations.

"Do you think more skotoi will come?" Timeus asked her. He should have been asleep by then, curled under his cloak on the opposite side of the hearth.

"And face Brother Timeus the skotos-slayer? I doubt it."

A muffled huff. She could practically feel the heat of his blush. "It was just an oil lamp," he said. "Not the holy flame."

"It was quick thinking. It was a deed worthy of an ashdancer. When I was a novice, the only thing I managed to set on fire was a tray of Sister Obelia's apricot cakes, and that was because I put too much wood in the oven."

Timeus stifled a laugh. Good. He needed his sleep, not a restless night worrying about unholy demons. That was Sephre's job.

But the laugh faded quickly into a too-thoughtful silence. "What about Nilos? Do you think he'll come after you?"

We'll meet again. You have something I need.

"Let me worry about that," she said, gruffly. "You should sleep. We've got a long day tomorrow."

"I know. Sorry. I keep thinking about what he said. Or what you said he said. How could anyone have a piece of the Serpent's power in them, and not know it?"

Sephre flinched, even though she knew he was talking about Castor and Iola. She hadn't shared Nilos's suggestion that she herself might also carry such a fragment. It was probably just another lie. She brushed her fingers over her arm, feeling nothing.

"And what do you think he did with it? Do you think he has a lot of them? I wonder how many there are."

Good questions. "I don't know," she said, wearily. "Try to clear your mind. Think about something peaceful. Count your breaths. Agia Halimede will know what to do."

Sephre had considered trying to chase after Nilos, but she had no idea what she would do if she managed to catch him. It was more important to tell the agia what they had learned. *You need to find the Faithless Maiden.*

Faith*less*. Not Faith*ful*. But he must be speaking of the same woman. Sephre supposed the Serpent would see the Maiden as his enemy, an ally of the Ember King. And it was she who had tricked him into yielding up what would become the Ember King's most powerful weapon.

There were several variations on the legend of Heraklion. In one, he was born a humble shepherd but was sought out by a soothsayer who foresaw his greatness in the stars. In another, he came from across the sea in a boat of whalebone and silk. There was even a version where he fell from the sky, and was found a naked child, alone in a hollow of melted glassy stone.

But all the stories agreed that Heraklion was brave and strong and true. And of course such a man must have a beloved who was equally superlative: the most beautiful and clever in all the land. So wondrous that even the god of death fell under her spell, and wished to claim her for himself. On the day Heraklion was to marry his beloved, the Serpent struck, stealing her away to his sinuous and poison-threaded labyrinth to be his own bride.

But this Faithful Maiden—unlike Heraklion, her name was not recorded, which struck Sephre as deeply unfair—refused to be seduced by the Serpent. Instead, she tricked him and managed to steal a fang from his own jaws. Escaping back to the mortal world with her prize, the Maiden found her way to Heraklion, gifting him the fang with her dying breath, telling him to turn it against the Serpent.

For the god of death had already begun to wreak vengeance on the living world, unleashing the terrors of the cataclysm. The earth shattered, sinking entire islands, burying others in ash and molten earth, tearing apart the old empire.

Weeping for his lost love, Heraklion crafted the fang into the blade Letheko, the dagger of oblivion, with the power to destroy a spirit utterly. Because of course the dagger had a name, while the woman who had sacrificed herself to gain it was left anonymous. With the weapon, Heraklion destroyed the Serpent, but was himself mortally wounded. He died promising that he would be reborn when next the world needed its most bright and shining hero.

So that was Hierax. And who was she to argue otherwise? Maybe the original Ember King had been an arrogant jackass too. She had seen plenty of terrible people accomplish great deeds in her time. Maybe you had to be a bit terrible, to make your mark on the world.

Or maybe the Ember King in those stories was a lie, as Halimede's oath suggested. If so, maybe the real Faithful Maiden was not the brave and loyal woman of legend. Maybe she was in fact Faithless.

Which led to the second part of Nilos's accusation. Another troubling tidbit she had not shared with Timeus. *The secrets of the Embraced are always held close.* Was he saying that the Maiden— whether Faithless or Faithful—had been Embraced? That instead of dying tragically in Heraklion's arms, she somehow managed to make her way to Stara Bron so that some long-dead agia—perhaps the Cerydon that Halimede spoke of?—could burn her past away?

Why? What had she done that was so terrible?

And if that was true, how had her bones ended up far to the south, in Bassara, so treasured that her defenders would rather fight a war than yield them to Hierax? That question rankled most of all. *Furies take the man.*

"You're right," said Timeus. "I'll try that. Sorry." A rustle, as he turned on his side. "It's just so strange, the way the world works. I thought when I came to Stara Bron it would be boring. Not boring in a bad way," he corrected, hastily, "but, you know, mostly prayers and chores. Not fighting skotoi and rescuing babies from serpent cultists! Rhea will be so jealous! She's probably still in training, sticking arrows in straw dummies."

"There's nothing wrong with prayers and chores. And you'd have been safer if you stayed at Stara Bron." She grimaced. "I shouldn't have gotten you into this."

"No," he protested. "This has been the best week of my life!"

She shushed him. "You'll undo all our goodwill if you wake that baby."

"Sorry," he whispered. "But it's true, sister. I never thought I'd actually do anything worthwhile. I once overheard Mother telling Rhea that I must have been a wastrel in my last life, because I wasn't amounting to much in this one."

"Your mother sounds like a fool," said Sephre, too tired to be tactful. "You're doing a fine job with this life, from what I see. Skotos-slayer, remember?"

Silence. Then, softly, "Thank you, sister."

And finally, blessedly, a rumble of sleeping breaths.

She ought to take her own advice. But Sephre had no peaceful thoughts. She tried to imagine herself in the garden at Stara Bron, the sunlight filtering green through the vines, the air heavy with pollen and summer sweetness. But dark coiling shapes rippled in the shadows. She could imagine she heard them now, beyond the tight stone walls of the cottage.

And when she counted, all she could see were the bodies, tumbled in the streets of a city across the sea. A city that no longer existed. A city she had helped kill.

Groaning, she flipped onto her other side. She needed sleep, or tomorrow would be unbearable. In spite of herself, she thought of Nilos's wine. His wry smile. *You needed the sleep.*

If she'd thought to bring dreamfast with her, she would have taken it. But instead, she had only the hollow echoes of her own skull, the rattle of her fears, and the holy flame kindling in her chest.

It was the flame she turned to, in the end, desperate. *Please. Make it stop. Just let me sleep.*

The sparks rose, warm and hungry. Her thoughts fell to ash, and darkness swam up to claim her.

CHAPTER 14

SEPHRE

Sephre released her breath as the heavy wooden doors of Stara Bron thudded closed behind her. It had been a long, tiring two days traveling back from Kessely, made heavier by the burden of everything Nilos had thrust on her.

The world needs the Serpent. The same way it needs the moon, and the sun, and the sea.

She did not want to believe it. She had no reason to believe it. Nilos himself had told her not to trust him. Fates, she'd come to Stara Bron to make things simpler. To remove herself from having to make decisions with fatal consequences. To grow old, pulling weeds and brewing tonics. A sulky outrage simmered in Sephre's chest. Damn that man, for dumping this tangle on her.

She needed to speak to Halimede. The agia would know what to do. She would take Nilos's searing accusations and render them into fancies, dust to be swept away from the clear path of the truth. Or, if it *was* true, if Sephre truly did carry some fragment of the Serpent's power within her, then Halimede would deal with it. She'd have no excuse not to grant her the Embrace. To burn away that impurity and prevent Nilos from claiming it and restoring the Serpent to power.

Pausing only to set down her travel pack, Sephre led Timeus from the courtyard, through the cloister, then up the steps that led to the heights. Halimede should be in her office, preparing for the evening prayers.

Sephre gave herself no time to rest, ignoring the stitch in her side as she propelled herself up the stairs, Timeus hastening to follow.

She barely even paused to rap at the door. Halimede would forgive her, when she'd heard their tale.

She thrust herself into the room. "Agia, I'm sorry to interrupt, but I have to tell you what—"

Sephre stopped so abruptly that Timeus, hard on her heels, slammed into her. Thankfully she still had some of her old instincts, and managed to catch herself against the doorway. All the air seemed suddenly gone from her lungs. She stared at the woman behind the desk.

"Beroe?" Sephre found a thimbleful of breath, rallying herself. The woman must be visiting Halimede on temple business. But then why was she sitting at the agia's desk? Why did she make Sephre think suddenly of a spider, crouched in the center of her web?

"Where's the agia?" Sephre demanded. "I must speak with her."

"I'm afraid that's impossible at the moment," said Beroe. "Agia Halimede is unwell."

Unwell. It could mean so many things. Sephre clenched trembling fists. "Where is she?"

"The infirmary. She—wait, sister! She isn't to be disturbed. We've given her poppy syrup."

Sephre whirled back from the door. "*You* gave her poppy syrup? How much? Why? What's wrong with her?" Accusation turned the words sharp.

Beroe's eyes narrowed. "Sibling Abas suggested it. The agia fell ill shortly after you left. Pains in her chest, and shortness of breath. You know as well as I that her health has been fragile, and no doubt the stress of recent events weighs heavily on a woman of her years."

"She was fine last time I last saw her." A bit of breathless on the stairs, that was all. Even Sephre had felt that climb.

"Which was five days ago," replied Beroe, coolly. "What kept you away so long? Did you discover more about the attacks?"

"Yes," began Timeus, helpfully, "There was another—"

"We'll report everything to the agia," interrupted Sephre.

"*I* am acting agia," said Beroe, chin lifting. "As senior yellow, it's my duty to ensure that Stara Bron does not suffer in Halimede's absence. And the others agree. It was decided yesterday, at summations."

Sephre's teeth were going to crack if she ground them any more tightly.

"I can see that the news of the agia's illness has distressed you," offered Beroe. "Very well, then. Go. See for yourself that she's in no danger. Minister to her as you see fit. I'm sure that Brother Timeus can provide me a full report of your activities in the meantime. Won't you, brother?"

Timeus gulped, glancing to Sephre.

Furies' tits. "That won't be necessary. Settle your things in the dortoir, Timeus. Then go and see that the mint hasn't taken over our garden. I'll meet you there once I've given Sister Beroe my report."

She waited until the boy had scuttled off, keeping her gaze fixed on the map table.

"I understand Agia Halimede sent you to Potedia to investigate another death," prompted Beroe. "Did the dead man have the same mark as the girl from Tylos?"

"Yes," Sephre answered grudgingly. "But his family had never seen it. I believe it was placed there by someone."

"Who?"

Her tongue felt heavy. Why? She owed Nilos nothing. And no doubt Beroe would ask Timeus to confirm her story. There was no point to lying. But what would Beroe *do* with the information? Would she send word to the king, telling him of the attacks?

Maybe that wasn't such a bad thing. Sephre might despise Hierax for an arrogant, self-aggrandizing fool, but he had far more power at his disposal than the temple. If the goal was to hunt down Nilos, the king was likely their best option.

She plunged onward. "We heard tell of a stranger who was in Potedia at the same time the shepherd was killed. We tracked him to Kessely. He kidnapped a newborn from the village. We confronted him and recovered the child. The baby's fine now, back home safe."

"And the man?"

"He gave his name as Nilos. He's trying to restore the Serpent."

Beroe's eyes narrowed. The sparks of yellow in their depths flared. "How do you know?"

"He told me. He seemed proud of it."

"Where is he now?" Beroe glanced past her, as if she expected to see the man bound in chains.

Sephre hesitated, wishing she had a better answer. "He got away."

"You let a minion of the Serpent escape you?"

"He was holding a child!" Sephre couldn't quite keep the ire from her tone. "Or do you think I should have incinerated the baby, too?" *Collateral damage, Captain. Unfortunate, but the victory is ours.*

Beroe drew in a long breath. "Of course not. But he could be anywhere now, murdering some other innocent."

"He claims the deaths aren't his work." Sephre spoke steadily. Her words were soldiers, a shield wall braced for assault, betraying nothing. "He says that the Ember King didn't truly destroy the Serpent, only shattered its power into fragments. And now all those pieces are here in this world, bound to mortals. Those are the people with the marks. The baby had one too, but it vanished when Nilos touched it."

"Then how does he explain the deaths?"

"He says someone else took over in the Serpent's absence, and is trying to stay in power. They're sending skotoi to kill anyone who carries the mark, to send the fragments to oblivion before Nilos can claim them. In the corpses of snakes, to cast the blame on the Serpent."

Beroe frowned. "Did you see anything to support such a notion?"

"Yes," Sephre admitted. "Skotoi. One of them tried to attack the baby. Brother Timeus slew it. He was a credit to the temple," she added, with a rush of pride for the lad.

"And the other?"

HOUSE OF DUSK 145

"The other?"

"You said *skotoi*. Plural."

A stupid slip. She'd no wish to tell Beroe what had happened in the barn. Any of it. But no doubt the woman would wheedle it from Timeus. Better to make the story her own, while she could.

"Oh. Yes. One of the serpent-skotoi attacked us while we sheltered during the rain. Nilos killed it."

"Why would it attack *you*, if it was seeking those with the mark?"

A chill rippled up Sephre's spine as Beroe's yellow-lit eyes skimmed over her. Lingering on her arm? No, she was being paranoid. Letting her own baseless fears rule her.

"I assume it was trying to kill Nilos," she said, briskly. "But they'll have to get in line."

"Indeed," said Beroe, smiling. "The king's soldiers will see to that."

"Soldiers?" Sephre repeated. "What soldiers?"

"The ones on their way to Stara Bron as we speak, accompanying King Hierax's royal emissary."

"You told the king about the attacks?" Sephre sputtered. "Halimede said—"

"I know what the agia said." Beroe's lips flattened. "I didn't countermand her decision. I didn't need to. Much has happened in your absence, sister. Brother Itonus sent a firespeaking from Helissa City four days ago, reporting an attack by risen skotoi near the necropolis. There were dozens of witnesses. It confirms what we all have long feared: the Serpent seeks to return, and the Ember King must make ready to stop him. The Sibyl of Tears has prophesied that Stara Bron holds the key to his victory, and now King Hierax sends his son here to claim it."

Heavy tramping steps, shaking the quiet earth. The rough clatter of bronze. Soldiers, marching through the broken gates to claim their prize from a silent city. Sephre shook away the memory. *That won't happen here. This is a temple. We aren't Hierax's enemies.*

But they could be. Sephre would have bet her entire stock of medicinal wine that this "key to victory" was the same mysterious something that Halimede's oath bound her to keep hidden. And then what? Soldiers tramping through Sister Obelia's scrupulously organized kitchen? Panicking the novices, smashing the ancient tiled walls of the cloister in search of their prize? No. Not on her watch. These were her people. She had prayed with them, laughed with them, tended their wounds and coughs and cramps. And she would not see them brutalized.

Sephre licked her dry lips. "What key?"

"I'm sure the prince will make that clear when he arrives," said Beroe. "It should be any day now."

===

Halimede was dignified even in slumber, her long gray hair combed back neatly, her arms folded across her belly, her lips slightly parted in the slow breath of deep sleep. Natural sleep, for Abas had agreed with Sephre that three days of the poppy tincture was enough. Now, they must see if she would wake, or drift forever deeper.

Come back. Sephre held the old woman's hand in her own, watching the rise and fall of her thin chest. *We need you still.* I *need you.*

But Halimede slept on. And might never wake. It was her heart, Abas said. *There is no herb that can cure time.*

She felt a pinch of guilt over her suspicion of Beroe. Only a small pinch. The woman hadn't scrupled to take advantage of the situation. But Sephre had to admit that Beroe was keeping the temple running smoothly, even with all the additional preparations for a royal visit. And she'd come every day to visit Halimede, a golden flame cupped in her hands as she whispered silent prayers at the agia's bedside.

Sephre would have given much to know exactly what Beroe prayed for.

Something tickled her palm. Halimede's fingers, moth-soft,

fluttered briefly against her own. Sephre squeezed the old woman's hand in answer, hope lodged so tight in her throat that the word came out a whisper. "Agia?"

Time hung, a wheel spinning in the mud. Halimede slept on. A piercing pain gripped Sephre, chased by anger. It wasn't fair. Halimede sent her after Nilos, gave her the task of chasing down answers. And all she had found were more questions.

The sensible thing would be to ignore everything Nilos said. It was clear he was trying to manipulate her. Sliding his taunts under her skin like splinters. He wanted them to ache. To fester.

And yet she had to admit there might be some truth to them. Perhaps the Maiden had been faithless. Perhaps the Ember King wasn't the hero the stories claimed. And that was why Cerydon had set an oath on the agias of Stara Bron. An oath that no one but Sephre knew about. "Acting Agia" Beroe certainly wouldn't hesitate to grant whatever the royal emissary asked of her, seeing it as a means to gain power and influence for Stara Bron. And Sephre doubted anything she said to the woman would convince her otherwise.

Which meant it was up to Sephre to keep Halimede's oath. A throbbing ache began in her temples. She forced her jaw to unclench. What now? How could she thread this maze, and bring herself and her fellow ashdancers safely past the demons?

She needed answers. And Nilos had told her where to look for them. *The secrets of the Embraced are always held close.*

If so, maybe that was where she should start. By speaking with one of them.

=====

"Sister Sephre, what brings you to my domain?" Brother Dolon smiled broadly from behind his desk as she entered the archives the next afternoon.

Like the rest of Stara Bron, the library echoed with unuse. There must be thousands of scrolls filling the compartments along the walls. Several tall ladders gave access to the highest shelves. There were a half-dozen worktables filling the center of the room, lit by bright shafts of morning light that slanted in from the windows high above. Sephre could imagine them filled with ashdancers copying out records and accounts of the dead. Once, the temple had served as the primary source of such information, but the duties had shifted over time into secular hands. The king's offices of taxation handled it now.

"Good morning, brother." She met Dolon's smile with one of her own, though it felt tight on her lips. She had always liked Brother Dolon. He was a sturdy, unflappable man with a deep interest in the smallest details of the world and a contagious joy for knowledge. He always set aside any records he came across in his work that might be of use to her. Herbal recipes, medical tomes, and once the journal of an ashdancer who visited the hidden city of the Idrani and documented their ingenious water systems, which allowed them to cultivate glorious gardens even in the seemingly barren Bleeding Sands. Spending time with him always made her feel as if she'd gained a new pair of eyes, that she could see all the intricate beauties of the world, the patterns shaped as if by some unknown, numinous architect.

She had no wish to hurt him. To poke at old scars. Though if it was true, what Beroe told her, maybe there would be no hurt. That was the whole point of the Embrace. To burn away the shame and pain and corruption of spirit. Even if so, she feared it would be an awkward conversation. And so she'd brought a gift. Or maybe "bribe" was the better word for it.

She set the small glass jar on the table between them. It had taken her most of the morning to compound. "I brought you something."

Dolon's eyes went wide with delight. "Is it . . . did Abas remember the recipe?"

"I think so. You'll be the best judge."

He plucked it up reverently, tilting it to catch the slanting afternoon light. The substance inside glittered, sparkling a pure, bright blue. "Azarine ink! Hah! I can finally finish!"

She had her doubts about that. Dolon had been working on his treatise on the children of Chaos for as long as Sephre had been at Stara Bron. She'd helped Abas to produce a number of other dyes and inks for the man over the years. The perfect gold for the Sphinx's wings. Just the right glossy blue-black for the Beetle. Every time he'd claimed that the work was *almost* done.

"It's exactly what I need for the waters of the Lyrikon," he went on effusively. "Thank you, sister!"

Sephre winced. Part of her wanted to turn and walk away. Leave Dolon happy and untroubled. She gathered her courage, and forced herself to speak. "There's another reason I'm here."

"Of course." Dolon was still swirling the bottle, admiring the brilliant blue. He gestured vaguely in the direction of the shelves that held the botanical scrolls.

"It's not about the herbarium. It's . . ." Her mouth was dry. She licked her lips. *Just spit it out.* "It's about the Embrace."

Dolon's grip on the jar of ink faltered. Sephre lunged forward, snatching the glass bottle from the air. For a long moment they stood in silence, though she could hear the man's quick breathing. She set the ink on the desk between them. "I'm sorry. I wouldn't ask if it weren't important. And I'm not asking you to speak about . . . yourself."

A sigh. Dolon reached for the jar. His pure joy in the ink had fled. Now, he cradled it like a talisman. "There's little I could say. But go on. Ask, and I will do my best to answer."

She'd already decided it was best not to repeat Nilos's suggestion that the Faithful Maiden had come to Stara Bron to seek the Embrace. She hadn't told Beroe either. If it was false, then no one else needed to know she had been duped. If it was true, then it was likely connected with the secrets of Halimede's oath.

Either way, she needed a different excuse for her questions. There had been plenty of time to plan a nice, composed, reasonable speech while she decanted the ink, but now the words turned to stones in her mouth. "I . . . it's for me. I want the Embrace."

"Ah." Dolon turned the jar in his hands. He cleared his throat. "I'm not sure how I can help, sister."

Fates, he looked miserable. "I just . . . I thought you might be able to tell me what it's like. Whether you're glad you did it."

The question had nothing to do with the Faithful Maiden, but it flew out of her lips unbidden.

"You're assuming I had a choice." He kept his gaze fixed on the ink.

Oh. Right. She hadn't even considered that option. Dolon might have been sent to the Embrace as a criminal. The question hovered on her lips, unspoken.

"I don't know," he said, after a moment. "I don't know if I asked for it, or if it was a punishment."

"Do you *want* to know?"

"No." The answer was quick, sharp, certain. "It's done. It won't change anything to know who I was."

A wild goat had broken into Sephre's garden last fall. By the time she chased it out, it had torn its way through the beds, heedless, snapping up tender shoots and vulnerable buds. She'd wanted very much to wring the creature's neck. And yet here she was, ripping and chewing her way through Dolon's past.

"So . . . you don't remember any of it?"

"Only the flames." His gaze went distant. "Blue flames. I stepped out from them and Halimede was there. I was at the shrine. On the mountaintop. And I felt . . . free. Like I'd just set down a boulder."

Sephre hunched, feeling crushed and sour. It had been a mistake to come here. All she was doing was tormenting herself and making poor Dolon uncomfortable.

"I'm sorry I can't help you, sister," he said. "I'm not sure anyone can. The Embrace is personal. Although I suppose . . . But no, they're sealed for a reason."

She jerked her chin up at his thoughtful tone. "What are sealed?"

Dolon looked as if he regretted opening this conversational

door. "Anyone who comes to Stara Bron seeking the Embrace is required to leave an account in the archives. But it wouldn't be right to read them. They're memories of lives that are gone now."

A tremor shook her, as if one of the Fates had just tapped her on the shoulder. "How old? How long have they been kept?"

"Oh, centuries. We lost most of the records from before the cataclysm, of course, but there are some from not long after, I believe. I don't visit those shelves often," he admitted.

"Then the people who left those accounts are long gone to the labyrinth," she said. "Most likely their spirits have been reborn a half-dozen times since. Surely it would do no harm to read them. I . . . I need this, Dolon. Please. There's nowhere else I can go for answers."

It wasn't a lie. And it was more truth than she'd meant to give him. She felt suddenly naked as a bare root pulled from the dark earth.

A brief struggle contorted Dolon's round face before he nodded. "I suppose . . . I suppose it's a reasonable request. Come, I'll show you where to find them."

====

Sephre had skimmed two dozen codexes in the past three hours, and each one felt like a violation. Some were tragedies of fate, but many more were the brutal, hideous acts of people. Swabbing her fingers over her weary eyes, she half expected them to come away bloody.

And yet she could not stop. She told herself it was because of Nilos, because she had to learn whether his taunts had any truth to them. But she knew it was more personal than that. She was looking for justification. Proof that she was no different than any of these long-dead folk who had been reborn in flame. She squinted at cramped lines of faded ink, puzzled out archaic spelling, drowned herself in ancient pain, trying to measure it against her own.

Except that you couldn't set your sorrows neatly onto a scale. There was no metric. How could she compare her own shames to that of a woman who accidentally poisoned her five children, mistaking dropwort for parsley?

Sephre closed the tormented mother's codex and sat for a time, filling her lungs with the dry, cool air, tinged with the bitter scent of the pressed sheets of oilpith meant to protect the codexes from mildew and vermin. She was beginning to think this was a hopeless quest, on all counts.

Oilpith could only do so much. Many of the oldest were barely readable. If the Maiden—Faithful or Faithless—had left her story here, it might already be lost in a lacework of mice nibbles and blooms of mold. .

Standing, she collected her current batch of codexes and returned them to the shelves. It was late afternoon by then, the shadows stretching. Carefully, she cupped a handful of flame in her left palm, kneeling to scan the lower recesses for any volumes she might have missed.

The flame wavered. Strange. She felt no breeze. Sephre swept her hand slowly, following a draft that only the fire seemed to feel, until she knelt beside the farthest niche.

Reaching into the shadows, she felt dust, slippery under her fingers. Then something more solid: a small oblong. She pulled it out.

A codex, barely larger than her palm. She traced the knot of twine twisted around the leather cover. She'd worked out the meaning of the colors over the past hours. It had been a small relief to discover she could skip over those tied in white thread. Those belonged to children, and the two she'd skimmed before realizing the pattern had been devastating enough. Sephre doubted that the Faithless Maiden had been Embraced as a child. If there was some secret here, it belonged to the woman grown.

That left only the gray-knotted accounts of the criminals, and the handful of volumes bound in black. Testaments of adults who had sought the Embrace willingly. Like this one.

She tried to work the knot free, but the years had settled the cord like stone. Carefully, she pressed one fingertip to the binding. Not one of the traditional uses of the holy flame, but then, it was the flame that had guided her to this book. A hum filled her chest as she tugged loose the singed cord. Pages thin as onionskin fell open, and Sephre nearly dropped the codex to the floor.

The Serpent's star sign stared up at her. Seven points, joined in a faceted ring, drawn carefully in black ink.

She searched the facing page for some explanation, but found the paper mottled with mold, barely legible. Only bits and pieces remained.

> *. . . knew what I had done when I took my vows, yet*
> *still calls me sister . . .*
> *. . . the terrible cost of my betrayal . . .*
> *. . . trusted one who loved me too well . . .*
> *. . . could slay death itself, and break the cycle of . . .*
> *. . . yet his mark lingers on my skin even now . . .*

A paltry handful of clues, but enough to set her pulse jittering. Was this it? The writer spoke of slaying death. Was it a reference to the Ember King? The Faithful Maiden had given her lover that power, when she gave him the means to craft the dagger Letheko. But the woman who left this account had clearly been an ash-dancer. She spoke of vows, of being called sister.

Sephre's chest was a prison, locking her breath tight. She had no word for what she was feeling. Kinship? Was that it? For so long she had felt alone in her grief and shame. But here, in these tattered pages, she saw it reflected. A woman who had come to Stara Bron with some terrible weight on her soul.

She skimmed onward, fingers trembling so badly she tore one of the pages. There *must* be more. Every blotch of mold and bleary line of text taunted her, until she flipped to the last page in desperation.

It was almost completely illegible, only a few scattered words winking out like stars in the deep of night.

. . . Cerydon . . . request . . .
. . . blade . . . hidden . . . only agia . . . claim it . . .
. . . will ensure . . . never . . . again . . .
. . . faithless . . . no more . . .

A light scuff of approaching footsteps made her jump. Instinctively, she tucked the small codex into her sleeve, just as Brother Dolon appeared at the end of the shelf. He hovered there, averting his eyes from the shelves that held the secrets of the man he had once been. "Did you find what you were looking for, sister?"

Her heart thudded. Foolish to let the ancient, mold-riddled text turn her into some sort of sneak-thief. But even more foolish to ignore the truth simply because she didn't care for the messenger.

"Most of these old codexes are unreadable," she answered, hoping he wouldn't notice the evasion. She didn't want to lie to Dolon. But the words in the codex—scattered and shattered as they were—had done nothing to cast doubt on Nilos's accusations. Instead, they had given shape and form to Halimede's ghosts. To the oath sworn all those years ago by Agia Cerydon, and passed on to each of the agias after them.

A woman who called herself faithless had come here, to Stara Bron. She had taken the Embrace, cleansing herself of some deep shame. But before the flames took her past, she had given her agia a blade to keep hidden, so it could never be used again. It must be Letheko.

And now King Hierax's son was on his way to Stara Bron, guided by the words of a prophecy, to claim it.

She needed to speak with Halimede. *Fates, let her wake. I need her more than ever.*

"I'd best get back to the garden," she said, starting to move past Dolon. "Thank you, brother."

HOUSE OF DUSK 155

He held up an arm, staying her. "Of course, sister. But the garden will need to wait. Sister Beroe has called an assembly."

Wonderful. The last thing she needed right now was another tedious summations meeting, especially one led by "Acting Agia" Beroe.

But summations was always early in the morning, directly after dawn prayer. Not late in the afternoon, with the sun slanting toward dusk. And she could think of no other reason to gather all the ashdancers except—

"It's the royal party," said Dolon. "They've arrived."

CHAPTER 15

YENERIS

At least this time they both had proper disguises. Yeneris had insisted on it, once she'd heard Sinoe's plan. It had taken some digging in the princess's wardrobe to find something suitably plain. And still more effort to convince her to leave behind her trinkets.

"I don't see why I couldn't wear my amber earrings," said Sinoe. "You can't even see them when I have my hair down. They're good luck. And they bring out the color of my eyes."

Yeneris scanned the street ahead, then glanced back to check that no one was following. The only people she saw were clustered around the open front of a taverna, passing a large wine cup around as they played some sort of dice game. "You can't walk through the city as if it's the palace. You *do* realize just one of those earrings is worth three years' wages to most people?"

Sinoe sighed. "Spoilsport."

"And your eyes are fine as they are," she added. *More than fine. Maybe too fine.* Yeneris tensed as two young men stumbled out of the taverna, laughing. One of them tugged on his friend's sleeve, nodding appreciatively toward Sinoe. They changed course.

"Two beautiful ladies like you shouldn't be—" The man yelped as Yeneris's dagger appeared under his chin.

"Shouldn't be bothered by random men with no respect for personal boundaries?" She forced him back a step. He had been reaching for Sinoe's arm.

The man looked more outraged than alarmed. "You think you're too good for us?" he spat. "You think you're tough because you have a little knife? You're nothing, girl. Someone ought to—"

She kicked, sweeping his legs out from under him. By the time he hit the street—with a quite satisfying thump—she was already hustling the princess away.

"I told you this would be fun," said Sinoe.

"This is not my idea of fun."

"Isn't it?" Sinoe cast her a sidelong glance. Yeneris was suddenly highly aware of her own hand, resting lightly on Sinoe's shoulder. How close she was standing. For safety, of course. To make sure that if the men followed, her body would block the princess.

But they weren't following. Yeneris and Sinoe has passed into a bustling night market, a patchwork of brightly colored stalls lit by pierced-copper lamps, the air smelling of smoke and burnt sugar and fried onions. Yeneris dropped her arm to her side.

"What *do* you do for fun, then?" Sinoe traipsed along one of the aisles, pausing to ogle a display of glass beads, then an array of cosmetic pots.

The question rattled in Yeneris's mind. She had fun. Of course she did. Just not recently. Training had been fun, sometimes. Sparring with Mikat, when she managed to actually land a hit and cracked a smile from the older woman. When she was little she'd loved the sea, loved the swell of water lifting her. But the last time she'd gone swimming she'd hated it. Hated the way it made her feel so small, so powerless. The hungry abyss cold below.

"That wasn't supposed to be a stumper."

She blinked, and found Sinoe watching her curiously, a tiny dent between her brows.

"I like doing my job," Yeneris said, finally. That was a good answer. "I like being useful. I don't have time for fun."

Sinoe arched a brow. "That sounded like a challenge."

"It wasn't," said Yeneris, hastily. "Where are we going? You said your vision was of someone who could help us learn what Lacheron is up to. Are they here?"

Sinoe did not answer, having been distracted by a nearby vendor whose stall was heaped with scrolls and bound codexes.

On the surface, at least, the market didn't seem particularly dangerous. No doubt a good chunk of the goods had been smuggled into the city. The import taxes were notoriously high since the war. But they were mostly small luxuries. She hadn't smelled a single whiff of medena. There were few visible weapons. The only raised voices were friendly shouts and boasts.

Still, there was something about the place that set Yeneris's skin humming. What was it? She let her gaze wander, trying to find the source of her unease.

There. So small she'd almost missed it. A symbol carved into a corner of the bead seller's stall. A stylized bee. She scanned the other nearby stalls. More bees. Now that she'd seen one, they were everywhere, even painted onto some of the walls.

Yeneris had memorized a detailed map of the city as part of her training. Had spent hours reciting different possible escape routes from the palace. The locations of three different safe houses. Places she could go for supplies, for healing, for weapons. Places where rules could be bent and laws could be broken without fear of notice. This was one of them.

She turned on Sinoe, who was sorting through a basket of scrolls. "Look!" she squealed, unfurling one. "It's the Epic of Swords and Fire! One of the copies from the library of Melicarum. Ooh, and there's even illustrations. This is my favorite part, when the heroine is poisoned and—"

"Where did that bangle come from?"

Sinoe arched her brows innocently, as if there weren't an enormous golden bracelet decorating one of her shapely wrists. "You're not the only one who can hide things in interesting places."

"Princess," Yeneris began, pitching her voice low, glancing to see if anyone had noticed the thief-bait. "This market belongs to the Queen of Swarms."

"Of course it does," said Sinoe. "That's why we're here." She turned and signaled to the merchant.

Yeneris swallowed a curse. It was her own fault. She should have demanded more details. This was what came of trusting

Sinoe to be in any way sensible. "She's the one you had a vision about? You want to meet with of one of the most notorious thief lords in the city?"

The princess completed her purchase, not bothering to hide her silver coins any more than the gold bangle. Yeneris saw the merchant's eyes linger on the trinket.

"Don't frown, Yen," Sinoe said. "This is important."

"Fine. Then tell me where I need to go. I'll take you back to the palace and get the information myself. You can't be here, Sinoe."

Maybe it was the fact that she'd used her name. Or maybe Sinoe finally heard the edges in her voice. She regarded Yeneris steadily. "I have to do something, Yen. You've seen what it's like. Fates, you know. You're—did you lose people? Because of my . . . in the war?"

It took Yeneris several heartbeats to find her tongue. "Yes." *Everyone. Everything.* That was how it had felt at the time.

"Then you understand. You're the only one who does."

There were thousands. Not just the few who had escaped the destruction of the city, but those who fled before the siege, those who were already living elsewhere, the diaspora that had begun three centuries ago during the cataclysm. So, no, she was not the only one. But perhaps she was the only one in Sinoe's narrow world.

"What about your brother?" Clearly Sinoe hadn't told Ichos about her clandestine activities.

Sinoe rolled her new scroll between her hands. "My mother told me a story when I was a little girl, about scorpion mares. Have you heard of them?"

Yeneris shook her head.

"They live in the far eastern steppes. They're beautiful, tall and graceful, and they have coats like molten metal. Fast as the wind. There's a story that they're the daughters of the Sphinx."

"What does this have to do with your brother?"

"Scorpion mares can't be tamed. There's only one way to catch one. You need to hunt down one of their foals. And you kill it. You murder it and tear out the baby's heart and you take that, and you show it to the mare, and she will submit to you. She will let you ride her, because you hold something that is precious to her. But she will never love you. She hates you, even as she serves you."

Yeneris shook her head. "I don't read poetry, princess. You'll have to speak plainly."

"Ichos is the scorpion mare. He hates Father, but he'll never turn against him. And he doesn't understand what it's like for me. He's not imprisoned in the palace."

"Because he's not valuable enough to keep locked away," said Yeneris. That must be a wound as well. Ichos was as much his father's tool as Sinoe. Just not one as highly valued. Awkward, to say the least.

Yeneris couldn't help feeling that none of this was what she'd volunteered for. When Mikat had recruited her from the camp—hungry and desperate for purpose—it had been to restore Bassara. For the past seven years she'd imagined this mission. Herself, brave and capable and cool-eyed, silently working in the shadows to regain the kore's bones. She'd understood that doing so required getting close to the princess. She'd been prepared to lie, to manipulate, to gather secrets.

She hadn't realized that witnessing someone's hidden truth could be a mirror. These were not things she could simply scribe into the tablet of her memory, to be spilled back out to Mikat.

Yeneris cared. That was the solid, shameful truth of it. She cared about Sinoe. Fates, she even felt a pang of pity for the brother.

Fine, she told herself. *Feel it. Feel it and then lock it away.* Emotions weren't shameful, unless she let them rule her. And she most definitely could not afford to be ruled by these emotions.

Which was made abundantly clear a moment later when she noticed a tawny-haired boy of about eleven bump against Sinoe on his way through the market.

"Not so fast." Yeneris caught his arm just as he was about to slip away into the crowd. He gave a squawk, fighting her, but she was stronger. He was a skinny thing. She relaxed her grip slightly. No need to hurt the boy. "Give it back."

"I didn't take anything!" His eyes went wide, actually welling with tears. He was good. But not good enough.

Yeneris patted the boy's sleeves, then the scarf tucked around his shoulders, where she found the suspicious lump. She pulled loose the gold bangle and held it out to Sinoe. "I told you this would happen."

"And I told you to trust me," said Sinoe, archly. She took the bangle, then held it out to the boy. "Here. You can keep it, if you take us to the Hive. We need to speak with the Queen of Swarms."

"I don't think this is a good idea," said Yeneris, scowling around the dim hall. The clatter of dice thrummed in the air, twining with the reedy hum of pipes. The high, curved walls were painted a rich saffron, decorated with a pattern like honeycomb. The Queen of Swarms clearly valued a strong and consistent aesthetic. Yeneris wondered if she would be wearing a striped black and gold gown. Perhaps jeweled wings. Or a poisoned blade she called Stinger.

"You're just grouchy because they made you leave your weapons at the door," said Sinoe.

"Not all of them," countered Yeneris. She'd managed to keep two of her most well-concealed blades. A small comfort, given that others here had no doubt done the same. "How exactly do you plan to get the queen to speak with us? If she's working for Lacheron, don't you think she's just going to tell him about all this?"

Her belly went cold at the thought. At best, she'd be fired from service. Ruin any chance she had of rescuing the kore's bones. At worst, she'd be executed. No, worst of all, they might suspect her. And what then? Would she be the one bound and bleeding, with Sinoe thrust into the thick smoke to spill her secrets? Reveal Mikat and the others?

Sinoe waved a dismissive hand. "Not if we give her a good reason."

"What reason?"

"We're going to save her life."

Yeneris forced herself to take a long, deep breath. Then she drew Sinoe to the side, into an alcove beside one of the large braziers that warmed the room. "Tell me everything. Seriously, princess. This isn't a game."

"I know it's not a game," Sinoe bit back. "I saw the blood. I saw a woman twitching on the ground, trying to breathe through a severed throat." Her voice trembled slightly. "I'm sorry. I should have told you everything sooner. I should have trusted you."

Yeneris winced. "It's fine. It doesn't change anything. Let's just focus on the mission." Good advice. "Did you see the assassin?"

"No. The visions weren't clear. But I know the words. I wrote them down." She tugged a bit of paper from her sleeve, holding it out.

Yeneris took it, careful not to brush Sinoe's fingers. The prophecy was short. *The Queen of Swarms will die by an unseen blow, her hives dripping secret honey into the jaws of the wolf.* "And you know it will be tonight?"

"No. But we can warn her."

Fates, did she really believe it was that easy? That a woman who controlled everything remotely illicit in five different districts would simply believe their warning? And then *reward* them with information?

A week ago Yeneris would have called Sinoe naive. Her world so limited, so confined, even with its comforts. But she wasn't naive.

Hopeful. That was a better word. Even now her brown eyes held Yeneris's own, brimming with certainty that they could do this. And Fates curse her, that hope was catching.

"All right," she agreed. "We'll find the Queen of Swarms and warn her."

"Warn her of what, exactly?" said a sharp voice behind them.

Yeneris's heart plummeted. Two figures blocked their alcove, both wearing light leather armor, both with swords drawn.

CHAPTER 16

YENERIS

The man on the left was the weakest link. Someone needed to teach him how to brace properly. Yeneris could kick his legs out, then one good shove and the brazier would block the other for a few heartbeats. It might be just long enough to get Sinoe out of the alcove. One of her daggers to drive back pursuit, the other to get through the outer door.

Still nearly impossible. But better than being taken prisoner. Sinoe was a rich prize, even without her jewels. They needed to get out of here before she was recognized.

"Well?" demanded the other brigand, a tall, pale woman with a scar across one cheek that hooked her lip into a perpetual snarl. "Who are you to threaten our queen?"

"It's a warning, not a threat," said Sinoe, somehow managing to look down her nose at them even though she was the shortest person in the alcove by a good handspan. "And it comes from the Fates themselves. I am Sinoe, daughter of Hierax, the Sibyl of Tears."

Yeneris stifled a sigh.

"The princess never leaves the palace," the pale woman scoffed.

"We should bring them to the queen," said the man. "She's worth something to someone. Might even score a nice cut for ourselves."

"The queen has enough to worry about, Antioc," the woman replied. "She doesn't need to be bothered with by a pair of grifters. Best get rid of them before they cause any more trouble."

"Pff. What trouble?" Antioc sauntered forward, reaching for Sinoe. "Come along now, *princess*."

Yeneris stepped into his path, palming one of her two hidden daggers. A ridiculous thing to face off against a pair of swords but she'd damn well make it count. "No one touches the princess."

Antioc laughed. "You think that toy will stop us? Give it here, I need a good nail trimmer."

Yeneris held her ground. "Try it and I'll trim something else you might miss more."

A husky laugh filled the alcove, rough and smoky. It came from a tiny woman who seemed to have appeared out of nowhere. She was soft and rounded as a clot of wool, with no sharp edges except for her smile. Frail wisps of gray showed at the edges of her dark headscarf. Her light brown skin was crinkled like fine linen.

She was the oldest person Yeneris had ever seen. And almost certainly one of the most dangerous.

The Queen of Swarms dipped her head to Sinoe, her smile glinting in the firelight. "It's a pleasure to meet you, Princess Sinoe." Her gaze turned to Yeneris next, lingering on her dagger. "Impressive. It's been a long time since anyone managed to get a weapon past the door."

"Thank you." Yeneris had a brief struggle with her pride, but succeeded in keeping the other, still-hidden dagger to herself. This wasn't over. If anything, it had only gotten more dangerous.

"But I would prefer if you turned it over to one of my wolves," she went on, gesturing to the brigands.

"Wolves?" repeated Sinoe. She gave Yeneris a significant look.

"That's right," said Antioc. "So best not give us reason to bite." He held out a hand to Yeneris. "Give it here."

"It's all right, Yen," said Sinoe. "We came to speak with the queen and here she is. Let's be good guests."

Yeneris did not lower her blade. "*Are* we guests?" she asked, looking to the queen.

The old woman tilted her head. "For now. I'd like to hear what brings you here."

"Lies," said the pale woman. "We can handle them, Melita."

"Stand down, Lykia." The queen lifted a hand, and the woman subsided, her lips pressed tight. Yeneris lowered her blade as well. She had a bad feeling about this. Flipping the blade in one hand, she held it out hilt first to Antioc.

"Thank you." The queen—Melita—continued on, her tone still conversational. "I assume your father doesn't know you're here, princess?"

"No," Sinoe admitted. "I'm here on my own business. And that of the Fates."

Melita arched a thin gray brow. "Yes, I'd heard you're a sibyl. Very convenient for your father, to have the Fates anoint his rule."

"The princess has true power," said Yeneris. "You should listen to her."

"I've lived quite a long time," said Melita. "I'm quite curious why the Fates would take an interest in me only now."

"Because you're in danger," said Sinoe, bluntly. "Someone is going to kill you."

Melita laughed, the same husky rumble that was so dissonant coming from her small, soft body. "My dear girl, I don't need the Fates to tell me *that*. I need them to tell me what socks to wear to stop my toes from aching. Or how to convince my granddaughter that just because a man is pretty doesn't mean he's worth keeping around. I know, I know, I could just get rid of him, but she'd never forgive me."

Yeneris watched the two brigands. The man, Antioc, glowered at Sinoe, as if it was her fault. Lykia's expression was more serene, but Yeneris caught the tap of her fingers against her sword hilt, and the way she was still holding herself on the balls of her feet. Was it only wariness?

Sinoe stood straighter. When she spoke, it wasn't the otherworldly voice of prophecy, but it was clear and strong and unwavering. *"The Queen of Swarms will die by an unseen blow, her hives dripping secret honey into the jaws of the wolf."*

Melita no longer looked amused. "One of my own people?"

Antioc flushed. "It's not me! I swear it, Melita. Why would I bring the princess to you if I was a traitor?"

An excellent point.

"It'll be one of those new fellows we brought in last month," said Lykia. "I'll go round them up right away. Before word spreads."

She was stepping back. Starting to turn. Sword still bare. The blade had just begun a neat and fatal arc when Yeneris's last hidden dagger caught her in the shoulder.

Lykia screamed, dropping her sword. It rattled across the stones, spinning to rest at Melita's feet. By then Yeneris had slammed into the brigand, one sharp punch to the throat, another to the gut, then a sweeping kick. Lykia slammed to the floor, her head cracking against the stones. She slumped, wheezing and groaning.

Melita had not moved, had barely flinched. But her gaze was like ice. "Antioc," she said. "See to it."

The man gathered himself, then went to crouch beside Lykia and began binding her arms.

"You have my thanks," said Melita, returning her attention to Sinoe and Yeneris. "And my attention. But I suspect there's something more?"

"Yes," said Sinoe. "You have some information we need."

"Then we should speak further. Somewhere more private."

=

Sinoe sank into the plush couch with a deep sigh of contentment. Kicking off her slippers, she curled her legs up beneath her, seeming utterly at peace with the fact that they were now deep in the thief lord's lair. Yeneris did not sit. She stood beside the arm of the couch, watching as a servant set out a silver carafe and platter of tiny cakes oozing honey from layers of thin pastry. Melita sat across from them, ensconced in a plush couch of her own. She did not speak until the servant had departed, closing the heavy wooden door.

"So," said Melita. "I am in your debt. But I'm curious what information I could have that you might require. Especially given that you have the Fates to call upon."

"I can call on them, yes," said Sinoe. "But they choose whether or not to respond."

"What can I offer that the Fates cannot, then?" asked Melita.

"You can tell me what you do for the Heron."

Melita leaned back against the couch, folding her hands together in her lap. "That is a dangerous question."

"As dangerous as an assassination attempt?"

The Queen of Swarms was silent for a long moment. "Mm. Quite possibly." She narrowed her gaze at Sinoe. "What do you plan to do with this information?"

Sinoe hesitated, glancing to Yeneris. A questioning look, as if she actually wanted her opinion. Or her help. As if they were . . . partners.

Yeneris took a breath to quiet the thrum of her pulse. Best not to commit. "That depends on what it is."

Melita gave a wry smile. "I see. In that case . . ." She pursed her lips, then gave a small nod. "Bodies."

"Bodies?" Sinoe repeated. "You mean you kill people for him?"

"No." A strange look passed over Melita's face. "He wants bodies. Dead bodies."

Prickles flickered over Yeneris's skin. "Why?"

Melita shrugged. "I didn't ask. It's not my business."

"But acquiring dead bodies is?" asked Sinoe. "Where did you get them?"

"In my line of work, we do occasionally find ourselves in the possession of corpses," said Melita. "And there are always folk who die with no kin to pay the grave-tenders for proper funerary rites."

"So you step in and pay the grave-tenders for their bodies. And then what?"

"I have someone deliver them."

"What, like a load of cabbages to market?" Sinoe's lip curled. "How many?"

"Roughly four dozen in the past year." Melita took a sip of tea. The scent of honey was thick in the air. It had been sweet, before, but now it turned Yeneris's stomach. She thought of the ghouls in the necropolis. If the grave-tenders were holding bodies for Lacheron, if they had not been given proper rites, it might explain why they had become ghouls. Yeneris was no expert, but from the stories she'd heard, that was how ghouls came to be. If a demon from the underworld found a spirit that was weak enough—as one deprived of the rites would be—they could consume it, opening a sort of doorway into the spirit's corpse and allowing the demon to inhabit it.

Which meant there might be four dozen other ghouls out there, somewhere.

"Where?" Yeneris asked. "Where do you deliver them?"

Melita tapped a finger against her cup. "I'm afraid I can't share that. It's risk enough to tell you this much."

"Somewhere in the city?" Sinoe uncurled her legs, leaning forward beseechingly. "I know you're a thief lord, I know you've probably done all sorts of wicked things, so maybe this is just all part of a normal day's work for you, but this is . . . very important. You must have heard about the skotoi at the city necropolis?"

Melita nodded grudgingly. "Yes."

"The Fates are trying to warn us," said Sinoe. "Something terrible is coming. If Lacheron is part of it—if he's using it for his own gain—then I need to know."

Silence. A lump filled Yeneris's throat. Then finally Melita spoke. "Six went to the Heron's workshop, in the palace. The rest were to be taken north, into the mountains. My people left them at the drop-off, and that's all I know."

Sinoe sat back, her brow furrowed. "Thank you."

Melita shrugged. "I owed you a debt. That debt is now repaid."

"Then we should go," said Yeneris. She was itchy to get Sinoe out of this place. Melita had treated them fairly so far, but best not to press the limits of the woman's sense of honor. She was still a criminal who had been willing to steal corpses. And to create them.

"Indeed." Melita smiled. "I'm sure Hierax would be . . . displeased to discover his sibyl was missing. He must value you highly."

Sinoe's jaw tightened. "He values his sibyl, yes."

"A shame," said Melita, taking another of the cakes. "I could use such wisdom to guide my business. And I would pay quite handsomely for it."

For a moment Yeneris thought Sinoe might actually be entertaining the offer. Sinoe's eyes widened. Her lips parted. Then she shook her head sharply. "My visions aren't something to be bought and sold. They belong to the Fates."

"Do they?" Melita tilted her head. "It seems to me that they belong to the king."

Sinoe said nothing. Only stood, and dipped her head to the old woman. "Come, Yeneris. We're done here."

<hr>

Sinoe said very little on the journey back, and Yeneris was too busy ensuring that they weren't murdered, robbed or recognized to make conversation. Or at least, that was what she told herself.

It wasn't until they'd finally made it back to the palace gardens below the north wing that Yeneris cleared her throat. "Princess, are you all right?"

"You mean aside from the fact that there are apparently six dead bodies hidden in Lacheron's workshop?"

Fine. So she didn't want to talk about it. Just as well. She'd stick to business, then. "So you didn't know? Your father didn't speak of it?"

Sinoe had halted beneath a trellis of night-blooming jasmine. "Not with me. But Lacheron's always been in love with alchemy and sorcery. Maybe he's using them for his research. Brewing up some new poison to destroy Father's enemies."

Yeneris said nothing. But maybe her silence was enough. Sinoe drew in a sharp breath. "Furies scald me. I'm sorry, Yen. I shouldn't have said that."

"It's fine," Yeneris lied.

"No. It's not. None of it is fine." Sinoe began to pace, slippers crunching against the white gravel of the path. "Maybe he was trying to find a way to revive the dead. To give my father what he wants: the Faithful Maiden at his side." Scorn turned her voice sour.

Yeneris counted to five, keeping her breathing slow. "I thought your father wanted the agia of Stara Bron to do that."

"Yes, well, that would be ideal, wouldn't it? One of the gods incarnate granting him her holy blessing? No one could question him then. It's exactly the sort of grand spectacle he likes."

And even now Lacheron and Ichos were on their way to Stara Bron, armed with Sinoe's latest prophecy. What if it was enough to sway the agia? Even so, it should be impossible. The kore had dedicated her bones, her spirit, to the Scarab. Gave her flesh and soul to calm the roiling, broken earth and preserve Bassara during the great cataclysm. But the Phoenix was sister to the Scarab. Equal in power. And if the agia willed it, that might be enough to undo that sacrifice. And then what? Would even the broken remnants of Bassara fade to nothing? Sink beneath the sea with no hope of rising again?

All the more reason to act now, while they had the chance.

Sinoe continued to pace, growing more agitated with every step. "He's up to something. You feel it, too, don't you, Yen? There's something going on."

"Stealing four dozen corpses is a fairly obvious sign that something's going on, yes." But it wasn't the only question gnawing at Yeneris. "Why is your father so convinced that he needs to have the Maiden at his side? Was that in your original prophecy?"

Sinoe shook her head. "I don't remember. But it was clear enough three days ago."

"Was it? You said the Maiden would step from flame to take her rightful place. It doesn't say her rightful place is with King Hierax. We don't even know if it's the kore or some other maiden." Yeneris held her breath, watching the princess.

Sinoe groaned. "You'd think the Fates would make it more clear if it was so important." She wrapped her arms around her midsection. She looked very small, a dark shadow in the moonlight. "I'm sure it will all make sense, after it happens and we can't change anything and the world is falling to cinders around us."

"That's not going to happen." Yeneris wished she had a blade sharp enough to slice away Sinoe's despair. "Look at what you did tonight."

"You did most of that. I was just getting in your way."

"You weren't in my way."

The space between them had narrowed. It made it even more obvious how tiny Sinoe was. The top of her head was barely level with Yeneris's chin. She remembered another girl teasing her, once, saying that Yeneris was so tall she'd need to carry a step stool for her lovers to stand on when she went courting. She cleared her throat, knowing she ought to step back. Her feet wouldn't move. "You don't belong to him," she said. "He doesn't own you. Or your visions. You are no one's tool."

Sinoe tipped her chin up, hazel eyes turned to dark and mysterious pools, her creamy skin gleaming as if she'd swallowed moonshine. "Thank you, Yen."

Her fingers brushed the back of Yeneris's hand, tracing her knuckles with fire. "It felt good to do something. To choose something for myself. I know . . . I know I make things hard for you. But I want you to know I appreciate it. I appreciate you."

"I appreciate you, too." Yeneris winced inwardly. The words sounded so silly, so meek and colorless. When inside she was awash with color. When what she wanted, more than anything, was to reach out and twine her hand in Sinoe's. To know the feel of her skin. But that was impossible. And so maybe it was all for the best that she lost her tongue around Sinoe.

Because if she ever did find it, she might speak the truth.

CHAPTER 17

SEPHRE

Beroe could have welcomed the royal party in the courtyard, with basins of water to refresh them and strike the dust from their hands and feet. Or at the summit, where the holy flame blazed from the blessed stone, cracked open by the Phoenix herself, when she first burst free of the underworld and was reborn to bring life to the mortal world. Or better yet, the Great Hall, the largest room in the temple, where the ashdancers gathered for daily prayers and tedious summations meetings.

Instead, she chose the Chamber of Doors.

Sephre stood in the tight press of her siblings, wondering if Beroe had picked this room specifically to make their slim numbers appear greater. Or maybe she thought the royal emissaries would be impressed by the tilework that covered every single surface. It was a beautiful room, one of the oldest in Stara Bron. Windowless, and without any niches for lamps or braziers. In fact, the only light came from the ashdancers themselves, each kindling a spark of crimson or gold, ranged on either side of Beroe like the wings of a flaming Phoenix.

Sephre had to admit the effect was stunning. Even the novices had been given small lamps to hold. She saw Timeus among them, eyes wide, no doubt straining for a first glimpse of the guests.

The Chamber of Doors did not, ironically, have more than a single entrance. Sephre had asked Abas about it, during her novitiate. *The other doors have been closed since the cataclysm,* they'd said. *Those ways are lost.*

The walls held no sign of any closed archway or sealed passage, only glittering mosaics showing the first four gods rising from primordial Chaos, each to shape some part of the world. To her right, the Beetle, iridescent black against the dark loam of the earth, beneath a midnight sky. To her left, the Sphinx, sunburnt bronze, proud beneath the noonday sun. Before her, above the lone arched doorway, the Phoenix blazed crimson and gold as she rose with the dawn.

Behind her, the Serpent's coils gleamed blue and green beneath a dusky sky, like the ripples of an endless pool. And within, the faintest outline of towering dark walls, an endless maze haunted by the spirits of the dead. Turning. she stared at the two bright fragments of green set into the Serpent's diamond-shaped head, and heard Nilos's voice. *The world needs the Serpent, the same way it needs the moon, and the sun, and the sea.* Her body rebelled at the thought, shivering. The Serpent was the bringer of death. The corruptor. Cruel and hungry, feasting on human suffering. Surely the world was better off without him.

Bitterness clogged her throat. Was it, though? A better world where an entire city could be slaughtered without mercy, to grant a king his prize? Even now she heard the beat of marching feet. The rattle and clang of bronze.

Her eyes flew open. Not a memory. The soldiers were there before her eyes, a dozen of them, marching through the arched doorway, bronze chest plates and gilded faceplates gleaming bright as the tiled walls. Crimson crests spurted from their helms.

She hadn't wanted to believe Nilos about the Maiden, either. But the slim codex tucked into her sleeve was proof that there was more to her story. She felt like a branch blocking an eager stream, the water surging and tugging, the pressure building and building. Soon, it would shove her aside. Or carry her, spin her onward, to new and unknown waters. Fates, she wasn't ready for this.

The soldiers parted, revealing a man in richer garb, his tunic embroidered with gold thread, his armor embossed with lions, his head uncovered, clasped by a circlet of beaten gold leaves.

"Prince Ichos, son of Hierax Heraklion, the Ember King

reborn," announced one of the soldiers, her voice ringing like a drawn sword.

Sephre studied the prince. She knew little of Ichos. He was eclipsed by his father, even in a mere introduction. No doubt he had been there at the victory parade ten years ago, standing with his father to welcome home the bones of the Faithful Maiden. She couldn't recall. Her earlier memories were sharper. Sephre had been part of the honor guard escorting Kizare north to the Vigil Gap, after Hierax divorced her. It wouldn't do to have a living wife when he sought his eternal bride's bones, even if that wife was the mother of his children.

The twins had watched from one of the towers as the former queen departed. Kizare was Scarthian, so she had ridden openly, on horseback, her flaming hair a shock of brightness against her gray mourning garb. She had turned back once, lifting a hand to her children. She must have known there was little chance she would see them again, but Sephre saw no tears on her pale cheeks.

The little princess, Sinoe, had held herself stiffly erect, and the only tears on her face were paint, the weeping mask of the sibyl she always wore in public. But the boy beside her had scrubbed his eyes. Sephre had seen it, and felt a twist of sympathy.

Now, here he was, a grown man. Lavishly handsome, but with a petulant jut to his chin, as if he expected disappointment. His bow to Beroe was all courtesy.

"Agia, thank you for opening your gates to us."

Beroe smiled, no doubt tempted to let the prince continue in the misunderstanding. But apparently that was a step too far, even for her ambition. "You honor me, Bright One, but I am Sister Beroe. Our beloved Agia Halimede wished very much to welcome you personally, but her poor health prevents it. I stand before you in her place, acclaimed as the most senior of the yellow order. As acting agia, I offer you all the resources of our temple." Beroe swept her arms out, golden flames snapping dramatically as she gestured to the gathered ashdancers. "We are yours to command, my prince."

Sephre bit her tongue. Halimede would never say such a thing. She would never be so fawningly deferential.

Even Ichos seemed taken aback, though he recovered quickly. "I'm glad to hear it. I didn't realize Stara Bron was such a loyal friend to my father."

Was she only imagining the twist of mockery in the prince's tone?

For one breath, Beroe hesitated. Then she lifted her chin, resolved. "Stara Bron recognizes King Hierax as the Ember King reborn. In these perilous times, it is our duty to support him however we can. When skotoi dare to spread their foul corruption even in the royal city, how can we do less?"

Insufferable woman. It was a blatant overstep, but then, Beroe had never questioned her own righteousness.

Ichos huffed. "Indeed. Well, that should make this easy, then." He lifted a languid hand. "Lacheron?"

A stir of movement, behind Ichos. Another man stepped forward, looking dull and colorless beside the gleaming scarlet and gold prince. A man with an unremarkable face, lank and faded hair. The sort of person who could slip from memory without a ripple, but Sephre knew him instantly. She had seen his face too often in her nightmares to ever forget.

The general's tent is hot, the air heavy with sweat and impatient glory. A map lies spread across the table, taking up most of the room. She stands stiffly, hands behind her back, waiting for orders. She is so weary, it feels as if her bones could break. The losses weigh heavy, each one a stone settled in her gut. If she falls into the sea, she will sink, be lost in the abyss. But she is a soldier. She has pledged to serve.

The man speaking is not the general. They call him the Heron, though she thinks it an injustice. Herons are elegant birds, and hunt only to feed themselves. Lacheron hungers for something more. It glitters, deep in his dull gray eyes. He slides a single crimson token across the map, past the city walls, toward the round basin that holds the Bassarans' water, the reservoir that has allowed them to endure the siege for two full years. It will end the war in a day, he says. Here is what you must do.

The scrape of unfurling parchment broke Sephre from the memory. She focused back on Ichos as he brandished a scroll to the ashdancers. "These are the words of the Sibyl of Tears. This is the prophecy that brings us here. Listen, now, to the voice of the Fates."

Sephre shivered. One prophecy had sent her to Bassara, had poisoned everything she thought she believed. What new disaster might this one bring? She held herself still as the prince read the scroll.

"*Long has the old enemy watched and waited. Now he seeks to strike his second blow, and the world will not survive it. The first light must reveal the weapon of unmaking. When it is found, when the Maiden steps forth from flame to take her rightful place, only then shall the old enemy fall.*"

Ichos let the parchment close with a snap before handing it to Lacheron. "You must understand why we have come, given such a prophecy. The signs are clear. The Serpent seeks to return. My father must be prepared to meet him and banish him once again. Only Letheko has that power. The first light is dawn, and you are the House of Dawn. So. Where is the blade?"

Sephre felt as if she'd run twenty leagues in the space of time it took Ichos to read the sibyl's words. She'd make herself dizzy if she didn't control herself. She drew in a deep, slow breath. Then another. She held her arms loose against her side, keenly aware of the codex hidden there. The codex that spoke of a blade concealed somewhere that only the agia could claim it.

There was so much she still didn't understand. How could the same woman be called faithful by some, and faithless by herself? How did her bones end up in Bassara, if she had chosen the Embrace and life as an ashdancer? Who was she, truly, with all the stories and legends stripped away? The one clear truth was that the long-dead woman had not wanted the blade to ever be used by the Ember King again. And had sworn the agias of Stara Bron to help her. This was why Halimede had held the temple apart, had distanced herself from Hierax.

Something that Beroe had just undone, very grandly and publicly. Did the "acting agia" know where the blade was? Had she already found it, snooping through Halimede's chambers?

But Beroe looked as confused as the rest of them by the prince's demand. "Of course we will do whatever we can to assist in your quest. But I've never heard anything that would indicate that Letheko is at Stara Bron."

Relief threaded through Sephre. If Beroe *did* know where the blade was, she wouldn't keep it a secret. More likely she'd present it to the prince on a golden pillow, with a chorus of ashdancers singing the hymn of dawn and maybe a hired harpist for good measure.

Ichos narrowed his eyes. "Perhaps we need to speak with Agia Halimede."

Beroe remained calm, though her shoulders stiffened slightly. "I'm certain the agia would be most honored to offer her wisdom on the matter. But as I said, she is unwell. She sleeps without waking, and we fear her spirit may soon depart to seek the cleansing flame of rebirth."

The prince was less practiced at controlling his expression. Or maybe he just didn't care if they saw his impatience. "You speak pretty words of support for the Ember King, but words are nothing without action."

He shifted his stance. Firelight caught the gilded hilt of the sword at his hip. The bright crests of the soldiers blazed behind him. Tension clotted the air. It reminded Sephre far too much of a battlefield, just before the first charge.

She scanned the firelit faces of her fellow ashdancers. Timeus, earnest and wide-eyed. Sister Obelia, her round face gone very pale, her usual smile fled. Stern Sibling Vasil, setting a steadying hand on the shoulder of the trembling novice beside them.

Sephre had never meant to care for them all so much. It was part of the reason she'd thrown herself into her work in the herbarium,

HOUSE OF DUSK 179

where the company was green and silent and did not judge her. But they had all dug roots into her when she wasn't watching, rather like the mint when she ignored it for too long. Too late to dig them out, even if she wanted to. And she would fight anyone, anywhere, to keep them safe.

A sentiment that Beroe apparently shared. To Sephre's chagrin, the woman didn't simper and grovel as she'd expected, but stood taller, meeting the prince's gaze fully. "Stara Bron stands ready and willing to fulfill our sacred vows, as we have for centuries." She was doing something with her voice, making it deep and thrilling, so much that even Sephre found herself leaning forward to listen, her skin prickling with gooseflesh.

"The Phoenix trusted the ashdancers above all," Beroe continued, "so much so that she gifted us with her holy flame. The Serpent and his skotoi will not find this world unguarded. Tell us where we are needed, Prince Ichos, and we will go. We will march forth as the ashdancers of old, to do battle with the creatures of the netherworld."

All around her, Sephre felt the other ashdancers stirring. The room brightened as every flame leapt higher. It was well done. A neat reminder to both ashdancers and royal party that they stood on holy ground. That Stara Bron held the blessing of the Phoenix.

And it worked. Ichos removed his hand from the hilt of his sword, though he still looked annoyed. "And Letheko?"

"You are welcome to search our archives, of course," said Beroe. "Search all Stara Bron, if you believe the dagger to be hidden here. We have no secrets from the Ember King."

Sephre fought the urge to hunch. Dolon had no reason to connect her research on the Embrace with this, and she hadn't told either Timeus or Beroe about Nilos's final taunts. So long as she remained beneath royal notice, there was no cause for anyone to suspect she knew more.

"You might also wish to consult with Sister Sephre," said Beroe. "Agia Halimede sent her on a mission to investigate a series of deaths we believe to be the work of serpent cultists. She spoke with one of them."

So much for remaining anonymous. "Sister Sephre?" repeated Ichos. The name clearly meant nothing to him. He was too young to remember her from the war. She doubted even Lacheron would remember, any more than he'd recall which stylus he'd used to jot down a note ten years ago. She had been a tool, not a person.

But even before Beroe lifted a hand to identify Sephre, Lacheron's eyes found her. His gaze seized her like a grasping fist, unfathomable. Was it shock? Surprise? Did he remember her from the war, after all? Whatever it was, it set her pulse pattering, her coiled muscles humming with the impulse to flee or fight. And it wasn't just her imagination. To her left, she felt Sister Obelia stiffen. On her right, ancient Brother Petrus shifted closer, as if he meant to cast his old bones in front of her if the Heron attacked.

A painful jab caught Sephre in the chest. Fates, she did not deserve these people. She gathered her courage, gently moving past Obelia and Petrus, stepping to the front of the line of ashdancers. She bowed to the prince. She was an old woman to him, nothing but a humble ashdancer, no one important. "I am here, Bright One."

Ichos waved aside the niceties. "Tell me about this serpent cultist."

"He called himself Nilos," she said. "He claimed to be trying to restore the Serpent by gathering pieces of the god's power that are scattered in the mortal world. Hidden in mortal souls. I saw him take one from a baby."

"Where?" snapped Ichos.

"In the village of Kessely. But that was two days ago. No doubt he's fled far by now."

Lacheron spoke for the first time, his voice low and smooth, as bland as every other part of him. "Prince Ichos, I believe your father would like to speak with this man. Will you see to it, while I remain to continue the search for the dagger here? Perhaps, as Agia Beroe says, there might be answers in the archives."

Ichos clenched his jaw. He didn't care for taking orders, even if they were made to sound like questions. But he nodded. "Better that than poking around a bunch of dusty scrolls." The prince addressed Beroe again. "I ask your hospitality for Lord Lacheron in my absence."

"Of course," Beroe nodded. "For as long as he needs."

"I am a patient man," said Lacheron, his tone mild as milk. His gaze skimmed back to Sephre. No longer shocked, but grimly satisfied. "Some secrets take longer than others, but they all reveal themselves in time."

━━━

Perhaps Halimede would awaken. It was a vain hope, but Sephre clung to it, as she made her way along the hallway to the infirmary. Grunts and shouts echoed from below, where Lacheron had already set the soldiers to work digging up the Terrace of First Light. She winced at the cruel crack of hammer against stone. The overlook was one of the most beautiful spots in Stara Bron. Sephre herself had spent many a morning there, watching the dawn burn away the mists that clung to the eastern hills. Admiring the perfect, careful work that had fitted the paving stones just so. Feeling their gentle smoothness beneath her thin sandals.

Another crack. Sephre hastened her steps, pressing one palm to the angry thrum of her chest. If Halimede were awake, she would never allow such an outrageous desecration.

But Halimede was not awake. Sephre saw that the moment she crossed the threshold into the infirmary. The agia lay as still and silent as ever in her narrow cot. And she was not alone. Prince Ichos stood beside her, one hand outstretched toward the agia's face.

Instinct sent her surging forward, turned her voice to an accusing lash. "What are you doing?"

Ichos jerked back. A flush darkened his cheeks. "Nothing. I thought . . . I was checking that she was still breathing."

Sephre strode to the side of the cot and pressed her fingers to one of agia's thin wrists. Relief flooded her as she felt the flutter of a heartbeat. "She lives."

If the prince was disappointed, he hid it well. He only pressed his lips tight for a moment, then asked, "Will she wake?"

"Only the Fates know that."

He drummed his fingers against the hilt of his sword. "You're Sephre. Aren't you some sort of physician?"

He was a royal. Not for her to snipe at. No matter how irritating and entitled he might be. "Sister Sephre," she said. "But I'm only an herbalist."

"And yet Agia Halimede trusted you to investigate these serpent-cultist murders."

Sephre said nothing. It hadn't been a question, and she wasn't about to give this boy anything more than necessary.

"Tell me about this man Nilos. Did he say anything about where he might be heading next?"

"No."

Ichos grimaced. "But you last saw him in Kessely? Where exactly?"

"On a ridge to the east of the village. He ran away north."

"Ran away?" Ichos gave her an amused look. "From you? I should have no trouble taking him, then."

Fates save her from the arrogance of youth. Though she'd probably been as bad or worse. Full of her own fresh power, invulnerable to time. Even now she struggled briefly with her own pride, and managed *not* to toss a nice fat fireball at the prince's feet.

"So you mean to kill him?" she asked instead.

"Do you have a problem with that?"

She bit the inside of her cheek. "He claimed he wasn't responsible for the murders. He might not be our enemy."

Ichos regarded her for a long moment. "It's not my job to decide that. My job is to serve the Ember King."

Was there the faintest twist of bitterness on the words? Maybe even despair?

"Does your father often send you to kill his enemies?" she asked.

There it was again, in his eyes. It was achingly familiar. For a moment his jaw worked, and she thought he might answer. But all he said was "Good day, sister," as he quit the room.

====

Sephre glanced around the garden. She could almost slip right back into her old, comfortable groove. The mint needed thinning, and there was plessuda root to grind. Timeus was with the other novices, enduring one of Sibling Vasil's notorious meditation exercises. The herbarium was serene and quiet.

Instead, she held her breath and slipped the codex out from the jar of exceedingly well-named offalwort leaves where she'd been keeping it hidden, trusting that the noxious stench would ward off both overly curious novices and nosy royal advisors.

Not that Sephre had seen much of Lacheron in the past two days. He spent much of his time in the temple archives, and she had invented a plethora of urgent tasks that kept her busy in the herbarium and safely out of sight. The short interview in the Hall of Doors had been more than enough.

Ichos was likewise absent, having departed in pursuit of Nilos soon after their awkward conversation in the infirmary. And there was absolutely nothing she could do about that. She certainly couldn't warn Nilos, even if she wanted to. Which she didn't.

What she wanted was answers, but thus far the codex had not given her anything but more questions. She flipped through the mold-mottled pages, but they were as impenetrable as they had been the last dozen times. The only clues were the tantalizing handful of fragments she'd already gleaned.

She smoothed a hand over the battered leather case. *Who were you? What did you do? Where did you hide it? And why?*

Only silence answered her. She snorted. What was she expecting? She was no sibyl, just another flawed and foolish mortal. It hadn't been the Fates that led her to the codex. Only her own curiosity and a draft in an old building.

A gust of wind stirred the drying sheaves of thyme and sage, the long loops of shagvine hanging from the rafters above. The lanternflowers rattled their crimson globes. Gooseflesh shivered up her arms. The garden was too quiet. Sibling Vasil was keeping the novices busy with training. If the world was tilting toward oblivion, Stara Bron needed every fully ordained and fire-wielding ashdancer they could muster.

Fates. Did she actually *miss* Timeus's ceaseless chatter? No. It was only that he'd become a habit, in the past weeks.

And because he reminded her of Zander.

And because—she forced herself to admit the truth of it—Sephre had never been a solitary creature. She'd been forever envious of the other village children who had siblings. Maybe that was why she'd enlisted. The promise of comrades close as kin.

And she'd found it. Zander and Vyria and Calchas. The bonds between them forged in the crucible of the training camp, then tested by war.

Then broken. Only Vyria was still alive, last Sephre knew. She wondered if she'd gone back to the sweetheart she'd left behind. Cybele? Cylene? Sephre ought to remember. Vyria had the girl's name tattooed across her wrist. She used to kiss it, for good luck, before battle.

Did Vyria still have nightmares too? Maybe Calyce—*that* was the name—chased them away.

Sephre had never visited them. Best not to trespass on whatever joy and peace Vyria had managed to reclaim. *Coward,* she told herself. *You're not that noble. You're just afraid she'll ask what really happened.*

What really happened. That was the question, wasn't it? No one wanted to bare their shame to the world. Better to burn away the mistakes. Like the author of the codex. Sephre echoed with that yearning. And yet . . . she needed to know, if she was going to

HOUSE OF DUSK 185

keep Stara Bron safe. No one else was going to suffer because she made the wrong choice.

She flipped the codex open to the last page.

> *. . . request granted . . . faithless . . . no more . . .*
> *. . . blade . . . hidden . . . only agia . . . claim it . . .*
> *. . . will ensure . . . never . . . again . . .*

Sephre had considered a number of possibilities as to where the blade might be hidden. Perhaps it was sewn into the heavy golden mantle that was kept sealed away in the temple treasury, brought out for the high holidays. Or secreted into a hidey-hole in the walls of the agia's office. In either case, she doubted it would remain secret for long. Lacheron's soldiers had spent the last two days digging holes throughout the Terrace of First Light, heedless of the priceless tilework crafted by Kalanthe herself. Where would they dig next?

She closed the codex and went to replace it in the jar. Halimede still clung to life in the infirmary, but she had not woken. There was no one to guard the blade.

No one except Sephre.

And it was time to act.

═══

She decided to start with the agia's office. The treasury was locked, and the main gates barred at night, but none of the other doors at Stara Bron were ever sealed. And it was nearly time for the chorus of high sun, which meant Beroe should be in the Great Hall.

Even so, Sephre crept up the stairs, careful to muffle her footfalls, an excuse sheathed behind her lips, just in case. Five steps from the top, she heard voices. She nearly retreated, but the words were faintly muffled. Coming from inside the agia's office. She crept closer, listening.

"The blade isn't in the treasury and there is no record of it in the archives," Beroe was saying. "Nor is it hidden beneath the Terrace of First Light, as your soldiers so helpfully proved with their extensive excavations, Lord Lacheron."

If there was any sarcasm in her tone, she had done an excellent job filing it away. "Indeed," said Lacheron. "Your solicitude has been most welcome, Sister Beroe. The Ember King will need allies like yourself in the days ahead. People who are not afraid to act. If only Agia Halimede were so brave."

If it were Sephre, she would have socked the man on the jaw for such an insult. Beroe, of course, was more politic. "Agia Halimede's devotion is beyond question," she answered carefully.

"I mean no slight to your predecessor," said Lacheron, smoothly. "No doubt she had her reasons for rejecting the king's request."

A pause. "What request?"

"Oh," said Lacheron. "I assumed she had shared the matter with you, sister. You *are* her anointed successor, after all." He added just a tiny twist of doubt to the words.

Beroe clearly felt the sting. "She did not," she answered flatly. "But perhaps you would enlighten me. Given that I act now in her place."

This was the Heron she knew. The man who could convince you to do anything, could make you believe that whatever solution he offered was the only real option. And Beroe was falling for it. Too lost in her own sense of injury, her entitlement, her ambition.

"To restore the Faithful Maiden to life," said Lacheron.

"You mean to free her from the curse that traps her spirit in her bones," said Beroe. "So she can finally be reborn into a new, unblemished life."

"No," said Lacheron. "Not reborn. Restored to life, so that she may be reunited with her lost love, as was prophesied."

Impossible. Unthinkable.

On the other side of the door, Beroe drew in a sharp, scandalized breath. "Not even the holy flame has that power."

"But the Phoenix does," said Lacheron. "And if the agia of Stara Bron summons her, she will come."

"In theory, yes," admitted Beroe. "The Phoenix promised the first agia that she would return, if ever there were a time of great need. But the Blue Summons has never actually been used. It's . . . it's . . ."

"Unprecedented," said Lacheron. "Yet we live in unprecedented times. The Ember King has returned to us. Skotoi walk the mortal world, and the minions of the Serpent seek even now to restore him to power."

"Yes." Beroe sounded wary. "But even so, only the agia has that power."

Only the agia.

The rest of the conversation slid away, muted by those three words. That was it. The treasury, the terrace, the agia's office, none of those were truly beyond reach of someone with enough determination and a handy company of soldiers with no scruples about destroying priceless architecture.

The certainty clicked into place, a well-fitted boot. Sephre knew where to find Letheko. She turned away from the door to the agia's office, toward the narrow archway to the left, the one that led out onto the mountainside, where a set of well-worn steps carved a path to the summit, and the flame that burned there.

CHAPTER 18

SEPHRE

The wind caught at Sephre's hair and whipped her gray robes against her legs as she crested the stone-carved steps. The summit was utterly bare. There were no golden ornaments, no rich tapestries. Even so, her breath always caught at the sight of the enormous boulder perched there. A great crack split the stone, cleaving it into two equal halves. And through that fissure blazed the holy flame.

A pressure hovered in the air. A feeling of being watched, as if this bare stony bowl was the navel of the universe.

Sephre put the setting sun behind her and faced the burning channel. Eight and a half years ago she had taken a single step into the blaze. Crimson flames danced over her skin, anointing her a red sister. A second step, four years ago, had made her a yellow sister. But only the agia could take a third step, into the blue heart of the flame.

Sephre thought of the fragile form lying in the infirmary. When Halimede died, Beroe would be the next. She would stand here, in this exact spot, and take three confident steps forward. Or maybe she would go slowly. The woman did love a dramatic moment.

Either way, the dagger would not remain hidden much longer, if it was here.

If. That was the question.

She had to learn the answer. But the flames exacted a price. The pure light of this holy fire would expose every corner of her soul. All the places she had stuffed tight with her old shames and sorrows. All the poisoned flesh of her soul that she could not wash clean, no matter how many tonics she brewed, no matter how many ills she soothed. No matter how she tried to forget.

She had done it before. She could do it again. Maybe it would even be easier, this time. Sephre sucked in a breath of the chill mountain air and stepped forward.

Crimson light curled around her. At first, instinctively, she flinched from it. Wary of what it might awaken. But she had passed this challenge before. All that came to her within the red flames were dim voices murmuring in a distant room, while her father sang a lullaby, the one she liked best, about a lost sheep and a faithful hound. Her eyes stung. Her chest stung. *Papa.*

Another step. Yellow light veiled her world. She was out in a flower-spangled meadow, racing through the tall grasses, breathless with laughter as a woman with merry brown eyes chased her. *You can't run from the tickle monster!*

Sephre breathed deep. So far, so good. But what lay before her now was a trial she had never endured. The blue flame. It was like staring into an endless summer sky, with no cloud or bird to hook her gaze. A sky that would suck her in, split her open and expose her stinking entrails to the sun. But maybe she didn't need to go farther. She pressed one palm against the wall, feeling for any recess, any hiding place. Gingerly, she slid her hand along the cracked stone, closer and closer to the wall of blue. A single spark licked her fingertips.

The blood slicks the stones beside the wall, thick and dark. At first, she thinks she can stop it. She calls for Boros to give her the small kit, tears through it for bandages. Her fingers leave red smears everywhere. Zander gives another agonized groan. It echoes, too loud.

"They're going to hear," whispers Boros. "We need to keep moving. The mission—"

"I know." But Zander is all she has left. Calchas died two weeks ago, caught by a Bassaran arrow because he was too damned tired to keep his head down. Vyria is in the healer's tent with a shattered knee. Boros is a good soldier—they all are, the

last of the Seventh—but they don't have a piece of her soul, like Zander.

Sephre bit down on her lip, pain bringing her back to herself, shoving the memory aside. Inch by inch her fingers crept deeper. The fire gnashed at her. She was kindling, she was paper and oil, she would burn away to ash. Acrid smoke slid down her throat.

Then, finally, a crack in the stone. She followed it, heart thrumming.

The bandages are already soaked through. She smells something more than blood. Sees slippery coils of viscera, spilling out from the deep slice along Zander's belly, where the Bassaran guard's spear found the gap between backplate and breastplate. He never buckled his armor tight enough. He always said he was too fast, the enemy would never touch him, not with the winds of the steppes to protect him.

Another groan, almost a scream. Boros swears. "If they catch us, we'll never make it to the cistern, captain."

She doesn't look at him. She leans closer, gripping a flailing hand. "Zander?" His fingers close over hers, clamping painfully. She grits her teeth, leaning close.

His blue eyes devour her, wide enough to drown in. "Please, Seph. Help me. It hurts. I don't want to die. I haven't . . ."

Her fingers tighten. She holds on, as if she can keep him in this world with the force of will alone.

Yes. Hold on. The flames were testing her, but she was stronger. The crack deepened, becoming a narrow recess. Her fingers dug into it, skittering over bare stone.

Then something else. Something familiar. A hilt, fitted neatly against her palm, as if the two had been wrought as one.

She hides the dagger against her side. "I'll help you. I promise." She keeps her voice calm, so that his blue eyes stay fixed on her. So he doesn't see.

So that he gives only a small, soft sigh as her blade slices him free.

Her fingers spasmed. A guttural cry wrenched from her chest.

She was floating outside herself. Then slamming back to painful reality, the cold stone of the summit hard and unyielding under her, her hands empty.

She hunched against the stones, listening to the rattle of her breath, rough with smoke and heat. Her palm throbbed. She had felt the hilt against her skin. That had been something more than memory. The dagger was there, just as the codex promised. Letheko, the blade of oblivion, killer of gods. That should mean something, and yet her brain refused to move on. To stop circling over the carcass of her old pain. Plucking at it. Feeding on it.

Hss. A shadow flickered in the corner of her eye. Focus returned with a rush of nerves and pulse and coiling strength. Sephre rolled herself upright. Golden flame wreathed her hands. Let the demons come. She could use a good fight.

But this was a different sort of demon.

Lacheron squinted, shielding his face from the blaze of light in her hands. "Peace, Sister Sephre."

How long had he been lurking there, watching? Jaw clenched, she willed her flames back to a handful of sparks. Fought to make herself still and peaceful, no one of any interest.

"I . . . apologize," she managed. "I thought . . ."

"There's no need to explain," he said. "I'm glad the ashdancers stand ready to smite the evils of the netherworld. And you clearly still have the reflexes of a soldier." The intensity of his gaze was even more unnerving up close. The weight of it made her chest ache, turned each breath into a struggle.

"You remember me," she managed, stupidly.

"Not at first," he said, sounding oddly chagrined. "Fates. I should have. But you've changed." His not-gray, not-brown eyes continued to rove over her face, but she had the strangest sense that he wasn't truly seeing *her*. That she was only a mirror, reflecting something back at him. "Do you remember me?"

A jar, pressed into her hand. They will have no choice but to surrender, he says. They cannot endure without water. It will end the war, spare countless lives. It is all up to you, captain.

Sephre found her tongue. She wanted to spit, to clear the bile in her mouth. "I remember the siege," she said, roughly. "I remember what you did." She ought to bow, but her spine refused. He wasn't her lord anymore.

Lacheron stared at her another endless heartbeat. When he finally nodded, she couldn't tell if he was disappointed, or relieved. "I'm glad the Fates placed us here," he continued. "I've been wishing to speak with you further, captain—sister," he corrected himself, glancing to the gold sparks flickering at her fingertips. "But you seem to be an exceedingly busy woman."

"Yes." If he was going to give her such an opening, she would gladly take it. "In fact, I should be—"

Lacheron spoke over her. "I understand you were in the archives recently. Looking for information on one of the Embraced."

Careful. Sephre tensed. If she'd had a sword, she would have drawn it.

"Yes," she answered. "I was hoping to learn more about those who seek it. For . . . myself."

She couldn't tell if he believed her. He tilted his head slightly. "For *yourself*. Because you regret what you did in Bassara."

Curse the man. He didn't deserve to even ask such questions. But at least she had led him away from the hidden blade. And she would answer him truthfully.

"Yes."

"Would you rather the war had gone on? That they died of hunger, slow and aching? That parents had to choose which of their children to feed?"

Sephre stiffened. "I'd rather it ended without anyone dying."

Lacheron arched a brow, studying her with an intensity that made her skin crawl. It was a look she'd seen before.

The Heron had arrived in Bassara late in the second year of the siege. Whispers flitted through the camp that he had brought some new weapon, one that would end the war by winter. They had joked about it. Vyria had guessed it was a battering ram, powerful enough to take down the giant bronze gates. Calchas thought it was a spell—even then there were rumors that the man was a mage who spoke with the voice of the abyss. Zander said it was trained ferrets that would sneak in and steal the reliquary.

Even Sephre had been hopeful, though she suspected a battering ram was more likely than trained ferrets. Then one day she was summoned to his tent, to report on a scouting mission along the western ridge.

She found him at a worktable. There was a rat—the camp was thick with them—splayed out before him. Dead. Sliced open, organs neatly parceled out. Sephre had no idea what the man was doing. But the look on his face haunted her. A fierce, pitiless focus. An absolute dedication to tearing free the answers he sought.

He had the same expression now. She was the rat, and he was trying to flay her open, to weigh and measure her organs. To catalogue all the deepest parts of her.

"The Bassarans could have ended it," he said. "All they had to do was return the Faithful Maiden's reliquary. They were the ones who stole her from her people, who cursed her spirit. We were there to bring her home. To set her free."

Sephre bit the inside of her cheek. She'd believed it, once. That the war was a holy thing. She'd stood at the railing, watching the black prow of the warship slice through the waves toward the isles, her brow slippery with a smear of ash. The priests had smudged each of them as they filed onto the ships, destined for glory. *And if you fall, know that your spirit will rise anew, and be rewarded in your next life. For this is a holy quest, to restore the Faithful Maiden to her home, and to her eternal beloved.*

But no war was ever holy. She knew that now. Those bones so many had died for might not even belong to the unnamed woman who wrote that journal. It was sickening. All those lives, spent on a lie.

"Is it the Bassarans you mourn?" asked Lacheron. "Or your own people? There were many losses, I recall."

Zander's blue eyes held her, agonized, pleading. *Please, Seph.* She drew a shuddering breath.

"But they were soldiers," said Lacheron. "They accepted the sacrifice."

"And what have you sacrificed?" The question wrenched out of her.

For the first time, she saw something raw break through his careful mask of disinterest. Pain. Regret, even? Had she actually hurt him? It seemed impossible. And yet the way he stared at her, she might have been holding a dagger to his throat. Finally, he tore his gaze away. "I lost the one person who mattered most to me. And I know I will never get her back."

She took hold of herself. She had no sympathy for this man. None. "I'm sorry, I don't think I can help you. Unless you need something from my herbarium? I have a very good cassia and broadleaf tea, excellent for the bowels. My secret recipe. It'll clear you right up."

Foolish words. But better he think her a fool. Let him take insult, and go.

Lacheron didn't look insulted. He looked . . . thoughtful? Suspicious? She probably shouldn't have mentioned bowels. Still, he did not press the matter, only nodded. "No, thank you, sister. You've already given me enough of your time."

He skimmed away back down the steps, leaving her alone with the flame.

———

The wine wasn't working. It was supposed to dull the pain, and yet the ache was as sharp as ever. How many cups had she had? Sephre tried to lift the jar. Her fingers slid off the slick clay, nearly toppling it. *Too many, apparently.* And not nearly enough.

If anything, she felt worse. It didn't help that she'd spent the night on the summit, keeping watch. Drifting at the edge between sleep and panic, expecting Lacheron to return with a dozen strapping soldiers wielding pick-axes and hammers, come to claim the Ember King's prize.

But the Heron had not returned. Maybe even he drew the line at desecrating a holy shrine. Or maybe he already had some other plan in motion. All she knew for certain was that he would not give up. She had seen the conviction blazing in his colorless eyes, there on the summit. It frightened her.

Maybe it was pure self-interest. Lacheron had helped make Hierax into a king, after all. Sephre had been, what—twenty-four, twenty-five? A simple soldier, her days full of training and duty and her own personal ambitions. Even so, she'd heard the mutterings, watched the officers leaning close over braziers late at night, trading the latest news of the ailing queen, Erycina.

Erycina had three children, but succession in Helisson was often a messy business, given that an inheritance of spirit could be as—or more—important than mortal parentage. The fates of Erycina's blood heirs was proof enough of that. One dead, having eaten "bad snails." Another disappeared, supposedly fled across the sea in a fit of religious fervor to walk the Bleeding Sands. The third bundled off to the flying hills for his own safety, having been identified as the most recent incarnation of Lygo the Luckless.

And into that void stepped Hierax. He'd always been popular with the generals, in large part due to his family's monopoly on the trade in tin, so vital in the forging of bronze for weapons and armor. He'd even married a Scarthian bride, to ensure he alone controlled the imports from the northland. But even that might not have been enough to open the door for Hierax, if it weren't for the prophecy of his Fates-touched daughter proclaiming him the Ember King reborn.

Convenient, of course. Even Sephre—naive and desperate to believe in something—had wrinkled her brow over it. But only briefly. Because the streets were full of bards singing the tale into surety. Every trusted soothsayer confirmed it. If there were any voices of dissent, they went silent.

On the day before the royal investiture, Sephre had stayed up half the night polishing her armor, combing out the crest of her helm so it would fall in a perfect crimson cascade. It had been exciting, thrilling. There was eager talk of new campaigns, new chances for glory under King Hierax, who promised that Helisson would rise as a second empire under his rule, regaining all that was lost in the cataclysm. It sounded rich and fine, something to be carved in stone for all the ages to witness.

That eager girl with her shining armor and her shining notions felt like another person to Sephre now. Not a stranger, exactly. More like . . . a younger sister. If only she could reach back through time and shake her. Tell her that glory was a sword with no hilt. That it sliced you open if you tried to wield it.

What would have become of her, if she'd been less naive? Would she have left the army? Returned to her father, to sheep and high mountains and the life that had once chased her away with simplicity and tedium?

Or maybe she would be dead. Hung from a thorn tree with a severed tongue, like the governor of Tarkent, and her husband, and two of her children. Because the governor's teenaged son had sung a ridiculous song about the Ember King trying to woo the Faithful Maiden with a series of increasingly large and suggestive vegetables. Because anything that questioned the glory of the Ember King was a threat to Hierax's power.

Like, say, the fact that the Faithful Maiden had not died in her supposed lover's arms, but had instead fled to Stara Bron and hidden his most powerful weapon beyond his reach and named herself faithless. That the bones he had waged a war over might not even be hers.

"Sister?"

Timeus stood in the herbarium doorway, the early evening shadows etching his cheeks and wide eyes. The knot in her belly relaxed, just slightly. She could use a distraction. Something uncomplicated that even she couldn't corrupt. He was a good lad, and she'd missed him. "You've excellent timing, Brother Timeus." She set her palms to the table to hold her wine-soaked world steady. "How would you like to learn the proper way to grind plessuda root? I promise, it's not nearly so tedious as it sounds."

He shifted his weight, reminding her of the first day he'd shown up in her garden.

"What's wrong?" Her voice went sharp, honed by a series of terrible possibilities. Halimede, dead. The dagger, found.

"N-nothing, sister," he stammered. "I'd be happy to learn how to grind plessuda. But . . . I was wondering . . . that is . . . I need your advice."

Sephre blinked. Since when was *she* wise enough to give out advice? "Did you forget how to tell the difference between the skinbite and the mint?"

"Smooth must shun, jagged harms none," he recited. "No, it's that . . . well . . . Sibling Vasil wants me to take the crimson vigil. They said we need every ashdancer we can have ready to face what's coming."

Sephre let out her breath, caught by an unexpected burst of pride, sweet enough to drive back the despair that had been swamping her. "When?"

"Tonight." His smile flared and faded. "Or . . . some other time . . . whenever I'm ready."

"Vasil thinks you're ready."

"I suppose so." He eyed her. "But do *you*?"

"That's not advice," she said. "That's permission. And you don't need it."

His expression twisted, wrestling with this. He didn't believe her.

"Do you *want* to be an ashdancer?" she asked, more gently.

"Yes," he effused, his certainty a delight and a terror. "I want to help people. To be the flame that stands against the skotoi. Now more than ever. It's just . . ." He sagged slightly.

"It's dangerous," Sephre finished.

"No. I mean, yes, it is, and I'm not brave or anything. I still have nightmares about Kessely. But even so, I helped stop it. I did something good. I want to keep doing that. Even if it's dangerous."

"So, what, then?"

His cheek dented, caught between his teeth. "I just keep thinking about everything I've done wrong in my life. How many mistakes

I've made. I know you said we all make them, that we learn from them. But how do you know when you've learned *enough*? I don't know if I'm—if I'm good enough. For the flame. What it . . . what if it doesn't want me?"

She laughed. A short, sharp bark, wild with disbelief. This pup. This lovely boy, thinking that anything he had done in his short, innocent life could *possibly* be so terrible.

"I mean . . . I'm not like you," he said. "I'm not a hero. I keep hearing my mother's voice, telling me—"

"Lies," Sephre snapped, abruptly furious. At his mother. At herself. At a world where someone like Timeus thought that he wasn't good enough. That she, Sephre, murderer and despoiler, was a hero.

"Sit," she said, roughly.

Wordless, big-eyed, he slid onto the seat across from her. The nearly empty wine jug sat reproachfully between them. Sephre fought the urge to sweep it away. Instead, she poured the dregs into two cups, then pushed one across the table. "Drink. It's medicinal," she added, before he could protest. She lifted her cup. "To Zander."

It was the first time she'd said his name in ten years. It should have shattered her. Instead, here she was, a mouthful of wine sloshing down her throat.

"Who was he?" asked Timeus.

"A soldier. We served together, during the siege. He's dead now."

She wanted to say more, but words couldn't hold a person, a life. It was like trying to describe a beach with a few grains of sand. Zander was the one who invented filthy songs to cheer the rest of them during long nights on watch. The one who saved a bit of every meal to feed his favorite hungry camp-dog. The one who had gifted her a bottle of Scarthian milk-wine after she was promoted, then drank most of it himself to "save her from behaving in an un-captain-ly manner." The one who started a brawl with the entire fifth wing after one of them called her a joyless harpy. *Everyone knows you're a joyful harpy,* he said, lips split, cheeks battered, eyes already masked with bruises.

Sephre coughed, as if it might make the words come easier. It didn't. "Our unit—my unit—was given a mission. They said it would end the siege in a day."

She kept her gaze fixed on the table, but she heard Timeus draw in a breath. She wondered how much he knew. Which stories he'd heard. The ones that left the nature of the Helissoni victory conveniently vague, or the ones that told the truth.

"It was Lacheron's plan," she said. "All we needed was to get a small team over the city wall. There was a spot we'd found, along the western ridge. Near the city's water supply. So. That was us."

"The seventh wing?"

"What was left of it." She grimaced. "There were six of us by then. We started the war as fifty."

She braced herself for the boy to say he was sorry, but he held his tongue. She went on. "It was a simple enough mission. Carry the flasks of poison to the cisterns and dump them in."

Another sharp breath. She paused, waiting.

"Poison?" He made a noise, something between a huff and a sigh.

"You were expecting a glorious charge?" She couldn't keep the bitterness from her voice. "The valiant Helissoni battering down the gates and marching into Bassara to rescue the Faithful Maiden?" She shook her head. "It wasn't anything like that. What we did was horrible. Unforgivable."

"I . . . I didn't know." He swallowed. "But it was Lacheron who ordered it."

"That's no excuse." Sephre laced her fingers together, staring at her pale knuckles. "I just wanted the war to be over. I told myself there would only be a few deaths. Then they'd see the danger, and surrender. I didn't let myself imagine the worst. That . . . that so many would . . ." She gave a sharp shake of her head. "The point is, don't measure yourself against me. I'm not a hero. I'm not even sure I belong here. I didn't come to Stara Bron to fight skotoi and save the world. I was running away. I just wanted to—" Her throat clamped. Weariness stained her gray and listless.

After a moment, Timeus spoke. "I broke my sister's arm." He frowned into his cup. "We were six. I was angry she wouldn't let me have my turn with the toy horse. I shoved her, and . . . I guess she just fell wrong. I heard the snap. I was crying before she was. I hadn't meant it to happen." He hitched his shoulders, as if the story was an old, itchy blanket, hard to settle.

"Mother slapped me, and then she locked me in the cellar. She said I'd best learn to behave, or the skotoi would find me and eat my soul. It was the worst night of my life. It was pitch black. And I kept hearing them. The demons." He huffed wryly. "Probably just mice, but they were skotoi to me. I was terrified. My bones practically rattled out of my skin. And that wasn't even the worst part."

Sephre waited, watching the old fears twist the boy's face like storm clouds.

"I could hear Rhea, upstairs, weeping. I think she was trying to be quiet—she's always been the brave one—but I guess it hurt so much she couldn't help it. And she was all alone. Mother must not have heard. Maybe she'd had too much wine." He carefully slid his own cup away, lacing his long fingers together and staring into them instead. "I finally managed to shake the latch loose. I went to Rhea, and I told her I was sorry again, and I stayed with her all that night and told her stories so she wouldn't think so much about the pain."

He drew in a long breath. His bony shoulders heaved, as if casting something off. "It wasn't willowbark tonic, just a bunch of silly jokes, really. But still. I think it was . . . good." He unlaced his fingers and met her eyes. "I'm going to do it. I'm going to sit the red vigil."

Sephre doubted anyone had ever called Timeus handsome, with his gangly limbs and his wine-jug ears and overlong, over-lean face. But in that moment he was utterly beautiful and she was so, *so* proud of him.

"You're going to make an excellent ashdancer," she told him, croaking past the lump in her throat.

He smiled, swift and sweet. "Thank you, sister."

"You should go," she told him, before he could further unravel her. She nodded to the darkening sky. "You're supposed to start the vigil at dusk."

So he went, leaving her alone in the shadowed workshop with only the moths for company. She watched them flutter around the single small oil lamp. Drawn to the light, heedless of how it might singe their soft wings.

She waved the blundering insects away, then snuffed the flame.

It was time to stop wallowing. Time to act, while she still had the chance.

CHAPTER 19

YENERIS

Yeneris crept into the garden early the next day. Exhaustion bit at her bones, and her eyes felt crusted with salt. She could have put it off, but that would only give the weasels in her brain more time to chew her excuses to guilty shreds.

I was following orders. They said to make her trust me, and I did. She cares for me, because I made her care. Because we need her for the mission.

She had done nothing wrong. So why did she feel like a child stealing sweets?

Because she was lying to herself. It was more than just the mission now. It had been ever since the night she followed Sinoe to the necropolis. Even now, on her way to possibly be reamed end to ear, she couldn't help smiling when she passed the jasmine trellis where Sinoe had taken her hand.

So where did that leave Yeneris? There were tiny hooks embedded in her skin, tugging her in two different directions, and if she wasn't careful they were going to flay her alive. But that was the trouble. She *wasn't* being careful.

Sinoe was the problem. Being around her was making Yeneris soft. Making her dream of things she could not have. So it was good she was seeing Mikat. Mikat made her hard. Mikat reminded her that she was not a feather. She was a sword.

I am a sword. She sliced through the gray pre-dawn gloom. A damp mist hung over the garden, gemming the leaves and vines with soft pearls. Her sandals were wet, squelching in the spongy mats of purple-blooming groundcover. She thought she'd seen someone moving past the line of statues that bordered the rose garden, and was heading that way when Mikat spoke.

"You're up early." The woman stepped from a gap in the sweet-smelling hedge. She carried a ewer of water, freshly filled judging by the way she rested it against one hip. "Especially for someone who was gallivanting about the city all night."

The words jabbed her chest. "You know?"

Mikat's lips quirked. Was she amused? Angry? "You're a valuable resource, Yeneris. We worked very hard to place you in the palace. With the princess. And we want to make certain you have all the support you need to pursue the mission."

Yeneris cleared her throat. "Of course. Thank you. Yes, I . . . accompanied the princess into the city."

She laid out the events of the previous day, though not in strict order. Better to begin with the visit to the Queen of Swarms, then finish with an account of the family luncheon, the king's sacrilege. It would horrify Mikat, and focus them both on what mattered most. The kore.

Mikat's expression, already dour, turned to stone as Yeneris described the desecration of the kore's bones, turned into Hierax's puppet, his plaything. Yeneris felt her own blood thrum, and she welcomed it. Welcomed the fury that would keep her fixed on this path.

When she finished, Mikat turned away and spat. "Abyss take them all."

Yeneris held her tongue, bracing herself for more questions.

"You've done well," said Mikat. "The princess trusts you. She cares for you."

"Yes." Best to keep her answers short.

"But she doesn't suspect you?"

"She knows I'm Bassaran," Yeneris admitted. "But she doesn't seem to care. She's sympathetic to our cause."

"Or she's just having a bit of fun," said Mikat. "You say she's been kept caged. A caged bird only wants to get free. It doesn't care what hand opens the door."

She swallowed a protest. Mikat was right. Perhaps she was only that. An open door. A chance to escape for a little while.

Mikat tilted her head. "That bothers you."

Furies take me. She should have guarded her expression. Shoved the feelings down, trod them to dust under the heel of her duty.

"I'm not angry." Mikat tapped one finger against the handle of the water jug, making it chime faintly against the morning silence. "It means you're doing the job we sent you to do. It means you've committed yourself, fully."

Yeneris opened her lips, but nothing came out. She was too relieved to speak.

"I trust you, Yeneris," said Mikat, holding her gaze steady, speaking her name with the same inflection her mother had used, rather than softening it, as the Helissoni did. "I wouldn't have asked this of you, otherwise. But I know that it is a hard task. A painful one. And for that, I'm sorry."

Finally, Yeneris found her tongue. The words sputtered out, too fast. "I swear, Mikat, I will free the kore's bones from this place."

"I know." Mikat gave her a considering look. "But remember that you are not alone in this. There are others standing ready to play their parts. We are stronger than the Helissoni think. Already our agents in the south have finished constructing the first five ships for the return. More of our people join the cause every day. They may not know your name, they may not know your mission, but they are all with you, Yeneris. Dreaming of the kore's return, and the renewal of our home."

Yeneris shivered. The thought was both reassuring and over-whelming. Which was probably exactly what Mikat intended. And it was what she needed to hear, she told herself ruthlessly. *This mission isn't about you. It's about the kore. It's about hope.*

There had been other attempts to return to Bassara since the war. But none had succeeded. The first had been a fine vessel, sponsored by a wealthy Bassaran merchant from Urabas. It was meant to be a proof of concept, led by the daughter of one of the

Nine Elders, stuffed full with bards and nobles and dreams. But the ship had been lost in a storm with all hands. Had never even touched the shore, so far as anyone knew.

The second had gotten farther, actually grounding on the curved, white beach sheltered by the eastern headland. The crew managed to last almost a full month, before a mysterious illness ravaged their nascent settlement, and they were forced to abandon it.

Since then, no one had dared attempt the return. Some said that the island was haunted by the spirits of the thousands who had died there. Others claimed that the kore herself was angry that her people had not protected her, had let her be stolen away.

Yeneris had never dared ask Mikat what she believed. She wondered, sometimes, if the older woman's reasoning was more pragmatic. She was fairly certain that several of the major investors in the expedition would withdraw support if the mission to recover the kore failed.

"Our priority is the kore," Mikat said. "See if you can encourage Sinoe to visit again. Preferably without her father. Use her doubts. If she suspects that Lacheron has corrupted her visions, she will be easier to manipulate. And she may be the key to unlock our future."

You are no one's tool. Her own words to Sinoe haunted her, made her stomach twist with guilt. The hooks in her skin tugged again, sharper now.

"What about the bodies? The ghouls? The Heron is plotting something."

"Concerning, yes," said Mikat. "But if some new cataclysm is about to fall, then it's all the more reason to reclaim the kore. To restore her and ensure our people have a home. A refuge."

Of course.

"It is curious, though," said Mikat, "how they control the sibyl's visions. They can direct her gaze, with pain? All they need to do is force her to weep, with the smoke, and she cannot stop the words?"

"Yes." The word felt like a hot coal on her tongue, but Mikat didn't seem to notice. She was nodding to herself.

"Very good," she said, finally. "Go, then. Continue the work."

=====

For the next two days, that work involved mostly standing around. Nocturnal adventures aside, Sinoe's life was highly constrained by protocol and the seemingly endless rituals of dressing, grooming, and prayers to whichever greater or lesser god the star-seers proclaimed to be in ascendence, punctuated by a handful of carefully curated social engagements that Yeneris suspected served primarily to remind Hierax's court that his daughter spoke for the Fates.

Standing stiff-backed against the wall while two handmaidens dried Sinoe's hair, Yeneris could almost imagine that none of it had happened. The necropolis, the visit with Melita. The bloom of jasmine and Sinoe's upturned moon-bright face and the brush of her seeking fingers.

Maybe Mikat was right. Maybe this was all just a game to the princess, a distraction.

Coward, Yeneris told herself. It would be easier, that way. It would mean she didn't have to feel guilty. She could pretend that they were both using each other, that no one would be hurt when this all ended. Because it would end. Yeneris would reclaim the kore's bones and be gone, and Sinoe would still be here, in her cage, aching to fly free.

Unless Yeneris set her free, as well. Found some way to remove her from the palace. A tremor rippled through her at the thought, the wild and completely impossible dream. Sinoe beside her on a swift ship, sailing down the river to the sea.

"Yen?"

She startled, drawn out of the vision into a present that was equally unnerving. Sinoe, alone now, standing before her in her silky sleeping gown, face unpainted, her hair twisted up in bits of cotton cloth. Tomorrow they would spill down in long dark curls.

"Where were you?" Sinoe asked.

Yeneris coughed, shaking her head. "I'm sorry, princess. What do you need?"

"Mm. An intriguing offer. Honestly, a sound night's sleep. But this is our chance, so I doubt I'll get one."

"Chance for what?" Yeneris corralled her mind very sternly.

"To sneak into Lacheron's workshop of course."

"Oh. Yes."

"You sound disappointed. Did you have something else in mind?" Sinoe waggled her brows. "We have a mission, Yen. Lacheron must be at Stara Bron by now. We need to find out what he's up to."

═══

"I didn't realize picking locks was a standard part of bodyguard training," Sinoe said as she leaned against the doorframe outside Lacheron's workshop, watching Yeneris slowly work her thinnest dagger into the iron keyhole.

"I didn't realize sneaking into the workshop of your father's spymaster was a standard part of princess training, either."

"Oh, yes. They teach it right after comportment and before mathematics."

"You studied mathematics?"

"I'm quite good at it, thank you very much," said Sinoe. "If I ever wash out of being Sibyl of Tears, I'd make a respectable accountant."

Click. Relief melted through Yeneris as the door swung open. She slid inside, moving slowly, cautiously. Lacheron seemed the sort of person who might well leave unpleasant surprises for unwanted guests. And there were the corpses to consider.

But there were no poisoned darts. No ghouls. Only a lofty chamber lit by thin shafts of moonlight lancing through the high windows. A couch stood against one wall, but the heaps of storage baskets piled atop it made it clear no one had sat there in a long time. The desk showed more signs of use. Wax tablets lay neatly stacked on one hand, while the rest was covered in a large square of parchment. Yeneris padded closer, studying the squiggling lines and dots curiously.

"A map." Sinoe's breath tickled Yeneris's cheek as she bent close to whisper. "What do you suppose these marks are?" She reached out, tracing the scattered black dots from the southern coast all the way north to the Veil.

Yeneris shook her head, already moving on, taking note of the shelves full of scrolls and codexes that marched along the far wall. The long workbench cluttered with jars and pots and small braziers. A large trunk in another corner, bound in bronze. And the arched corridor that must lead to the inner chambers, veiled in a darkness so deep it seemed to devour her vision.

Then a spark of light bloomed, chasing them back. Sinoe held up a tiny oil lamp, the flame half shielded by her hand. Together, they advanced on the corridor.

The quivering light glinted off a bronze gate, a crisscrossing web of bars sunk into the stone. Yeneris could see no lock, no mechanism of any kind. Sinoe swore so colorfully Yeneris turned to make certain it was truly the princess beside her, and not a sailor from dockside. "Can you open it?"

"I don't even see a lock," said Yeneris. "It must be hidden. I'll keep looking."

Sinoe nodded, drifting away toward the shelves, where she began riffling through the papers.

Yeneris searched the gate from top to bottom, feeling for any secret latch, any loose twist of metal that might be the hidden key. She found nothing. It could be elsewhere in the room. Or maybe it was something the man himself carried. Yeneris had no idea what the true extent of his abilities was.

Hsss.

Yeneris tensed. Was it only her imagination? The echo of Sinoe's movements? Or had something moved in the darkness beyond the gate? She leaned closer, pressing her ear to the bronze bars. All she could hear was the thud of her own heart.

Up until now, Yeneris had thought the greatest risk was discovery. Being spotted by one of the household, caught by a patrolling guard. But looking into the darkness beyond the gate, she felt a deeper, nameless terror. Like staring up into the depth of the night sky, not at the stars but at the darkness between. A sense of something her mind could not fathom.

Sinoe gave a small cry of triumph, dragging Yeneris back from the void. She shook herself. Just a fancy. Just her mind spinning to fill the unknown. She left the gate and went to see what Sinoe had discovered.

The princess had pulled a large scroll from the shelf and unfurled the bottom, revealing a series of short stanzas inscribed in ink.

"Poetry?" Yeneris asked, dubiously.

"No," Sinoe breathed reverently. "Prophecies."

"Your prophecies?"

"Yes. Look, here's the last one." She ran a finger along the lines, reciting them. "*Long has the old enemy watched and waited. Now he seeks to strike his second blow, and the world will not survive it. The first light must reveal the weapon of unmaking. When it is found, when the Maiden steps forth from flame to take her rightful place, only then shall the old enemy fall.*"

Even in Sinoe's own natural voice, the words seemed to hum, to have weight and heft. Yeneris shivered, thinking of the man with the Serpent's mark. The blood. The smoke. The screams.

She swallowed the sour taste of the memory. There was something else written below. "What's that? Another prophecy?"

"No." Sinoe bent closer, reading. "*Her rightful place? At his side, or mine? Is it possible she might finally—No. Enough, old man. You lost her long ago. This is no time for foolish sentiment.— The dagger is all that matters now. And she will lead me to it, just as the first prophecy foretold. I have only to go to the House of*

Dawn and find her. But I must be cautious. If she remembers too much it could unravel all I've worked for."

Yeneris shook her head. "I understand the part about the dagger and the House of Dawn. That was in your prophecy. But what's the rest of it mean? What first prophecy? And who's the 'she' he's talking about? It can't be the Maiden. They already have the kore's bones."

Sinoe's brow furrowed, her lips moving slightly as she reread the notes. "Unless . . ." She looked up then, hazel eyes catching the glint of the oil lamp, so that she seemed to be a flame herself. "'*We don't even know if it's the kore or some other maiden.*' That's what you said the other day."

Yeneris sucked in a breath. Then blew it out. "But if it's true, if Lacheron *knows* it, why take the kore's bones in the first place? Why go to war? Spend thousands of lives?"

"That's a very good question," said Sinoe. Her jaw tightened, and she turned back to the scroll. "Let's see how far back this goes. Here, hold the lamp."

Yeneris took the small bronze vessel, holding it aloft as Sinoe unfurled the scroll with a feverish energy. For several heartbeats, there was only the slap and ripple as a long spool of parchment snaked loose across the stones.

"Here," she said, finally reaching the beginning of the scroll. "My first prophecy." Her jaw tightened, her eyes stormy. "I was only five. I remember Father saying he had someone who wanted to meet me. A sort of physician, who could help me with my bad dreams. All I had to do was breathe in some smoke and it would make me feel better. He promised. But I was so scared. It smelled bad, and I didn't want to have any more nightmares, and they wouldn't even let Mother hold my hand."

Yeneris flexed her own chilly fingers, seized by a wild urge to reach out and take Sinoe's hand in her own. A belated comfort. But the princess had already lifted the parchment. "*Long has the Ember King waited, denied his final victory. But what was shattered shall be remade. The Maiden who once turned from the world has* now returned, to reveal what has long been hidden. And if he claims it, even the gods shall tremble before him."

"Is there another note?" asked Yeneris.

"Yes. But all it says is, 'Finally. Finally it will end.' Not ominous at all." She began furling forward. "Let's see if he has anything more to say about the war. It should be somewhere around—ah, here."

Yeneris leaned closer, following over her shoulder as Sinoe read the words. "*The Maiden shall grant him power, or deny it. He will not know her at first, for she bears another name now. But what she faces across the sea will unmake her, and she will return to seek rebirth in flame. Only then, at last, shall they be reunited.*"

"That's it?" Yeneris scoffed. "Three sentences. That's what sent Hierax to war? To destroy a city?"

"There's another note," said Sinoe, reading on. "*A new name. And new memories. Remember that. All she is now is a tool. A way to claim what I need to finish this, and end the tyranny of the gods. Very well. I will wait if I must. But Hierax will not. The man is desperate for legitimacy. So. We will give him his bride. One maid is as good as another, and my allies will feast well.*"

The scroll hung like a long pale tongue, silent now. After a long moment, Sinoe began to roll it up again. She did not look at Yeneris.

Yeneris had been angry for years. She'd held her fury close, turning to it whenever the training seemed impossible, on the dark mornings when she'd risen before dawn to meet Mikat, driving her body to become a sharp and deadly thing. It was a constant, steady burn, familiar if not comfortable.

What she felt now was something new. A flare that shook her, set her limbs trembling, made her want to crash out into the hall and murder every single person who stood in her way, until she found the king and jammed every one of her seven blades into his flesh.

"*One maid is as good as another,*" she repeated, the words snapping out of her.

Sinoe flinched. Her fingers tightened on the scroll, crumpling the smooth parchment. "Yen, I—"

"Don't apologize. It wasn't you."

Sinoe let out a single soft sigh. She shoved back her shoulders. "So what can we do?"

Yeneris began to pace. This was the downside to training her memory to record every detail. The words were inked into her mind now, a jumble of clues, fragments of a larger picture she could not see. *You don't need to understand the whole story. You only need to play your part. Rescue the kore.*

She tensed and relaxed her muscles, limb by limb, a small ritual Mikat had taught her to center herself. Sinoe watched her, waiting, wounded, wanting to do something to help.

So give her something to do. Use her. Yeneris could almost hear Mikat's orders.

She licked her lips, then spoke. "You were right about Lacheron, princess. He's been manipulating your prophecies all this time. Using them for some purpose of his own. But we can set things right. The Fates can guide us."

A faint relief bloomed in Sinoe's face. "Yen, I—yes, I want to help. I want to fix this."

"Can you get us in to see the kore's bones? Alone? Without your father?"

Sinoe frowned. "Why?"

"You could do a scrying." The lie slid off her tongue, leaving a bitter taste. But even now—especially now—she couldn't risk the truth. Sinoe was the key to the kore. "You said you want to fix this. Maybe the Fates will show you how?"

Sinoe nodded slowly. "Yes. There might be a way." But her lips had an unhappy twist.

"Is it dangerous?" Would it matter? She had to do this. No matter the cost.

"Not dangerous. Just . . ." She shook herself. "I'll do it. The day after tomorrow. Ambassador Opotysi is hosting a hawking exhibition. I can arrange it then."

HOUSE OF DUSK 213

So that was it. Sinoe had agreed. There was no need to demand any other details. Or to worry over the shadow in her eyes.

Clack.

They both turned toward the bronze gate. "What was that?" whispered Sinoe. She started to step forward, but Yeneris caught her elbow.

"Wait." Heart thudding, she lifted the small oil lamp. The single thin flame had been bright enough when they were using it to read the scroll. Now it seemed such a small thing, so easily snuffed.

The thin fingers of gold light reached through the bronze bars, only barely scraping the darkness on the other side. Nothing moved. But the air felt thick, oppressive, heavy with a whiff of rot.

Something glinted, deeper in the shadows. A reflection of the lamplight? No, it was the wrong color. Almost purplish.

Yeneris thought of the ghouls in the necropolis with their bruised eyes. Of her swords slicing them, only to spill out more and more shadowy tendrils. Flame was the only thing they feared. And all she had now was an oil lamp with a flame no taller than her thumb.

"We should go," she said.

"Yes," agreed Sinoe. They began to retreat toward the door. Yeneris's eyes burned from staring into the darkness. Every muscle quivered. The door creaked open, letting in a draft of clean air. The throbbing in Yeneris's head lifted. She pressed Sinoe outside and slammed the door. The lock clicked shut and they fled together down the hall.

Behind them, from inside Lacheron's workshop, came a low, hungry howl.

CHAPTER 20

YENERIS

Yeneris did not trust Sinoe's brightness. It was a mask, like the paint that had taken three handmaidens an hour to brush onto her face, turning her creamy skin a cold ivory, her lips blood red, her eyes enormous, rimmed in kohl with a single blue tear marking each cheek.

"Will you be scrying?" Yeneris asked softly as they made their way along the path of heroes, watched only by the golden eyes of the statues. It was the first time they'd been alone in nearly a day. Two servants trailed behind them, but neither was close enough to overhear, and they were fully occupied pushing a handcart that held a boxy shape covered in a rich gold cloth. Faint keening noises came from within, and the rustle of feathers. Sinoe had ordered that Tami be brought along to the hawking exhibition, but clearly the ailouron was not pleased with her current situation.

Neither was Yeneris. The last thing she wanted right now was to be surrounded by Helissoni. She didn't blame Sinoe. It was Lacheron—and potentially Hierax, though the full extent of the king's involvement was unclear—who had twisted the sibyl's prophecies. Used them to excuse the war that had destroyed Bassara. She knew Sinoe regretted it. But Yeneris had too much fury in her now to bear Sinoe's guilt.

Yet Sinoe had promised a way into the south wing. Yeneris couldn't afford to let that opportunity pass.

"No," said Sinoe. "Father just likes to remind everyone that he commands the voice of the Fates."

"Does he?" Yeneris asked. "Command you?"

HOUSE OF DUSK 215

Sinoe glanced back to the veiled cage as Tami gave another piteous protest. "Sometimes. But don't worry. I haven't forgotten what I promised. I'll find a way to get you to the kore."

They walked on. The beaded hem of Sinoe's gown chimed softly. A gentle sound, but it rankled Yeneris's nerves, especially in counterpoint to the caged ailouron's keening. She would have pressed Sinoe to tell her the plan, but they had just emerged onto the open green where the hawking exhibition was taking place.

Sinoe was her usual smiling, sunny self once they joined the crowds gathered on the southern lawn, flitting between groups of Helissoni worthies in their garishly vivid tunics and gowns, reminding Yeneris of the hummingbirds she'd watched in her grandfather's garden as a girl.

Yeneris followed Sinoe's flight, skin prickling in spite of the clear blue sky, the brightly striped Scarthian tents, the heaps of soft pillows and jewel-colored carpets, the tables full of honeyed nuts and cheese tarts and roasted lamb. There was an edge to Sinoe's brightness. It was honed too sharp. Yeneris saw that sharpness whenever the princess glanced back toward the cart. The servants had drawn it onto the green, but halted along the edge. Waiting.

There were people all around. Even so, Yeneris leaned closer, murmuring, "Princess? What's wrong?"

Sinoe turned to her, hazel eyes swimming in the dark ring of kohl. But she didn't respond, only gave a small shake of her head. Then the mask was back, her smile hooking into place as she fixed on a stranger walking toward them across the grass.

He was tall, with deep brown skin, merry eyes, and a tumble of black curls that somehow managed to look more artful than messy. Judging by his dress, he was Scarthian. Only the northerners wore trousers like that, and in such striking geometric patterns, like bits of a language that her mind was forever at the edge of under-standing.

Yeneris retreated a few paces so that Sinoe could greet the man. Which she did with considerable affection, flinging her arms around him and giving such a sincere cry of joy that Yeneris wondered whether she had just imagined Sinoe's earlier disquiet. "Hura! I didn't expect to see you back until fall!"

The man, Hura, laughed, returning the embrace. "I live to surprise you, Noe."

Noe? How well did these two know each other, exactly? Not that it was her concern. Sinoe could hug whomever she liked. For as long as she liked.

But Yeneris was not the only one frowning at the princess and the young man. Several of the nearby Helissoni guests had also taken notice. The man's glance slid past the princess briefly, taking in the disapproving looks, and some of the brightness faded from him. He pulled gently back from Sinoe, still smiling, but more reserved. He dipped his head.

Sinoe seemed to catch the shift in tone, drawing herself in, speaking more formally, "And how is your father?"

"Very well. Very pleased with himself for negotiating a new trade agreement with the Idrani. And they've finally finished work on the temple. Urabas feels like a true city now."

A thrill quivered through Yeneris. She knew that name. Urabas had been part of the old empire, though it was only a small trading outpost even before the cataclysm, eclipsed by Bassara in size and population. But it had been growing in size even before the war. Afterward, it was one of the few places where those who had escaped Bassara could find a refuge. Mikat scorned them. *If they were true Bassarans, they would be fighting for our home, not casting up some pale shadow.*

Yeneris understood who Hura was now. She ought to have guessed. Now that she knew what to look for—to listen for—it was clear as the bright blue sky above. The sharpness at the ends of some words, the edges she had so carefully filed off her own voice. He might be wearing Scarthian garb, but Hura spoke with the traces of a Bassaran accent. He must be Ambassador Opotysi's son, the one Sinoe had spoken of, who was both Scarthian and Bassaran. And a friend of Sinoe's as well. It made sense. Yeneris forgot, sometimes, that Sinoe also lived a doubled life, Helissoni and Scarthian.

"Is your brother here?" Hura was asking.

Sinoe arched a teasing brow. "Am I such poor company? I should be insulted you can't go five minutes without asking about Ichos."

Hura seemed flustered. "You're excellent company, of course. I only wondered . . . that is . . . the prince is an admirable sparring partner."

"Mmm. Yes, I'm sure he is. He's very good with his spear," said Sinoe, giving Hura a wicked smile.

The ambassador's son choked, cheeks darkening. "And how are things going with Tami?" he asked, clearly eager to change the subject.

He succeeded. Sinoe's mirth melted, leaving only a stony sort of resignation. "She's lovely. Adorable and fierce and—" Her voice quivered. She drew in a breath, and the next words were harder, sharper—"I can't keep her. I'm returning her to your mother today." Sinoe nodded toward the covered cart at the edge of the field.

Yeneris stiffened in shock. Sinoe had given no hint of this earlier. She had let Yeneris believe she was bringing Tami to fly her in the exhibition. Not to banish her. And as little as Yeneris cared for the destruction of her tunics and the piercing sharpness of the ailouron's claws, she knew how Sinoe loved the silly creature. And how the beast loved her in return. She couldn't possibly give Tami back.

Hura seemed equally shocked. His brows lifted. "Why?"

Sinoe was biting the inside of her cheek. And Yeneris saw the way she clenched her fists, though she tried to hide them in the pleated layers of her gown. Yeneris found her own fingers clenching in sympathy. She wanted to charge forward, to fight something, to protect Sinoe. To stand between her and anything that shadowed her joy.

"Because of him," Hura answered his own question. He glanced away, across the green. Following the look, Yeneris saw King

Hierax had just arrived, surrounded by soldiers and attendants, the weight of his presence already drawing the crowd closer.

"She'll have a better life back in Scarthia," Sinoe said. "She's too closed in here. She can barely fly at all."

"She's not the only one," said Hura darkly. Sinoe's eyes went wide with alarm, but he held up a hand. "I know. I know."

Sinoe drew in a quick breath. "Please. Tell Mother I—"

She broke off. King Hierax was approaching, a storm cloud crackling with the promise of lightning.

"Daughter," he said. "You shouldn't take too much of Lord Hura's time."

"Of course," Sinoe replied smoothly, her expression tranquil. "I only wanted to request an audience with the Scarthian Ambassador. To arrange for the return of their gift."

"Ah." Hierax nodded. Placated. "Yes. Very good."

"Here's my mother now," said Hura, as a tall woman strode to join them from the direction of the striped tents.

Opotysi was as impressive as Yeneris remembered, the sort of woman who could crush you with her mind as easily as with her fists. Her flaming hair was braided into a complex web of interweaving coils, decorated with small disks of hammered silver. Triangles of dark blue ink patterned her pale cheeks and ran up her arms. Yeneris had heard the marks were some sort of holy invocation. Scarthians honored the four god-beasts and the Fates, along with a host of other spirits and lesser gods. There were jokes about it. The Scarthian sailor who drowns because he makes a prayer to the god of waves rather than the god of tides.

"King Hierax," Opotysi said, dipping her head to the king, and then to Sinoe. "Princess. What's this about returning a gift?"

Sinoe stood stiffly, as if someone had replaced her spine with a spear. She gestured toward the waiting cart, the covered cage. "The gift is too great an honor. I cannot accept the ailouron. I have brought her here so that you can take her home."

The faintest of dents dove between Opotysi's brows. Yeneris couldn't read her expression, but the beat of silence spoke loud

HOUSE OF DUSK 219

enough. "You are a daughter of the steppes," she said, finally. "Surely it is only fitting that you have an ailouron as your companion."

Yeneris saw Sinoe's shoulder hunch slightly. As if she was preparing herself for a blow. And again, Yeneris fought the urge to spring forward. To shield Sinoe from this. "No. I am a daughter of Helisson. My father is the Ember King. And my true mother—" there was no hesitation, only the faintest flex of Sinoe's fingers as she spoke—"is his Faithful Maiden, who has returned to us, and praise the Fates, will once more stand at his side."

A murmur rippled through the various nobles who had gathered. Yeneris saw cautious smiles and nods from those in Helissoni garb, but the Scarthians were less pleased. Some frowned. Others shook their heads.

The only person who seemed completely satisfied by Sinoe's proclamation was Hierax. That was when Yeneris understood the point of all this spectacle. The truth of it sliced her, sudden and unexpected, like the slip of a paring knife. And for a long moment she could only stare at the blood seeping from the wound. *This* was Sinoe's plan to convince her father to allow them to visit the kore's bones alone. The princess had publicly rejected her mother, had cast off her beloved ailouron, all to help Yeneris rescue the kore. All to win King Hierax's approval.

And it had worked. Hierax gave Opotysi a triumphant look. "Indeed. As my daughter says, Ambassador."

"Very well," said Opotysi, her voice clipped, her expression cool. "I'll make sure your message is delivered." She gave another nod, then spun away. She paused briefly to speak with Hura, before heading off toward the Scarthian tents.

Hierax reached for Sinoe, one heavy hand wrapping her arm. "Come, General Fortus is about to fly his hawk."

Sinoe glanced back as the king swept her away, her eyes hunting, landing on Yeneris. "See to the transfer, Yen. She trusts you."

And then she was gone, leaving Yeneris to grapple with the aftermath. With the hard knot tied into her chest. This was the mission, she reminded herself. And why shouldn't Sinoe make sacrifices? Yeneris surely had.

"Yen, is it?" Hura had lingered. He was watching her now, a little too curiously for her comfort.

"Yeneris," she answered, painfully aware of her own voice, and how it might betray her. Hura might not think anything of it, of course. There were thousands of folk with Bassaran heritage scattered across the lands of the Middle Sea. She didn't think he would suspect her mission. More likely he'd simply think her desperate, to take service in the household of the man who had destroyed their city. Or maybe he didn't even care. Urabas had remained neutral during the war. Choosing to save themselves, rather than risk being attacked.

"Yeneris," he repeated, speaking her name as she had, in the softer Helissoni way.

The name wasn't unusual. The languages—like the people—of the Middle Sea had much in common. They had all been part of the old empire, after all. Before the cataclysm. *Stop fluttering,* she told herself. *Stop acting like you have something to hide.*

"May the kos bless you." Hura gave the greeting casually, as if it meant nothing. And maybe it was true. He was half Bassaran, so no strangeness that he might offer her a Bassaran greeting.

She nodded in return, then turned and began marching toward the cart. The sooner this was over, the better. Tami was keening again, a plaintive wail that scratched her nerves raw.

This was all for her. No, that was presumptuous. It was for the kore. Sinoe needed to win her father's trust, to gain access to the south wing. Still, Yeneris wished there were an easier way. One that didn't require Sinoe to give up Tami. The princess hid her feelings well, but Yeneris knew she must have sliced out her own heart to make that speech. To know that her mother—her true mother—might think it was real. That Sinoe had so thoroughly rejected her.

She halted beside the cart. The two servants stepped back at her approach. Bracing herself, Yeneris tugged aside the cloth. Tami

HOUSE OF DUSK 221

gave a bright chitter, uncoiling from a tight ball at the bottom of the cage and flinging herself at the bars closest to Yeneris with a piteous wail.

"Shhh," she hushed the creature. "It's going to be all right. You're going to go home now."

But Tami continued to wail until Yeneris opened the cage door. With a creel of triumph, the ailouron leapt onto her shoulder, nestling her beak beneath Yeneris's ear. She began to purr.

"She likes you," said Hura.

Yeneris shrugged. "I'm familiar."

The man arched a brow. "Ailourons aren't particularly friendly with anyone other than their chosen person. Or people their chosen person cares about. Their hearthkin."

Another Bassaran word. Hearthkin and heartkin. The two kinds of family, her mother had taught her. Those you were born to, and those you chose for yourself. A foolish heat spread up her cheeks. Yeneris reached for Tami, unwinding the ailouron's claws from her hair, ignoring her squawk of protest. She held the creature out to Hura. "Then she'll be very happy with you. Princess Sinoe clearly thinks very highly of you, Lord Hura."

Hura took Tami, who in fact did submit easily to his touch, and had soon nestled herself onto his shoulder. Yeneris told herself sternly that it was ridiculous to feel jealous.

"I should go." She started to stalk away.

"A moment, Yeneris."

She halted. Not because of his raised hand, or the entreaty in his brown eyes. It was her name. Even on Sinoe's lips, her own name still sounded strange to her, just slightly dissonant. But this time Hura spoke it properly, the way her mother had said it. The way Mikat said it. It must be deliberate. *Calm*, she told herself. *Give nothing away*. It could be simply a slip. He was half Bassaran, after all.

"What is it, my lord?"

"I have something for Sinoe," he said. "Another gift. One that I hope she will keep. One to give her hope."

Yeneris hesitated. Unease crawled over her skin. Hura had positioned himself so that his back was to the crowd. His short cape hid his arms as he drew something from his brightly patterned tunic. "Will you see that it reaches her safely?"

"What is it?"

"A trinket from Lady Kizare. She wishes her daughter—" He spoke the word very deliberately—"might know that she has not forgotten her. That she thinks of her. That she prays every day to the four winds that they be reunited."

The unease became something sharper. Yeneris stared at the small packet in Hura's outstretched hand. What would Sinoe want her to do? Taking it endangered Sinoe. And Hura too, for that matter.

And it endangered the plan. Sinoe needed her father's trust. She had just sliced out her own heart for the chance to visit the kore alone.

She started to step back. Hura's gaze narrowed. "Please, take it. You strike me as a woman who knows how to keep secrets. And if you help me, I can help you someday. Perhaps you understand the desire to return someone beloved to their home?"

Ice spiked her chest, but Yeneris kept her expression impassive. He could simply be fishing, tossing chum into the water to see if she'd bite. She would not bite, even as her mind spun through possibilities. If she denied him, did he have the power to reveal her? Hierax clearly didn't trust the Scarthians. But Hura could seed doubt. Whisper in the right ear, and raise enough concerns that she might be fired from her post.

If she accepted, she would need to thread a very narrow course. Clearly Hura wanted to whisk Sinoe out of the palace, off to Scarthia and her mother. If not for her own mission, Yeneris would want that too. To get Sinoe as far away from her father and this cage he kept her in. To give her space to spread her wings and fly. What a sight that would be.

But Yeneris needed Sinoe, too. The princess could take her to

HOUSE OF DUSK   223

the kore. Help her ensure that the reliquary returned home, that whatever desecration Lacheron planned would not come to pass.

Still, if she could balance things just right, maybe she could have both. Rescue both Sinoe and the kore.

Carefully, Yeneris turned and went to collect the small leather bag that hung beside Tami's cage. Returning, she held it out to Hura. "Here," she said. "Tami's favorite treats. The princess would want her to have them."

As Hura took the parcel, he pressed his own into her palm. She tucked it away in a smooth movement, slipping it into her sleeve like one of her hidden daggers.

"Thank you," said Hura. Turning, he ambled off. Tami craned her neck, bright golden eyes fixing on Yeneris. She began to keen again, riffling her wings, but Hura distracted her with one of the bits of dried meat until she quieted. And then he was gone, and Yeneris was truly alone.

CHAPTER 21

SEPHRE

This was, quite possibly, the worst idea she'd ever had. And Sephre had had her fair share of bad ideas. Letting Zander order drinks. Bowing to fashion and bobbing her hair, then having to endure a year of looking like some weird overgrown mushroom. Or that time, early in her soldiering career, stupidly eager to prove herself, when she'd challenged her greatest rival to a race through the Razorfells. *Barefoot.* She still had a scarred divot cut out of her left heel.

The stairs up to the agia's office were not lined with thornweed, but even so, Sephre's feet flinched from them. But she climbed, grimly, aware that she was out of other options. Halimede might never wake. Like it or not, Beroe held power in Stara Bron.

And yet Sephre had not shared any of this with her. She'd told herself she was being cautious. That Beroe's ambition made her untrustworthy. It might even be true. Beroe might scoff at her concerns, do nothing. Or turn on her. Call her traitor, summon Lacheron's soldiers to cast her in chains.

Or she might listen. She might be an ally. She might keep Halimede's oath, and send Lacheron away empty-handed.

Sephre paused at the top of the steps, letting her breathing slow. Her heartbeat was a lost cause, still rattling as she finally rapped at the door. "Beroe? It's Sephre."

"Come in." There was a sigh in the words.

Sephre pushed the door open to find Beroe at the agia's desk. A stack of wax tablets teetered before her. A half-drunk cup of tea abandoned near her elbow. The spill of golden light from the nearby lamp traced deep shadows under her eyes. She looked pale and tired and worn.

"I'm sorry to interrupt," Sephre offered.

"It's fine. The numbers aren't going anywhere. Unfortunately. Sometimes I think I'd far rather wage battle with a host of skotoi than with the temple ledgers." Beroe gave a weary laugh, then seemed to remember who Sephre was, her brow furrowing. She took a deep breath, as if to brace herself for something unpleasant. "How can I help you, sister?"

Sephre swallowed the sting of that breath. She couldn't blame Beroe. They had been prickly as cats together ever since Sephre had come to Stara Bron. *Because she's an ambitious, headstrong fool,* whispered a petty voice at the back of her skull. *Just like you were,* Sephre whispered back. This time, she forced herself not to squirm away from the truth. Beroe raised Sephre's hackles because she reminded her of herself.

She could do better. She, who *knew* what it felt like to have Lacheron's fingers twitching at you, plucking out the tune he wanted. But instead of reaching out, instead of trying to help, Sephre had written the woman off. Measured her by all her worst aspects, and ignored the good.

"The temple is lucky to have you," Sephre said, partly because it was true, and partly in the hopes of softening that suspicious frown. "I can't imagine how much work it must be, managing Stara Bron."

Beroe's brows arched, and for a moment she looked pleased. Then her gaze narrowed again. "Thank you. Though I'm sure it's nothing to commanding an entire wing of soldiers."

"I'm serious, Beroe. No one else could do what you're doing right now, especially not me."

Beroe studied her a moment longer. "You didn't climb halfway up the mountain just to compliment me. What do you want?"

Now it was Sephre's turn to draw a steadying breath. She hadn't planned the words. Better to speak plainly. She wasn't Lacheron.

She didn't want to pluck strings and poke wounds. She just wanted Beroe to believe her.

"I need to tell you something," she began. "We've had our differences, but I know that you care about Stara Bron. About the vows we swore. That you would fight to the last against any skotoi that dared enter this world."

"I would." Beroe's shoulders relaxed slightly. She was wary, but curious.

"Before she sent me to Potedia, Agia Halimede told me about a vow she swore to the agia before her."

"What vow?"

No going back now. "To keep Letheko hidden at Stara Bron, and make sure the Ember King never used it again. Because doing so would cause a second cataclysm."

Beroe stared. Blinked. Then carefully folded her hands together in front of her. "So the dagger is here at Stara Bron? You know where it is?"

The words were flat, colorless.

"Yes," admitted Sephre.

"But you're not going to tell me," Beroe added. "Because you think I'll give it to Hierax."

"He would be a powerful ally for Stara Bron." Sephre gestured to the wax tablets. "Make all those accounts a lot easier to manage."

"I don't care about the accounts," said Beroe. "I care about keeping my vow to the Phoenix. I care about guarding this world from the demons of the labyrinth. I care about stopping a second cataclysm."

"Then we can't let Hierax claim the dagger. I don't know the full truth, but I've learned enough to know that something's not right. The Ember King wasn't the hero we think he was. The Faithful Maiden herself brought the dagger here and swore Agia Cerydon to keep it safe. And every agia after them has kept that oath."

Beroe's fingers knitted tighter. "And why, exactly, did Halimede share all this with *you*?"

"Because she knew how I felt about Hierax."

"You could be lying. You could be inventing all of this."

Sephre blew out a breath of frustration. "Here." She drew the codex from where she'd tucked it in her sleeve, then set it on the desk between them. "I found this in the archives. I think it was written by the Faithful Maiden, before she took the Embrace."

She curled her fingers into fists as Beroe reached for the codex. It felt like a violation to share it, but if it would convince Beroe to believe her, it was worth it. She waited as the other woman flipped the fragile pages, frowning at the mold-spattered paper. A breath of despair blew up her spine. The words had seemed so powerful, earlier. But what were they, really? A thimbleful of whispers.

Beroe's expression was unreadable.

"Maybe you don't trust me," said Sephre. "Fine. But you trust Halimede, don't you? You know she refused to recognize Hierax as the Ember King. She must've had a reason. It's dangerous to deny him. If you love Halimede, if you still respect and honor her as your agia, then at least consider that she did it for a good reason."

"A reason she neglected to share with me."

Sephre clung doggedly to her patience. "Are you really going to ignore all this because your feelings are hurt? Look, I don't know the full truth either. Halimede didn't tell me everything. But something terrible is coming, Beroe. And I'd rather not face it alone."

She searched the other woman's face, hunting for any sign that the words had reached her. Was that a softening in her jaw? A spark of thoughtfulness in her eyes?

A bell began to toll. Sephre bit her cheek in irritation. Surely prayers could wait for this. But the bell rang on, no mellow call to worship. This was sharp and strident. A warning. A call to arms.

Stara Bron was under attack.

The bells were still ringing when they met Brother Dolon in the cloister. His round face was grim. "It's skotoi. I don't know where they all came from. There must be a dozen of them. Obelia managed to close the outer gates, but they're coming over the walls. She and Vasil and some of the reds are holding them in the courtyard for now. But I don't know how long they can last. They . . . they just kept coming. What do we do?"

"We do our duty," said Beroe, unwavering. If she had doubts, she hid them well. "They will not claim this holy place. Not so long as we hold the flame."

The acting agia led the way onward, down the passage that led to the courtyard and the gates. The bells had stopped ringing, but Sephre could hear the dim screams and shouts from below, mixed with other noises, slick and slithering, inhuman. Whatever ash-dancer had been raising the alarm was now dead, or fighting for their life. Sephre's nerves crackled. She held flame at the tips of her fingers. It must be enough.

"Do you know where Lacheron is?" she asked Dolon.

"No. I haven't seen him. Or his soldiers."

So much for the Ember King and his glorious defense of the mortal world.

They emerged beneath the pillared portico of the temple, above the wide, shallow steps that led down to the courtyard.

A pall hung over the sky, turning the world dim and smoky. The air was heavy and hot and thick with decay, turning Sephre's stomach. It took her a moment to understand what she was seeing.

The outer gates were gone, the oak beams torn apart. And through them surged a flood of corpses. Many of the skotoi no longer looked even remotely human. Some hunched like crabs, scuttling on multiple needle-thin legs. Another rose tall but limbless, a mountain of flesh that surged slowly but inexorably across the stones, shifting like molten wax. And yet here and there she caught a glimpse of something terrifyingly, wrenchingly human. A hand, reaching from a slurry of meat. A single eye, wild and brown. A row of perfect white teeth rippling along the tip of a tentacle.

A dozen ashdancers formed a line along the base of the steps, holding back the monstrous tide from the temple. Flames spattered her vision with crimson and gold. Squinting, she made out the sturdy figure of Sibling Vasil, sweeping a lash of flame to drive back a skotos with wide strips of gray, flaccid skin hanging from its shoulders in a gruesome mockery of wings.

Someone called a warning as the limbless mountain fell upon the center of the line. It swarmed over a young red sister, enveloping her like a rising tide. Then Sister Obelia was there, shoving gouts of flame at the monstrous thing, driving it back so that two other ashdancers could pull the girl free. The rotting hulk turned on Obelia, surging over her. Sephre's breath caught. Her hands jerked up. But she was still too far away. She could only watch as the other woman fell, crushed beneath the relentless tide of flesh.

"Fates have mercy," murmured Beroe.

Sephre bit down on something much less holy. But her body did not betray her. Or maybe it was a betrayal, how *well* she remembered this: the flicker of lightning along her nerves. The quickening of her heart. Her mind slowing, clearing, focusing. No sword now, but the flames were in her hands, and in her heart. She threw herself down the steps and into the fray.

She took the place of one of the red sisters, holding the left flank. And then there was only the battle. The slap and groan of unliving flesh, the taste of ash coating her tongue, the dazzle of flame in her eyes.

And the weariness of her body. The strain of each step. The tremble in her arms. *This is nothing,* she told herself grimly. *Remember the Scrimfang raiders? You held them off all night. You didn't even go to the privy.*

Granted, she'd also been twenty years younger. At least this battle wasn't likely to go on so long that she'd piss herself. Thank the Fates for small mercies. The flames of the ashdancers were doing their job, destroying the smaller skotoi easily. But the shifting hulk that had killed Obelia was proving harder to vanquish.

Sephre edged closer to the thing, chafing at the bite of wrongness. *Of course this feels wrong. You're surrounded by demons trying to destroy your home.*

Except that they weren't. The skotoi had taken the courtyard easily, and yet they weren't advancing up the steps, into the temple. Even that horrible boulder of flesh seemed to be . . . holding back? Were they simply conserving their numbers? Were the skotoi clever enough for such things, without the Serpent to command them?

She remembered Nilos then. What he'd said to her, at Kessely. That the skotoi had found a new master. Was he the one who had sent this host to attack Stara Bron? To destroy the ashdancers?

The truth struck Sephre in the gut, driving out her breath. She understood the wrongness. Why the flow of the battle itched at her.

Because it *wasn't* a battle. It was a distraction. A feint. But what was the true goal, if not to simply wipe out the ashdancers? What did the demons want?

To stop the return of the Serpent. But Nilos wasn't here. Sephre considered her own fears that she carried a piece of the Serpent's power. If so, it didn't seem to be drawing the skotoi to her at the moment. At least, no more than to any other ashdancer.

Could the skotoi be after the dagger? Were they slithering up the mountain even now to claim it? Impossible. The Holy Flame would guard it. Only the agia could claim it. And the agia . . .

Horror seeped through her.

"Fall back!" she bellowed. "This is a distraction! They're after Agia Halimede!"

Beroe turned toward her, face clouded by confusion. There was no time to explain further. She'd have to trust Beroe to marshal the defenses. It might already be too late.

Sephre spun on her heel and dashed up the steps, heading for the infirmary.

====

The broad hall was echoingly silent. Dark, with only a faint glow from the brazier along the far wall. No movement. Nothing.

That was a bad sign. If nothing else, surely the bells would have roused Abas and the other retired elders. Well, aside from Sister Ketis, who could probably sleep through a second cataclysm.

Maybe not the best thing to joke about right now. Sephre padded deeper into the still room. Her breath strangled as a dim shadow along the ground resolved into a crumpled heap of cloth. A body.

A keening cry escaped her clamped jaw. Then the heap shifted. A groan. Sephre kindled flame in her hand, advancing quickly. "Abas?"

Fates, let them be alive, not corrupted into some soul-riven thing. She held the golden sparks before her. She could do this. If she must, she would.

"Sephre?"

Her legs melted. She fell to her knees beside the old ashdancer, finding an arm, a hand reaching for her. She gripped it, squeezing tight. Another groan, tinged with pain. "Are you—?"

"Only bruised and battered," Abas replied, grimacing. "Skotos. It came through the window. I tried . . . it was so fast. It knocked me down. Ketis too. I think . . . I think it killed Jovan. He tried to burn it, when it went for the agia."

Jovan. The oldest of the ashdancers. He'd told her a story once about nearly getting eaten by a sphinx when he was a boy. He'd tricked it into letting him escape by giving it a riddle with no answer.

"The agia?" she asked, bracing herself for the shattering.

"It took her. Carried her off." Abas gestured toward the door on the far side of the hall.

The possibilities coiled cold in Sephre's belly. Were they taking her to the summit even now? Did they think they could force the agia to claim the dagger for them? But how had skotoi known Halimede was here, in the infirmary? Nilos had suggested they served a new master now. Had he sent them here?

Lacheron's absence was a seed in her teeth. Could he have known about this attack? He always had plans within plans. She shivered, feeling invisible hands shoving her across the game board.

Someone was directing the skotoi. It seemed ridiculous that it could be Lacheron. And yet, it would explain much.

"Stay here," she told Abas. "Others are coming. Tell them what happened. I'm going after Halimede."

Abas squeezed her fingers, nodding, then let her go. She moved quickly, smoothly. No time for panic. There was only the mission. Only the faint trail of ichor and ash that led out from the infirmary, along the corridor. Her mind parceled up the questions for later. She stopped once, leaning out from a window to try to see whether the fighting continued below, but the bulk of the lower temple hid her view of the courtyard. She pressed on. No time to wait for reinforcements.

The dark spatters did not lead her to the mountaintop, as she'd expected. Instead, they took her to the Hall of Doors. Good. The chamber had no other exits, no windows. No way out. The skotos was trapped.

Sephre paused at the threshold just long enough to kilt up her skirts and roll back her sleeves. To limber her shoulders and settle the knot in her chest. Then she stepped within, hands wreathed in flame.

The tiled walls reflected her light into a thousand watchful eyes. There were no other lamps or braziers. She held herself still, poised, ready.

A shadowy bulk shifted against the gold. A voice whispered.

You failed, baleful one. We know where you hid it. And now, our master will claim it.

"You'll burn to ash first, demon." She raised a flaming hand, spreading the pool of golden light. But what it revealed made her breath catch hard and sharp.

This skotos was not some shambling corpse. It was lean and powerful, smooth white bone wrapped in tendrils of darkness. Human-shaped, and yet there was something inhuman in the way it held itself. Skull too broad, jaws overlong, the eye sockets narrowed to slits. The teeth sharpened to fangs, split wide as it spoke. A horrible rasping formed without lips or tongue.

No closer. Or we destroy the blue one.

It shifted, showing her the agia, caught under one bony arm, limp and thin and undefended. Halimede gave a faint groan. Fates, was she awake?

Sephre held her ground, groping for a plan. The thing was smart enough to speak. She could take advantage of that. Keep it talking until the other ashdancers found her. "Why do you need Halimede?"

The skotos cocked its head. *Our master promised us a feast.*

"She's the agia of Stara Bron," Sephre scoffed. "She'll turn your stomach. If you have one."

It snickered. That was a bad sign. Something was wrong.

Not the blue one, whispered the skotos. *She dies, as he commands. She has served her purpose.*

It happened in a blink. So fast Sephre stared, the image making no sense, a jumble of white robes and sharp black spines and crimson splatters. Then it resolved into Halimede, hanging loose as a bit of washing out to dry, the front of her pale robes dark with blood, and a strange sharp, black flower bursting from her belly.

The skotos hissed, retracting the sinuous arm that had sliced into Halimede, then cast the agia aside like a bundle of rags. Fury burst from Sephre, a wordless cry. She hurled herself at the skotos.

The air around her filled with slithering shadows. Too late, she realized that the demon had been playing the same game she had. Keeping her talking, as it wove its tendrils close enough to strike. Now they snatched out, one coiling around her midsection, another catching her arm. Then tightened, squeezing her breath away.

She scrabbled at the thing, calling the holy flame to her palms. But she felt only the faintest flutter of heat. It was hard to think. The skotos shook her, making her body snap. Pain exploded along her side, through her skull. It must have slammed her into the wall.

Stars spun, an entire constellation filling her vision.

So much pain. So much shame. And this. The shattered heart of a dead god. Do you even know that you carry it? And why?

Perhaps we will tell you the truth, as we strip the flesh from your bones and flay every sorrow from your soul. Something cold wrapped around her arm. Prickles raced over her skin. Not pain, but a shifting, sand under her feet, melting away. She tried to scream. It was like being underwater. Bitterness filled her mouth, her throat. If she breathed, she would drown.

Then the world burst into crimson flames. A wrench, and she was free, falling, caught in warm arms. Human arms that lowered her to the stones gently. She blinked, and looked up into a pair of familiar brown eyes, in a familiar brown face framed by dark braids.

"Timeus!"

He smiled. It was brief, and sweet, and she could not bear it. "You shouldn't be here," she croaked. "You're a novice."

"No," he said. "I'm a red brother now."

Crimson flames sparked in his eyes. Sephre's own flame blazed in answer, filling her with hot pride. Of course he was. Brave, wise boy.

"Come on," he began, gripping her shoulder. "We need to—"

The words cut off as a thick, oily tendril of shadow lashed around Timeus, tearing him away. Sephre shoved herself upright, cursing.

Timeus dangled in the air just beyond her reach, coiled in the grip of the skotos. The demon gave a sharp shake, making the boy flop. Sephre bit down on a shriek of outrage. It was like watching a hound with a baby rabbit.

"Let him go!" Fire wreathed her hands, snapping to match her fury.

You only delay the inevitable, the skotos hissed. *We will consume you, baleful one. You will be nothing but dust and dying memories.*

"If I'm the one you want, then fight me," snarled Sephre. "Not that boy!"

The skotos only snickered. *You care for this one? Good. Then come and claim him.*

Damn right she would. She flung a handful of flame at the skotos, aiming low.

The bolt spattered against empty stones. The demon was retreating. Where? The only door was behind Sephre. Surely it couldn't—

A frail gray light split the darkness, somewhere along the western wall. The Serpent's wall. She blinked, vision foggy, barely making out the shape of an archway. And beyond, nothing but mist. Or was it a river? A lake? A darker smudge loomed over it. Walls. Endless maze-like walls. A place she had only ever seen in ancient carvings, in nightmares. The Labyrinth of the Dead.

The skotos plunged into the apparition, with Timeus still struggling in its grasp.

And then it was gone. Winked out of existence. Sephre was alone, with a handful of golden flames, a dead agia, and her apprentice stolen.

CHAPTER 22

SEPHRE

Sephre lunged forward, wrenched by the fishhook of loss lodged in her chest. She dug her fingers into the tiles of the western wall, searching for some crack, some seal, some way to tear open whatever uncanny portal the skotos had used to spirit Timeus away. Leaving her alone with that challenge. *Come and claim him.*

Oh, she would. And she'd rip apart every slithering, rotting corpse that tried to get in her way. Once she found the damn door. She slammed a flaming fist uselessly against the western wall, swallowing a curse. There must be another way to get into the underworld. Aside from the obvious.

Footsteps echoed behind her. Gasps of alarm. A ragged cry that she thought might be Beroe. Exclamations and invocations. Dolon's low rumble, saying something urgent.

The pulse of battle in Sephre's blood began to dim. She tried to cling to it, to hold onto the focus, the sharpness. To keep running ahead of the tide of grief and loss. Dolon was speaking to her, but the words were part of that grief, and she could not afford to listen.

Then, a faint, wet cough.

"Agia? Can you hear me?" Beroe pleaded. "Fates, Sephre, get over here and do something!"

Hope spun Sephre away from the wall to find Beroe kneeling beside Halimede's crumpled, bloody form. Dolon stood nearby, while Vasil lingered by the door, holding back a handful of the reds.

"What can we do?" Beroe demanded, her face pale and streaked with ash, her eyes still bright with golden flames. She pressed a wad of Halimede's robe against the gaping gash in the woman's belly. It was already sodden with dark red blood.

Sephre's hope winked out at the sight. Nothing. No poultice or tonic could cure a wound like that. It was a wonder that Halimede had not already slipped away. And yet she could see the rough rise and fall of the woman's chest. Her mouth working, as if she was trying to speak.

"Agia?" Sephre knelt opposite Beroe.

Halimede's eyelids fluttered open. The blaze of blue light behind them made Sephre's breath catch. She seemed to be nothing but flame thinly veiled in mortal skin. "The Embrace . . . burned away . . . But I would know her by the signs . . . by her wounds . . ."

The words spattered from her lips like embers, each one catching in Sephre's chest. Halimede grimaced, teeth clenched, sparks dribbling between them. When she spoke again, her breath came in ashen puffs. "Your wounds . . . Must face . . . what you did . . . waters . . . remember . . . you can end this!" A groan. Blue sparks skittered over her skin like raindrops. Beroe made a high keening noise.

Sephre leaned closer. "Remember? Remember what?"

Halimede's eyes went wide, drowning her in depthless blue. "Remember!"

And then there was nothing but flame. Sephre flung an arm across her face. Felt a pressure in her ears, against her skin, like some great hand gripping her tight. Then releasing.

Darkness fell. Sephre blinked, and saw only a loose heap of ashes against the stones. Halimede was gone.

But Timeus was still out there. He needed her. Surely no mortal could survive for long within the Labyrinth of the Dead. It was a place of spirits, of sorrows, where all the cruelties of a thousand generations had seeped into the stones. Where the skotoi now ruled, feasting on misery and despair. Sephre managed to get one arm under herself, shoving against the stones. Her legs were shaky. "I need to go," she croaked. "They took Timeus into the labyrinth. I have to—"

She broke off at the sound of heavy footsteps. The clatter of metal. It was all the warning she had before Lacheron swept into the hall, followed by six of his soldiers. "There," he snapped coolly, jabbing a finger at Sephre. "Take her. She is a creature of the Serpent."

"What?" Sephre took a step back as two of the burliest warriors moved toward her. Her palms itched to bloom with fire, but it would be sacrilege to turn the holy flame against the living. No matter how infinitely boneheaded they might be.

One of the men tried to reach for her, moving lazily. Not seeing a threat. She ducked his grasp. Much good it did her. The other soldiers now blocked the door.

Fine. She had nothing to hide. It was Lacheron who should be answering for himself.

"I'm no one's creature." She kept her voice calm. He would not provoke her. "I was out there fighting skotoi. Which is more than I can say for you." Her withering glare took in Lacheron and his soldiers. A few of the latter had the decency to shuffle their feet or glance away, but Lacheron was unmoved. She wanted to fly at the man and claw the rotted half-smile from his lips. Was it Halimede's death that cheered him?

"That mark suggests otherwise," said Lacheron, nodding.

"Mark?" Sephre tasted sour panic. She swallowed it. Forced herself to look down.

Suddenly the world was spinning, and there was only one fixed point. The ring of dark lines, just above her right wrist, linking what had once been merely freckles. The Serpent's star sign. She remembered the skotos, wrapping its dark tendrils. The cold. The drowning. The horrible voice, whispering. *Do you even know that you carry it? And why?*

So. Nilos was right. She had been carrying the Serpent's essence all this time. And now it was clear to all the world, etched remorselessly onto her skin.

"I—" She licked her lips, tried again. "It's not . . . it doesn't mean . . ." She had to stop stammering. It made her sound guilty.

HOUSE OF DUSK 239

She focused on Beroe, on Dolon. Sisters, brothers, siblings. Her family. "It means there's a fragment of the Serpent's power in me. But I'm an ashdancer. I serve the Phoenix." She raised a hand. Held her fear between her teeth, biting hard until yellow sparks kindled in her palm.

A tremor passed over Beroe's still face. She drew in a breath, as if steadying herself. "Lord Lacheron," she said. "I am acting agia. Sister Sephre is a daughter of Stara Bron. I have authority here."

"The woman is a danger to all Helisson," said Lacheron. "Her very existence is an invitation for the Serpent to return. In the name of King Hierax, I demand that you turn her over to me."

Beroe drew herself taller. "I will do no such thing."

Lacheron's smug certainty crumbled slightly, and Sephre almost cheered. She had never been so grateful for Beroe's high opinion of herself.

"What will you do then?" Lacheron demanded. "You cannot allow her to walk free."

"No," agreed Beroe. She turned to Sephre. "Don't worry, sister. I understand, now. How this has been poisoning you, filling you with lies. Those things you said, earlier."

"That was the truth." Frustration boiled up her throat, spilling out. "He's the liar." She jabbed a finger at Lacheron. "He's behind all of this. Just like in Bassara. He wanted Halimede out of the way because she refused to recognize Hierax as the Ember King. Because he wants someone he can control. Don't let him use you!"

She could practically see her words bouncing off Beroe. In her eyes Sephre was raving. A child throwing a tantrum.

"We will do as Agia Halimede commanded, with her dying breath," said Beroe, finally.

"What?" Sephre was honestly confused, trying to recall Halimede's last broken words. Something about facing what she'd done, and remembering. And . . . water?

"We will burn away the taint," said Beroe, simply. "You'll be cleansed of the Serpent's mark, and released from the pains and fears of your past. Just as you've long wished, sister. You will be Embraced."

———

Sephre had never begrudged her small, windowless bedchamber before. It was warm and snug, and her hours in the garden offered all the fresh air and sunlight she could want.

Now, it was a prison. Complete with a chamber pot and a ewer of water. She counted the passage of time by the rotation of the soldiers standing guard in the hallway outside. It must be well past dawn by now. Half a day since the attack on Stara Bron. Since Halimede died and Timeus was stolen.

He was alive. He must be. The skotos wanted her, not the boy. They would not kill him. But what else might they do? Torment him? Feed on his spirit? At least she could take some comfort in the fact that he was a red brother now. He had a spark of the holy flame to protect him.

Frustration itched over her. She wanted to hit something. Lacheron's face would do. Or Beroe's.

Sephre grimaced. She had tried, but it was too little, too late. Maybe if she'd approached Beroe sooner, told her everything that first day after she returned, she could have convinced the woman to trust her.

Probably not. Sephre barely trusted herself. She sat on her cot, weary from pacing the five steps between the narrow walls, and angled her right wrist to catch the light of the small lamp. The mark was a shock, no matter how many times she studied it. It reminded her of the first time she'd seen her own reflection after the war. The fine lines around her eyes. The threads of wiry gray at her temples.

She understood what Beroe feared. Fates, Sephre feared it herself. What if the mark *was* changing her? But it wasn't as if the Serpent was whispering in her head, telling her to release a tide of demons into the world. And her own spark of yellow flame remained as strong as ever.

She summoned it, now, to brighten the cell. To drive back the gnashing images of Timeus being tormented by skotoi. Sephre might never understand the grand shape of the world, the machinations of the Fates, the epic struggles of the gods. But she knew that a boy she cared about, her apprentice, a young person placed in her charge, was in danger. Whatever else, she had to find him. Free him. Return him safely to Stara Bron.

The Embrace would steal that from her. She would lose her memories of Timeus. She would forget that he had been taken, that she had ever cared. This pain in her chest when she imagined him suffering would fall to ash.

But Timeus would still be a prisoner. The skotos had taken Timeus to lure Sephre to them. Because apparently she was so dangerous to them that they wanted not just to kill her, but to consume her spirit. To destroy her beyond any hope of rebirth, as they had Iola. Perhaps that was only possible within the labyrinth?

Or maybe she was giving the skotoi too much credit for tactical thought. Regardless of why they wanted to lure her to the labyrinth, if she failed to show up, they might simply consume Timeus, and annihilate his spirit instead.

She forced the thought back, buried it deep. That would not happen. She would find a way into the labyrinth and bring him out again. She would dare those drear dark walls, she would walk those mist-shrouded passages. She would face her own demons if she must.

Maybe she *had* wanted the Embrace once. Maybe a part of her still did, even now. To be free of her shame, of the terrible things she had done. Zander's eyes. The silent streets of Bassara. But those weren't the only things the flame would burn away. And she needed to remember.

Sephre might not recall Halimede's dying words exactly, but she didn't credit Beroe's interpretation. It hadn't been a command, but a warning. Did she know about the Maiden burning her own memories to ash, leaving the world to believe the Ember King's lies? Had that been one of the secrets Agia Cerydon had passed down?

If so, she could have been asking Sephre to discover the truth of what really happened three centuries ago. But even so, why tell her to *remember*, unless . . .

Halimede said she was watching for signs foretold by Agia Cerydon. *Many things may be reborn, not just the Ember King.*

Such as the Maiden herself?

When she was ten, her father had caught Sephre play-acting the Trials of Telemena, using a purloined melon to represent the Unequaled Pearl and his walking stick as the Swan-Wing Sword. He'd laughed, stinging her young pride, and she'd shouted at him— Fates, she had been a handful—that she could be a great hero reborn. He'd only shaken his head, gesturing to their humble home, their stark mountain. *You think a great hero would be reborn to this?*

Yes, she'd felt a pang of familiarity, reading the Maiden's codex. Yes, they carried similar burdens. Similar wounds. But that didn't mean she was the Maiden reborn. It would be too cruel an irony, even for the Fates. And it had nothing whatsoever to do with rescuing Timeus. He was her priority.

She heard movement in the corridor outside. Sephre carefully rolled her shoulders. Shook the tension from her arms. This could be an opportunity. The soldiers outside were well trained, strong, quick. She was out of practice, old, and exhausted. But highly, highly motivated. And they had already underestimated her once. She gave herself even chances of breaking past them. But then what? Back to the Hall of Doors to see if she could somehow open the same portal the skotos had?

Or should she flee Stara Bron entirely? Where would she go? She had no allies.

She could think of only one person who might help. Who might

HOUSE OF DUSK 243

know how to enter the realm of the Serpent. Nilos. If she could find him. If he even still lived, with Prince Ichos hunting him.

"It's food. Nothing more." Someone was speaking in the corridor. A mellow, gentle voice, but with a core of iron that Sephre recognized. "Agia Beroe made it clear that Sister Sephre is to be treated with compassion and respect," said Brother Dolon. "Now step aside, please."

Some grumbling. Then the creak of the door. A shadow, cutting the brighter light that spilled in. Sephre hesitated, measuring the distance to the door, taking note of the soldier just outside, a spear ready in his hand. No. Better to learn what she could from Dolon first. Maybe Beroe had reconsidered. Or, even better, maybe the blue flame had rejected her. Only a full agia could grant the Embrace. It would at least give Sephre a bit more time.

Also, she was ravenous. And the platter in Dolon's hands was heaped with rounds of bread, a bowl of oily, herb-flecked cheese, boiled eggs, and even one of Sister Obelia's apricot pastries. Memory gripped her throat in a vise, and she blinked hard. Obelia was gone. Murdered by the skotoi.

The door swung closed. Dolon sat beside her on the cot, his brown eyes soft, their golden spark muted. Grief and pain carved his normally jolly features, but at least he looked uninjured, save for a few scrapes and bruises.

"Who else?" Sephre asked. "Aside from Obelia and Halimede."

"Jovan and Actia," said Dolon, gravely. "And . . . Timeus."

"No," she swung the word like a sword, driving back the possibility. "Timeus isn't dead. They took him to lure me. I can still save him."

Dolon pressed his lips together, not arguing, but not agreeing either. He nodded to the tray of food. "You should eat. Have you slept?"

She gave a hollow laugh. "Have you?" But she tore a bit of bread, scooped some of the cheese, and forced herself to eat. The pastry sat untouched.

Dolon watched her. She swallowed her mouthful. "You're not afraid to sit here with me? With this?" She turned her right arm, brandishing the mark.

"You're my sister," said Dolon, simply. "The flame hasn't abandoned you. Neither will I." He hesitated then, glancing toward the door. When he spoke again, his voice was softer. "It's not right. The Embrace isn't meant to be forced."

Sephre frowned, thinking of the gray-knotted volumes in the archives.

"Even when it's a punishment," Dolon went on. "I . . . looked into it. I wanted to understand. And there's always a choice. Not a good one, perhaps, but a choice. The Embrace or death. The Embrace or twenty years of hard labor. I still don't know *why* I made the choice. But I know it was my decision. And it should be yours."

She held his open brown gaze. "I don't want it, Dolon. Not anymore. I need to find a way into the labyrinth. I need to find Timeus and bring him back. And I can't do that if they burn away my memories." A breath, a brief plea to the Fates. "Will you help me?"

Dolon looked away, and her heart cracked. But it wasn't a rejection. He was thinking. He always tilted his head like that when he was deep in thought, dredging up some reference, or the name of an obscure scroll. "Why are you so certain he's in the labyrinth?"

"The skotos took him there. From the Hall of Doors. It opened some sort of . . . magical gateway?" It sounded ridiculous even to Sephre, who had seen it with her own eyes. The portal had closed before the others arrived. He had only her word for it.

"Truly?" Dolon sounded delighted at the idea that a door to the underworld could pop open inside the temple at the whim of a demon. "Fascinating! It suggests the damage might not be as severe as we thought. Or that there was some other reason the paths were disabled."

"The paths?" Sephre prompted, before he could wander off into even more obscure academic musings.

"Connections binding the four great temples. Stara Bron, Stara

Vex, Stara Mhyr and Stara Sidea. There's evidence that prior to the cataclysm, there was considerably more communication among the four orders. Imagine it!" His expression lightened. "A dustspinner from Stara Vex borrowing a book from our archives. A balewalker, stopping by to take tea."

"It didn't look like a temple. More like a cave, and a pool, or maybe a river?"

"It must have been Stara Sidea," mused Dolon. "Just as Stara Bron was built to defend the Holy Flame, the temple of the balewalkers supposedly guards the mortal shores of the Lyrikon, the river that carries the Serpent's power. Still, I'm surprised you saw anything. According to all the contemporary accounts, the House of Dusk was destroyed utterly during the cataclysm. Of course, some say the Ember King slew them all and toppled their temple, and others claim it collapsed in one of the earth-rendings, and still others say the balewalkers all perished with the god they had bound themselves to." Dolon shook his head regretfully. "A shame. They were our allies, once. Our mirror order, patrolling the labyrinth itself to ensure that no evil escaped."

The details slid through Sephre's mind, but she seized on just one. "Can we open the door? Can I follow them?"

"I've no idea," said Dolon. He gave her a wan smile. "I'm afraid there's no manual in the archives on opening portals to the underworld. And there are . . . other difficulties." He glanced significantly toward the door.

Sephre ground her teeth. She could risk it. Knock down the two soldiers, if she was lucky. Run for the Hall of Doors. But with no way to open the portal, she'd likely just get trapped there. There must be another way. "Do you know where Stara Sidea is?"

"No." Dolon shook his head regretfully.

Sephre straightened her shoulders. "That's fine. I think I know someone who does." So long as she could find him before Ichos did. Or hope that he found her, as he'd threatened. But either way, she had to leave Stara Bron. And for that, she was going to need help.

"Tell me what you need," said Dolon, so simply and earnestly that Sephre's eyes prickled. "You're not alone," he went on. "You still have siblings here. Not just me. Abas. Vasil. Even Beroe, in her own way."

Sephre snorted, swallowing hard to clear the lump from her throat. "Right. Except that her own way involves burning away my memories to save my soul. But . . . thank you." She reached out, gripping Dolon's hand. It could work. If Dolon could distract the soldiers, she might be able to slip out, reach the stables. Be gone before they knew it.

A tread of boots in the corridor crushed her frail hope. When the door swung open, she counted six soldiers, all of them hard and grim-faced. "Come," one of them ordered crisply. "Your agia awaits."

===

With every step up the mountain, the possibilities for escape dwindled, and Sephre's desperation grew. Even in her prime and fully armed, she could never have stood for long against six armed opponents. Her only hope now was to convince Beroe to release her. Which was about as likely as convincing a fish to breathe air.

Still, she held that hope as an ember against despair. Until she reached the summit, and saw Lacheron. He was as nondescript as ever, fading into the stones beside Beroe, resplendent in her new robes of office. And yet the triumph blazing in his eyes was as bright as the blue flames in Beroe's.

He'd won. She understood that, with the last crumbling of her hopes, when she saw the slim, sheathed blade Beroe held before her. The new agia lifted her chin as the soldiers escorted Sephre to stand before her. "You see, Lord Lacheron. All will be well. The Phoenix has gifted us the tools we need to address this matter without further pain."

Lacheron stared at Sephre for a long moment, his expression strangely tense. Then he gave a short shake of his head. "Yes.

Perhaps that is for the best. So long as she is Embraced, the Ember King will be satisfied that she is no longer a threat."

"Then I will entrust you with this, to deliver to him." Beroe held out the dagger.

As Lacheron took the blade, a ripple of something—pain? hunger?—passed over his face. He tucked the weapon away, into the folds of his tunic, then nodded to Beroe, all calm civility again. "King Hierax will be pleased to know he has an ally here in Stara Bron. And I know he will be eager to show his thanks, should you accept his offer."

"What offer?" Sephre demanded, alarm shrilling through her.

"That is not your concern." Lacheron frowned at her, and she had that same sense that he was searching for something, that she was a mirror granting him only a dark and blurred reflection. "I pray that the flames of the Embrace grant you peace. Goodbye, daughter of flame."

He couldn't possibly mean it. He wanted this, damn him. If there was any trace of regret in his voice, it was because he'd lost his chance to be the one to murder her.

Beroe, meanwhile, had extended her hands, cupping blue flames in each. She looked radiant, resplendent, terrible. "Come, sister. Be free."

Sephre lurched back, panic beginning to dig claws into her, tearing at her muscles to run. The soldier farthest to the left wasn't properly braced. Could she knock him down? Run for the stairs? She forced calm into her voice. "No. Please, agia."

The tiniest flash of impatience wrinkled Beroe's brow. "You want this, sister. You told me yourself."

"Yes," Sephre admitted, sliding a single step to the left. "I did, once. But I can't. I need my memories. I need to go out there and rescue Timeus!"

"You should accept your mercy and be glad of it," Lacheron chided her. "The boy is dead. As you would be, if you were so foolish as to enter the labyrinth. No living thing can endure that foul place."

"The balewalkers did," Sephre countered, and saw the man flinch. Beroe remained unmoved, still a beatific vision of unrelenting redemption.

But Sephre didn't want redemption. She wanted to find Timeus. Not to make amends, not for absolution, but because it was the right thing. Let her own spirit be devoured, but she would not abandon that boy.

She bolted. Shoved her shoulder hard into the leftmost soldier, who gave a gratifying yelp as he toppled. Two more bounds, and she was halfway to the steps.

More hands grappled her. A fist slammed into her belly, leaving her gasping. They wrenched her back, spinning her to face Beroe.

"It will all be over soon, sister." The new agia's eyes burned full blue now. Her hands were wreathed in Phoenix-fire as she reached out to gently touch Sephre's cheek. "You are still an ashdancer. You swore to honor your agia. Trust me to do what is best for you. To save you from this corruption."

"I. Don't. Want. It." Sephre ground the words out. "And you can't Embrace me if I don't accept it. Please, Beroe. You're not stupid. You saw that codex. You trusted Halimede. Lacheron is *lying*."

For a moment, she thought the words had reached Beroe. The blue veil parted, and she glimpsed the woman's true, mortal eyes, brown and clever. Then the celestial flames roared back. And Sephre knew there was no hope. Whatever was in Beroe now was something more than mortal. And it wanted only to consume. To purify. To burn.

"You don't know what you're saying," said Beroe, inexorably. "I have to save you from yourself."

And then the blue flames were in Sephre's eyes. Dancing over her skin. Hungry, searching, yearning. A brilliance that stole away all shadow. There was no place to hide. No place for those old shames and pains to shelter. All of it burst into sharp relief. She screamed as heat flared through her.

No. Not now. She could not lose herself. She shoved the flames back, casting them away. *My name is Sephre. I murdered a city and betrayed a friend, but I will carry all that if it means I can save a boy's life. My name is Sephre, and I will not forget. Sephre. Sephre. Sephre.*

The grip of the flames loosened. She took the opening, lashing out. Kicking. Wrenching. Biting. Beroe screamed.

Blood. She tasted blood and ash. But she was still Sephre, and Sephre she would remain, until death took her. Which might be very soon, if she didn't get out of here. Beroe was no longer a figure of gentle release. She was wrath and fury. Sharp white teeth that bit off each word as if it were fresh meat.

"Keep your memories, then! Keep the taint!" the new agia spat. "But you will not despoil the flame!"

The fire flared higher, brighter. A whirling inferno that held no kindness, no gentleness. It clawed at her relentlessly. Sephre clung to the only thing she could. Herself.

There was a rushing, like the indrawn breath of a great beast. Then, nothing. She was still chanting her own name as she fell to the stones, shivering and gasping. Her teeth chattered. "S-Sephre. I'm Sephre."

"Yes," said Beroe, her voice cool, tinged with regret. "Sephre. *Only* Sephre."

Sephre couldn't make sense of the words. She lifted her hands. Her palms were cold. Her entire body was so cold, so cold.

Something gold glimmered in Beroe's cupped hands. A ball of soft yellow flame.

Understanding howled through Sephre then. *Her* flame. Beroe had taken it. Even now, the agia was turning, holding the handful to the split stone, feeding the yellow sparks back to their source.

When Sephre had first come to Stara Bron, she had overheard two of her fellow novices gossiping about a red brother who had left the order three months prior. Apparently a soothsayer had named him the reborn heir to a powerful cloth merchant. The merchant had given a large donation to Stara Bron, and the red brother had given up his flame in order to accept his new role. But he had done so willingly.

Don't, she ordered herself. She couldn't stop to mourn. She had to go. *Timeus*.

Lacheron was frowning. "Agia, she must not be allowed to—"

Sephre stopped paying attention. All that mattered now was escape. She spun, kicking out, catching one man in the knee. Slammed a fist into the neck of the woman beside him. Then threw herself toward the stairs.

"Stop!" shouted Beroe.

Sephre did not stop. She pelted down the steps, ignoring the throbbing of her head, the ice in her chest. A bolt of blue flame exploded against the stones beside her. She ducked, and ran on. If she could just reach the ridge below, she could cut across the mountainside. It would be a rough scrabble, likely too rough for Beroe, especially if she meant to keep her new robes pristine.

There. The last turn. Just a few more steps.

Pain exploded across her shoulder. Blue sparks danced in her eyes. Her next breath was like sucking down a storm, lightning hammering her chest. She smelled burning hair. Burning flesh.

Then she was falling, slamming into the stones. The world stuttered, shadows grasping at her vision.

Death. This was death. She thought that naming it might make her less terrified, but no. She was trembling. She'd always thought she would meet her death bravely. *Fates. Forgive me, Timeus*.

She could beg it of him. Not the others. But Timeus, at least, she had tried to save.

Darkness fell over her. This was it, then.

Hands grasped her arms. The shadow shifted, becoming a man. "Not so fast," he said. "You've still got something I need, sister."

That voice! Sephre blinked, her vision still bleary.

"Did you miss me?" Nilos stood over her, his green eyes wickedly bright.

She couldn't work her lips, not even to curse him. He gave her a wry smile. "I told you we'd meet again. We've much to discuss, you and I." He crouched, hefting her into his arms. The movement set off a spiderweb of pain. Her shriek came out a tormented croak. "Shh."

Was he really trying to *shush* her? She tried to glare at him, but the shadows returned, swarming over her vision. Her body went limp, and darkness took her.

CHAPTER 23

YENERIS

"Well?" asked Sinoe. "Do I look like a dutiful daughter about to visit her stolen corpse-mother?" The princess spun round in the center of her dressing chamber, setting the long pleats of her gown swirling like wisps of clouds around the dark eye of a storm. Her hair hung long and loose at the back, the curls pulled out into rippling waves, glossy and dark. Even the bright slants of late afternoon sunlight found no hidden sparks of red, thanks to the oakleaf treatment her handmaids had applied earlier, in preparation for this visit.

She looked beautiful, as usual, but Yeneris couldn't say that. There was too much between them. If they had been born into other lives, maybe they could have been friends. Or lovers. But not in this life. That was clear.

When Yeneris was six, she had told her mother she was going to become a dustspinner. They'd just visited the Scarab's Grotto, to lay flowered garlands at the kore's shrine. Her fingers smelled of hyacinth, her eyes peeled wide to take everything in. The shaggy cavern above, dripping fingers of old stone that glimmered in the lamplight. The veins of silver in the stone walls, a finer and more fitting adornment for such a holy place than any tiled mosaic.

But even more impressive to her child self had been the woman standing guard. Strong and sturdy, as if she might have been carved from the stone herself, clad in an iridescent habit the exact blackish-blue of a scarab's wing and armed with a glossy black blade. The dustspinner was everything Yeneris dreamed of being: beautiful, powerful, and heroic.

HOUSE OF DUSK 253

To her credit, her mother hadn't laughed when Yeneris declared her intention. She had always taken Yeneris's dreams seriously. *I think you would make a fine dustspinner, Ris,* she said. *But it's a hard path. And it requires sacrifice. You would need to travel away, far to the south, to be trained in the House of Midnight.*

That had given her some pause. *Could you come with me?*

Her mother shook her head. *No. I'm sorry, love.* And a shadow had passed over her face. A rare thing. Her mother was a great one for laughter, for smiles and jokes. Even when she spoke of Yeneris's father, who had gone to rejoin the kos before Yeneris had even been born, she smiled.

What's wrong? Yeneris asked, shaken by this rare glimpse of sorrow. *I don't need to go. I can stay.*

Her mother slipped an arm around her shoulders then, tucking Yeneris close. *No, love, that's not it. I want you to go out into the world and make a life for yourself. It's only . . .* She laughed ruefully. *I wanted to be a dustspinner, too. When I was just a little older than you. I even began the training. But I had to stop.*

Why?

Because your grandmama got sick, and it was more important for me to come home to take care of her. Sometimes the world is like that, love. We can't always get what we want. We have to choose one path, and give up another.

Yeneris had nodded dutifully, but secretly she resented the idea that the world might force such a choice. Surely her mother could still have pursued her dream. She could go now. They could go together.

But they hadn't. And in time, in sorrow, Yeneris understood better. Some dreams, some desires, had to be set aside for the sake of other callings.

"Do you want your amber earrings?" Yeneris asked, fishing the trinkets from one of the bowls of other ornaments set out along the nearby table.

Pain flashed across Sinoe's face. "No. Those were a gift from my mother. If Father sees me wearing them, he'll suspect something.

You should wear them. They'll bring out those pretty glints of gold in your eyes."

Yeneris hadn't realized that Sinoe was paying such close attention to her eyes. Heat fluttered up her throat, over her cheeks. She set the earrings back into the bowl resolutely. "I'm sorry about Tami," she said, chasing away the warmth with a dose of cold, brisk guilt. "But your mother will know the truth, won't she?"

Sinoe's lips pressed to a thin line. "I had to do it. Father's more than happy to have me spend time with my beloved 'true mother' now. This is our chance." Her gaze transfixed Yeneris. "You want to do a scrying on the bones, don't you?"

"Yes."

"Then this is the way." She swept past, heading for the outer room, the door to the hallway. Yeneris followed, pinning her feelings very firmly in place. *Do the job. This is why you're here.*

She brushed a hand over the lump at her waist, where she still had the parcel from Hura—or rather, former queen Kizare—tucked into her sash. She had opened it, earlier, while Sinoe was being bathed and having her hair dyed. The gift was an amber hairpin shaped like a bee, a match to the earrings. And a short note, a message of affection that seemed harmless enough.

It had taken Yeneris an hour to work out the hidden words. Bassaran and Helissoni were sister tongues, easier to move between. Scarthian was an entirely different beast, and Yeneris knew only a smattering of the language. Still, it was enough to wrangle the intent. *Come to me. Wear this, and my friends will show you the way.*

Confirmation of what she'd already suspected. Kizare was working through Hura to get Sinoe out of the palace.

Hura said he could help Yeneris, if she helped him. But if Sinoe vanished, Yeneris would lose her access to the kore. And quite possibly her own life. She was meant to be the princess's bodyguard, after all. Hierax was not a forgiving man. Briefly, she entertained a vision of fleeing with Sinoe, of the two of them riding together, her arms tight around the princess's waist, chasing the winds to the far, free horizon. But that was not the path she had chosen.

So she would keep the gift and the message to herself, at least until after the visit to the south wing. This could be exactly the chance she had been waiting for.

===

Yeneris braced herself as she followed Sinoe into the queen's receiving room. The room itself was inoffensive—pleasing, even. Less garish than some of the other chambers she'd seen in the palace. The walls were a mellow gold, painted with vines dripping pendulous clusters of dusky violet grapes. The furnishings were exquisite: couches carved of some dark wood with an almost purplish grain, silk pillows, a scattering of low tables inlaid with ivory. A beautiful silver tea service and a platter of small cakes decorated with gold leaf.

And there, in the midst of it all, sat the bones of the kore.

What did the servants think? Yeneris glanced toward the three women standing along the edge of the room, heads slightly bowed. Did they believe Hierax's claims? Did they think that the bones were their true queen? Or was this a joke to them?

She wasn't sure which answer she preferred. If they believed Hierax, at least they might have treated the bones reverently, as the kore deserved. It curdled her belly to think of the alternative. The secret jokes, the shared looks passed between them as they pinned that precious gauzy gown around the kore's bones and set those winking jewels on her bony fingers. The rolled eyes as they propped her into place on the finest couch.

Her mind swam with childhood memories of the grotto, the veins of silver, the stern resolve of the dustspinner with her scarab-black habit and obsidian blade. All lost now. The grotto had been defiled. Its guardians slaughtered.

"Thank you," Sinoe said, nodding to the servants. "You may leave us."

The princess waited until the door closed behind the women. Then she spoke, her voice loud enough that Yeneris knew it must be for the benefit of anyone listening. "Hello, Mother. It's lovely to see you. This looks marvelous. Are those pistachio cakes?"

She drew in a breath then, and turned to Yeneris. "All right. Go ahead."

"Go ahead?" Yeneris shook her head, confused.

"Go ahead and take your kore. We've got at least an hour before anyone will suspect anything. And if I know you, you've already plotted at least three different ways to get out of this room other than by that door."

Yeneris gaped. In fact, she'd been doing exactly that. This was her chance to fulfill her mission. To seize the stolen kore and return her home. And yet she stood frozen.

"What?" Sinoe asked. "*More* than three? If you're considering the sewers, I advise against it. They say there are crocodiles down there. It could be just a rumor, but why risk it?"

"I . . . I hadn't thought about the sewers." Her lips felt rough and stupid. The words weren't the right ones. She had to master this. Yeneris bit the inside of her cheek, a pinch of pain to center her. She turned her gaze to the kore. Remembered words spoken in a dark room. *Let the Scarab herself bear witness: I swear I will set the kore free.*

But she had sworn another vow, hadn't she? Unthinking, but sincere. *She'll be safe with me. I swear it by the Fates.* The words she'd spoken to Ichos whispered in her mind, along with the memory of the princess in her arms.

Sinoe stood tall, chin lifted, as if bracing herself for something terrible. "Goodbye, Yen."

We have to choose one path, and give up another. Her mother's words came back to her. But so too did her childhood defiance. There had to be another way. A path where she could keep both vows.

"No," Yeneris said. "Wait. Here." She tugged the parcel from her sash, thrusting it out. "Hura gave this to me. It's from your mother. They have a plan to get you out of here. To Scarthia. You'll be free."

A faint frown creased Sinoe's brow, but she took the gift, unwrapping it carefully. At the sight of the amber hairpin, her lips parted in a silent *oh*. She unfolded the note, reading it. She swallowed, then gave a small shake of her head.

"I can't just leave. I need to stop Lacheron. Whatever he's planning, it's something terrible. And he's using my prophecies to do it."

"All the more reason for you to leave, then," said Yeneris. "Please, Sinoe. I need to know—" Her throat clamped shut.

"To know what?" Sinoe's eyes seemed darker now, the pupils wide. Clouds had dimmed the light streaming through the windows.

"That you'll be all right." She winced, hearing how useless the words sounded.

"You don't have to worry about me, Yen," said Sinoe, softly. "You were never really my bodyguard, were you? You don't have to lie. I always knew it wasn't real. I was a means to an end."

Yeneris opened her mouth to agree. To admit that she had used the princess to reach the kore. That always and ever, that had been her only mission here. The only thing she cared about.

But for all her training, the one thing she couldn't do right now was lie. That vow hadn't been a stupid slip of the tongue. She had meant it. Even then.

"It *was* real," she said. "I want you to be safe, Sinoe. I want you to be happy. I want . . ." *Something I can't have.* "You're not what I expected."

Sinoe gave her a wan smile. "I'm much more beautiful in person, yes?"

Yes.

"You're clever and stubborn and wicked and brave," said Yeneris, before she could stop herself. "And you're one of the most generous people I've ever met. I'm not sure how you fit such an enormous heart into such a tiny person."

If she reached out now, she could brush the loose curl at Sinoe's temple. And Fates help her, she wanted to. That, and more. To trace the curve of Sinoe's cheek. To test the softness of her lips. To squeeze the space between them to nothing but heat and skin.

Sinoe stared back, eyes liquid, shimmering. "Yen, I—" She drew in a ragged breath. "Oh!" She lifted a hand to her cheek as a single tear slid free.

Yeneris was still staring stupidly at that lone jeweled droplet, her brain too slow to recognize what was happening, when the uncanny, inhuman voice of the Fates began to spill from Sinoe's lips.

"*Two maidens shall be bound, but only one shall walk free if the divided heart remains.*" Sinoe shuddered, her back arching, quivering in the grip of the prophecy. "*The key lies hidden. Hidden . . .*"

She gasped, twisting, as if caught in the crash and surge on an invisible sea. Yeneris thought of how Sinoe had described it earlier. A *single ewer trying to pour out an ocean.*

"Sinoe!" She seized the princess's hand. It was cold and stiff, the hand of a corpse. Her eyes were wide, unblinking, streaming tears, melting the kohl into dark rivulets.

"*Hidden behind the gate with no lock,*" she went on, "*opened only by the blood of the Ember King. Only . . .*" She gasped again, shoulders hunching, body curling in on herself.

"That's enough!" Yeneris pleaded. "Please, Sinoe. Stop. *Stop!*" The last word came out a shout, flung into the air, at the Fates themselves.

But the words rolled on. "*Only the right key can set the future free. And only then shall the old enemy fall.*"

Desperately, Yeneris cupped Sinoe's cheek, trying to turn the princess's face toward her. Her fingers slid, damp and crimson. Yeneris stared stupidly at them before the meaning struck her, turning fear into horror. Blood. Sinoe was weeping blood!

Oh no. No no no. And then she was fumbling for the pouch, the one she'd carried always, ever since her first day of service. The one that held Sinoe's elixir. The only thing that could stop the blood tears, before Sinoe wept herself into oblivion.

HOUSE OF DUSK 259

Yeneris cursed, fingers slipping on the seal. She drew one of her daggers, slashing it clear. With one hand, she tipped back Sinoe's head. With the other, she pressed the vial to her lips, dumping the contents past her chattering teeth.

Everything smelled of blood and honey. She held Sinoe tight as a promise as the woman shivered and moaned. Her secret dream, warped to this horrible nightmare.

Sinoe gave one final shudder, then went abruptly, horribly still. The empty vial cracked against the marble floor as Yeneris hugged the princess close, lowering her softly to the ground. *Please. Please be alive. Please don't take her.*

"Sinoe?"

Nothing. The barest of breaths. So slow, so shallow.

"Help." The word came out a croak. She coughed. "Help!" Stronger then. She heard the voices in the hall, a thud of heavy footsteps. "Please! Send for a physician."

The door crashed open, and suddenly the room was full of people. And yet Yeneris could not move. She could only kneel there, with Sinoe cradled in her arms, praying to the Fates that she might keep her vow.

═══

It had been nearly a full day, and Sinoe still hadn't woken. Yeneris watched from her position along the wall in the princess's chamber, as the physician pressed her fingers to Sinoe's wrist. "Her heart is strong. I believe the danger is past."

King Hierax let out a long breath. "Good. Thank you, doctor."

He sat hunched beside Sinoe's bed, his eyes never leaving his daughter's face. He'd burst in shortly after the princess had been carried to her bed, and had barely left her side, a solid rock amid the swirl of servants and handmaids and three different physicians. Yeneris could almost believe that he truly cared for her. And maybe he did. She supposed you could be an arrogant, self-important ass but still love your daughter. You could love someone, and still use them, still sacrifice their happiness for your own. An imperfect, incomplete love.

It was a bitter irony that she would feel any shred of kinship with Hierax. But hadn't she done the same? She cared for Sinoe—no sense denying it now—but she'd used her. Sinoe was laying there pale and still as a corpse because she had wanted to help Yeneris. Easy enough to excuse it, to convince herself that it was for the greater good, for Bassara, for the mission. Hierax probably had excuses too.

But if Yeneris truly cared only for her mission, she wouldn't even be here now. She'd have taken the kore and fled. Now that opportunity was gone. Probably forever. Even once Sinoe recovered—*please, please let her be well again*—Yeneris doubted there would be any more unsupervised visits to the south wing. In fact, she suspected Sinoe would be watched even more closely.

Yeneris held her breath, testing herself, feeling for the bite of regret or guilt for choosing Sinoe.

She felt none. Because everything she'd said to the woman was true. And she had to believe that if the kore's spirit still clung to her bones, that she would not want Yeneris to abandon Sinoe either. Mikat was another story, of course, but Mikat didn't need to know any of this. Well, likely she would hear rumors, but it would be easy enough to explain.

There was a way to save both the princess and the kore. Sinoe's own prophecy had said as much. *Two maidens shall be bound, but only one shall walk free if the divided heart remains.*

Yeneris was fairly certain the two maidens were the kore and the princess. Both were grasped tight in Hierax's hands, closely guarded treasures. But what did the Fates mean about a key and a gate with no lock? Was Hierax going to move the reliquary to some impregnable storehouse? Or was it Sinoe who would be locked away? She chewed the inside of her cheek, watching the doctor sorting through a box of medicines and wishing again that the Fates could make things a little more clear.

On the other hand, *only one shall walk free if the divided heart remains* was painfully clear. But Yeneris had chosen to stay. Was that enough? No, clearly not, given all the rest about keys and blood. Still, there was hope.

A moan drew her attention back to the bed. Sinoe's eyelids fluttered. "Fates. How much wine did I drink?"

Hierax leaned over her. "No wine, daughter. The gift of the Fates."

Sinoe's eyes opened fully at the sound of the king's voice. Her fingers spasmed, trying to push herself into a sitting position. "Father? What are—*oh*!" She twisted, her eyes darting around the room, before they found Yeneris and the wildness softened. Only for a heartbeat, but enough to make Yeneris straighten, for her throat to go suddenly dry.

Sinoe flopped back into her pillows. "I . . . I'm sorry, Father," she said. "I was so overcome, seeing the Faithful Maiden, knowing how painful it is for you—for her—to be divided as you are. But the Fates granted me the most beautiful vision."

Hierax blinked. His large hands curled slowly, as if he were seizing the hem of destiny. "What vision? Tell me."

Yeneris tensed, but Sinoe didn't even glance toward her now. Her expression was utterly serene, utterly innocent. "I saw the Faithful Maiden restored to life, and garbed in fine linen. A wedding veil, I think."

How had she ever thought Sinoe simple? Even now, groggy, ill-used, and battered, the princess was quick-witted enough to weave such a lie. It was exactly the sort of thing the king would believe. It was what he wanted. That was obvious in every eager line of his body. "You're certain? You saw her? Alive?"

"Standing at your side." Sinoe gave her father a wan smile. "You both looked so happy."

Hierax swallowed, his lips pressing tight for a moment. Then he reached out, taking Sinoe's hand. How easily he could crush her fingers. But he only gave a gentle squeeze, then leaned closer, pressing his lips to his daughter's forehead.

The physician and servants had withdrawn. Only Yeneris

remained close enough to see Sinoe's face. The spasm of emotions. Pride. Love. Sorrow. It occurred to Yeneris that if a flawed man was capable of love, he might also be loved in return. Even if that love was imperfect and wounded.

Voices sounded in the hallway. Yeneris tensed at the impatient rumble, a louder protest from one of the guards. "The princess is ill. The king does not wish to be disturbed. You can't—"

Yeneris shifted one hand to the hilt of the dagger hidden along her thigh just as the door to Sinoe's chamber burst open and Lacheron strode into the room.

CHAPTER 24

YENERIS

The Heron carried a crackling charge, like a storm cloud sweeping across the sky. It was unnerving. Before, he had been so slippery, fading into the walls, easily overlooked. He still wore the same simple stone-colored robes, still had the same paper-pale skin and colorless eyes. But somehow, now, he seemed taller. He moved with purpose and power.

It sent a chill down Yeneris's spine.

He paused, scanning the room, then gestured to the remaining servants and the physician. "Leave."

Yeneris jerked her gaze away, pretending not to see the command. She felt his eyes rest on her briefly, then shift away. She was unimportant. She let out a thin breath, watching him from the corner of her vision.

"Lacheron." Hierax stood. "What's wrong?" He glanced past the man, to the door, now shut behind him.

"Where is Ichos?" Sinoe demanded, her voice threading higher. "Is he—?"

"Your brother remained in the north," said Lacheron smoothly. "He hunts your enemies, sire. Others who bear the Serpent's mark. Who plot his return."

"Then why are you here?" Sinoe inched herself higher, scowling. "Why aren't you with him?"

Lacheron ignored the princess. He bowed deeply to Hierax, tugging something from the folds of his robe: a sheathed blade about as long as Yeneris's forearm. "My king. Letheko, the blade of oblivion, at long last restored to its rightful wielder."

The leather was old and dark, with no ornamentation, but Hierax accepted it as reverently as if it were forged of gold. He sucked in a breath, then pulled the blade free, holding it aloft.

The dagger was obsidian, deep as the darkness between the stars. It seemed to drink in the light of the room. Like the sheath, the blade itself was simple, with no etchings, no gems, a bare hilt bound with black leather.

"So. The ashdancers had it all along?" Hierax grimaced, snapping the blade back into the sheath.

"Yes. To their own detriment. If Agia Halimede had revealed it sooner, we might have been able to prevent the tragedy."

"What tragedy?"

"An attack. It seems that one of their number was corrupted by the Serpent. She summoned a host of skotoi to destroy her own temple. The other ashdancers defended themselves well and bravely, but several perished, including the agia."

Yeneris felt the world shift slightly. It seemed impossible. The ashdancers were holy warriors of the Phoenix. They carried the sacred spark of the god-beast within them. Surely if anyone could stand against an attack of ghouls, it was them. There must be more to the story. She was sure of that. The agia must have had good reason to keep the blade from Hierax. Yeneris would have liked to meet such a woman, someone willing to stand up to the king.

But now she was dead, and the blade was here, in the king's hands. Nothing suspicious about that. Yeneris wanted to ask how many skotoi there had been, but she dared not draw the Heron's attention. She was fairly certain she knew the answer already. Around four dozen.

"Fortunately Agia Beroe has taken charge of the temple," Lacheron continued, "and she stands ready and willing to do her part to ensure the Ember King's victory, by reuniting him with his Faithful Maiden at long last."

A sick feeling spun through Yeneris. It took all her strength to hold herself still, to keep her expression cool, especially when she felt Sinoe's eyes turn to her.

"That's . . . wonderful news," the princess said, brightly. "It's just as the Fates decreed. Is she here now?"

"No," said Lacheron, and Yeneris was finally able to suck in a breath. "The ashdancers needed time to tend their wounded and mourn their dead. But I expect Agia Beroe and her party will be here by the solstice. A fitting day for your wedding, sire."

Yeneris ground her teeth. The solstice was in five days. Five days to puzzle out Sinoe's vision and ensure that both she and the kore were free of this place, of these men and their dreams of glory.

Was it glory that Lacheron dreamed of? Hierax did, no doubt of that. It was in his every movement, the way he was constantly watching to see that those around him paid him heed, gave him the admiration and respect he thought he deserved.

The Heron, though. What *did* he want? It was still a mystery. And more and more, it was a mystery that had its teeth in her, in Sinoe, in all of them.

"Just as our Sibyl of Tears has foretold," said Hierax, nodding proudly at Sinoe. "And now I have the power I need to protect our people. This attack on Stara Bron only confirms our fears. The Serpent seeks to return, and his minions will lay down a carpet of blood and tears before him. But we will not allow him to bring another cataclysm to the world!"

It would have been a thrilling speech, if Yeneris believed one word of it. But it was all lies. True prophecy twisted to serve some other purpose. She watched Lacheron, and thought she caught the faintest hint of a smile twitching his lips.

"Indeed, my king."

"But Ichos is the one who's out there fighting them," Sinoe protested. "If he's hunting down these serpent mystics, why doesn't *he* have the fancy serpent-slaying dagger? Why is it here?"

"Because your brother is not the Ember King."

"So you'll just let him go off alone to fight your enemies?"

"Calm yourself, daughter," said the king, all traces of his former indulgent concern gone. "You don't want to upset yourself again."

"So it's true?" Lacheron turned to Sinoe. "I was informed that there was an incident in the Queen's Chamber. You were gifted a vision?"

"Yes," Sinoe replied brightly. "I saw my father united with the Faithful Maiden. She stepped from a pillar of flame, gold and silver in her bridal veil. It was beautiful."

"I'm sure it was." Lacheron's words were oddly clipped. He shifted his gaze to Yeneris so suddenly she startled. "You. You were with her?"

Yeneris coughed. "Yes, my lord. It's as the princess said."

"What *exactly* did she say?"

Fates. Calm. Calm. Surely he wouldn't expect her to remember that. She let a trace of shame into her voice. "I don't recall the exact words, sir. I'm sorry. It was so quick, and then the princess was weeping blood and I had to give her the tonic."

Lacheron frowned. Maybe she shouldn't have mentioned the blood tears. Then again, this was the Heron. He'd probably already heard a full report.

"Yes," said Sinoe. "It was very distressing. But I'm fine now. Only sorry to have caused such a fuss." She gave a light, brittle laugh.

It did nothing to soften Lacheron's expression. "You must take better care, princess. The gift of the Fates is a heavy burden. Even the strongest of men would find it a challenge to bear."

Oh? Not so great a challenge as my dagger in your throat, you miserable git. Yeneris caught herself just in time to keep from reaching for the blade tucked under her sleeve.

Sinoe, too, was clearly fighting for control. Her lips pressed tight and she was plucking at the coverlet. "Yes. Of course."

Lacheron turned to Hierax. "Perhaps it's time to consider the measures we spoke of, sire. For your daughter's safety."

"Measures? What measures?" Sinoe's gaze flashed briefly to Yeneris, then back again. "I'm fine, Father. It won't happen again."

"No." Hierax nodded to Lacheron. "It will not. How long will it take to prepare?"

"I took the liberty of stopping at my workshop on my way here," said Lacheron, drawing a pouch from his belt, tipping the contents into one hand.

At first Yeneris feared it was the amber hairpin from Kizare. But that was safely tucked back into her own sash along with the note promising Sinoe's escape. This was something else.

A golden band, etched with curling lines that drew her eyes like clouds, seeking a pattern that wasn't quite there. Sinoe looked as confused as Yeneris by the trinket. She looked to the king. "Father, what—" She yelped, trying to pull back as Lacheron began to slide the bracelet over her hand.

The king's heavy hand fell onto her shoulder, holding her. "It's for your own good. A protection to keep you safe."

There was a sharp click and Lacheron withdrew. Hierax released Sinoe's arm, and she stared at the bracelet. "Wh-what is it?" She touched the band, only to pull back with a sharp cry.

Yeneris started forward, to do what she had no idea, except that she would very much like to punch the king in the face. But Sinoe's warning look halted her.

"Since you cannot control your gift," said Hierax, "Lord Lacheron offered a way to control it for you. The bracelet will silence the voices of the Fates."

Sinoe's lips parted. She gave a strange, high laugh. "You think you can bind the voices of the Fates? You think it's your place to silence them?"

"Only temporarily," said Lacheron. "Your father may remove it when there is need." He twitched the folds of his robe, tugging free a slender amulet dangling from a fine chain. He held it out to the king. Yeneris had a brief glimpse of what looked like writing or possibly star signs painted onto the red clay, before Hierax's hand closed around it.

"How does it work?" the king asked, frowning at the thing.

"A simple resonant binding," said Lacheron. "Break the amulet, and the bracelet will open. I'll prepare another, so it's ready, should we have need of it."

Sorcery. Yeneris bit the inside of her cheek. What sort of power could do this? Nothing that came from the god-beasts. Was it true, then, that the Heron treated with the nameless powers of the abyss?

Clearly Hierax did not care. Or at least, not enough to reject the magics. He nodded, returning his attention to Sinoe. "You carry a sacred gift, daughter. We cannot allow you to squander it. Or bring yourself to harm."

Sinoe said nothing. She wrenched her gaze down, staring at the bracelet.

"The bracelet serves another useful purpose," offered Lacheron, his voice smooth as oil now. "It will allow us to find you, should any harm befall you. As much as we trust those who guard you—" his muddy gaze shifted to Yeneris briefly—"we must be wary of the danger. There are many who might seek to gain control of your visions, princess. Selfish folk, who want them only for their own power. Not like your father, who seeks only to protect not just Helisson but the entire world from an ancient evil."

"Of course." Sinoe's voice was a tiny thread, so defeated it nearly broke Yeneris's heart. "Of course, Lord Lacheron. You are wise. Thank you. Thank you, Father."

She flung her arms around the king then. He startled at the touch but didn't seem displeased. "Of course, daughter. You are the jewel of my—"

He broke off with a grunt of what sounded like pain.

"Oh!" Sinoe fluttered, pressing a hand to her hair, tugging at a long golden hairpin. "Father, I'm so sorry. I'm still in such a state! Did my hairpin get you?"

"I'm fine," said the king, sounding more irritated than upset.

He glanced toward Yeneris. "You, girl, see to your mistress. Make certain she doesn't impale herself next."

Yeneris darted forward, taking the pin from Sinoe, noting the glint of crimson at the tip as she folded it into her sleeve.

The king was already rising, moving to the door, with Lacheron in his wake. "Rest, daughter. We have much to do. Preparations for a royal wedding." Then he left.

Neither she nor Sinoe spoke for several long breaths after the door had closed.

"You didn't go," said Sinoe. There was something breathless in her tone. It almost sounded like she was insulted.

Yeneris hesitated. The thing between them was so new, so fragile. It felt as if the wrong word might shatter it. "Did you expect me to? Is that what the Fates told you?"

"No. I just thought . . ." Sinoe grimaced, giving a small shake of her head.

"I couldn't. Especially not after—" Now it was Yeneris's turn to grimace. "I'm sorry." She stared at the gold bangle on Sinoe's wrist. "If I hadn't asked you to take me to the kore, this wouldn't have happened." She reached out, not quite touching the thing. "Does it hurt?"

"Not as much as Lacheron is going to hurt once I rip out his tongue and feed it to the eagles," said Sinoe darkly.

A choked laugh wrenched from Yeneris. It left her slightly breathless. "I'm not leaving you alone, Sinoe. I'm going to rescue my kore. But she's not the only one I—" She caught herself. *Too much.* "She's not the only one who needs to be free," she finished instead.

Sinoe arched a brow, as if she somehow knew. Then she closed her eyes, resting her head back against the pillow. "So. There's two maidens who need to be freed. There's a key to free one of the maidens behind a gate that can be opened by the blood of the Ember King. And then the ancient enemy can be defeated, or something like that, yes?"

"Something like that." Yeneris cleared her throat, nodding to the bangle. "I think it's pretty clear which maiden the key will free. You're the sibyl, the future-teller. *Only the key can set the future free.* Lacheron said he was going to make another one of those amulets, so we just need to get into his workshop and find it, and then we can get that thing off you."

Sinoe wrinkled her brow. "Yes. We need to get the right key." She gave a small shake of her head, as if casting off an unwelcome thought. "And there's nothing to stop us, now that we have the blood of the Ember King."

Yeneris extracted the pin from her sleeve, turning it to catch the bloody glint of Hierax's blood. "That was quick thinking."

Sinoe sniffed. "I do have some skills aside from declaiming the words of the Fates. We should probably use it soon, though. I'm no sorceress, but I imagine the fresher the better."

Silence stretched between them again, but it felt warmer now. Even with everything that stood before them. Maybe because of everything that stood before them. They were truly allies now.

"I promise you, Yen, we will get your kore home. This wedding business, I know it's sacrilege, but it could be the chance you need. Knowing Father, he'll want a spectacle. He's not going to smuggle Agia Beroe into the south wing. He'll do it somewhere grand and public. Which means he'll need to have the bones there."

It made sense. It was clever thinking, on Sinoe's part. "What about you?" she asked, finally daring to drop onto the edge of the bed, though she made certain there was still space between them. "Once we get that key from the workshop—"

"This is my home," said Sinoe. "I'm not letting Lacheron have his way with it. I'm not letting him bind my voice and my power. I'm not his tool."

Yeneris drummed her fingers against the silken threads of the coverlet. "He's even more dangerous than I thought. The attack on Stara Bron—those must be the corpses he had sent north. And all the effort to bring the new agia here, just to restore the kore. Why?

HOUSE OF DUSK 271

Why does Lacheron care so much about the kore, when he knows that she's not even truly the Faithful Maiden? It can't be just to plump the king's pride." She shivered.

"And if he cared so much about the Serpent's return, he wouldn't have sent Ichos after that mystic alone," Sinoe said. "We need to find out what he's really up to. We need to see what's behind that gate."

CHAPTER 25

SEPHRE

Sound came first. Crackling flames, jumping her heart to a gallop. Light blazed somewhere to her left. She tried instinctively to roll away, only to groan in pain.

"Better not to move," said a voice. "The burns are still raw."

The dazzle resolved into a modest campfire. She lay a few feet from the flames, belly pressed into a woolen blanket, softening the lumps of stones beneath. Her body felt as if someone had broken off her limbs, then tried to knit them back together again using threadbare string and cheap glue. Even lying perfectly still, a deep ache throbbed across her right shoulder.

A chill, too. She was still wearing her habit, but there was something wrong with it. One shoulder was torn away, leaving her skin bare to the night.

And it *was* night. This was not the darkness trying to tug her back to oblivion. Gingerly, she turned her head, spying a stream of milky stars above. And closer, a man sitting cross-legged beside the fire, using a sanding stone to smooth the flanks of a small wooden horse.

Nilos tilted his head, eyes reflecting the flames, so that for one brief moment he looked like an ashdancer. Pain flared, deep in her chest this time. She moved her lips, her parched tongue, trying to speak. It came out a hiss, like dry grasses rattling in the wind.

He tucked the wooden horse away. Shifting closer, he slid one hand around her midsection, deftly avoiding the aching swaths of what must be a highly impressive burn. "Here."

She was too weak to pull away, could only grit her teeth as he helped her to sit, then pressed something cool to her lips. A clay cup. Water. She drank eagerly, too thirsty to mind the indignity of it, to think of anything but her body's needs.

But when the cup was empty, she had to face the rest of it. Why she was here. What Nilos wanted. She tensed, trying to turn her right wrist to look for the Serpent's mark, but the movement triggered another sickening wave of agony.

"I haven't taken it," said Nilos.

Sephre tried again, moving more gently this time. The truth of it was there on her skin. She let out a breath. "Why not? Do I need to be awake?"

His hand tensed on her waist. He was too close. She could smell him: sweat and incense and a sharp, herbal scent. She would've pulled away if she thought she could do so without falling over. Furies' tits, she'd forgotten how damned miserable burns could be.

"No. I've taken most of the others that way. Far easier to slip dreamfast into someone's drink than to explain the metaphysics of restoring a dead god." The corner of his mouth quirked wryly. "But it's harder, the older the mark. Easy enough to remove it from a newborn babe. More of a challenge with someone like you."

"I think you just called me old."

"It's no insult to be old. Especially considering the alternative."

Yarrow, she realized. That was what he smelled like. And sunbane. Together they made one of the best salves to treat burned flesh. He hadn't only rescued her. He'd treated her wounds.

"Is that what this is?" Some of her strength was returning now. She coiled it tight, used it to prop herself further upright, away from his hand. "You need to keep me alive long enough to finish your work?"

"It's not the only reason," he said, with an infuriating smile.

She refused to ask him to explain. It was what he wanted, no doubt. Instead, she scanned their surroundings. How far had he taken her from Stara Bron? Judging by the sky, she'd been unconscious for at least eight hours. Carrying her would have slowed Nilos down some, but she'd already seen how fast the man could move.

They were camped against the hillside, on a narrow shelf of rock scrubby with short pine and tanglekiss. To the west, the deeper darkness of a tall hill chewed the edge of the night sky. She recognized the outline, though it looked less like a sleeping lion from here. They were well south of Stara Bron. She saw no other lights against the hills. Villages were sparse in these parts. There might be no one else around for miles.

She fought the urge to curse, aware that Nilos was watching her keenly, for all that he made a show of tending to the pot bubbling over the small fire.

"Did anyone follow?" she asked, finally.

"No one from the temple," he said. "Though there's been a young man with a very fine sword at my back for the past three days, until I left him a false trail heading north."

"Prince Ichos," said Sephre. "Did it work?"

"For now." He bent over the pot, tipping the contents into two bowls. Returning to her side, he held one out. She hesitated only a moment before the growl of her belly forced her to take it. If he'd wanted to kill her, he'd had plenty of chances. She'd been utterly at his mercy. Sephre took a tentative sip. The soup was good, filling her with deceptive warmth.

"I could take your mark now," he said. "If you're willing."

"Willing?" She seized on the word like a dog after a bone.

He had his own bowl tilted up, so that she couldn't see his face, only the bob of his throat, swallowing. When he lowered it, his expression was inscrutable. "It's easier that way. And you'd be free. You could return to your temple and beg forgiveness. Go back to stifling yourself."

"*Stifling* myself?" She set down her bowl, half finished. "The holy flame is a blessing!"

He said nothing, only took another sip of the broth. She narrowed her eyes, understanding this feint. He was trying to draw her out. To trick her. "That's what you want, isn't it? For me to let you take the mark so you can go and bring back the Serpent."

"The world needs the Serpent," he said. "You see that now, don't you? The lies you've been told?"

He assumed too much. Yes, she had been lied to. But that didn't mean she was ready to embrace the return of the god of death. Her breath swept in and out, too fast. She fought to slow it, to regain control. Instinctively she reached for the holy flame, but that place inside her was cold and chill and clogged with ashes now.

Nilos was silent as a still pool. It made her feel loud and unseemly.

"I . . . I agree that there's more to the story." A deep breath. "You told me the Maiden came to Stara Bron. That she was Embraced. And you were right. I found her journal in the archives. She . . ." Her throat spasmed. She swallowed. Went on. "She called herself faithless. Said that she had betrayed someone. She seemed . . . full of regret."

She watched Nilos as she spoke. Saw the catch of his breath. The slight pinch of his lips.

"You seem surprised," she said. "Didn't you know all that?"

For a moment she thought he wouldn't answer. He seemed to be gathering something, deep inside. "I . . . wasn't certain. How she felt about what she'd done."

"What *did* she do?" Sephre asked. "Who did she betray?"

Silence.

"You know the truth," she accused him. "Just tell me."

"The truth." He huffed, giving a small shake of his head. "I'm not sure I can claim that. I don't have—" He bit down on whatever he was going to say—"I only have fragments. Shards of a shattered vase, pieced together. There are still gaps. It won't hold water."

"You know more than I do." Why was he hesitating? Not just uncertainty. "Are you afraid you'll lose your dashing aura of mystery and danger?"

That won her a small smile. "I did work rather hard to cultivate that. But you're right. You deserve answers. I'll tell you what I can."

He leaned back, staring into the fire. When he spoke again, his voice had the lilt of a storyteller. "Centuries ago, when the old empire ruled the Middle Sea, there was a terrible illness in the land. It ravaged the weak and the strong, the old and the young. And each of them the Serpent took, into his domain, to pass through the labyrinth and cleanse their souls of all mortal dross, so that they might be reborn in his sister's pure flame."

The flames of the campfire snapped. Sephre shivered, her chill still bone deep.

"In that time, a man called Heraklion ruled. He was, by all accounts, a good king. He wept to see his people suffer. He cast himself down in ashes, begging the Serpent not to claim any more innocents. Yet still his people died, and he could do nothing. Some began to call him the Ember King then, for he ruled a dying land."

"Why didn't the Serpent help?" Sephre asked.

"He did, in the only way he could, by keeping the skotoi in check, by easing the passage of the spirits that passed through his realm. Even the Serpent cannot alter the cycle of mortal life and death."

"But the Ember King didn't believe that?"

"Apparently not. He decided the only way to end the plague was to slay the Serpent. But it's no small thing to kill an immortal. To craft a suitable weapon, the Ember King sought out the most rare and alien of metals, taken from a forbidden crater far to the north, where it was said a star once fell. For a full month he labored, crafting the blade of oblivion, which you call Letheko. Infusing it with ancient magics of the abyss, binding it to his terrible purpose. But the Ember King knew the Serpent would never allow him close enough to strike the blow. He would have to send another in his place. Someone the Serpent would never suspect. A young woman."

Sephre shifted so sharply she nearly upended her bowl of soup.

"You're saying the *Maiden* is the one who slew the Serpent? Not Heraklion?"

Nilos prodded the fire, staring into the leaping sparks. "Yes."

"So the world nearly ended because the Serpent couldn't resist a pretty face?" She huffed, shaking her head. "The Maiden must really have been something. Let me guess. Was she beautiful as the dawn? Gentle as a dove and pure as cream?"

"No." Nilos's smile was crumpled, as if he'd left it wadded in a chest for too long. "She wasn't beautiful. And she belonged to the dusk, not the dawn."

"The House of Dusk?" Sephre frowned. "She was a balewalker?"

"A novice. Newly arrived from the royal city with a large dower. Not gentle, but fierce and wise and full of love for the world. And the Serpent was weary of his work. Weary of the pain, weary of the constant vigilance required to guard his realm, to keep the skotoi in check as the plague sent more and more spirits for them to feast on. She was his one solace."

A muscle in his cheek flickered. He was clenching his jaw. "She brought him songs and stories from the mortal world. She told him of sunset and stars and the infinite swell of the sea. The perfect sweetness of a ripe peach. The utter contentment of a long day of work and a warm fire at the end of it. She made him laugh. And she made him want something more."

"But it was all part of the Ember King's plan," said Sephre.

"Yes. The blade of oblivion would only work if the Serpent took mortal form. Knowing this, the Maiden begged him to come to her in the mortal world, in mortal flesh. Just one day. Even one hour."

He was silent so long that Sephre coughed. "And then?"

"Then the Serpent fell, his power shattered. That's all I remember."

"You *remember*?" Sephre repeated, warily.

There were all sorts of tricks that could supposedly awaken memories of past lives. Sephre had tried her fair share of them as a girl, staring into still pools, walking backward holding her breath. Hoping to catch a glimpse of herself doing great deeds, fighting alongside Breseus and Polypox, voyaging to the Pillars of Eternity. Or even something more mundane, but worthy: bringing healing and comfort as a physician, growing old with a large family she had nurtured and kept safe.

All it got her were damp tunics and several painful lumps on the back of her head. She searched Nilos's eyes. "You have the Serpent's memories?"

He nodded, something flitting across his face too fast for her to catch. "More with each mark I take."

"How many *have* you taken?"

"Not enough. Not all of them."

"So you don't remember why she went along with it? Did she know slaying the Serpent would cause the cataclysm?"

Nilos gave an eloquent shrug. "She had lost much. Suffered much. But she still loved the world. I don't think she knew the devastation she would cause. She believed the Ember King's lies."

"Which would explain why she fled from him, afterward. Why she took the Embrace. She regretted what she'd done."

His gaze shuttered.

"Do you remember her name?"

"No. Not yet."

Sephre shifted, trying to ease the pain chewing at her shoulder. "And what about the rest? Everything that happened after the Serpent was destroyed? How do you know that someone took the Serpent's place?"

"Most is rumors and whispers and bits of old histories pieced together into a ragged cloth. The skotoi themselves have revealed some of it."

"Like their new master."

"Yes."

"Did you know the Maiden brought Letheko to Stara Bron and made the agia swear to keep it hidden from the Ember King?"

Nilos sat straighter, jerking his green gaze back to her. "The dagger of unmaking is at Stara Bron?"

"It was. But Beroe gave it to Lacheron. He was planning to bring it back to Helissa City, to give it to Hierax. Though if he's so set on stopping the Serpent, you'd think he'd be trying to use it on you. He's the one who set the prince on your trail."

"Yes, an unfortunate complication." Nilos grimaced. "It's part of the reason I wasn't able to reach you sooner. I'm sorry for that." He frowned into the flames. "I should have been there."

She squeezed her eyes shut against the images that swam up. Obelia, crushed under a mountain of rotting flesh. Halimede, her chest shattered. Timeus, torn away. Vanishing into a strange and baleful land, in the grip of a demon.

Timeus was so young, sap-strong and overgrowing himself with eagerness. She could not fathom it, all that life trapped within the grimness of the labyrinth. Every story of the land of the dead spiraled through her skull like a flock of corpse crows. The luminous pools that slaked no thirst. The endless passages that taunted you with the promise of an escape that was always just beyond reach. The strange, spectral gleam of the duskflowers that bloomed only in the netherworld. She'd teased Abas about it, once. *I swear one day I'll go out there and find that you've managed to cultivate duskbloom.*

The joke felt sinister now.

"It's not your fault," she said roughly. "And I can still save Timeus. The skotoi took him. They said I could have him back, if I followed them. Into the labyrinth."

"You know it's a trap."

She rolled her eyes. "Of course it's a trap."

"But you're going anyway."

"Yes. But first I need to find a way into the labyrinth. Preferably one that doesn't involve dying. I heard there might be an entrance at Stara Sidea."

"There was." He winced as if the words were thorns. "But the House of Dusk was destroyed in the cataclysm. It's only ruins now."

"But you know where it is."

"Yes," he admitted.

So. That was it, then. This was her best option. A man who by his own admission was trying to restore the god of death, who already carried bits of divine memory and spirit. And yet, she could see no other way to reach Timeus.

"Take me there," she said. "Help me get my novice back, and—and I'll give you what you want." She held out her wrist, the black lines of the Serpent's mark standing out against her lighter skin.

His lips parted around a silent huff. Had she surprised him? Misgivings chased her, but she drove them back. Waited for him to speak.

"The ruins are to the south," he said. "It should take us no more than a few days."

Us. She drew in a breath, feeling the weight of it in her chest.

"So we go together," she said. "We . . . work together."

His smile winked at her, and for a heartbeat his teeth looked sharp as fangs. "We work together."

"Does that mean I can trust you now?" she asked. "You still haven't explained who you are. Who you were, before all this. How you ended up collecting the memories of a dead god. Did you grow up in a cult of serpent mystics?"

He didn't answer, only turned his face away, staring into the fire. A tiny thorn of guilt pricked at her. Still, she would not take the words back. She waited.

"Trust is too easily broken," he said. "You know my goal. I know yours. That will have to be enough for now."

He stood then, turning away. "You should sleep. You'll need your strength to reach Stara Sidea."

=====

Her burns were already substantially better by the next day. Instead of feeling like she was being flayed with a dull knife, it only felt as if hungry rodents were nibbling at her. She'd endured worse,

HOUSE OF DUSK 281

had marched on feet so raw her footprints were scarlet. Held her post through the night with an arrow in her shoulder, the shaft broken off because there was no time to seek a physician.

"Do you need to rest?"

She stumbled to a stop, blinking past the late-afternoon brightness to find Nilos halted on the path ahead. Concern crinkled the corners of his eyes. She almost believed it.

"I can keep going," she said, grimly.

The corner of his mouth quirked up. "I've no doubt you *can*. But that doesn't mean you *should*."

She huffed out a breath, aware that her legs were trembling, that some part of her had collapsed with relief just to have this small break, halting to argue. "Shouldn't you be encouraging me to keep going? More pain and suffering to feed the Serpent?"

"The Serpent wasn't the one that burned you."

She clamped her lips tight, trudging onward. Nilos joined her, keeping pace, radiating an infuriating aura of smugness.

They continued south, into softer, greener land. She'd spotted a few curls of smoke, heard the soft bells of goats. There were people here, somewhere.

"We're nearly there," said Nilos, nodding along the gray-green slope. "See?"

Sephre squinted ahead, but all she saw was a small stone-crafted shelter with thatched roof, so covered in lichen and moss it seemed just another large boulder.

"Stara Sidea is an old shepherd's shack?"

His bark of laughter surprised her. "No. It's another day by foot. But we can shelter here tonight. Your burns need tending. And sleep is the best physic."

That might be true, assuming she could in fact sleep. Last night she'd been so exhausted that sleep was deep and dreamless. Tonight would be different. And if the nightmares came, she had no holy flame to drive them back.

But the shelter was snug and warm, and Fates, she did need the rest. She didn't even have the heart to muster up a protest when

Nilos left her there, saying he had to fetch supplies. Supplies from where, she wondered. Did he know this place?

She wakened from a doze at the sound of footsteps, blinking groggily to find Nilos returned with an armful of blue and tan cloth. "New clothes," he said.

She frowned at the bundle, running a hand over the sleeve of her habit, picking at the yellow flames.

"Unless you'd prefer to walk around in charred rags?"

"No," she said, the word rough.

"Turn round," he told her. "I'll check the burns."

If she had longer arms she might have refused. Instead she did as he asked, trying not to flinch at his touch. He was gentle—probably gentler than she would be if their positions were reversed—but the bandages clung in places, and she couldn't help hissing as he removed them. Then again, at the numbing relief of the salve, the soft sweep of his fingers across her skin. She caught herself against the maddening and utterly ridiculous urge to lean into his touch.

Instead she stared ahead, biting her lip, searching for something to distract her.

There were carvings in the stones that formed the walls of the shelter. A few rough outlines of animals and people, but mostly words, some foul, others nonsensical. Then one she recognized.

Nilos. The name had been carved carefully into one of the smoothest rocks, just beside the doorway. And under it, more roughly: *is an ass-faced weasel.*

"Is that you?" she asked, nodding to the graffito.

A beat. Was he trying to concoct a lie?

"Yes."

She cocked her head, trying to see his face, but he shifted, bending closer to bind the fresh bandages across her burns. His breath brushed over the nape of her neck, making her skin prickle.

"Bold to tell the whole world how you really see yourself."

"My brother added that part." He sounded faintly irritated. Sephre hid her smile.

"So you have a brother? And . . . a home? Here?" She supposed even wandering serpent cultists came from somewhere. Still, it was a strange thought. Imagining Nilos as a boy.

More silence. There was a heaviness to it, a space that held pain or loss. "Cardis and I grew up in this village." He drew on a smile. "Not quite the secret serpent-mystic temple you were expecting?"

No, it wasn't. And it only seeded more questions. How had a boy from a village like this ended up on a quest to restore the Serpent? Then again, her own home wasn't dissimilar.

"Is your brother still here?"

"No." He moved more briskly now, securing the bandages. "How does it feel?"

Fine. What did it matter who Nilos was? Let him keep his secrets, so long as he took her to Stara Sidea and Timeus. She rolled her shoulders, cautiously at first, then with more confidence. There was still pain, but it was the dull tug of healing skin, not the raw agony of the previous day. "Better." Better than it should. She turned, frowning at him. "What exactly is in that salve? Aside from yarrow and sunbane?"

"Ah." He smiled, completely ignoring her question. "You're an herbalist."

"Which is how I know even yarrow and sunbane don't heal burns overnight."

"Then you still have something to learn."

"Your brother had it right," she told him sourly, but it only made him laugh.

CHAPTER 26

SEPHRE

Nilos was gone the next morning. She rolled up from her blanket, only biting her lip once at the ache of her healing skin. A quick survey of the shelter told her he must not be far. His pack was propped against the wall, and there was even a pot bubbling in the embers of the campfire, smelling of oats and honey. But the man himself was nowhere to be seen.

He'd left his sword beside her blanket. For her? In case the skotoi grew impatient of waiting and came hunting?

She stared at the weapon for a long moment. Bending, she brushed her fingers just above the leather-bound grip. It had been over nine years, but she still remembered the feel of a sword in her hand. The strength and surety of it. *False strength*, she reminded herself. *False surety*. Then drew her hand away. He'd probably just gone off into the scrubby woodland to piss.

She busied herself putting on the new clothing. It was unnerving, to look down and see no gray, only muted blue and warm brown. It made her feel displaced, unreal. The same feeling she remembered from those first weeks after the end of the war, missing the heaviness of her armor, the routine of her soldier's life.

Sephre glanced at the brightening horizon. Either Nilos had a bladder the size of the moon, or he was off on some other business. *Trust is too easily broken*, indeed.

She set off down the slope, toward the village.

It was the dog that led her to him. She heard the excited barking even before she reached the edge of the brushy woods. Then Nilos's voice, warmer than she'd ever heard it.

"Hush, Turtle. You're going to wake the village, silly girl. I know, I know, I'm glad to see you too. There you go. Good girl."

Sephre halted behind a screening hedge of thornflower, watching as Nilos hunkered down in the dust, rubbing the belly of the wiry, brindled hound writhing ecstatically at his feet.

Well. Hardly the dire secret meeting she'd feared. She watched, bemused, as Nilos continued to lavish the dog with attention, murmuring indulgently.

Then abruptly the hound—Turtle, for reasons Sephre could not fathom—rolled back onto her feet, cocking her head toward the nearest cottage. She gave a small, hopeful yip.

Nilos stood, suddenly tense. He backed away a single step. Someone was moving inside. Sephre heard the murmur of voices. Nilos spun on his heel then, darting away with the same speed she remembered from their fight. By the time the cottage door opened he was gone, fled up the slope to Sephre's left. No doubt heading back to their shelter.

She ought to go, too. But curiosity held her. Why had he come here? Clearly it was a familiar place, judging by the dog's reaction. He'd said his brother no longer lived here, but perhaps he had other family still?

An old man stepped out into the dawn, blinking owlishly. "Turtle? What's wrong, girl?"

The hound came to him, yipping, tail spiraling with feelings clearly too large to be contained by her small body. He rubbed her ears. "Was it a wild boar again? I hope you left it well alone. Eh? What's this?"

"Grandfather?" Another voice, high and sweet. A girl appeared from inside. "What is it?"

The old man had stooped to pluck something from the ground. Sephre leaned forward, trying to see.

The girl gave a squeal of delight as her grandfather held up the object: a small wooden horse. "Is it for me? Where did it come from?"

The old man let the girl take it from him, his attention shifting to the hillside. Sephre shrank low as his gaze skimmed over her hiding place.

"I . . ." He coughed, clearing his throat. When he spoke again, his voice was firm. "From the forest nymphs, no doubt. They must be trying to lure you away to join their revels."

"Ooh!" The girl looked delighted by this possibility.

"But a strong nymph needs a good breakfast," said the old man. "Back inside now. Go show your gran."

The girl giggled, disappearing back into the cottage. Her grandfather lingered another few heartbeats, still staring at the hillside. Then he, too, returned within. The door clattered shut. And Sephre crept away, her mind full of questions.

Nilos was tending the fire when she emerged from the woods near the shelter. He watched her over the pot of oats. "You followed me."

Just as well he'd guessed. It spared her having to use the frankly ridiculous story she'd come up with about getting lost trying to find a spot to relieve herself. "Who are they?"

"My parents." He dished porridge into a bowl for her.

She took it. "And the little girl?" The child looked nothing like Nilos, but perhaps she took after her mother. Though what had the old man said? *Go show your gran.* No mention of a mother.

A smile crept onto Nilos's face, like a relentless sun, rising even on a day of mourning. "My niece. Cardis's daughter. My parents took her in, after Cardis died."

So the brother was dead. She cleared her throat. "Why didn't you stay to see them?"

Nilos gave a small shake of his head. "It's too late for that. I've changed too much. They wouldn't know me."

The words were a puzzle. Changed how? "Your dog knew you."

"Turtle loves everyone." His expression had closed, snapping tight. Maybe *he* should be the one named turtle.

She stirred her oats. The steam brushed her cheeks. She waited until he hunkered down with his own bowl cupped in his hands. A tactical move. It might make him less likely to flee her next question.

"How did it start?" she asked.

He frowned at the porridge. "Well, in the beginning the world was tumult and void, and Chaos ruled all."

She rolled her eyes. "I meant collecting the marks."

"Ah." He took a spoonful of the oats. "Are you sure? Did you know that in the Bassaran tellings, Chaos births five children, not four? But the first is wicked and selfish, and devours his younger siblings rather than share creation with them. They escape— messily, I imagine—and cast the firstborn into the abyss for all eternity."

Sephre waited. His humor melted away, leaving only a tense jaw, eyes that fixed on the middle distance.

"About four years ago," he said. "My brother was living in Helissa. We had word he was sick. By the time I reached the city, he was already gone. His wife was ailing, too, and Gaia was only five, so I stood the tomb vigil alone. That's when it happened. When he . . . came back."

A cloud passed over the sun, the shadow making her shiver.

"At first I thought it was a miracle. Or a mistake. The physicians were wrong. He hadn't been dead, only asleep. He even knew my name. But it wasn't him." Nilos grimaced as he spoke, as if the words were rancid.

"A skotos," said Sephre.

"He said I was marked. He touched me, grabbed my arm, and—" Nilos paused, setting his bowl down. He tugged up his left sleeve to reveal a familiar seven-sided ring.

"And then?"

"And then he tried very hard to kill me. It was probably a good thing I didn't know how to fight back then." He gave a bitter laugh. "I couldn't think of anything better to do, except to toss my lamp in his face. Not quite as effective as the holy flame, but it works, in a pinch. He burned to ash. I killed him."

She managed to keep her voice steady. "It wasn't your brother."

"I know," said Nilos. "I know, but it doesn't . . ." He broke off, shaking his head.

Her heartbeat thrummed in her ears. She gripped her bowl, knuckles pale. "It doesn't make you feel any less guilty. I . . . understand."

He met her gaze for a long moment, then nodded.

"So, that was that," he said. "I really did collect stories, at first. Legends of the skotoi, of the Serpent. It was only later I learned how to find others like me. The first mark I took was from a little girl, in a fishing village on the southern coast. I was a blundering fool, and nearly got myself gutted and smoked by her family. But with each mark I understood more. I learned tricks to make it easier, like the dreamfast."

"But why you?" Sephre asked. "What made you so special?"

He laughed. "We all want to think that we're special, don't we? That the Fates chose us for something great?" He shook his head. "It's why so many soothsayers can make their living telling people that they're this or that hero reborn. But we're just mortals, Sephre. All we can do is to act based on what we know. What the world gives us. If I hadn't been so curious, if I hadn't started looking for answers, maybe none of this would have happened. Maybe someone else would be here in my place. Sometimes I wish . . ."

She held her tongue, waiting. But he swallowed whatever he'd been about to say, and continued, "There were others before me. I found records, most of them useless, but enough to scrape together an understanding of what the mark meant. There was a scribe in Tarkent accused of a series of murders, thirty years back, who claimed it was the work of demons and that she had been trying to save the victims by cleansing them of the Serpent's mark. She was executed," he added, grimly. "I knew that might be my fate, as well."

"But you didn't let it stop you. You became a traveling crusader. I ran away," she said, bleakly. And she'd once been so convinced he was a villain. "Do you know what I did? Before I came to Stara Bron?"

"Do you want to tell me?"

The question took her by surprise. That he was giving her a choice. Her past had never felt like a choice. "I poked my nose into your life," she countered. "Spied on your family."

He regarded her steadily. "Maybe you did run. I can't judge that. All I know is that you didn't stop caring. That you're here now. Because you refuse to abandon the boy with the big ears and all the questions."

"Timeus." She set down her bowl, gripping her knees instead. "I thought if the flame accepted me, if I could just be good enough, it would . . . make things right. But it never will. Saving Timeus won't balance some set of cosmic scales. It won't change the fact that I killed my best friend. That I helped destroy a city."

"No," agreed Nilos.

She flinched. What had she expected? That he would argue with her?

"But you're doing it anyway," said Nilos. "You could have let your agia burn this all away. Forgotten the pain."

Like the Maiden. Yet how could it be so wrong to remove pain and suffering?

She felt something building in her, an understanding, as if someone had been showing her bits and pieces of a horse—a hoof, a mane, an ear—but only now was she seeing how they formed a complete creature. Maybe there was a difference between the pains that were done *to* you and the ones you inflicted on yourself. The pain that was pure suffering, and the pain you could learn from.

Fates, if she went on like this, she might as well run off to the flying hills and become a sage. Introspection was all well and good, but unraveling her feelings wasn't going to save Timeus.

"When we first met, you told me that something—someone—had taken the place of the Serpent. That the skotoi had a new master. Could it be Hierax? The Ember King reborn?"

Nilos shook his head. "I don't know. The skotoi never speak of him by name. But I have my suspicions."

"Because of what you remember?"

"In part. But also the stories I gathered, even if most of them had been destroyed by those who wanted us to believe a different history."

"What sort of stories?" Sephre sat, holding her porridge, waiting.

"An old Scarthian man told me one of his clan legends. He called it the story of Death's Bride. It starts with a maiden leading her family's horses to their summer grazing grounds. The sky is just sinking into dusk when she comes upon a stranger—a man with emerald eyes."

He lifted his gaze from his bowl, his own green eyes holding hers. "The man had been injured by some wild creature. But the woman tended his wounds with healing herbs. And they fell in love and decided to marry."

"Just like that?" Sephre scoffed. "A few hours together and they're ready for that sort of commitment?"

"Well, I'm leaving out the parts about how attractive they both were. Apparently she had hair black as night, and lips as red as pomegranates. And you know it's very hard to resist a man with green eyes."

His lips quirked teasingly, and she was suddenly far too warm. And not just because of the bowl of hot porridge. *Have some dignity, woman.* She cleared her throat. "Not in my experience."

He pressed a hand to his chest, as if wounded, but continued on. "But there's a shadow upon their love. The stranger makes his bride promise that she'll tell no one about him. He tells her that if anyone discovers their love, he'll be forced to leave her forever. She tries to honor the promise, but she wants more than a handful of stolen, secret hours."

Nilos lowered his gaze then, stirring his cooling bowl of oats. "The maiden seeks out a witch, and begs for a way to ensure she and her green-eyed stranger can be together forever. The witch gives her a dagger, and tells the maiden that she need only spill a single drop of her lover's blood, and it will bind him to her, so that he can never leave her again."

"Something tells me that the witch was lying."

"The witch had guessed the true nature of the green-eyed stranger. When the maiden goes to her lover and spills that single drop of blood, it reveals his true form. He transforms into an enormous serpent, only his emerald-green eyes still holding any echo of the man she'd loved. The man she'd betrayed. Because of course the witch had placed a spell upon the dagger, to destroy the Serpent-god and steal his power. And so the Serpent dies, and the Maiden is left to wander the world, weeping for her folly and her loss."

Sephre leaned back. "But that can't be true. It doesn't match the other story you told me. What you actually remember."

"No. But I think it holds fragments of the truth."

Sephre combed through her own thoughts uneasily, wondering if any of them were alien. Tiny snippets of divinity. Perhaps her single shard of the Serpent's power wasn't enough. And maybe that was a good thing. What was it like, to carry the memories of a god?

Uncomfortable, to say the least, judging by the tightness around his lips, the shuttering of his eyes. A strange thing. She could almost see the man he would be, without their weight. A man who smiled generously, who laughed at the antics of a faithful hound. Who spent his lean grace in earnest labor, or spinning his partner through the breathless pulse of a village dance. In another life they might have danced together.

Stop staring. He already thinks far too highly of himself. "So you think that's why the Ember King sent the Maiden to slay the

Serpent," she said. "He wanted the Serpent's power for himself? Meaning that it's Hierax commanding the skotoi now?"

"I think it's possible."

"For what purpose, though?" She chewed her lip, thinking. "If Hierax could call upon an army of skotoi, why not send them to Bassara? And why does he even want the Maiden restored? If he remembers his own past, he must know she's not really his beloved. She's just some girl he used to get power. She's already served her purpose."

But Hierax wasn't the only one who used people like that. And maybe that was her answer. "Unless Hierax *isn't* the Ember King reborn?"

The words had felt like a joke inside her own mind. A ridiculous notion. But now that she had spoken them aloud, they felt heavy enough to crush her. She despised herself for what she had done in Hierax's service. But some small part of her had—not excused, not justified—*accepted* that he asked those terrible things of her because of who he was. Not just her king, but the great Heraklion reborn.

If that was a lie, did it make her own crimes worse? Fates, she wanted to throw up. To curl into a lump with a cloak over her head and sleep this all away.

Nilos gave her an inscrutable look. "Who, then?"

She swallowed the ugly lump in her throat. *Get it together. Haven't you wasted enough time on self-recrimination? You still have an enemy to fight. One that's been right in front of you this whole time.* Because of course it was him. It was the only answer that made sense. She took a breath, then spoke his name.

"Lacheron. The king's spymaster. He's the one who helped Hierax gain the throne. He's the one who commanded the final assault on Bassara. And he was there in Stara Bron during the attack. He wanted Halimede out of the way." Her voice roughened, trying to hold the enormity of what she was suggesting. "And now he has his own pet agia. Look at what she's already done for him. Given him the dagger. Tried to . . ."

Sephre trailed off, remembering the regretful look the man had given her, on the mountaintop. So strangely personal. "He wanted me Embraced. Why? Was it just to keep you from getting my mark?" Her hand strayed, covering the dark ring on her own wrist briefly. "Would the Embrace truly remove it?"

"I don't know," said Nilos. "Phoenix-flame burns away all that binds a spirit to mortal life. To prepare it to be reborn. But the mark isn't a mortal thing. It came from the Serpent. I'm not sure if it can be so easily removed."

So the Serpent's mark might have remained fixed to her soul. Stayed with her even if she was reborn. "It doesn't make sense. It almost felt like it was *personal*. Is it because I've got a piece of the Serpent's power?"

Nilos tapped his fingers together thoughtfully, and now his green eyes seemed to be looking everywhere but at Sephre. "Possibly. Especially given that . . ."

"That what?" she prompted, as he continued to avoid her gaze.

"Your fragment is . . . particularly potent."

"Why would that be, if none of us is special? Am I just unlucky? Or—" Fates, she felt like a fool to even say it. But what had that skotos said, about the shattered heart of a dead god? *Do you even know that you carry it? And why?* "Or is there a reason? Something I did?" She drew a breath, to steady herself. "Am I the Maiden reborn?"

That made Nilos look at her, finally. A single flash of those green eyes, before he veiled them. He stood, collecting the bowls. "Only you can discover what you are, Sephre."

"That wasn't a no."

"I don't know for certain what you carry. You might find answers in the labyrinth. Just . . . be wary of what memories you wake."

She glimpsed a slice of his expression as he started to step away. So grim. So heavy.

"Nilos?"

He halted, shoulders tensing. Did he know what she was going to ask? She hadn't known, herself, until just now.

"Have your eyes always been green?"

He drew in a breath. Released it. "No."

There was another question on her tongue, but she could not bring herself to ask it. And so he left her by the fire, and went to wash the bowls.

CHAPTER 27

YENERIS

The day was hot already, though the sun was only just creeping over the eastern wing of the palace. But the lily garden still held onto some of the night's coolness, in the damp breath of the pool and the shadows of the boxwood hedges. Yeneris found Mikat there, her feet sunk into the shallow mud, pulling out the reedy stems of intruding grasses and weeds from among the water lilies.

As always, she listened impassively to Yeneris's report, giving only a faint stir at the mention of the wedding.

"Five days," she said, after Yeneris finished. "No more than five days."

"Yes. They plan to hold the ceremony at the Temple of the Fourfold Gods, outside the palace walls. The kore will travel by palanquin. It could be the chance we've been waiting for. Can our people be ready to take her then?"

"We must be. The sibyl has spoken. This is our chance."

"So you believe her?" Yeneris had expected this to be harder. In fact, she and Sinoe had spent several hours the previous night plotting how to convince Mikat to go along with the plan. Of course, she still hadn't broached the subject of what would happen *after* they had reclaimed the kore. Mikat would expect Yeneris to leave the city, to come with her.

Mikat looked up, lancing her gaze into Yeneris. "I have no reason to doubt that the princess speaks for the Fates. Unless you think the prophecy she made before the kore was a pretense? Could it be a trick?"

"No." The blood tears had been horribly real. And the words

Sinoe spoke felt painfully true, still echoing inside her. *Only one shall walk free if the divided heart remains.* She still wasn't certain what it meant. She cared for Sinoe. And she cared for the kore, for Bassara. Of course she did. She was human; she would never love only one person, only one thing. The Fates would never ask a child to love only one of their parents. Maybe that was the point. She had thought she had to choose between them, but in staying, she'd chosen both. The kore *and* Sinoe. Though that was a decision she had *not* included in her report to Mikat.

Mikat bent over the water again, jerking sharply at one of the weeds. "Can she learn more? Either through prophecy, or from her father? What route they'll use to take the kore to the temple? The number of guards? What sort of pursuit we might expect?"

"With luck there won't be any pursuit, at least not for some time," said Yeneris. "The princess promised to hide the truth from her father for as long as possible. She said we might even be able to use a set of decoy bones."

"We have no wish to hide it." Mikat crushed a handful of slimy roots, tossing them into her basket. "Everyone must know. There can be no suggestion of deception. Let the Helissoni know the truth of their defeat. And let our people know the truth of our victory. They need that, as much as they need the kore. To know that we are not powerless."

The words chewed at Yeneris, poking at memories she had scuttled and sunk deep, long ago. Ironic, considering it was Mikat who had taught her to set them aside. *Focus on what you can do now. You grow stronger feasting on fresh meat than on bitter bones.*

But the memories were always there. Ready to entangle her in past pain, to drag her down into the depths of that terrible day. Waking to cruel silence. To her mother, cold as shadowed stone. She had thought it was a nightmare. Had run through the streets, calling and calling, her voice fracturing, until at last she could only gasp, a horrible mewling noise like a half-drowned kitten. It had been a bright blue day, but to Yeneris, it was night, and all the stars had been struck from the sky.

A hand gripped her shoulder. She blinked, finding Mikat standing beside her. Watching her. There was no judgment in the older woman's expression, only a weary sympathy.

It took Yeneris three long breaths to center herself, to tense and release each muscle. Mikat was right. Their people needed this. To know that they still had the will and the power to shape their future.

Mikat had returned to her weeding. "So then. Will your princess scry for us?"

"She can't. The Heron has bound her sight."

Mikat went briefly still, her fists full of streaming muddy roots. "Bound her how?"

"With some sorcery. A bracelet that blocks the voices of the Fates."

"Can it be removed?"

"Yes. He gave the king a sort of key. And he's crafting another. In his workshop." Yeneris bit the inside of her cheek. She hadn't expected Mikat to care. Had, in fact, thought the woman might think it a distraction, which was why she hadn't mentioned her plans to break into the workshop, to find out what lay behind that bronze gate.

"You can obtain it?" Mikat dumped her muddy handful into the basket, then stooped again, plunging her hands into the water. A few pinkish-pale fish darted away, riffling the water.

"We can try. Lacheron has a nightly appointment with the king, at the eighth hour."

Mikat's sharp gaze settled on her again. "We?" Her tone was carefully curious.

Yeneris swallowed her instinctive protest. She had nothing to hide. She was doing exactly what Mikat had asked of her. "Like I said, Sinoe wants to help. To make amends for how her prophecies have been misused. And . . ."

Mikat waited, seemingly as tranquil as the pool.

"And she's concerned that Lacheron is planning something more. Some . . . great evil. She believes that's what the Fates are warning about. If so, we could learn more about that as well. I know it's not my mission," she added quickly. "But it could still threaten our people. It could threaten the entire world."

She braced herself, already imagining Mikat's response. *The world is not our concern. Only the kore. Only Bassara.*

Instead, the woman nodded, looking thoughtful. "Very well. I trust you to keep yourself safe, Yeneris. You're not our only blade, but you are the one closest to the heart of our enemy. Remember that."

═══

Yeneris could hardly forget. She turned Mikat's warning over and over in her mind throughout the day. There was little else to occupy her. The physician had decreed that Sinoe should stay in bed, which meant that the chamber was fluttery with handmaidens fetching tea and cakes, opening and closing shutters, and dramatically reading a selection of the princess's favorite poetry.

It was a warning. But what sort? Simply a caution to be safe, to keep herself ready? Why the bit about her not being the *only* blade? That felt like something more. Not a threat, exactly, but . . .

Yeneris shook herself. She would spin herself dizzy with it. It was almost as bad as trying to unravel the words of the Fates. At least the part about Lacheron's workshop was fairly clear. *The key lies hidden behind the gate with no lock, opened only by the blood of the Ember King.* Thanks to Sinoe, they had that blood. The hairpin was tucked into Yeneris's belt pouch. And it was almost time to use it.

At the seventh hour, Sinoe began to complain of a headache, banishing the handmaidens from her chamber so that she could sleep.

"We won't have long." Sinoe bounced from the bed and began to strip off her sleeping robe. "I think Alcis suspects something. She'll be back here with one of her horrible headache tonics, just you see. Why are you staring at the wall, Yen? I know that color is hideous, but I hardly think it's a threat to my person."

"I—" Yeneris coughed—"You were dressing." Or rather, undressing. And revealing a considerable swath of bare flesh in the process. Skin softened by endless baths in milkroot and salt-of-dawn. Yeneris rubbed her own fingers together, feeling the calluses from her years of training. No doubt Sinoe's skin was silky as rose petals.

And *that* was why Yeneris was making such a fixed study of the far wall.

"Ah. Yes. I forgot how very proper you are. Don't worry, I'm quite decent now. At least on the outside."

Yeneris turned back resolutely, to find Sinoe now garbed in one of her more sensible gowns. Though in this case, "sensible" still meant that it was composed of a half-dozen layers of thinly pleated linen with whispery folds that clung to her like clouds veiling a crescent moon.

"Are you sure about this?" Yeneris asked. "You don't need to come with me."

"And let you have all the fun?" Sinoe grinned. "I may not be very useful in a fight, but you'll be glad I'm there if you get caught by the palace guard."

"I wasn't planning on getting caught."

Sinoe tilted her head. "Were you planning on being thwarted by a foxwing the other night?"

Yeneris sighed. It was a fair point. And . . . she wanted Sinoe with her.

"All right," she said. "Let's go see what's behind that gate."

=====

This time, Yeneris came prepared. The flask of oil wasn't as dramatic as an entire jar of naphtha, like she'd used at the necropolis, but she hoped it would be enough to drive back any ghouls lurking on the other side of the bronze gate. She'd also taken the precaution of coating her sword in emberwax. It wouldn't last long once ignited, but it was better than bare bronze. She'd also borrowed a torch from the lower storerooms.

"Here." She handed their small oil lamp to Sinoe, gesturing for her to stand to one side of the gate. The sulky flame did little to light the chamber, and did not penetrate the deeper darkness beyond the gate at all. But Yeneris saw no uncanny gleams, heard nothing but her own steady breaths.

Sword in one hand, hairpin in the other, Yeneris stood before the gate. She looked to Sinoe. "Ready?"

Sinoe's eyes were huge, but her lips firm. "Ready."

Gingerly, Yeneris extended the hairpin, brushing the crust of dried blood against one of the bronze bars.

Nothing happened.

She tested the bars, but they held firm.

"Maybe it needs to go in a particular spot?" suggested Sinoe. She held up the lamp, directing the frail beams over the gate.

Possible. Yeneris leaned closer, squinting at the bars. "I don't see any old blood."

She tried prodding the pin at several other spots, then gave up and slid it more quickly across the grill, filling the air with a dissonant chiming.

Still nothing. Yeneris blew out a breath in frustration. "It's not working. Maybe the blood is too old. Or we're misunderstanding the prophecy." She glowered at the pin. *Opened only by the blood of the Ember King.* There didn't seem to be any other reasonable interpretation. But who knew what was reasonable to the Fates. "Maybe it's talking about *your* blood? You're his daughter."

"Why would Lacheron seal his secret workshop with *my* blood? It's not as if he can stop by for a vial whenever he needs it. Also, *ugh*."

Yeneris stared at her, the words tugging at her. "You're right. It makes no sense to use your blood. *Or* your father's." She let out a low laugh as the truth finally tore free. "This isn't going to work. We've got the wrong blood."

Sinoe frowned. "What do you—"

"Shh!" Yeneris tensed, cocking one ear toward the outer door. "Someone's coming!"

Sinoe started toward the door, but Yeneris caught her arm as a key clattered. "We need to hide." She tugged Sinoe toward the desk that held the map. It was solid enough they might just escape notice, so long as whoever it was didn't stay long.

They ducked behind the heavy mahogany. Sinoe shuttered the lamp just as the outer door creaked open. Someone paced into the room. Then halted. Yeneris held her breath, her entire body tense and fluttering. It did not help that Sinoe was curled against her, shoulders pressing into Yeneris's chest. She could feel her soft, shallow breaths. And her hair, sweet with rosewater. Fates, what if he could smell it? Surely he must; it seemed to be everywhere, filling her nose, her mouth, her chest.

If they were discovered, she would fight. She would drive her sword into the man's lying throat and let him choke to death on his own blood.

A murmur. Words she couldn't make out, that might have been in another tongue for all she knew. Then a flare of strange, sickly light.

Sinoe trembled. Yeneris's free arm tucked around her. Their fingers met, lacing together. The bruised light cast strange shadows against the wall. Yeneris watched them, gripping the hilt of her sword. There was a faint grunt, the noise a person might make bumping his head. Or pricking his thumb. Then a grinding creak of metal.

Then footsteps, receding. The odd light had also fled.

Yeneris eased herself free of Sinoe, though their hands remained inextricably linked. Now that they had touched, it felt impossible to break apart fully. To deny either herself or the princess the comfort and steadiness of that bond. Cautiously, she craned her neck to glance over top of the desk. The room was empty. But the gate was open now, the passage oozing a heavy, purplish light. In the glow, Yeneris caught a single glimpse of a figure stalking away from them down the narrow passage.

"Lacheron," she whispered, helping Sinoe to her feet.

She shook her head, frowning. "How did he open the gate?"

Yeneris crept closer, taking the lamp, releasing a single thin bar of light to shine across the open gate until she found what she was looking for: a smear of fresh crimson blood.

"With blood," she said. "*His* blood. Your father isn't the Ember King reborn. Lacheron is."

CHAPTER 28

YENERIS

"You should go back," Yeneris whispered. They stood at the threshold of the open gate, confronted by the shadows of the corridor. "It's too dangerous."

"I'm not leaving you." Sinoe squared her shoulders, then gave Yeneris a teasing smile. "Besides, you're my bodyguard. You can't send me back to my room. What if I was attacked?"

"By what? Lady Alcis and her headache tonic?"

"You wouldn't say that if you'd ever tried it." Sinoe made a face.

"Does it taste worse than your half-rotted fish sauce?"

"It's not rotted, it's *fermented*. And it's a delicacy. And you should know by now that I'm not going to agree to run away, so why stand around wasting more time when we could be spying on the Ember King?" She spoke the title with a twist of bitterness, shaking her head. "Fates. *Fates*. Why? Why let Father believe it's him?"

Yeneris chewed the inside of her cheek. She'd been asking herself the same question. There were several possible answers. "When someone wants something desperately, it makes them easier to manipulate. And it's a sort of shield, too. Lacheron can stay in the shadows, doing what he wants. Whatever this is," she added, gesturing ahead.

There was just enough of the queasy light to see their path, to avoid bumping into the walls.

"Do you hear voices?" Sinoe asked, her voice barely a whisper.

Yeneris nodded grimly. She couldn't make them out, but one

sounded like Lacheron. The other was barely a whisper. Even so, it set a host of spiders crawling over her skin.

They edged further along the passage, the light brightening, until they reached the threshold of another chamber, larger than the outer workshop, but windowless, with low, oppressive ceilings. A handful of braziers provided a sullen veil of light. The air was heavy, thick with incense and a fouler scent beneath. It nearly made Yeneris gag. Sinoe made a face, pressing one of her silky sleeves to her nose.

Six waist-high stone plinths stood in neat rows, filling the center of the room. On three of them lay a still form wrapped in linen. Corpses. Presumably some of the six Melita had arranged to have delivered to Lacheron. But where were the other three?

Swallowing a swell of unease, Yeneris edged through the doorway. The plinths would be good cover, so long as the bodies didn't rise up and try to chew her face off. Warily, she slid into the shadow of the nearest stone table. Beneath the shroud she could just make out the suggestion of a nose, a chin. But no movement. She counted five breaths to be sure, then waved for Sinoe to join her.

The princess looked pale and ill and furious. "This isn't a workshop," she whispered. "It's a tomb."

Yeneris grimaced. "In a tomb the bodies would be treated with respect. These are . . . something else."

Lacheron spoke again, somewhere deeper in the chamber. He sounded frustrated, angry. "—no business luring her into the underworld. I told you I would take care of her! All you had to do was kill the agia."

Yeneris peered past the plinth, finding the Heron on the far side of the room. He stood with his back to them, some twenty feet away, speaking to a shrouded figure. Another of the stolen corpses. But this one was not silent or still. It shifted restlessly, pinpricks of purple light gleaming from its rotting, misshapen face.

A slithering whisper came from the dead body. From the ghoul that now inhabited it. Horror crawled over Yeneris's skin like a host of spiders.

She is too dangerous. You would be foolish to let her live. We will consume her utterly, and ensure she can never again betray you.

"It's not your place to question me," snapped Lacheron. "Not if you wish to remain free of your old master."

A ghost of rosewater tickled her nose. Sinoe leaned close, not speaking, but her eyes were wide dark pools in the shadowlight. She pointed toward the wall to their left. Yeneris followed the gesture, and saw a long worktable, lumpy with glassware and scrolls and other tools she did not recognize. Sinoe arched her brows, twisting her hand, as if turning a key in a lock.

The key. According to the Fates, the key was here, somewhere. And this was their best chance to claim it, while Lacheron was distracted. Yeneris nodded. Together, they crept over to the table.

Lacheron's ghoul spoke on. *She comes to us. And she brings the seeker with her. Once they pass into the labyrinth, they will not leave again.*

Who were they talking about? A woman. Maybe one of the ashdancers? It couldn't be the old agia. She was dead.

Yeneris netted her thoughts, tugging them back from the sea of speculation. The key was what mattered most. Freeing Sinoe from the Heron's cursed bangle. It must be here, somewhere.

The worktable was cluttered with oddities. Strange devices of metal and shimmering black stone, bundles of feathers, baskets of claws. A jar of liquid that spun sluggishly by unseen currents, gleaming blue. But nothing that looked remotely like the red clay amulet she'd seen Lacheron give to Hierax. Her pulse skittered, beating a warning. They'd need time to escape.

"How close is he?" Lacheron was saying. "How many has he managed to find?"

We have stolen those we could, came the corpse-voice. *But he has many. Already he changes. You must keep your promise, Ember King. Give us the abyssal blade. We will end him.*

"No. I have need of it. And I've given you more than enough already. You've feasted well. Grown strong."

A feast. Cold fury shook Yeneris, as she considered what that might be. A war? An entire city, fallen in the sweep of one day? *Later*, she told herself. She could be angry later. Right now she had a job to do.

Sinoe had moved down the table to the left. Yeneris continued her search to the right, running her fingers lightly over a collection of glass lenses set in brass, a heavy clear stone that seemed to hold a dragonfly at its heart. An old wooden box, beautifully inlaid with a pattern of leaping waves. There was a word—a name?—worked into the waves. She thought the first letter might be an M, but it was hard to be certain, as the script was old Imperial. It reminded her of the tilework that decorated the Blue Palace, inscribed with ancient invocations. Her mother had taken her there a handful of times when she was a girl, before the war. It wasn't a true palace any longer. Bassara had no king, only the Nine Elders. But it had once been a part of the old empire. No one knew exactly what the Blue Palace had been, before the cataclysm, only that it had clearly been treasured. She remembered running her hands up one of the old pillars, finding traces of gold still speckling the pale stone, outlining the ancient, impenetrable words.

Because the past was always with them. Bassara endured. Even when the earth had cracked open and devoured half of their island during the cataclysm, her ancestors had not abandoned their home. They had rebuilt. And they would do so again. The next expedition to Bassara would not fail, not with the kore's bones to protect them. It might be only a small settlement, at first. But it would grow. And ultimately create a safe haven for all Bassarans to return to.

She held that vision, briefly, sweetly. Herself, standing there in the Blue Palace, no longer a child but a woman grown. That was the future she was here to earn for herself, and for her people.

Yeneris slid the latch open, then gingerly tilted the lid. Her breath caught in surprise. Of all the things she might expect to find in the unholy workshop of an evil sorcerer, a child's doll was not remotely on the list. And yet here it was. A delicate, lovely thing.

And much loved, judging by the smudges of small fingers scattered across the smooth clay limbs and sweetly painted face.

Was it cursed? Or could it be some sort of weapon? Maybe there was a poisoned needle hidden under the doll's lovely embroidered tunic.

Or maybe it was exactly what it looked like. A beloved keepsake from three centuries ago.

For all that the Helissoni went on about being this or that famed person reborn, Yeneris had never truly credited the notion. No spirit returned to the world whole and intact like that, with full memory of some past life. It was a typical Helissoni view, of course. To think oneself so important, so unassailably independent from the rest of the world. Even if Lacheron carried some fragment of the spirit that had once belonged to Heraklion, he surely could not have his memories, let alone his keepsakes. Maybe the man had found the artifact? It might've been stored here, in Helissa City, in some old treasury or storehouse.

She recalled what Mikat had said. *The man has an uncanny ability to survive.* Maybe it was more than luck. But surely even a sorcerer could not extend his life for three full centuries.

The slithering voice of the skotos pierced her musings. The creature seemed to be growing angry. *We have done all you asked. We slew the blue one. We come here, into this decrepit form, to speak with you. And yet you plot in secret. You give the abyssal blade to the fool who believes himself king. What purpose does this serve?*

A very good question. Yeneris carefully closed the box, sealing away the doll. Something red winked at her from further along the table. Her heart jogged faster.

A half-dozen clay amulets were laid out on a waxed cloth. Yeneris snatched one up with trembling fingers. She turned, catching Sinoe's attention with a sharp wave. The princess joined her, breathless, eyes wide as she took in Yeneris's discovery.

Break the amulet, and the bracelet will open.

She didn't think. Her fingers simply moved, twisting the clay sharply. The crack echoed, too loud. Foolish. She was a fool. And yes, she couldn't regret it. Not if—

Sinoe lifted her wrist to display the golden bangle, still ruthlessly whole.

Yeneris's hopes plummeted. She studied the snapped bits of clay, only realizing now that they were unmarked. No star signs or sigils, only plain red clay. "He hasn't finished them," she whispered. "We'll have to try to come back later."

"Enough," Lacheron's voice rose again. "You have your orders. Do this, and you will have what you wish. The interlopers will rule you no longer. We will all be free. Now go. I have work to do."

A long, slow hiss spun out. Yeneris craned her neck, trying to see the ghoul, but all she could see now was Lacheron, standing alone. And a faint ghost of black smoke drifting to the floor. Having served its purpose, the ghoul had returned to the netherworld, destroying its temporary form. Yeneris ducked back down, gripping Sinoe's arm, holding her still, panic jolting through her veins. They'd delayed too long. Lacheron's steps approached from the far side of the room. Toward the door? Fates, she hoped so. She didn't relish being locked in here with a host of sleeping skotoi, but it was better than being caught.

"He's coming this way!" breathed Sinoe.

The princess was right. The steps were not moving toward the door. They were coming straight toward the worktable. Keeping hold of Sinoe's arm, Yeneris scuttled along the plinths, as if they were children playing catch-me-if-you-can. Except that getting caught would be deadly. For Yeneris, at least. Sinoe had value, as Hierax's daughter, and more so as a sibyl. Lacheron would not kill her. Probably.

Heart thrumming, Yeneris pulled Sinoe beside her just as Lacheron reached the worktable. She could see him standing there for a long moment. Heard the faintest rasp of an old latch. Then words, too low to make out.

More steps. He was pacing along the worktable. Yeneris sent a

HOUSE OF DUSK 309

plea to the Fates. Sinoe's hand slid into hers, gripping tight as the Heron passed by on the far side of the plinth where they hid.

Sinoe's grip spasmed. Yeneris turned, meaning to reassure the princess that she would keep her safe. But it wasn't fear that had gripped her fingers so tight. She pointed to Lacheron, who had paused beside one of the braziers, and made the key-turning gesture again.

Yeneris squinted. It was hard to see. Lacheron had done something to the brazier. More incense, maybe, to hide the stench of the corpses.

Then she saw what Sinoe had seen. The wink of something red, tucked into the Heron's sash. The key! But how could she possibly get it?

Yeneris rested a hand on the hilt of her favorite dagger. The one so sharp it could slice flesh like a ripe fig. Easy enough to slit the man's throat. Destroy the Ember King here and now, before he could do whatever horrible, blasphemous thing it was he planned with the kore's bones.

A breath, close beside her ear. "Wait. Look."

Easier said than done. Yeneris's eyes stung, tears blurring her vision. The smoke had thickened, thanks to whatever Lacheron had cast onto it. It reminded her of Sinoe's prophesying. Even more so when she realized that Lacheron stood close beside the brazier, arms spread, muttering. An invocation to the Fates? Was he praying?

Then a new voice spoke. It came from nowhere, and everywhere. It seemed to be inside Yeneris's skull, to fill it until there was no room for her own thoughts. And yet she could not fathom a single word. It was no language she knew, or even recognized. She looked to Sinoe, who shook her head.

Lacheron swayed slightly as the terrible voice droned on. Yeneris watched in fascinated horror as flames leapt from the brazier—strange sparks of dark purple radiance that seemed to suck her eyes into them, tiny windows into some other world. One of the sparks landed on Lacheron's wrist, flaring, singing his skin, and yet he did not even flinch.

Like Sinoe in the grip of prophecy, the man was in some sort of trance.

Yeneris knew what she had to do. "Stay here," she breathed to Sinoe. "I'm going to get the amulet."

Sinoe's expression pulled taut with worry. "He'll notice."

"He's in a trance," said Yeneris, praying she was right.

"He'll notice it's missing," the princess persisted. "Later."

It was a fair point, but Yeneris didn't see any other option. They needed that key. "Maybe he'll think he dropped it?"

"Could you swap this?" Sinoe held up one of the unfinished amulets. She must have taken it from the worktable. Clever woman. A flutter of warmth chased back the tension grinding Yeneris's belly as she took it.

"Yes."

Carefully, she crept forward. Every nerve flayed. She was a living scream clenched between sharp teeth. A teetering goblet above cruel stone. And every step brought her closer to the Ember King.

The smoke fell silent. Yeneris froze, poised to rabbit away. She was so close she saw the rise and fall of Lacheron's chest as he breathed, deep and slow. He spoke, and these words she understood.

"Yes, my lord. I have reclaimed your gift. And I know what to do with it now. I know how to break the cycle."

Yeneris sidled closer. She held the blank amulet lightly in her left hand, limbering the fingers of her right. She could do this. She'd lifted heavier purses from far more attentive marks. Though not recently. But as she lifted her hand, reaching for the slip of red clay, she froze.

There were two.

They looked identical, but then, she couldn't see more than the top inch. She glanced back to Sinoe. Found the princess frowning. Biting the side of her cheek, as if puzzling out a bit of one of her prophecies. Then she pointed to the right.

HOUSE OF DUSK 311

It made sense. The other was probably just another backup. And Yeneris only had one decoy. She drew in a steadying breath, breathing in calm and certainty. Then quickly, neatly, smoothly, she made the swap.

Lacheron shuddered. Yeneris grasped for the hilt of her dagger, had it half unsheathed before she realized the man was speaking again.

"Five days," he said. "Five days and it will be done. The interlopers will rule no more, and the world will be yours, as it was always meant to be."

The brazier began to pop and shudder, more and more of the strange purple embers flaring out. Yeneris backed away, but she was too slow. One of the sparks grazed the tip of her thumb.

A terrible roiling caught her, like being spun by the waves in a storm. Like when she was sick with the flux back in the camps, nausea turning her inside out, making her feel as if her body belonged to someone else, to another world with different rules. She was lost.

Until cool slim fingers wrapped her own, steadying her against the maelstrom. A breath of jasmine drove back the smoke. Sinoe's shoulder lodged under her arm, and together they scrambled away, out of the chamber, away from the Ember King and his nameless master.

===

"Are you all right?" Sinoe still hadn't released her grip on Yeneris's hand, though they were well away from Lacheron's workshop of horrors by then, safe in the dim sweetness of the rose garden.

"I'm fine." Yeneris tugged her fingers free. She didn't want to, but the tip of her thumb still throbbed. When she turned her hand to catch the moonlight, though, she saw no injury, not even a bruise. Which was almost worse. "What was that?"

Sinoe shuddered. "Something I never want to see again. Fates weep. And I thought the talking corpse was bad." She halted in the shadow of one of the painted statues standing guard over the flowers. The bright colors were muted in the darkness, making it hard to identify the figure. Probably Breseus, though. Half the statues in Helisson were Breseus.

And yet the most heroic person she knew was standing before her. No statue, but a living, breathing woman. Having survived the last hours of fear and horror, something in Yeneris surged up, hungry for life. For something pure and brave and vivid. She tucked her hands behind her back before she did anything foolish. Clearing her throat, she said, "Thank you. I'm—I'm glad you came with me."

Sinoe laughed. "Me? Honestly, I was just trying my best not to shriek and wail. You were the living shadow. And so quick and clever with your hands. It's very impressive."

Yeneris flushed. This was verging a bit too close to some of her more interesting dreams. She cleared her throat, thrusting the clay amulet at Sinoe. "Here. Let's see if it works."

The princess took the amulet, her expression thoughtful. Then she shook her head. "I think we should wait. It's not as if I need to do a scrying this very instant. Lacheron said they can use the bracelet to find me. For all we know, he might be able to tell if it's removed."

"But . . . it hurts you." Sinoe had tried to hide it, but Yeneris had seen her chafing at the wrist, seen the pinch of pain on her brow, even if she smoothed it away a moment later.

"I can bear it. I'm stronger than I look," said Sinoe, grinning immodestly.

It was true. The princess might look as if she were made of thistledown and poetry, but she was stronger than that. A sudden memory invaded Yeneris's thoughts. Her mother, smiling at her, as they knelt in the soft earth beside her father's tree in the eternal garden, one of the fruits open between them, spilling the red-jeweled seeds. *Look how strong it grows, Ris. Just like your father. Strong and sweet.* She'd broken the seeds between her teeth, and the tart juice had run down her throat, and she had known that was what she wanted, too. What she would dream of. Someone strong and sweet, with deep roots and dusky secrets. A lioness.

"Oh, really?" purred Sinoe. "A lioness. I like that."

Had she said that aloud? Fates take her. She started to retreat, but Sinoe caught her hand, threading their fingers together as she had before. And just as before, it set the universe in its proper place, set every star ablaze.

Yeneris sucked in a breath of the night air, but it was full of roses, and there was a drumbeat of longing in her chest.

And then, abruptly, a very different drumbeat. Alarm.

"Someone's coming!" she hissed. The steps were faint, but clear. Approaching from the direction they'd just come. Could it be Lacheron? Had he discovered the missing amulet? Was he coming to reclaim it even now? Even if it was only one of the palace guards, they couldn't afford to be seen. It would raise too many questions.

"Come on," she said, "we need to—wait, what are you doing?"

Sinoe was pulling her sideways, behind the statue. Yeneris found herself pressed against the cold stone base, which only made her even more aware of the heat of her own body. "I thought you said you were going to defend me if we ran into guards?" she whispered.

"I am. Shush, or they'll think we're up to no good."

"We're hiding in the shadows in the garden in the middle of the night," Yeneris pointed out. "Of course they'll think we're up to no good."

"Yes. But not the kind that gets us dragged in front of my father."

Sinoe pressed a hand to her shoulder, a fairly pointless gesture if she was trying to keep Yeneris from moving. But then Sinoe's eyes met hers, and Yeneris knew she could never move again, that she would turn herself to stone, and endure a thousand thousand years, anything not to break this spell.

Yeneris didn't know if she moved first, or if Sinoe did. She hoped that they moved as one. That Sinoe was as eager as she was for this.

For the softness of the kiss, for the press of warmth in the shadows, for an answer to a question that had been beating in her chest ever since the first day she saw those ridiculous twee hummingbirds and heard Sinoe sighing over a book of poetry.

And now she had her answer. Sinoe's skin was silk and hot breath and something even sweeter that had no name. Yeneris's heart spread new wings, fledging with urgency.

For long, aching moments there was nothing but Sinoe.

And then, on the fringes of her awareness, a slight noise—a grunt? A gasp?

Yeneris pulled away abruptly. Someone was walking away, continuing along the path.

"It's fine," Sinoe said, sounding breathless. "It wasn't a guard. Only one of the gardeners. Though what there is to do this late at night, I've no idea. Watering moonflowers? Chasing away night-catchers?"

Only a gardener.

But it wasn't fine.

Because Yeneris had seen the gardener's face, just as she slipped away. Mikat had paused to look back. Had no doubt wanted Yeneris to see. To know that she was being watched. That she was not the only blade hidden here in the palace of her enemies.

CHAPTER 29

SEPHRE

They reached Stara Sidea at dusk. The day's journey had been long, but not unpleasant, aside from the painful detour Sephre insisted they take along a bramble-choked riverbed, after spotting what might have been a skotos—or a bloodthirsty prince—on the trail behind them. Nilos had taken it well, had even laughed when it turned out to be nothing but a hungry goat. There had been no more talk of the past or future. Instead, she and Nilos debated the relative merits of catmint and spearmint, and whether the clouds in the west meant rain. It should have been punishingly dull, but Sephre welcomed it. Nilos was a surprisingly comfortable companion. He reminded her of Abas. Giving her space to be who she was, with no expectations.

She flattered herself that she might be offering Nilos a similar comfort. Back in the rain-drenched barn where they'd first met, there had been a sort of . . . distance . . . around him. A wall of clever words and that dark wool cloak drawn close. And why not? It was only now that she understood the risk he had taken, that day on the hilltop, telling her his truth. Challenging her to step outside her own understanding of the world.

And now she was here. Walking beside him. Teaching him one of Zander's favorite bawdy marching songs almost entirely for the pleasure of seeing him blush. Watching him scramble up a wild plum tree like a boy half his age, to harvest a bounty of dusky-purple fruit for them to share. He cut them for her, sweet, dripping slices of summer.

She almost regretted their arrival at the ruined temple. But she needed more than her own peace. She needed to rescue Timeus. She needed a way into the Labyrinth of Souls, and with luck the ruined temple of the House of Dusk would give her that.

Like Stara Bron, Stara Sidea had been carved into stone. But rather than being atop a mountain, it lay deep in a canyon of smooth red rock. Nilos led them into one of the narrow gorges, following the pebbled bed of a shallow river. High walls closed them in. Overhead, a narrow ribbon of sky glinted with stars. The only sounds were the eerie whispers of the wind over stone, and a faint skittering of falling stones.

She searched the heights above, but saw nothing. Probably just a rat, or a lizard.

Even so, her nerves thrummed, highly aware of just how easy it was to die trapped in a gorge, with nowhere to run. Was this where the skotoi planned to spring their trap? Nilos had said they were stronger within the labyrinth than without, but that didn't mean they wouldn't strike earlier, given a good opportunity.

She turned to tell him so. He was gone.

Sephre swore, imagining a hundred different ways he might be about to betray her. She was just reaching for a nice hefty rock, perfect for smashing traitorous ass-weasels over the head, when she heard his voice, muffled, coming from one of the vine-draped walls. "Sephre? Are you coming?"

The vines shifted, revealing Nilos peering out at her from a narrow archway cut into the stone. "Is everything all right?"

She glowered at him. "Oh, absolutely. I'm following a complete stranger into the ruin of an ancient temple dedicated to the god of death, and he decides it's a good idea to just *disappear without warning*." She dropped the rock. It clunked loudly, echoing from the high canyon walls.

Nilos tsked her. "I think we're well beyond 'complete strangers.' I did save your life."

"Because you need me," she bit back, though it was as much a reminder to herself as to him.

"Would you have told a complete stranger your secret recipe for bowel cleanser?"

All right. He had her there. But that was only because they'd seen a patch of broadleaf and she hadn't been able to help herself. It was nice to have someone to talk to about such things.

She stalked past him, through the archway. As the darkness swept over her, she lifted her hand to summon a flame. Then jerked it back down again, remembering. If Nilos noticed, he said nothing, but a moment later a spark flared, and he held up a copper lantern, spilling a golden glow over the passage.

They passed several small rooms that must have been sleeping chambers, judging by the bed frames and dusty heaps of cloth. People had lived here. Prayed here. Maybe there was even a garden. A workshop where some long-dead balewalker had dried herbs and brewed tinctures for her siblings' headaches. Homesickness twisted Sephre's chest, yearning for the simple beauty and peace of Stara Bron. For the people. For everything she'd taken for granted.

Eventually they came to a wider room, lit with a frail silver light filtering down from shafts in the ceiling. Three long tables filled it, set with bowls and platters and clay cups. Sephre peered into one and saw the dark, dried dregs of ancient wine. She suspected the platters had been full as well, before the mice had gotten to them.

"What happened to them?" She winced, her voice too loud in this forgotten place. "The balewalkers?"

"I suspect most died along with the Serpent." Nilos continued on, not looking at the tables, the empty benches. "Every balewalker carried a drop of the Serpent's venom, just as your ashdancers carry a spark of Phoenix-fire. And in the same way an ashdancer doesn't fear flames, a balewalker had no fear of poison. But when the Serpent was no more . . ."

She jogs along the street, chasing the wail. Surely she can save one life. But the cry cuts off, and she's alone, with only the dead bodies to see her weep.

She dragged in a long breath. Felt Nilos watching her. She gave him a dismissive half-wave before he could ask. Nothing to see here. "Which way now?"

He led them onward to a stair on the far end of the room that twisted downward in a tight spiral. "Most of the upper level collapsed during the cataclysm. But the lower levels are still passable. Mostly."

Mostly was right. Chunks of stone littered the steps. Dust clouded the air, raised by their descent. The lamplight seemed to be dimming, the deeper they traveled. And the occasional patter of falling rock sounded far too much like footsteps, sending prickles racing over Sephre's skin. Her knees didn't care for it either. But Furies take her if she slowed down now. They were close. She could feel it. The chill stones whispered with it. She could almost hear the trickle of ancient pools. Smell the funerary spice of a flower that bloomed only beneath the gray skies of the underworld.

The Labyrinth of Souls. Where spirits wandered in torment, until they found their way free and could be reborn into the world anew.

Zander had died ten years ago. Surely he wouldn't still be lingering. She'd never known anyone who lived his life with such relentless confidence, so few regrets. *I don't make mistakes,* he'd told her once. *I take exciting detours.* He didn't hold grudges. He loved freely. She'd never seen him afraid, until the end.

And what about Timeus? Was he afraid? Did he think himself abandoned? *I'm coming,* she thought fiercely. *Just hold on a little longer.*

At last the steps ended, spilling them out into a wide chamber. The lamplight glinted over a forest of stony teeth, damp and shimmering, rising from the floor. More fangs dripped from the uneven ceiling. This must be a natural cavern, older than the human-carved passages above.

A great pool filled the far end of the chamber. In the silence, Sephre heard the *plink, plink, plink* of falling droplets. Saw dark ripples chasing each other across the surface. She couldn't see the far side, only a vast dark mirror.

"What is this place?" she asked, the weight of the room pressing her voice to a whisper. Telling her she did not belong. That this was no place for anyone who wished to feel the sun on her skin again.

"The unwaking shore." Nilos halted in the soft, dark sand that edged the pool. "Those are the waters of the Lyrikon. The river that bounds the Labyrinth of Souls."

Sephre joined him, but when she would have bent to touch the water, he caught her, one arm clasping her waist, drawing her back. She had forgotten how strong he was. How uncannily quick. "Don't. The waters still carry the Serpent's venom. They're death to the living."

"The House of Dusk built their temple on top of a deadly lake?" She tried to make it a joke, to ignore the thrum of her pulse where his palm still pressed into her side.

"For the same reason the House of Dawn built their temple beneath a font of Phoenix-fire," he replied. "The balewalkers entered these waters as a trial, to prove themselves capable of carrying the Serpent's power. To bear witness to the pain of life, to protect and comfort the spirits that pass through the Labyrinth."

He released her. She scavenged her wits. Drew a breath to settle herself. "So how do we get across?"

Nilos pointed across the pool to a low shape Sephre had not noticed before. A shallow barge, floating about twenty feet from shore. "Does having a chunk of the Serpent's power give you the ability to move things with your mind?" she asked.

"Sadly, no." He gave her a brief smile. "But it does give me enough protection that I can enter the pool. For a short while, at least. In theory."

"And you think it's a good idea to test that theory now?"

"I don't see any other option. Just . . ." He suddenly looked deeply uncomfortable. "Would you turn around for a moment?"

Really? Fates, they weren't children. Sephre had seen at least a hundred naked men in her life, though granted a fair number of them had been dead at the time. Still, she did as he asked. She heard the clank of his belt and scabbard. A whisper of cloth. Then the splash of a body entering the water. She waited another few heartbeats before turning back.

He was waist deep by then, and still alive, so that was something. Sephre dug her fingers into her arms, hugging herself as she watched. He'd left the small lamp in the sand beside his sword. She considered picking it up, cupping it in her hands. It would be almost like holding the holy flame. She stared at the waters, thinking of what Nilos said. Remembered washing her hands after a long day working in the garden, the dirt worn into her skin. She could never get them completely clean. There was always a smudge, a bit of earth dug under her nails. Was that how the cycle of life and rebirth worked? You washed away the worst, and the rest of it just . . . stayed with you?

Reaching the barge, Nilos wrapped one arm through a rope that trailed from the side, then kicked away and began to tug it slowly back toward the shore. He moved cleanly, muscles shifting under amber skin, though she could only make out a few intriguing glimpses. Fates, it had been a long, *long* time.

It was with no small amount of regret that she turned her back to him as he began clambering back to shore. "I didn't take you for the shy sort," she said. "Or is it that you know you've got a spectacular body and don't want to tempt me into breaking my vows? Because you should know there's no expectation of celibacy at Stara Bron."

He made a choked noise. She wished she could see his face. He deserved it, after the way he'd taunted her ever since they'd met. "Are you all right?" she called. "Not collapsed and dying of poison?"

"I'm . . ." He coughed. "It's not either of those things. It's—" A pause. An indrawn breath—"Turn around, then."

He didn't sound embarrassed. He sounded afraid. Her humor

dimmed. She hadn't meant to torment the man, even if he did deserve it. She braced herself, uncertain what to expect. Then she turned.

He stood before her, almost as bare as a fresh-kindled flame. Sephre wasn't entirely sure whether she resented the breechclout or owed it a life debt. But it wasn't his sculpted thighs or his bare chest or the intriguing cut of the muscles at his hip that made her draw in a sharp breath.

It was the marks. Fates, there must be at least a hundred. Scattered across his chest, his thighs, his arms. Each a twin to the one on her own arm. A hundred fragments of the Serpent's power. When had his eyes turned green? At twenty? Fifty? She forced her gaze to his face. There was something achingly open there. No shadowed gaze, no inscrutable smile. She understood the gift he was giving her. Sharing this truth. Her chest clenched tight, and heat swarmed up her throat, her cheeks.

"Oh," she said, wincing inwardly at how foolish it sounded. "So. I guess this is why you can enter the water and I can't."

He actually smiled at that. "Yes."

"And . . . this is why you won't see your family?"

His smile vanished, and she cursed herself for it. But she needed to understand this.

He brushed a hand over his shaven scalp, sending a shower of droplets to the sand. "I . . . I still feel like myself. That's the problem. I don't know where I stop and where it begins. It's not as if there's a strange voice hissing inside me or anything like that. The last time I tried to visit, my mother cried because I hadn't eaten any of the almond cakes she'd baked. My favorite, apparently. But food doesn't taste the same, now."

"I'm sorry," she said, and meant it with every corner of her being. Then she cocked her head, curious. "Why didn't you want me to see the marks? Did you think I'd be frightened?"

That won her a faint smile. "I suppose. You're the first person who's seen them. I've been alone for . . . a long time now."

Yes. She knew something of that. She took a step closer. There were still droplets of poison beading his skin, but they would be dry soon. And she didn't want him to think that she was afraid of him. Even though a part of her was. Afraid of how much she'd come to appreciate his company in the past few days.

"I understand," she said, wanting to return his gift of trust. "Knowing people might see you as . . . tainted. If they knew the truth."

"Is that what you think?" He held himself still. Waiting.

"I only know who you are, now," she said. "And I like that person. That is, you're . . . a good companion. For traveling."

"For traveling," he echoed, but there was a trace of a smile on his lips now. "As are you."

She might have done something ridiculous, like reach out and touch his shoulder—a very fine shoulder, that she wouldn't have minded touching—but Nilos stepped to the side then, ducking to collect his abandoned tunic and sandals. "I should . . . We need to keep going."

"Er. Right. Yes." And she ought to stop ogling the poor man. Sephre wrenched herself back around and stared determinedly at the pattern of her own steps in the black sand. Listened as Nilos opened his satchel, a snap of cloth being shaken out.

And then another sound. A breath, sharply drawn. A thud that sent her heart galloping even after ten years. The sound of a body, falling to the ground.

Old instinct sent her diving for Nilos's sword. It took her a heartbeat to sweep it up from the sand. Another to pull it from the scabbard. Deep inside, something wailed. Was it truly so easy, to snatch up a sword again? To be ready to kill? Did the past ten years mean nothing?

It's not killing if it's a demon, she reminded herself. Spinning, she prepared to slash whatever skotos had come for them to tiny pieces. But it wasn't a demon from the underworld.

It was a man. Her fingers trembled. She tightened them.

Prince Ichos stood over the slumped body of Nilos, but his gaze was on her. His sword braced for her attack.

She risked a single glance to Nilos. No blood. And she thought she heard a groan. He was still alive, thank the Fates. She did not pause to interrogate the burst of relief that flared through her. The prince must be her focus now.

The boy stood well. He had been trained, she could see that. He was probably very good.

She had been very good too. But that was ten years ago. She clenched her jaw, watching for anything that might betray an imminent attack.

"Drop the sword," ordered the prince. "I'm not here for you, sister."

She did not drop the sword. It would be easier to simply attack, but all she could think of was that little boy, scrubbing at his eyes as he watched his mother sent away from him. No, she didn't want to kill Ichos. *Someone's awfully confident.* Right, well, she didn't want to get killed either.

"I know why you're here," she said, careful not to move, to hold this fragile moment, blades still bare of blood. That was another bolt of relief. He must have knocked Nilos over the head, or choked him to unconsciousness. "You're very good at following orders, aren't you? Letting other people use you to kill for them?"

"I'm the prince of Helisson," Ichos snapped. "I have a duty to obey my father."

"Is it duty?" she asked. "Or is it just easier this way?" This was the gap in his armor. The crimson flush spreading over his cheeks was proof enough of that. And if she could just strike true, she could end this without spilling blood. That would be nice.

He stared at her, brow furrowing. "You're an ashdancer. Why are you defending one of the Serpent's minions?"

Fates, the prince wasn't that much older than Timeus. Raw and eager and probably desperate to prove himself. Just as she'd been, when she was his age. "I know Lacheron," she said, pressing her attack. "I was his tool once. I fought in the war. I did—" her voice cracked, but this was the weapon she had to use—"I did terrible things. I let myself believe it was the only way. But it's not. You can choose your own path, Ichos."

Was she reaching him? It was hard to tell. He was a stranger. But he had lowered his blade a handspan. His jaw worked, as if he were chewing her words. Maybe getting ready to spit them back out. Who was she, after all? Just some nameless old woman. Sephre hadn't even listened to her own father. She doubted she could change the prince's mind. But maybe this seed of doubt would be enough to distract him. She risked a glance to Nilos, still crumpled on the sand. But breathing more quickly now. His eyes fluttered. Nearly there.

"I'm no one's tool." The prince glowered at her. "Everything I do is for the sake of Helisson. For my people."

The crumpled heap that was Nilos moved slightly. Sephre shifted her stance, to keep Ichos focused on her. She was his target now. And he was hers. He'd shown her where to strike.

"You want to do the right thing. That's how the Ember King works," she said. Might as well use everything she had. Fates, she hoped this would work. "He lies. He uses other people to do his dirty work, and then dresses it up as heroism and glory."

"My father never lied to me," snarled Ichos.

"Not your father," she said. "The true Ember King. The one who's been manipulating all of you, all along. Lacheron."

The prince stared at her. She knew that look. She'd had it on her own face, when Nilos had confronted her with similarly unwelcome truths.

"That's not—"

Sephre hurled her sword at him. The prince yelped, ducking. And Nilos shoved himself up from the sand. He was not quite as lightning swift as in the past, but for a man who'd just been half unconscious it was a fine showing. He was still faster than Sephre, which meant that she had to take a flying leap into the barge as Nilos took up the pole and began to shove the vessel into the deeper waters.

She rolled up, pulling herself onto the wooden seat. Looking

HOUSE OF DUSK 325

back, she found Ichos on the shore, his shoulders hunched, body coiled. For a moment, she feared he might leap into the water, to his own doom. *Don't do it. Be more than this.*

He couldn't possibly have heard her. And yet the prince suddenly shivered, as if casting off a wet cloak. Then he turned and stalked away from the shore. Sephre breathed out, her body loosening, melting.

"That was well done," said Nilos. "Thank you."

"No need to thank me," she replied tartly, to cover the unaccountable flush his words provoked. "Just stop going on about how you saved my life. We're even now."

Shadows enveloped them, as they drifted deeper. She couldn't see his face, but she heard the faint huff of his laugh, and it lightened her spirits. Which was probably a good thing, given where they were now headed.

The Labyrinth of Souls.

CHAPTER 30

SEPHRE

It began to brighten slowly. Not sunlight, not moonlight, not fire-light, but a pallid blue mist that hung over the Lyrikon like fog. Curls of it twisted around the pole, as if to tug it from Nilos's grip, only to fall in shreds as he drove the barge onward.

Sephre sat in the prow, watching the smooth water slide past, her attention drawn taut as a bow. It would be far too easy to let the lull of this place consume her. It seemed to go on forever, a luminous mirror under clotted shadows dark as iron. If there was a ceiling, it was lost to her sight.

But something else loomed on the horizon. Even at a distance, she knew it was massive. Like seeing a mountain range from across a wide, flat plain. The black, bleak wall of the Labyrinth of Souls.

"Is that it?" she asked. A silly question. What else would it be? But she needed to speak. To hear her own voice. And his.

"Yes."

She glanced back. He sounded weary. "Do you need me to take over?"

He thrust the pole into the water, giving a small shake of his head. "I heal quickly. One of the advantages of carrying around the power of a god."

Sephre brushed a hand over her shoulder, highly aware that the burn was barely even itching. If her own single fragment of godly power could do that, no wonder the man was so strong and quick to heal when he carried dozens, even hundreds.

Nilos's marks were hidden once more, but she was still aware of them. Aware of other things too. Like the smooth, capable way that he handled the pole, thrusting them unerringly onward. Fates, this was what she got for hiding away in a temple for ten years. She wrenched herself back toward the prow.

Surprise slammed a sharp breath into her lungs. The wall was no longer a smudge on the horizon. It was right there, towering over her, so tall she couldn't see where it ended. Smooth and glossy, as if carved from obsidian. It stretched away on either side, seamless and endless.

The barge bumped onto a crescent of white sand. Sephre stood warily, feeling the uneasy tilt of the boat beneath her. One slip, and she might topple into the poisonous waters. She doubted her single mark would be enough to protect her. Though Nilos had said the balewalkers of old had once entered the waters. How different was it, from the trial of the Holy Flame?

Nilos leapt lightly to the shore. She was bracing herself to follow when something caught her eye, shimmering in the strange, still waters of the Lyrikon.

At first she thought it was her own reflection. Coiled dark-brown hair, light olive skin, serious brows. But the woman looking back at her was barely half her age. Her eyes were gray, not brown. Her chin softer, her nose sharper. Her lips moved, but Sephre heard no sound. The woman in the pool frowned, reaching up. Trying to reach her? To tell her something?

"Sephre?"

The alarm in Nilos's voice jerked her back to herself. A sick horror washed through her as she realized she was poised at the edge of the barge, fingers barely a handspan above the deadly waters. She snatched her hand back with a shudder. But there was something beneath the horror. An unanswered question. A yearning.

Warm arms caught her, lifting her over the pool. Her feet sank into the white sand, and it was Nilos's worried face that filled her vision. The heat of his hands burned back the horror, reminding her that she was here, alive. That blood pulsed in her veins, that breath caught in her lungs. She leaned into his touch, and felt no shame.

"What happened?"

"I saw someone. A woman. In the water." Saying it aloud made it seem foolish. She grimaced, rubbing a hand over her eyes. "Or, I thought I did. It was probably my own reflection."

But Nilos was still frowning. "Or not. As I said, the waters of the Lyrikon are not unlike your Holy Flame."

Not mine. Not anymore. Though the loss of it no longer felt quite so sharp. "You said they held the Serpent's venom. So, death, basically."

Nilos grimaced. "Death is more . . . a byproduct."

"Of what? Time?"

"In a sense. Mortals interact with the world. We experience it, we feel it. Love, fear, hate, joy. Those things are spawned from our connection to the world. From change. From impermanence."

"So who was she, then? It wasn't me. Or—" She thought of the old child's game, sneaking glimpses in a still pool, searching for glimmers of some past life. "Could it have been one of my past lives?" One particular, painful life that quite honestly terrified her. *If* it was true.

Nilos shook his head. "I doubt it's as simple as that. You're a mortal, and this is a place not meant for mortals. As you may have noticed." He stepped away, releasing her back to the chill of the place. The sense that they were unwelcome. They did not belong.

She wanted to press closer, to reach for him again. *Get a hold of yourself, woman.* "I don't know," she said, making her voice light. "It could be a bit more ominous."

His laugh drove back the chill. "How?"

"Bloody waterfalls, towers of skulls, maybe some distant creepy drumbeats that sound like a beating heart? A terrifying guard dog?"

Zander would be proud of her, joking in the face of doom. But it was working. Her galloping heart began to slow.

"You'll have to take it up with the Serpent," said Nilos. "Once we restore him."

The words shook her, though maybe she should've expected it.

She'd promised him her mark, after all. "Are you really so close?" she asked. "Surely there are more marks than mine?"

His jaw tightened. "Yes. But as I said, the fragment you carry is . . . unusually potent. I suspect it will be sufficient to awaken him."

Awaken. An interesting choice of word. He stepped away before she could decide if she wanted to ask what it meant, heading for a gap in the wall roughly double the measure of Sephre's spread arms. He stalked up to the threshold, pausing to search the corridor within.

It was a bleak, barren place. A few trailing vines spidered over the stones, but she saw no hint of any bloom, only dry, leathery leaves the color of dried blood. Puddles of oily water sheened the earth, reflecting the pitiless sky above.

"I begin to see your point," Nilos told her. "There should be a guard dog, at the very least." His smile was brittle, but he was playing along with her so she would do the same.

"But it can't just be a normal hound," she said, joining him. "Not if it's guarding the Labyrinth of Souls. Maybe it could have a scorpion tail. Or three heads. Or bat wings."

"You were clearly wasted as both a soldier and an ashdancer," he said. "Obviously you were born to be an aesthetic advisor to the gods."

But humor was a fragile shield. The passage stretching away on either side was as endless as the wall without. Fates, how could they ever find Timeus in this place? She pressed her eyes closed, but it did nothing to stop the images chewing at her. It was as if some cruel artist had taken all her most terrible memories, all the ways that a mortal body could suffer, and painted the boy's face onto them. She saw his strong young body shattered. Bones broken, viscera streaming. Eyes wide and mouth a terrible rictus of pain.

"Which way?" she asked. "Where would they be keeping Timeus?"

"Most likely the center. The source of the Lyrikon. It's where the skotoi are most powerful. But the route to the heart of the labyrinth is different for every soul that walks it."

"Even us? We're not dead." She frowned. Nilos looked troubled, lips pressed together, the corners of his eyes creased as he squinted at nothing she could see. "Are you all right?"

"I'm . . . fine," he said, after a moment that felt like a year. "It's the spirits. I can—" he winced—"I can feel them. Because of the Serpent's marks, I imagine."

Sephre felt nothing. Or at least, nothing she could separate from the ambient dread of traveling the underworld. "This is the Labyrinth of Souls. Aren't there meant to be spirits here?"

She recalled a taverna that she had ill-advisedly allowed Zander to drag her to. It had been called the Necropolis, and was famous for offering free drinks to any soldier on the eve of a deployment. The entire place had been decorated like a tomb. She had laughed at it, back then. Downed a cup of the sour wine out of a skull-shaped goblet, watched Zander flirt shamelessly with a dark-eyed bard singing funeral dirges. She had even—she squirmed to remember it—joined the other patrons scrawling on the walls.

They had been painted with scenes of the labyrinth. Only a pale, mortal approximation, the maze, uneven, rough. Populated by spirits, roughly drawn by laughing soldiers eager to share their conquests. And she had been one of them, scratching seven awkward figures into one of those painted corridors. Zander had teased her, saying they looked more like bundles of sticks than people. That was before the war.

She had never gone back, after.

"Not this many," said Nilos, wincing again. "Too many. Something's wrong."

"Is it the skotoi?"

"We'll find out soon enough."

═══

Sephre trudged along yet another glossy black corridor, the walls slicing up to a narrow strip of iron sky high above, wondering where all the spirits could be. They had been walking for what felt like hours. The passages had begun to blur, each the same as the last, making it dangerously easy to lose focus. Twice, she'd nearly stumbled into one of the myriad small pools and streamlets that ran through the maze, no doubt chock full of deadly poison.

The place had the drifting, uncanny feeling of a dream. The sense of shifting. That the only surety was the ground directly beneath her feet. The air in her lungs. The man at her side. Sephre found herself staring at Nilos, her eyes hungry for anything other than gray grimness. For the burnished warmth of his skin, for the leaf green of his eyes. She felt him watching her, too. Keeping close. Two mortals, walking the paths of the dead.

She had no way to measure time except for her own body's needs, which had thus far consisted of a handful of walnuts and dried apricots, half a flask of water, and two highly awkward breaks to relieve herself while praying the Furies wouldn't punish her for defiling the underworld.

And in all that time they hadn't seen a single spirit. She paused to take another sip of water from the flask. "Where are all the spirits? Shouldn't they be here, wandering the labyrinth, being tormented with their regrets and sorrows and all that?"

Nilos halted, leaning against the obsidian wall, arms crossed. He'd refused her offer of food, and barely had a single sip of water since they crossed the Lyrikon. "That's not the way it works," he said. "Any torment a spirit faces in the labyrinth is something they bring with them. And they bring their joys and loves as well. Those are what give them strength to find their way through."

She arched a brow, taking another sip. "How do they ever find peace?"

"I'm . . ." Nilos shook his head. "I'm still just a mortal man, Sephre. I have some of the Serpent's power, but I'm no god. I don't think it's possible for a mortal to understand. To see anything more than . . . glimpses. But I don't think finding peace is the point. If it was, why would the Phoenix keep sending us back? Maybe peace is impossible. Or maybe it will only come at the end of the world, when the First One claws his way out of the abyss and eats the sun. That's another Bassaran legend, by the way," he added.

"Then what is the point of all this?" She gestured to the glimmering, poison-threaded maze that surrounded them.

"Maybe struggling *is* the point. Realizing that you can't win, you can't balance some great cosmic scale. You can't live a blameless life. You might never get forgiveness for your mistakes. But you keep going. You keep trying to be better anyway."

She stared at him. She felt like a bell on the cusp of tolling. It was that same sense she'd had earlier, of seeing parts of something greater that her mind could not fathom whole.

"But who am to say?" Nilos gave her a weary smile. "Like I said—" He frowned, turning abruptly to the left.

The passage looked the same as every other to Sephre.

"This way." He began to jog. She followed, wishing that she hadn't thrown their only sword at Ichos. What if they encountered a host of skotoi?

She was going to ask, but Nilos lifted a hand in warning, halting at a juncture in the maze. Sephre snapped her lips tight. Someone nearby was weeping.

"Please," said a man's ragged voice. "I don't want it. You can take it."

And so we will, mortal, came the sibilant reply. *We will take* all *of you. And then your mortal flesh will be our gateway to an even greater feast.*

They edged closer. Sephre pressed herself to the stones, then leaned out to glimpse what lay around the corner.

It took a moment to understand what she was seeing: a twisting clot of thorny shadows glinting with dagger-cut eyes. Skotoi, in their natural—or *unnatural*—form. There were at least five of the things, though it was hard to tell as they swarmed together, then broke apart, like storm clouds.

They surrounded a floating blur of gray. The spirit's features were hazy, yet familiar, for all that Sephre had only seen them once.

Castor. "That's the shepherd from Potedia," she whispered. The man they had both been too late to save. "What are they doing? I burned his body. They can't use him to enter the mortal world."

"They can still consume his spirit," said Nilos, grimly. "Destroy the fragment of power he carries, to keep it from me."

Sephre ground her teeth. How much weaker was Castor's spirit because of what she'd done? He had no prayers, no grave goods to give him strength. Twenty years ago, she might have charged out and began bashing heads. Or tentacles. Even demons from the underworld must have something bashable. But this was not the sort of fight you won by bashing. Damn Beroe. If only she still carried the holy flame, she could incinerate the lot of them.

"What can we do?" she asked. "I've got a packet of broadleaf, a crust of stale bread, and a few good curses."

"I don't think the skotoi will care if you call them ass-faced weasels."

"Can't you—" she gestured vaguely—"use your serpent powers?"

He shook his head. "I'm stronger than a mortal, and faster, and I can heal quickly. I could probably take on two of them. Maybe three. But there's at least six."

Sephre chewed the inside of her cheek. As much as she wanted to arrow straight to the center of the labyrinth, to Timeus, she would not abandon Castor. Even without her flame. And besides, every fragment of power Nilos recovered would make him stronger. Better able to help her rescue her novice. Laid out like that, the answer was clear.

"That's easy enough, then," she said, with more confidence than she felt. "I'll lead them away."

Nilos looked as if she'd just suggested she go for a pleasant stroll into the caldera of Mount Pirsus.

"They want me, too. And I'm still alive. Doesn't that make me . . . more tasty or something?"

"Yes. They'll no doubt want you, if they see you. But—"

"I can take care of myself," she overrode his protest. "I'll lead them away and then find my way back to you. Or you find me, since you're the one who can sense the fragments. And who knows, maybe if you take Castor's, you'll get some new power. Or grow fangs."

He winced.

"I'm sorry. I shouldn't have said that. I don't really want—"

"I know." He drew a bracing breath, and when he met her eyes again there was only a fierce determination in his gaze. "Let's do this."

======

Sephre pelted along the corridor, her breath tearing in and out. She'd lost track of the turns. As she flung herself around the next corner, she risked a glance back. The boiling darkness was still there. And the hissing whispers, even more relentless.

We know you, baleful one. Liar. Betrayer. Murderer.

Sephre gritted her teeth, running on. If she could just get far enough ahead, she might be able to lose the skotoi. She dove sideways into another passage, dashed ahead, turned. And again. And again.

No hope now of finding her way back to Nilos. She only hoped he would find her before her own flesh betrayed her. Her legs burned, each step setting something sharp stabbing in her side.

She was going to collapse if she didn't stop, if only for a few moments. She flattened herself against the wall, trying to still her breath. Listening.

Nothing.

Fates. She'd actually done it. She'd outrun the skotoi. *Well done*, she told her poor, trembling legs, promising them a long soak in the nearest hot bath if they got through this alive.

Sephre counted to a hundred, then slowly pushed herself away from the wall. Her breath sluiced out in a long sigh of relief, and she turned to see what lay ahead. No doubt yet another identical obsidian corridor.

HOUSE OF DUSK 335

But it wasn't. It was a street, broad and paved with neat squares of stone. Buildings rose on either side, washed pale with limestone, capped with bright blue domes. Vyria had told her the Bassarans believed the color brought good luck from the Sphinx, the mercurial god of the sky.

Heaps of cloth that were not cloth lay along the street, chillingly still. Sephre stood frozen, her mouth full of ash, tensed for what was about to come, what always came next, in her nightmares.

A baby's wail shivered through the silence.

CHAPTER 31

YENERIS

The palace was a flurry of activity, but Yeneris welcomed it. Sinoe was kept busy with fittings for an elaborate gown that she was to wear for the upcoming festivities, and had been charged by her father to oversee the construction of an even more elaborate costume for the bride.

It had been two days and they had not yet spoken of the kiss.

It was her own fault. Once or twice she'd thought Sinoe was going to say something, during the rare moments they were alone. But Yeneris found herself smothering the silence with questions about the king's plans, the location of the spectacle, when the kore might be vulnerable to rescue.

She told herself she was making things easier on Sinoe. In case it meant nothing. In case it was only a ruse, meant to cover their true reasons for being out and about illicitly. Yeneris would simply pretend it had never happened. If it was more than a ruse, well, then Sinoe could bring it up. She was the princess, after all. Maybe she went around kissing all sorts of people. Maybe she considered it a royal prerogative.

Listen to yourself, you coward. That isn't even a good excuse. Just admit that you're scared to ask. Scared to find out if it really did mean something, because if it did, then you're sunk, aren't you? Because she's still the princess of Helisson, and you're still an enemy spy who's about to liberate the sacred bones of your people so they can restore your homeland.

Star-crossed romances were all well and good in epic poetry, but they were less comfortable in real life. Especially given how many of them ended tragically. So. Yes. Even in this, she would do her job, and protect Sinoe from danger.

But while Yeneris could wrestle her mind into some semblance of submission, her body proved unwilling to go along. She found herself vibrating, a taut string ready to be plucked, just watching Sinoe brush her hair. It was bad enough that she took to going to the training yard any chance she could, driving herself through endless exercises as if she could sweat the infatuation out of her skin.

That was where Mikat found her, thrashing a padded straw dummy soundly with a practice sword.

"You've been avoiding me." Mikat padded out into the training yard. It was dinner hour. The last palace guard had left a quarter hour earlier, after Yeneris had beaten him in a practice bout for the third time.

Yeneris lowered her sword, chest thumping, breath raspy and hot. She gave herself a moment to recover, stalking over to the large stone basin and dipping up a copper ladle of water. She drank, clearing her throat, so her words would be firm and solid. "No. Only busy with preparations."

"Mmm. You mean busy seducing the princess?"

Yeneris bit her cheek, dashing another cup of water across her face. At least she was already flushed from exercise. She stared into the rippling water, counted three breaths, then turned back to face Mikat.

"Yes," she said. "As you ordered me to do."

"I don't think I ordered you to stick your tongue down her throat."

Yeneris strangled a protest. The more she fought, the more Mikat would jab at her, searching for weakness. Maybe it had been only a ruse, maybe it would never happen again, but she would not allow Mikat to turn it into something sordid. Something untrue. It *had* been true for Yeneris.

"There's still no word on the exact route the kore's palanquin will take," she said, deciding the best course was to act as if the previous conversation had never happened.

Mikat nodded. "There are only so many possibilities. We'll have scouts posted. Keep our people ready in a central location."

Yeneris let out a slow breath, relieved that the woman had accepted the change in topic. "There's more. Sinoe and I snuck into Lacheron's workshop looking for the key. We—"

"You recovered the key?" Mikat interrupted.

Again, Yeneris's nerves prickled. The key had nothing to do with the kore. The key was for Sinoe, to ensure that she would be free when this was over. "Yes."

"Good. Be prepared to use it."

Yeneris drew a steadying breath, remembering alien words whispering from purple flames. The strange power that had nearly unmade her. And Lacheron's voice, promising that the gods would rule no more. That the world would belong to that nameless, terrible force. "I will. But Mikat, this is bigger than just the kore. We heard—"

"Yes."

Yeneris blinked. She had not expected the woman to agree so easily. Mikat fixed her with a narrow gaze. "We will liberate the kore, and see that her bones are returned to Bassara. That was your mission. That was why we sent you here."

Was? A chill raced over Yeneris.

"But thanks to your work here, we've become aware of another opportunity to ensure the renewal of our homeland. A secondary mission, if you like."

She did *not* like. In fact, her belly was already knotting itself in anticipation.

"What mission?"

Mikat gave her a slice of a smile. "Something that will shame Hierax still further. And gain a powerful tool for our people. He stole our kore. Now we will steal the source of *his* power."

"What?" asked Yeneris.

"Not what," said Mikat, triumphantly. "Who."

Oh, no. Fates, not this. But Mikat continued on, unstoppable as a prophet in the grip of the Fates. "The Sibyl of Tears."

HOUSE OF DUSK 339

In the end, it was easy.

Yeneris understood, the moment Mikat told her that she was to kidnap Sinoe, that there was truly only one choice. Her heart was not divided. And it filled her with a strange, serene surety.

The kiss was not a ruse. It had meant something. It had meant everything. And not just to Yeneris. It was only her own fears that had made her doubt. Because she'd been afraid of this very thing. Of having to choose between her mission and her heart.

She was no longer afraid. Her feet felt light. Her heart, too. All of her was lifting, billowed by the thrum of hope and expectation. Her quick steps carried her up to the door of Sinoe's chambers. There was a guard outside, the one who had taken the post while Yeneris had her hour of freedom.

"You can go," she told him, breezing past.

The door thumped closed. Yeneris crossed the outer chamber in a rush, flung herself through the inner door. It was as if her body were an arrow, driven by the bowstring of her nerves. There she was. Sinoe, seated cross-legged on her bed, with a heap of pillows piled behind her and a scroll open in her lap. The same scroll she'd purchased during their second outing to the city.

Yeneris remembered the arch of Sinoe's brow as she said, *That sounds like a challenge.* She flushed at the memory, but it was not shame.

"Yen!" Both Sinoe's brows arched this time, and her eyes went wide as Yeneris stalked across the room and reached for her. The scroll fell, rolling away across the carpet. Sinoe's lips parted. "Yen?"

"It meant something. That kiss was real."

The princess stared at her. The words had sounded so strong and certain in Yeneris's mind, had even felt strong and certain on her tongue. But the longer they hung unanswered, the more they began to sound like a question.

Then Sinoe made a noise. Not a laugh. Not a sob. "Oh. Yen."

Her lips trembled, as if she wanted to say more, but she only lifted a hand, pressing it to Yeneris's cheek. "Or course it was real. But if you don't believe me, you're quite welcome to—oomph!"

Her kiss silenced the princess, but Sinoe didn't seem to mind. Her hand slid back, threading into the tight mass of Yeneris's hair, spilling tendrils from her ponytail. A single kiss, or a dozen, threaded together like bright amber beads, each one perfect in itself, but together, something priceless, something that Yeneris could carry with her all her days, no matter what came of this.

It might have become a hundred, or a thousand, except for a faint scuff that suddenly sent Yeneris's nerves tingling for an entirely different reason. A sharp rap came from the outer door. Then the urgent voice of Prince Ichos. "Noe, it's me. I need to see you."

Yeneris wrenched herself away from Sinoe. It was agonizing, but it would be far more agonizing to be flayed alive by Sinoe's brother for taking liberties with the royal person. Even if Sinoe had most definitely been enjoying those liberties.

Not that anyone would know, to look at her. Yeneris's chest went tight with admiration, watching Sinoe do something quick and clever to settle her gown back into neat folds, tucking back a loose curl of hair. "Ichos? Is that you?" she sang out. Then lower, for Yeneris alone, "Don't worry. He won't be a problem."

Yeneris wasn't so sure about that. Ichos loved his sister, yes. She'd seen that. But what had Sinoe called him? Scorpion mare. *He hates Father, but he will never turn against him.*

"Of course it's me. What are you doing in there?"

Sinoe reached out, brushing one thumb across the corner of Yeneris's mouth, then flashed a wicked grin, showing the smear of lip paint that had come away on her finger. She turned and breezed over to the door to admit her brother.

Yeneris stood with her back to the wall, observing the greeting. The prince's clothing was travel-stained, his ruddy hair damp and coiled. A large purple bruise colored one cheek, though she judged it several days old. He must have only just returned from his mission. And come straight to his sister.

Sinoe flung herself into his arms. "You're back! But even grouchier than usual. Did you forget what I told you?"

"You told me to duck when I entered a cave," he replied sourly. "You didn't say it was because some fire-witch was going to throw a sword at me."

"An ashdancer?" Sinoe said, frowning. "I thought you were looking for a serpent mystic."

"They were working together. The woman was deranged. She said—" The prince broke off, finally noticing Yeneris lurking along the wall. "You. Leave."

"Don't speak to her like that." Sinoe's voice was too sharp. Too defensive. She nodded to Yeneris. "Yen, would you please bring some tea? And plenty of pastries. *Someone* obviously needs sweetening."

Yeneris nodded, retreating into the smaller side chamber where the maidservants kept a supply of treats and a samovar of hot tea to serve the princess's needs. She took care to rattle the cups as she set them on a tray, in case Ichos was listening. Then crept catlike back to the beaded curtain, angling her ear to listen.

"I don't trust that girl," Ichos was saying. "The way she watches you. The way she watches everything. She's probably one of Lacheron's."

"I'm the Sibyl of Tears," Sinoe replied, her tone light, teasing. Fates, she was good. "Don't you think I'd know if my own body-guard were a spy?"

Footsteps. The prince was pacing.

"What's wrong?" Sinoe softened her voice. "You smell like horse. Did you even stop in the bathhouse? Does Father know you're back?"

"No. No, I—" Ichos faltered. "I had to see you first, Noe. I had to know if it's true."

"If what's true?"

"I was so sure the fire-witch was lying. I mean, *of course* she's lying. She ran off with that serpent cultist into the Labyrinth of Souls. Fates. Father's going to flay me alive, isn't he?" There was a soft thump that Yeneris guessed might be the prince flopping himself onto Sinoe's couch. "I had them. I could have killed them both. And I let them get away. Curse that woman and her lies."

"What lies?" Sinoe prompted. "What did the ashdancer say?"

"Father will cut out my tongue if I repeat it."

"Don't you trust me?"

A huff. "More than I trust myself."

"So tell me." Sinoe again, more gently.

"She said Lacheron has been playing all of us. That he's just using Father. That *he's* the true Ember King." A long exhalation.

Yeneris held herself still. Things were about to go very, very well, or very, very badly.

"And you think it could be true?" asked Sinoe, her words carefully balanced, giving nothing away.

"No! I mean, maybe. I don't know. If it's true, it means Father's the biggest fool in the world. Which, yes, I've said myself more than once, but Fates, I didn't mean it like this. It changes *everything*."

Another beat of silence. "Well?" asked Ichos. "Aren't you going to say anything? You're the fabled Sibyl of Tears."

Sinoe's laugh lashed out, bright and fey. "And here I thought you missed me. That you wanted to see your big sister. But you don't. You just want the Sibyl of Tears, like everyone else. Well, I'm afraid she can't help you right now. Not until her master releases her."

There was a faint clink of gold. Yeneris imagined Sinoe lifting one delicate wrist to show off Lacheron's bangle.

"What master?" demanded Ichos. "What is that?"

"A 'gift' from Lord Lacheron," she said. "It binds me from prophesying."

A beat of silence. Then Ichos again. "So it protects you."

"No!" snapped Sinoe. "It's sacrilege!"

"But the blood tears could kill you, Noe. I'm sure Father only wants to keep you safe."

"Furies' teeth, I can't believe you're making excuses for him," spat Sinoe.

Yeneris's fingers twitched toward her sword, even as she reminded herself that murdering her beloved's brother was definitely not the best way to begin a relationship.

You don't have a relationship. You have a job. She curled her empty fingers, and forced herself to listen. She couldn't risk drawing the prince's attention. He already suspected her.

Yeneris angled her eye along a gap in the curtained door. Sinoe stood at the window, her back to the room. Ichos must still be on the bed.

"Do you remember when we rode out to the cataracts for the Fish Moon Festival?" he asked.

Sinoe's shoulders hunched.

Ichos went on. "It was the first time Mother let us ride our own horses. And we roasted apples over the fire."

"And you were a greedy-gut who got sick eating all the milk candy," accused Sinoe. But her voice gentled as she added, "Mother taught us the fishtail braid, but yours kept slipping out—"

"—because my hair was too short," finished Ichos.

Sinoe lifted a hand, touching her carefully bound curls. "We found that cave behind the waterfall, and I was convinced there must be hidden treasure in it and refused to leave, until you found that funny blue stone and told me it was a sapphire." She gave a wistful sigh. "I still have that, you know."

This time the silence between them was softer.

"I don't want it to be this way," said Ichos, finally. "I hate it."

"But not enough to do anything about it."

"What do you expect me to do?" Ichos burst out. "Father doesn't listen to me. I'm nothing. I'm not touched by the Fates. I'm not some great hero reborn."

Sinoe spun to face him, fists clenched, color burning bright in her cheeks. "Neither is Father!"

Yeneris held her breath. But Sinoe did not back down. If anything, she only blazed brighter with suppressed fury. "Well? You came here for answers. Now you have them. The ashdancer was right. It's all a lie."

"I thought your visions were bound," said Ichos, warily. "How do you know?"

"I know because I'm paying attention. If you opened your eyes and looked around, you'd know too."

"Sinoe, this is dangerous," Ichos began. "If Father suspects you're—"

"I should have stood up to Father a long time ago," snapped Sinoe, unrepentant. "But if you're too scared, then you should go. He's probably waiting for your report. You wouldn't want to make him angry, would you?"

Silence.

"Well?" said Sinoe. "Aren't you going?"

"No," Ichos released a breath. He sounded surprised. "No, I'm not." He rose from the bed and went to stand before Sinoe, arms loose at his side. "I'm with you. I swear it. By the Fates."

Sinoe quivered. Then gave a small cry, and flung her arms around him. Then punched him on the shoulder. Then embraced him again.

"So you might as well ask your bodyguard to stop plotting how best to murder me and bring the tea," Ichos added. "I suspect we're all going to need several cups while you fill me in on everything I've missed."

====

It was midnight by the time they finished filling in Ichos on Lacheron's manipulations of Sinoe's prophecies and the conversations they had overheard in his workshop. It had taken three carafes of tea, one jug of wine, a platter of fruit, and two baskets of pastries, one of which Sinoe had dumped over her brother's head to stop him swearing too vociferously after she described Lacheron's private stash of corpses.

"You took her into a dungeon full of skotoi?" He dusted the crumbs from his tunic, still glowering at Yeneris. "You're supposed to be her bodyguard."

"Only one skotos. The rest were just skotoi-in-waiting," said Sinoe, ignoring her brother's dubious huff. "And it was my choice. We needed to get the key."

"Which you still haven't used. Why wait to break the bangle? You said yourself that Lacheron needs Agia Beroe here to complete his plan. We should act now, before she arrives."

"It's a risk either way," said Sinoe. "If we accuse him now, we have no proof. Do you really think Father will believe that he's not truly the Ember King? After everything he's done in service to that lie?" She looked to her brother, who nodded grudgingly.

"Still, I don't see what we gain in waiting. You said you need proof, but what proof is there?"

Sinoe hesitated, glancing to Yeneris. As of yet, she'd said nothing about their plan to restore the kore, or Yeneris's true identity. Which was lovely and considerate, but Ichos was no fool. He must see the gaps in their story. She felt his gaze weighing on her even now.

"And why do you keep looking at your bodyguard like that?" he asked Sinoe. "What's *her* stake in this?"

Yeneris kept her face a mask. "It's my job."

"It's your job to keep my sister safe. Not to help her stage a coup. You must know Father and Lacheron would have rewarded you if you went to them with any of this."

She almost laughed at the absurdity of it. But Ichos was watching her too closely, too carefully. The chill in her belly slid up her chest, into her throat. She had trusted Sinoe with her secret. With her mission. But could she trust Ichos?

Maybe not. But he'd sworn by the Fates that he was with Sinoe. And Sinoe was with Yeneris. She was as certain of that as her own heartbeat.

And when it came down to it, the prince could be useful. They would need help to plan the kore's rescue. Information on what protections would be in place, what route would deliver the kore to the wedding. Ichos could get them that information.

Still, it took Yeneris a long moment to drag air into her lungs.

To shape the words. "I'm here to reclaim the kore's bones and return them to Bassara."

Ichos's brows arched. "You're a spy?"

Sinoe made a shushing gesture. "She's my *friend*, Ichos. And if you're going to keep your vow to stand with me, then I expect you to stand with Yen too. Because she's . . . important to me." A slight flush deepened Sinoe's cheeks. "And she's right. The Maiden—the kore—needs to go home. It's my fault she was taken in the first place."

"It was Lacheron," Yeneris growled, "twisting true prophecy into his own lies."

Ichos rubbed his temples wearily. "All right, let me see if I have this straight. Not only are we denouncing Father as the Ember King, now we're also stealing his bride?"

"Not stealing," said Yeneris. "She was stolen. We're bringing her home."

"And without her, Father has one less thing to legitimize him," added Sinoe.

"And then what?" asked Ichos. "What's the end goal? Cast Father down and take his place?"

"It would be you, not me, little brother," said Sinoe. "I already serve the Fates. I can't be queen. But that's putting the cart before the horse. Right now the most important thing is stopping Lacheron. And setting things right with the kore," she added, looking to Yeneris.

"But stop Lacheron from doing *what*, exactly?" asked Ichos.

Yeneris thought of the voice that they had heard, speaking in that strange and alien tongue. The one Lacheron called lord. How a single touch of the unseen power had nearly toppled her.

Judging by Sinoe's expression, her thoughts had followed a similar track. "Lacheron said he was going to break the cycle. That the gods would rule no more and that the world would belong to . . . to whatever that horrible voice was."

"*As it was always meant to be,*" quoted Yeneris. Ever since that night, she'd been twisting and turning the words. Trying to make sense of what they'd seen. She ground her teeth. She should have made Mikat listen. But the woman was so fixed on her own goals.

"And remember this lovely bit of prophecy?" said Sinoe. *"Long has the old enemy watched and waited. Now he seeks to strike his second blow, and the world will not survive it.* We all know what the Ember King is famous for."

"Killing the Serpent," said Yeneris. "The god-beast of death."

Sinoe rolled up from the couch and began to pace. "But now the Serpent is coming back, and it sounds like he's nothing but a distraction to Lacheron. I mean, yes, he sent you after them, Ichos, but he can't have expected *you* to destroy one of the gods."

Ichos huffed. "So much for sisterly loyalty."

"Pff. You know how good you are, you don't need me to fan your pride. Though, speaking of which, did you know Hura is back? And he asked about you. I think he missed your spear. In the sparring ring." She lunged away, snickering, as Ichos tossed a pillow at her, but the laugh turned into a groan. "Fates. It's just . . . too much. Every time I think we've got some inkling of all the moving parts, another one just pops in."

Yeneris cleared her throat. "Er."

Sinoe stopped pacing. "What?"

"There's . . . something I need to tell you." Yeneris glanced toward Ichos, who was just pouring a fresh cup of very hot tea. He arched a brow back at her. "But before I do, I swear by the kos, by the Fates, that I won't do it."

"Do what?" asked Sinoe.

"Kidnap you."

Ichos set his cup down with a clang that sounded very much like the ring of a sword being drawn. "What?"

"My . . . my contacts. The others I work with. They sent me here to rescue the kore. That was all. That was my mission. But now they want . . . you."

Sinoe blinked. Then understanding settled over her. "They want the Sibyl of Tears."

"I won't let them do it. I'll get them the kore's bones, but they won't get anywhere near you, Sinoe."

The princess frowned into her teacup. "I believe you, Yen. I do. *Two maidens shall be bound, but only one shall walk free if the divided heart remains.*"

"My heart isn't divided," Yeneris said. "It never has been. I love my people. And I love you. I don't need to choose. It's a false choice." She reached out, taking Sinoe's hand, lacing their fingers together. "I choose both."

"Love?" Sinoe's lips twitched, but there was something raw beneath the humor. Something tender and sweet that drew Yeneris like a bee to bloom.

"Love," she repeated, honing the word against her heart, making it sharp enough to slice through whatever trials the Fates threw before them. It was dizzying. To think she'd been afraid that giving in to her feelings might make her weak. Might somehow dilute her courage. Yeneris could have wrestled a lion. Could have leapt the Bleeding Sands in a single bound, if it lay between her and Sinoe.

But there *was* nothing between them now. All that was past. The world might be spinning toward a second cataclysm, but she was not alone. She would never be alone.

Sinoe made a sort of low growl, tugging Yeneris down for another kiss.

Ichos groaned. "Could we save the flirting until after the apocalypse is averted?"

"I think the eve of the apocalypse is the perfect time for flirting," said Sinoe, releasing Yeneris with a wicked wink. "Speaking of which. Ichos, brother dear, do you think you might arrange a sparring match with Lord Hura? He offered his help, and I think it's time we took him up on it."

CHAPTER 32

YENERIS

"Aren't you worried your father will find out?" Yeneris asked, as she and Sinoe made their way out along the gravel path to the athletic field. "I thought he didn't want you speaking with the Scarthian emissaries."

"We're not speaking with anyone," Sinoe said. "We just happened to be passing by on the way to the shrine, and saw my brother, and stopped to say hello."

"Your brother, who just happens to be sparring with the ambassador's son."

Sinoe rolled her eyes. "I know, yes, fine, it doesn't look entirely innocent, but Father's got plenty of other distractions right now. Agia Beroe's barge is nearly to the docks, and he wants a grand procession to welcome her. Get the people all fired up for their new queen's rebirth."

They found the prince and Hura in a wide sandy sparring ring, both armed with blunted spears. They were both quite skilled to Yeneris's eye, though her training had leaned more toward small secret blades than spears. Lord Hura seemed to have a slight advantage, landing a sharp crack to the back of the prince's knees as they approached. Spotting Sinoe, he broke off the attack, dipping his head. "Princess Sinoe. You bless us with your presence, as always."

Sinoe snorted. "It's certainly a blessing for my brother. It looks as if I just saved you from a proper trouncing, Ichos."

The prince scowled. "I was doing fine. That was a good trick there, though," he added, glancing to Hura. "I didn't even see it coming."

"Few do," said Hura. "But I'd be happy to teach you. Today seems to be a day for learning new things."

His eyes rested on Sinoe briefly, and his smile sharpened. "That's a lovely hair ornament, princess. Is it new?"

Sinoe brushed a careless hand over her dark hair, which had been twisted up atop her head, held by the amber pin. "Yes. A gift, from someone I love very much." Her voice wobbled slightly. "A generous gift."

"Ah. I'm sure they will be pleased to know that you appreciate it."

"I do," said Sinoe. "I would very much like to see them again. But that isn't possible right now. Perhaps after my father's wedding. I have duties here. Responsibilities I cannot abandon."

Hura's smile became slightly fixed. He glanced toward Ichos. "Yes. Your brother told me some of this. But princess, surely you can leave those duties to others. You have an opportunity now. It may not come again."

Sinoe drew in a breath, shading her eyes as she glanced around the empty field. "No," she said, her voice lower, serious now, for all that she continued to smile as if in the midst of some trivial conversation about the weather. "Ichos told you about Lacheron, yes?"

Hura tamped the butt of his spear into the sandy ground. "He told me a pack of wild-wind tales. The sort of thing my grandfather sang over the fire at midwinter."

"I know," said Sinoe. "But this is real. Yen and I saw it. Saw him ordering the skotoi. Heard him speaking with that nasty, nameless thing in the brazier." She turned to Yeneris for confirmation.

It was still strange to be a part of such conversations. Yeneris was so used to standing on the edges. Being unseen. Being the watcher, not the watched. But these were her allies now. And there was too much at stake not to speak plainly. As her full self.

She turned to Hura. "Did your father ever tell you the story of creation?"

HOUSE OF DUSK 351

It was Ichos who answered. "His father? What does that have to do with this?"

"It's an old Bassaran story," Yeneris answered, seeing Hura nodding to himself, a grim understanding hardening his expression. "My mother told it to me."

Her throat tightened. They all knew what she was. That this was a part of her. And the story was important. Still, she had a brief, terrible vision of Mikat, growling at her for every tiny lapse, every time she let a trace of her accent tinge even a single word. Slapping her hand when she started to make one of the old warding signs.

But she'd made her choice, and she would hold to it. She would show Mikat there was more than one path to a renewed Bassara. It was the kore she served, not Mikat.

"It's the story of how the world came to be," she explained. "All was churn and void, until Chaos birthed her five children, so that they might give order and structure to the world."

"Five?" Ichos repeated. "But there are four children of Chaos."

"The first one, the eldest, desired to shape the world to his own designs, alone. And because he was first, he was the most powerful. He devoured his younger siblings."

Sinoe poked Ichos in the shoulder. "Remember that, little brother."

Ichos rolled his eyes. "You're only ten minutes older than me." He looked back to Yeneris. "So then what? How did they escape?"

"By creating us. People. Mortals. The Scarab—or the Beetle, as you call her—gave us flesh, and the Phoenix gave us spirit, and the Sphinx gave us thought, and the Serpent gave us . . ." Yeneris hesitated, searching for the right word.

"Emotion is probably the closest word for it in Helissoni," said Hura. "And yes, I have heard the story. How mortal warriors freed the four younger children of Chaos, who then joined forces against their elder brother and cast him into the abyss and sealed him away forever."

"Not forever," said Yeneris. "He promised he would break free. That one day he would rise again and consume this world, and remake it alone."

"Fates." Sinoe looked slightly ill. "So that's who you think Lacheron is working for?"

"It's . . . one possibility."

"A horrible, horrible possibility. Which means it's probably true." Sinoe pinched the bridge of her nose. "I can see why the Fates want to stop it. So that's why the Ember King wanted the Serpent destroyed? Because he thought it would help the first one break free?"

"It would make sense," said Hura. "If the four younger gods sealed the first one with their power, then breaking that power might break the seal."

"Or weaken it," suggested Yeneris, thinking of the hazy lines of ancient palaces hidden below the sea. Of a once-mighty empire, shattered and fallen.

Sinoe looked to her brother. "Ichos said there's some mystic out there trying to bring the Serpent back. Would that help?"

"Lacheron doesn't seem to think so," said Yeneris. "He brought the dagger back here. He's got other plans for it."

"There are three more children of Chaos." Hura's knuckles had gone pale, gripping the spear.

"And if he has his way, one of them is going to manifest right here in three days," said Sinoe. "The Phoenix."

"It could be even worse than that," said Hura, darkly.

Sinoe gave a high, humorless laugh. "Really? Worse than breaking one more seal unlocking a divine power that wants to destroy everything?"

"The kore," said Hura. "She may not be the Helissoni's Faithful Maiden, but Lacheron could have another use for her. She was from the House of Midnight. Dedicated to the Scarab. According to our legends—" his gaze shifted briefly to Yeneris, and she felt the warmth of that *our*—"the kore bound herself to the god-beast of earth, to hold back the cataclysm. To quell the shaking earth and keep Bassara from falling into the sea like so much else of the old empire."

They all fell silent then. Sinoe pressed herself closer to Yeneris, who fought the urge to sweep an arm around the other woman. Ichos and Hura wouldn't care, but to any other eye she must be only a bodyguard. She cast her gaze across the training grounds, taking note of a handful of soldiers and servants. Any of them might be Lacheron's spy.

"There are too many eyes here," she said. "We shouldn't linger much longer, princess. You'll be missed."

Sinoe made an impatient noise. "Yes, yes, no time for war councils when there's a gown to be fitted. At least I'll look dazzling for the end of the world. Right, so, obviously we need to stop this." She looked at Hura then. "I know what my mother sent you here to do. But I'm not the one who needs to be rescued. We need to get the kore's bones away from here."

Her hand brushed Yeneris's, fingers twining tight. Hura's gaze slid from Sinoe to Yeneris, then back again. "We can do both. It would be the perfect opportunity for you to flee as well, princess. I can have my people ready to waylay the palanquin once it leaves the palace. Yeneris can return the kore to her contacts, and I can take you north. Your mother has already arranged safe passage, so long as we can reach Vigil Pass."

"No," Sinoe said, resolutely. "I need to face my father. He needs to hear the truth, for once. He needs to understand what Lacheron is."

Hura shook his head. "I don't like it."

Ichos crossed his arms. "I don't like it either. What makes you think Father will believe you? He's been the Ember King for half our lives. He's too proud to give that up. It's who he is."

"He'll believe it because the Fates will tell him so," said Sinoe. "And they'll do so in public, before his entire court, and the ashdancers. Even if he doesn't believe it, they will. Prophecy made him king. Now it can unmake him."

"And what about the real Ember King?" Hura asked. "He has the blade of oblivion. And Agia Beroe."

"But he won't have the kore's bones. Without a dead maiden to raise, he has no excuse to summon the Phoenix. So you see, it's all under control." She squeezed Yeneris's hand as she spoke, giving her a bright smile.

Warmth flooded Yeneris at the touch. Her chest ached. Maybe it would always ache at the sight of Sinoe.

And yet her nerves flickered. The smile was bright, yes, but brittle. She thought of how the princess had once teased her, telling her she wasn't afraid of dying because she'd seen her own death. She'd claimed it was only a joke.

"Sinoe," said Yeneris, "have you seen something?"

"I see a lot of things," she said. "I see a beautiful woman standing beside me who really shouldn't be frowning like that."

"A vision," Yeneris pressed her. "Something more about what Lacheron's planning?"

Sinoe huffed, brandishing her gold bangle. "I haven't had any visions lately, thanks to this. Don't worry, Yen. I don't need a vision to know that we're going to stop him. The kore will be safe, and so will my people. We know what we have to do."

She gave Yeneris's hand another squeeze, then pulled away. "Speaking of which, we really should leave you boys to your sparring practice. Be gentle with him, Hura."

Then she was sweeping onward across the field, and Yeneris had no choice but to follow. Sinoe's confidence should have cheered her, but she couldn't help thinking that the princess hadn't really answered her question.

━━━

The soldiers found them just as they passed back into the covered walkway of the north wing. Two men in bright bronze armor and bloody crests, their footsteps clattering like warning bells against the marble floor as they marched briskly forward. Sinoe muttered a surprisingly foul curse, then cast Yeneris a brief, worried look. But there was no time for words. The soldiers filled the passage, blocking their way toward Sinoe's chamber.

Yeneris ground her teeth. They had lingered too long. If the king suspected what they plotted, he could unravel everything. But how had he discovered it so quickly? They'd only just left Hura and Ichos.

"Yes?" Sinoe lifted her chin, her tone cool and untroubled, as if the men were small stones in her path, nothing more. "What is it?"

"Your father has need of you, Bright One," said one of the men.

The princess did not falter. "Very well. I'll be there shortly, but I have a fitting just now."

The soldier shifted his stance. "Apologies, Bright One, but the king said we were to accompany you directly to the great hall. Immediately."

Perhaps it was only some urgent detail of the upcoming festivities. Or the king wanted Sinoe to be there to welcome Agia Beroe. Yeneris studied the two soldiers. They were tense. One of them kept glancing down the nearby corridors. As if he expected they might be attacked.

Sinoe gave a breathless laugh of disbelief. "Do you know how hard it was to convince Mistress Cleia to come all the way here to the city to personally oversee my gown? I'm quite sure Father wouldn't wish me to insult—"

"They've caught a spy," said the soldier. "A Bassaran agent."

The words struck like invisible daggers, utterly unexpected, making Yeneris huff out a strangled protest. Fates, no. Mikat. Terrible images bled through her mind. Torment and torture. The woman was strong as iron. But even iron could be broken.

Yeneris strangled her horror. Held herself stone still as Sinoe likewise took in the unwelcome news.

"I see," said the princess. "And what does this have to do with me?"

"He wishes you to prophesy, Bright One. To learn the plans of your enemies."

Sinoe did not look at Yeneris. But one hand twitched, as if she wished to reach out. Then she curled the fingers into a fist, and nodded. "Very well," she said, and set off briskly along the corridor.

Yeneris knew it wasn't eagerness. She saw the strain in Sinoe's eyes, and matched her own pace. The soldiers, apparently taken by surprise, were slower to catch up. It gave Sinoe a single moment to speak privately, low and quick.

"The amulet," she whispered. "What if they discover the fake?"

Fates. Yeneris hadn't even thought of *that* complication. But Sinoe was right. Scarab's might, what a mess. There could be no scrying. A cold pit opened in Yeneris's chest. "They won't. I'll see to it."

Sinoe frowned. Started to open her mouth, to ask how. But it was too late. The soldiers rejoined them, and Yeneris was glad of it. Glad for the chill that was now spreading through her. Driving back fear and doubt and horror, and leaving only the certainty of what she knew she had to do.

By the time the doors to the great hall swung open, she was ready. Her fingers drifted, tapping each of her hidden daggers lightly. It had taken her five years to earn all six. Grueling hours of training, pushing her body past pain and exhaustion. She remembered the day Mikat had given her the last, a tiny blade no longer than her thumb. *Small. But as deadly as the rest. You need to be ready for anything, Yeneris.*

I am, she'd insisted. *Thanks to you.*

It had been one of the rare times Mikat actually smiled at her. A ghost of warmth pressed Yeneris's arm, the memory of strong, weathered fingers gripping her. *I chose well. Fates, you were a scrawny little thing. But I knew it, the first time I saw you. Brave, and bold, and stubborn. You were the one who could save our kore. No matter the sacrifice. No matter the cost.*

Yeneris braced herself and looked across the hall. It was not unlike the last time she'd been here. Hierax sat in his lion-guarded seat. Lacheron lurked beside him. And there was the scribe, ready to record Sinoe's prophecy. The brazier, already smoking. Two soldiers stood nearby, a prisoner hung limp between them.

It was a man. A boy, really. Younger than Yeneris, with clear olive skin and short, tightly curled black hair. He had been handsome. Now one cheek was split. His lips were puffy. It looked as if he'd lost a tooth. Sweat streaked his brow, mixing with the blood.

For a moment, she felt relief. It wasn't Mikat. She didn't even know this boy. But that didn't mean he wasn't one of her people. Yeneris knew only a handful of those Mikat had recruited. It was safer that way.

Either way, it didn't make this any less perilous. Even if the false amulet wasn't discovered, Sinoe's prophecy could doom them all. Shatter any hope of recovering the kore and thwarting Lacheron's plans.

She had to stop this. Every step brought them closer to the brazier. Sinoe's face was pale and pinched. One hand gripped her wrist, the bangle that imprisoned her visions.

"Good," said Hierax. "Now we'll have some answers. Hold your tongue all you like, boy. The Sibyl of Tears sees all. Your paltry schemes are nothing, when I command the voice of the Fates themselves."

Yeneris gritted her teeth. The breathless arrogance of the man. Lacheron might be plotting to destroy the world, and yet it was Hierax, pompous, vain, fool of a king, who made her blood boil. She'd bury every one of her daggers into that broad chest, that thick neck, those heavy-lidded eyes. But that would solve nothing. She'd be dead herself, a heartbeat later. Leaving Sinoe in Lacheron's clutches, unguarded. Ichos was a decent fellow, a good swordsman, but he'd lived too long in his father's shadow.

And as for Lacheron, she had no confidence even all six of her blades could end the man. Mikat had warned her that others had tried, and failed. Too great a risk, if there was another option.

Which there was. She saw it. Hated it. *A time will come,* Mikat had told her, *when you may need to make difficult choices. Sacrifice more than sleep and sweat and tears. Do not hesitate. I trust you to make the right decision, Yeneris. You know what's at stake for our people.*

There was no more time. It had to be now. Casting iron around her heart, Yeneris cried out her warning. "Knife!"

She was already moving, flinging herself toward the prisoner. His eyes met hers. Wide and brown and shocked. His lips parted, but the words were wet, red spatters. Did he know who she was? Hot blood gushed over her fingers, turning them sticky. No time for guilt. Yeneris shoved herself closer, so that his jerking movements hid her own.

Then her arms were suddenly heavy, supporting dead weight. She let it slump to the floor, bile surging up her throat. One of the soldiers was grappling the dead body. She heard one of them curse as he stooped to pluck a small dagger from the boy's limp hand.

"How did this happen?" Hierax demanded, glowering first at the soldiers, then at Lacheron.

One of the soldiers began babbling excuses, but they rang dull in Yeneris's ears. Or maybe it was guilt that silenced them. No doubt the men would be punished. Maybe even executed for the apparent lapse. She held herself still, even as she felt Sinoe's warmth at her shoulder. She couldn't risk looking at the princess. All her careful walls might crumble. And she needed them more than ever.

Lacheron was watching her. Not suspiciously, but with an intensity that froze her blood. She thought of the voice in the flames. The First One. The horrible sensation of unraveling.

"We are fortunate, it seems, that your daughter's handmaid is so attentive and quick to act," he said. "Even if she's deprived us of our answers."

Iron, Yeneris told herself. *Iron in your spine, iron in your bones. You did your duty, nothing more.*

"Better that than to deprive my father of his daughter," said Sinoe, with queenly disdain. "If there's nothing more, Father, I shouldn't keep Mistress Cleia waiting."

"No," agreed Hierax, grudgingly. Then he, too, fixed his gaze on Yeneris. "That was good work, girl. You honor Helisson with your service. Now, see that your mistress reaches her chamber safely."

===

They didn't speak. Partly because Hierax sent an additional complement of guards to escort them back to the north wing. Partly because Yeneris had no words. She was hollow as a broken shell, tumbled and cracked by the sea, cast up onto a dry and unforgiving shore. She kept seeing the boy's eyes. Wide and brown and terrified.

Good work, girl.

Sinoe set a brisk pace, but when they finally reached the princess's chambers, she sent her maids away, and even went so far as to spurn Mistress Cleia, pleading nervous exhaustion following the morning's "traumatic event."

Finally, they were alone. Yeneris followed Sinoe into the bath chamber, her own mind slow, thoughts curdling. Like the blood clotting her hands. "Go on," Sinoe prompted, gesturing to the steaming pool.

"I can't," Yeneris croaked. "I'm filthy."

"You do understand the concept of a bath, don't you? Hot water? Soap? Scrubbing?" Sinoe plucked a cloth from a nearby basket, snapping out the fabric, refolding it unnecessarily. "I don't need to stay. I know I'm probably the last person you want around you right now, after . . ." She coughed, then set the towel back in the basket.

Her tone pierced Yeneris's dullness. She lifted her head, forcing herself to meet Sinoe's eyes. "What? Why?"

"Because I'm—I'm the enemy."

A noise caught in Yeneris's throat. A wild sound that wasn't a laugh or a sob. She shook her head. "No. You're not. I don't blame you for any of that. I blame *him*. Lacheron."

Sinoe's expression softened, though the unhappy line of her lips held firm. "And my father."

"Yes," Yeneris admitted. "But we're better than them. We have to be. I won't let any of this drive us apart, Sinoe. I swear it." She started to reach for Sinoe, to prove the words with deeds. But the sight of the blood on her fingers froze her. No. She would not touch the princess with a killer's hands.

So it was Sinoe who fulfilled the vow. Gently, firmly, she set her smooth palms to Yeneris's cheeks. Then she drew Yeneris down. Their foreheads met, their breath mingling, their lips barely brushing.

"Good." Sinoe's voice was husky. "Then I'm not going any-where."

CHAPTER 33

SEPHRE

Sephre jogged along the tiled streets of the city. *It's still the labyrinth of the dead. It just looks like Bassara.* But telling herself that didn't quiet the thrum of her heart, the icy stab every time she heard another desperate wail. This place might not be real, but the spirits here were. And that cry sounded so anguished. So lonely.

Hold on, little one.

Sephre halted, holding her breath, listening. There it was again, more of a whimper now, but closer. She spun, scanning the street. Was it pulled from her memory, somehow? Mirrored back at her by the magic of the labyrinth? It looked, felt—Fates, even *smelled*—so real. It was only when she looked up that she knew otherwise. The sky above was the same dull, grim gray she'd seen in the underworld. So featureless it made your heart heavy to look at.

She was in a courtyard. Most of the Bassaran homes had these open spaces just inside the main entrance. This one even had a lemon tree growing in one corner, though the tree was brown and withered. There were several bodies. A woman curled near the tree, looking as if she were asleep. Two older men collapsed in a tangle at the base of the stairs that led to an upper level. A young man flung out more violently across the stones. There was a cracked amphora beside him. The other three were easier to ignore, but the man she could not help but see. The way his empty eyes stared so beseechingly up at the sky, the tongue swollen by poison.

These were the faces from her nightmares.

Another whimper. She spun, searching. It had come from the direction of the lemon tree. Sephre padded closer, eyeing the woman lying there, knees tucked, arms wrapped around herself. Like a child curled against a nightmare.

A flutter of movement, the faintest stirring. Sephre knelt, tugging at the dead woman's arms. Not shielding herself. Shielding a bundle of cloth. A bundle that whimpered in Sephre's arms. Fingers trembling, she plucked back the cloth, to reveal . . .

Nothing. A wisp of mist that spun away, leaving only the echo of a wail. The cloth fell from Sephre's hands.

You did this.

It was the dead woman. A gray shimmer had risen from her curled corpse, to hang before Sephre. The details were hazy, but the eyes were sharp. Pale silver, unblinking, they transfixed her.

More whispers, behind her. Sephre stood, spinning, found that she was surrounded. The young man, the two older men, and more. Dozens of spirits had gathered. She could see nothing but the mist of their formless bodies, the piercing brightness of their accusing eyes. *You did this. You.*

"I . . ." Her voice faltered. "Yes," she said. "I was part of this. I'm . . ."

She was going to say *sorry,* but her throat closed on the word. It wasn't what they needed from her.

"Are you real?" she asked. "Or are you just a memory?"

Your memories don't have faces, said the first spirit, the young woman. *Only him. Only the soldier you loved. The soldier you killed. But here, here we have faces. Here you cannot hide from what you did.*

Real, then. She caught another apology, swallowed it.

You torment yourself for giving him peace. And yet we are the ones in torment. Trapped forever in this place.

"Trapped?" Nilos had said there were too many spirits here. Was this why?

The wall of shadow binds the flame at the center of the labyrinth. We cannot be reborn. And the demons grow stronger, feeding on us. We grow weak. But you are strong. You could make us strong.

The spirits pressed closer. Sephre shivered at the touch of chill fingers. Then gasped in pain as they dug deeper, jabbing into her flesh. She wrenched away, teeth chattering as if she'd been caught in a winter rain.

Was this the answer? To give herself to these spirits? A sacrifice to balance what she did?

No. She thought of what Nilos said. *You can't balance some great cosmic scale. You can't win.* But she could keep trying. Keep struggling. Keep trying to do whatever good she could.

The hands had followed her, tearing, scraping painfully over her living flesh. Her body was ice. She could not move, but she could still speak. "I'll help you. Where is this wall of shadow? Can you take me there?"

A stillness. Then a sigh. The surging spirits subsided, like an angry sea turning calm. But they remained close, their chill seeping into her until she felt she had lost all sense of what it was to be warm.

Yes.

Steps cracked against stone. Sephre blinked, dizzy. The world had shifted again, the walls above her were black and glossy again. The sky above a dull gray. Somewhere, a faint trickle of water chimed, setting her teeth on edge. But the spirits remained, clotted close around her.

"Sephre?"

Someone was running toward her. Nilos. His clothing had seemed bland and forgettable back in the mortal world, but now the brown tunic was like a piece of rich earth. He was real and alive and the sight of him broke the rime of ice that held her.

The spirits retreated, opening a path between them. Nilos crossed it in three quick steps, and then he was there beside her, green eyes blazing into her with a mixture of alarm and relief. He reached for her, hands sliding along her upper arms, almost an embrace.

"Are you all right?" he asked.

She gave a hollow huff. "I'm still alive." And so was he. "You took Castor's mark?"

"Yes." A shadow passed over his face.

"Are *you* all right?"

"I'm still alive." His lips quirked, but she heard the echo of her own grimness in the words. Right now, being alive was the closest either of them could get to *all right*. He knew that as well as she did. She could see it in his eyes.

His grip on her arms tightened a fraction. She leaned into his warmth for a heartbeat. Two. Three. Then she pulled back.

"I know why there are too many spirits here," she said.

The gray mist still gathered around them murmured and muttered, pale eyes glinting in expectation. Sephre turned to them. "Take us to the center. Take us to this wall of shadow."

=====

"A wall of shadow?" Nilos asked, as they followed the host of shifting spirits along another featureless corridor. He paused, offering Sephre a hand as they came to one of the myriad pools. There seemed to be more of them now. She hoped it was a sign that they were drawing closer to the center of the labyrinth. The dread building in her was as bad as the tension before any battle. Not knowing what she might lose. Not knowing if she would be brave enough to survive it.

"That's what they said. It's blocking the way to the holy flame. Which means none of the spirits can reach the Phoenix to be reborn."

"For how long?"

"I don't know. Most of these spirits died ten years ago, in the war. Bassarans who died when . . . when the city fell." She kept walking, aware of his eyes on her. "But there are Helissoni soldiers too." She'd spent some time searching, while they walked.

She had not found Zander. And she could not bear to think what that might mean. Couldn't imagine him being torn by sharp teeth, his soul unraveling forever. They hadn't even been able to

HOUSE OF DUSK 365

shroud him. Boros had said a prayer, and Sephre had dabbed a bit of oil on his brow—lamp oil, not holy oil.

And likely she would never know if it had been enough. She'd simply have to live with it. Without any absolution, except what she gave herself.

But neither would she forget it. Because there was a difference. The pain of losing him was a torment, but only because of how much she'd loved him. She could not have one without the other.

"I'm sorry," said Nilos. He might not know all of her past, but she could feel the weight of his understanding. Though *weight* was the wrong word. It didn't hold her down. Nor did it lighten her burdens. She still carried them. But now he walked beside her on this path, and she was glad of it.

"I think you're right," she said. "About the labyrinth. About the struggle. About the holy flame and the Embrace. It's not always the wrong choice. But I—I don't want to forget. I want to do better. And I want to keep caring."

"We'll find the boy. His flame will keep him strong."

"Fates, I hope so. He's a good lad. A wise lad." She hesitated, but if she was going to bare her soul, she might as well go all the way. "But he's not the only one I care about."

Nilos coughed, and stumbled, though he managed to make it look like a sudden decision to drape himself against the wall. He eyed her warily.

She took a step closer. He did not flinch away, which was a good sign. She'd been afraid she might end up looking the fool. Which, granted, was probably the least of her concerns right now. Though not according to her thrumming heart, apparently.

The slim wedge of air between them grew warm. She hadn't seen him move, but he felt closer. When he sighed, it stirred the loose threads of her hair against her cheek. He reached out, tucking the strand behind her ear, fingers brushing her neck.

"Sephre, I—"

He broke off. Sephre shuddered at a sudden chill. The spirits pressed close around them, silver eyes bright, their whispers skittering over her skin. *We are here.*

=====

The heart of the labyrinth was an open space fitted like a bowl within curved black walls. It reminded Sephre of the shrine at Stara Bron, except at its center was a wide, flat pool. There was little else to draw the eye. A few gnarled trees bent along the edge of the pool, but they were dead and leafless. Dark red vines twisted across the stones, dry, leathery leaves rustling like half-heard whispers from another room.

A single span of stone arched across the pool, ending at a point in the exact center. From where she lurked, along the far side of the pool, Sephre couldn't see what lay there. A mass of rippling darkness obscured it. "Are those . . . skotoi?"

Demons, whispered one of the spirits. Sephre had given up trying to count how many there were. The mist shifted ceaselessly, trailing her and Nilos like a silver-gray cloak, more agitated now that they were so close. *They guard the flame. They make this place our prison.*

"It must be the flame of awakening," said Nilos. "Where the spirits go to be reborn. Blocking it would trap the spirits here. Make them easier prey."

Sephre gritted her teeth until her jaw ached. She wanted to look away, but she had to understand the ground. Especially given that she had good reason to believe this was a trap. At the very least, they were expected. Another, larger mass of skotoi had gathered at the near end of the stone bridge. Many were the formless slithering shadow-things that seemed to be the demons' natural form. But at least a dozen wore human flesh—a few shrouded corpses, more that had reshaped themselves, with long spiny fingers of bone, wings of flayed skin, extra limbs molded of melted flesh. One was a monstrous four-legged beast that reminded Sephre of an enormous skeletal boar. She shuddered at the sight of the sharp tusks.

But where was Timeus? Her heart lodged in her throat. Her fingers splayed, ready to tear her way through the lot of them.

"Your lad Timeus," said Nilos, pointing. "He's alive."

Her legs wavered with relief. He was. Overlarge ears and lanky frame and quivering braids and all. The skotoi had bound him to a stone pillar, arms wrenched up above his head. He was moving, albeit weakly. Horror clawed her throat as a spidery skotos—each leg tipped with a pale limp hand—pawed at Timeus, hissing hungrily. Sparks of crimson flickered around his fingers. The skotos snarled, retreating a pace, but flexing two of its legs, fingers growing long and thin as needles.

Sephre was about to lunge forward—caution be damned—when one of the other skotoi lashed the spider with a supple, boneless limb. *Patience. Soon the master will break the cycle. And then we will feast. Then they will all be ours.*

Hissing, the spidery skotos backed away. Timeus sagged against the pillar. Still bound, but no longer in immediate peril. *Hold on, lad. I'm coming.*

Sephre looked to Nilos. "So their master isn't here. Is that a good thing or a bad thing?"

"Good, if it means we only have to face that lot."

No. They were missing something. "But why? Their master wants to stop the Serpent from returning. So why isn't he here to do that? What does 'breaking the cycle' mean?"

She chafed her arms against the chill of the labyrinth. And the deeper chill of her own suspicions. Lacheron hadn't come to Stara Bron seeking only the dagger. He'd wanted the agia. He'd wanted Beroe to return with him, to summon the Phoenix so she might restore the Faithful Maiden to life.

"What if the Ember King wanted the dagger back for a different reason? What if he doesn't care about killing the Serpent? What if he's after a different god?"

Nilos stared at her. Then his green gaze shifted to the middle distance. Thinking. And not good thoughts, judging by the grim set of his jaw. "That would *not* be good. It would be . . . apocalyptic."

He gave a small shake of his head. "But there's little we can do about it now. What we *can* do is free your boy. And these spirits."

"Two unarmed mortals against two dozen demons of the underworld?" She grimaced. "I don't like our odds."

Nilos drew a short dagger from his belt, the one he'd used to carve the toy horse for his niece. He held it out. "Does this help?"

"I don't suppose you have anything a little bigger?"

He gave her a frankly wicked smile. "Maybe later."

She had to stifle a snort of laughter. Now they were both making terrible jokes. That was a bad sign. "What about you?" she asked.

"I think it's my turn to be the distraction," he said. "Get to Timeus. Cut him free. His flames should be enough to drive the skotoi from the center of the pool. From the holy flame. Then the spirits can reach it and be reborn. And . . . and you can reach it, too."

"Why would I—oh."

Beroe had stripped away her flame. But there was nothing to stop Sephre from reclaiming it. She had trained for it. She had done it once before. Surely the Phoenix would accept her return. *If* that was truly what Sephre wanted.

To return to a life of burning purity, a gorgeous, ruthless flame that cast all her sins in sharp relief. A brightness that focused her gaze always inward. What had Nilos said, about the balewalkers? That they bore witness to the pain of life. They served the spirits within the Labyrinth.

A lump lodged in her throat. She swallowed it. "And you really think you can handle the other skotoi alone?"

"I have the shepherd's fragment now," he said. "It will have to be enough. The others are gone. Consumed by the skotoi."

"Not all of them." She held out her arm. The ring was dark against her skin. "We had a deal. You kept your end of the bargain. Now I'll keep mine."

He tried to step back, the wall was behind him. "No."

She watched him. "You're afraid."

"Yes. I—" His jaw worked. "Fates, I can feel it. *Him.* I'm drowning in it, Sephre. It's so close."

She could hear the pain, the fear in his voice. Felt an answering echo in her chest. "What . . . what do you think will happen? Will you—" She forced herself to say it—"Will you die?"

He huffed, giving her a wry look. "Will the Serpent burst out of me like the Phoenix from the flames?" He shook his head. "I don't think it will be that simple. I'm—he's part of me. He's making me him. I'm not even sure how much of me is still Nilos. And I think it will only take a bit more to . . . tip the balance. And then I'll be gone."

Fates. She had feared the storm on the horizon, only to find a scorpion in her hand. Death was hard enough. Death meant rebirth. Meant that sometime, someday, they might meet again.

She took his hand. Still warm. Still strong and human. He smiled, but there was no humor in it. Only a terrible resignation.

"But that's not the only reason," he said. One of his fingers traced the veins of her wrist, prickling her skin, sending shivers along every nerve. "You're a mortal, walking in the labyrinth of the dead. The mark at least offers you some protection. Without it . . ."

"Don't worry about me," she said. "I can take care of myself."

"I noticed." He gave her a wistful smile. "I'm sorry we didn't meet in another time. Another life."

He raised a hand to her face, his palm smooth and cool against the flame of her cheek. There was a fire in her that had nothing holy about it. And a desperation. It could not end like this. She would not allow it.

"I'll remember you." Her voice wanted to crack, but she held it firm. "Even if you change. Even if you forget who Nilos is, I won't."

"Thank you," he said, and the simple words nearly broke her. There was nothing she could say. Nothing she could give him except the one thing that she had been so desperate to be rid of. The thing that might destroy a man that she . . . *loved* wasn't the right word. She had known him only a few days. And yet it felt like a lifetime.

So she gave him something else. A gift to herself as much as to him, if she was being completely honest. One memory, one moment, of what might have been. She had spent the last ten years wanting to forget. Now, all she wanted was to remember this, forever.

She kissed him.

He went still in surprise at first, which charmed her. Then he was moving, lips parting, hand sliding back to the nape of her neck, pulling her closer. Sweetness melted through her, and she was suddenly very aware that her body was a living thing. A hungry thing.

It was only a single kiss. But it was a kiss to last a lifetime.

Deep inside, she felt something tugging. A deep-buried splinter pulling free. She felt his sharp gasp, the air sliding over her own mouth. A part of her cried out in protest, but it was too late. She scrabbled to keep hold of Nilos, her fingers lacing through his, tangled tight to the hand that had carved a toy horse, sliced a fig, tended her wounds.

But the hand was gone. The man was gone. All she felt beneath her fingers were cold, smooth scales.

CHAPTER 34

SEPHRE

Sephre's knees cracked against the stones. She looked up, shivering, and felt as if the entire universe had somehow bound itself into those two green eyes. Utterly numinous, they loomed over her like the night sky, vast and timeless and cold.

He was beautiful, and terrible. Coils of shimmering darkness, glinting with a sheen of starlight. They wove and twisted endlessly, the patterns absorbing her mind, almost dragging her into a daze. She could not take his measure. He seemed to fill all the available space. To surround her, and encompass her.

She could only breathe, and blink, and tremble. It wasn't fear. Fear she knew. Fear she could overcome. This was something else. Awe? Reverence?

Or possibly her weary brain had simply given up, unable to fathom the fact that this was the god of dusk, the embodiment of death, right here in front of her. And she had kissed him. Well, not him. The human he had been.

"Nilos?" She finally managed to shape his name, though it came out a whisper. Did he recognize her at all? Did he remember?

Really? She scoffed at herself. *That's what you care most about? Whether the god of death remembers that you kissed him?* What mattered was the plan.

"Will you distract the other skotoi?" she asked, as if it were perfectly normal to be making battle plans with a giant serpent.

I will do far more than distract *them.*

His words whispered in her mind, which ought to have terrified her. But there was a dry warmth to it, almost amusement. It sounded like Nilos's voice. Just a little. Enough to unlock her frozen limbs.

Which was good, because the Serpent was already moving, rippling out into the center of the labyrinth. Now that Sephre had some distance, now that his eyes weren't haunting her, she could better comprehend his size. He was larger than any natural serpent, thick around as a horse at the broadest point. And endless. There were still dark coils rippling past her, though he had almost reached the bridge.

But would it be enough? The boar-skotoi was enormous, too. What if—

The Serpent struck swift as lightning. One moment he was rippling across the stones, the next moment his jaws were around the neck of the boar-skotoi, his coils winding around its rotting body. The boar bellowed. Bone snapped.

My realm. My rules.

Within the coils, the boar began to crumple. Bone and rotting flesh fell to ash, sifting gently to the earth. A slithering darkness tried to escape, but the Serpent snatched at it, jaw wide as the sky, before snapping tight. Swallowing down what remained of the demon.

The remaining skotoi shattered. Some of them—the smaller ones, she thought—simply fled, twisting away into the depths of the labyrinth. But others remained, including all those that had clothed themselves in flesh.

The Serpent gave a snickering hiss. He drew back, away from the bridge. Away from the stone pillar where Timeus still hung.

This was her distraction. Sephre crept out from the passage, hunched low, scuttling. She gripped the small dagger in one hand. It was better than nothing, and she'd always had a good kick. But even better not to get into a fight at all right now.

A daze still clung to her thoughts, and breathing was becoming more of a challenge. As Nilos had warned her, without the Serpent's mark, she was simply a mortal woman, walking the underworld. That was . . . not a good thing to be.

HOUSE OF DUSK 373

She quickened her pace, forcing her weary legs to a jog. Dimly, she was aware of black coils lashing and rippling. She heard the shrieks of the skotoi, the low, humorless rasp of the Serpent's hiss. And closer, the whispers of the spirits. They drifted behind her, as if she were a falling star, and they her silvery trail.

Then she was at the pillar. Staring up at a lanky boy with over-large ears who looked utterly astonished at her arrival. Though Timeus often looked astonished, so perhaps it had nothing to do with her.

"Sister Sephre? What are you doing here?"

"I couldn't lose my best apprentice." She climbed up onto the stone plinth. Stretching, she could just barely work the blade of the dagger under the cords that bound him. Not rope, she realized, shuddering. Tendon. She whispered a low prayer for the spirit of whatever corpse had been desecrated to provide them. "Then I'd have all the bother of training someone new."

He laughed, though it came out as more of a croak. The bindings parted, loosening his hands. The boy collapsed, but she was quicker, and managed to catch one long arm. Fates, he really was just a collection of knobbly knees and elbows.

"Can you stand?" she asked.

"I think so." He got his feet under him, easing himself upright.

"Can you call the flame? You need to get to the center of the pool. Drive off those other skotoi." She pointed. A sigh rose from the spirits drifting nearby.

Timeus turned to her, confused. "I—But you—"

She shook her head. "I can't do it."

"But—"

"I'm not an ashdancer anymore. It's . . . it's too much to explain right now. But we need to drive back those skotoi, so that the spirits can reach the flame."

He blinked. "Er. Right. So I guess I shouldn't ask about that, either?" He pointed past her, to where the Serpent writhed and coiled, snapping at skotoi.

Sephre gave a hollow huff. "I'll tell you everything later." If there was a later. She caught the edge of the pillar as another wave of dizziness washed through her.

Timeus made a noise of concern, but she pushed herself back to her feet before he could reach for her. "I need you to do this, Brother Timeus," she said. "You're the only one who can."

She stared at him, fixing his wide brown eyes with her own. She saw a flash of uncertainty—he still doubted himself—but resolve chased after it, and won. He nodded, lifting his palms, kindling handfuls of crimson flame. Then he turned and set off along the narrow stone bridge.

The spirits followed, their whispers louder now, eager. Silvery-gray mist buffeted Sephre as she tried to follow as well. Not that Timeus needed her. He was a red brother now. And in time, he would be a yellow brother. And who knew? Agia Timeus? That would be nice. He was wiser than she'd first thought. Wiser than her.

Sephre was midway across the stone bridge when a great flare of light blazed out. Crimson, edging into orange and gold. And with it, a wail of dismay, a flinching ripple of fleeing shadows.

She was on her knees by then, though she didn't remember falling. But it was fine. She could still see them. Sparks of brightness, ascending into that grim gray sky. First one, then two, then a dozen. Then hundreds. Like a rain of stars, but in reverse. Every spark a soul spinning out into the world, to be reborn.

She stared so long it made her eyes water. Or maybe she wept. The wetness slid down her cheeks, spattering her hands, lying loose in her lap.

"Sephre?" Timeus was back, leaning over her, eyes wide with concern.

"You did it," she said. "Good lad. I'm very proud of you."

His expression melted. Warmth flushed his brown cheeks. "Thank you, sister."

"Not sister," she reminded him. "Not anymore."

He tensed, looking past her. A faint whisper hissed over stone. Scales.

The Serpent wove toward them. Then her vision blurred. No, it was the Serpent blurring, shifting and contracting, becoming a man again.

Nilos. He looked the same as she remembered. All lean strength and smooth coppery skin, hair trimmed to a faint shadow along his scalp. But his clothing had changed. Gone were the simple tunic, the worn leather sandals.

He wore a long robe of some shimmering dark cloth, caught at the waist by a silver belt. It left bare a long triangle of his chest.

Sephre stared. The Furies would definitely curse her for thinking impure thoughts about a god, and yet she could not bring herself to look anywhere else. Certainly not his face. She thought of the eyes of the Serpent, so vast and unknowable.

I will remember you, she thought, blinking as the world spun.

Hands gripped her, lifting her. She forced her eyes open again, expecting to see Timeus. But it wasn't Timeus who held her.

"Nilos," she said, forgetting that he was gone.

Something flickered across his face, too quick to catch.

The Serpent lifted her as if she were a feather, setting her on her feet. Turned her gently toward the far end of the bridge, where a bright flame burned within a bowl of stone. Sparks rose crimson and gold, from an unwavering heart of palest blue.

She found the last of her strength, enough to step free from his hands. To stand alone, at the edge of the stone bridge, with the waters of the Lyrikon spread on either side, and the flame blazing bright before her.

"Go to the flame, ashdancer," said Nilos. She could call him that, in the privacy of her mind. She could believe that he was still there, some part of him. She had promised to remember. Just as she would remember Zander. And the woman with the baby. And the two men, who had died wrapped around each other, holding on.

She would never regret carrying the flame. Or her time at Stara

Bron. The place—the people—would never leave her heart. But it was time to walk a new path. *Assuming it doesn't kill me.*

She turned her back to the flame, shaky, but certain. "No," she said. "Not this time."

Then she let herself fall, backward, one step into empty air. A rush. A cry that was probably Timeus, because why would the Serpent cry out for her?

Then the waters of the Lyrikon caught her, and pulled her down.

———

Sephre had expected pain. Instead, she drifted, her limbs loose and soft and untethered. Even the ache in her knee was gone. She floated in a wavery, watery light. It reminded her of a day they had been patrolling along the eastern shoreline during the siege, and had found a tiny sandy cove tucked into the sharp crags, practically invisible from outside. It was hot as blazes and they'd been hiking since dawn. She'd planned to keep going for another hour, but Zander had been very convincing about the tactical necessity of a swimming break. *The Bassarans might be using underwater tunnels,* he'd said, already stripping off his tunic. *We need to make a thorough search.* Vyria had added, *Just as well we take a dip. Some of us are starting to stink like the Beetle's ass,* which had led to a long debate about whether beetles had asses, which had only ended in a water fight.

The sea had been such a vivid blue-green that it was like floating in the heart of a jewel, the world a bright and glittering place that could do no harm to anyone. She had held that day like a treasure, locked away deep. This was the first time she'd thought of it since the end of the war.

The rippling light surrounded her, but it had no source. Her feet touched no sand, no stone. Then something shifted, the light thickening before her, taking form.

HOUSE OF DUSK 377

It was the woman again. Younger than Sephre, but no willowy girl either. Unremarkable, with curling dark hair that hung to her shoulders, held back by a twist of blue cloth. Freckled olive-toned skin, a hawkish nose that might have seemed too sharp on another face. Thick, dark brows and a pair of clear gray eyes that regarded Sephre steadily. Not beautiful, but compelling.

It wasn't her own face, but it was close enough they might be mother and daughter. "Who are you?" she asked.

"An echo of a memory," the woman said. "I have no name. I gave it up. Burned it to ash."

Sephre breathed in. Strange that she could breathe here, in this watery realm. But she felt her chest rise, felt the flood of coolness in her lungs. "You're her. The Maiden."

Not some shadow named faithless or faithful to serve those who survived her. Not a legend or a story or a half-remembered tale. This was the woman herself. Or some part of her.

"Why can I see you?" she asked.

"You know why." The woman regarded her steadily.

Sephre had suspected. Had seen the shadow of this truth in Nilos's eyes. Even so, her lips did not want to move. To speak it. "I'm . . . am I you? Reborn?"

One corner of the woman's mouth tilted up. "*Reborn*. A mortal word, for something beyond mortal ken. You carry something of me."

Even so, if that was true, it had other implications. When a spirit was reborn, any trace of the old body fell to ash. Sephre forced herself to ask the question. "Then the bones, the reliquary we took from Bassara . . ."

"Are not mine. They belong to another."

She had expected it. Still, it shook her.

"If you wish to aid her," said the woman, "then you must finish the work I could not."

"What?" Sephre asked. "You mean the Ember King? Stopping him from breaking the cycle? What does that mean?"

A shadow passed over the woman's face. "It means the end of all this. The return of something old and terrible."

"That's all you can tell me?"

"I'm sorry." The woman shook her head. "So much is ash. I couldn't . . . I needed to forget."

"I understand." Sephre had almost done the same. And who was she to judge another's pain? Pain was not some coin to be counted and measured and tallied up. It just *was*. You endured or you escaped.

"But . . ." The woman frowned, lifting one hand, brushing her fingers close beside Sephre's temple. She thought of Nilos, cupping her cheek, and breathed deep again. "There is a face. In your memories. A face I know."

"That makes no sense," said Sephre. "You died centuries ago. Everyone you knew is dead." Even the Serpent wore Nilos's face, now.

The woman didn't seem to be listening. She twitched her fingers. "This one. This one I know." Her voice trembled with an emotion Sephre couldn't name. A tangle of love and loathing.

She stepped back, clutching what looked like a bundle of quivering threads. When she opened her hand, they wove themselves into an image.

Sephre stared into the colorless gray eyes, the bland, forgettable face that had sent her to poison a city. "Lacheron." She blinked. Breathed in the certainty of it. "He's the Ember King. He's the one who commands the skotoi. But . . . how can it be him? Still living? After three centuries?"

The woman was still staring at Lacheron's semblance. It reminded Sephre uncannily of the way Lacheron had stared at her, on the mountaintop. A hungry, searching look.

Then she blinked, shook her head, and the vision of Lacheron unraveled. "His vengeance drives him. And his master preserves him. So that he in turn will preserve his master."

"His master?"

"The First Power. The eldest child of Chaos. The destroyer."

What had Nilos told her, earlier? A legend of five children of Chaos. A murderous firstborn god, sealed into the abyss, who threatened to one day rise and claim the world for himself.

"Why would anyone serve a god who wants to destroy the world?" That was the part Sephre had never fathomed. "Vengeance is one thing, if he blamed the Serpent for not sparing his people during the plague. But isn't this . . . overkill? Is there more to the story?"

There must be. Like the unseen roots of an ancient olive tree, driven deep, tangled into stone, anchoring the silver leaves above. But she could not see the shape of them. Only a barest inkling, sieved from a dozen different—and often conflicting—legends. A maiden who fell in love with the Serpent. A king who sought to slay death itself. A witch who stole the power of a god. The haunted expression in the gray-eyed woman's face. And Lacheron himself, telling her what he had sacrificed. *I lost the one person who mattered most to me. And I know I will never get her back.*

"Was the Ember King . . . someone important to you?" she asked. "Is that how he convinced you to slay the Serpent?"

The woman hesitated. Trying to remember? Or trying to forget? "I'm sorry. My memories are ash. All I can tell you is that his face is . . . familiar."

Sephre clenched her fists, nails biting into her palms. "Never mind. It doesn't matter why he's doing it. What I need to know is how to stop him. Especially if I can't just stab him."

"You can. With the right weapon."

"Letheko? You're talking about the blade of oblivion?"

The woman shook her head. "It had a different name, once. So much has been forgotten. Cast into the flames and burned away. I . . . I was not strong enough. And now I may have doomed the world I sought to save. Deprived you of the weapon you need most desperately."

"No," Sephre said. "You did the best you could. And it's not your concern anymore. It's mine. I'll get that dagger back. I'll stop him."

"You can't stop him if you are dead."

"I'm not—" She broke off as a wave of nausea suddenly swept over her. The luminous waters buoyed her, but they were no longer mild and gentle. She felt herself leaching into them. Like salt, dissolving into the sea.

"You are mortal," said the woman, sadly. "And you no longer carry the flame."

Sephre struggled briefly with her heavy tongue, her numb lips. "I don't want the flame. I want this." She thought of her pain, her sorrow, her guilt, all of it. And the love too, the gem-bright water, the smiles, the laughter, the warm touch of gentle fingers on her back. It was who she was. She would carry it.

"Ah." The woman nodded. "Full circle, then. What I destroyed, you will renew." She reached out, lightly, as if she meant to press her thumb to Sephre's brow. But she was already fading. Or maybe it was Sephre's vision turning hazy.

Let go. Let it be. Let yourself feel.

Feel what?

Everything.

Was it her own mind? Or some other voice, the wisdom of the waters themselves? Did it matter? She felt the truth of it. And obeyed.

Her life. All of it, crashing through her, fresh with pain and joy. Her choices. Her losses. Her mistakes. None of it could be undone. This was no absolution.

But it was change. Time spun on, and in it, a chance to make things better.

Then she was surging up, buoyed by a great swell. Water filled her mouth, her ears, her nose. She sputtered, beating her arms, and found herself standing waist deep in a dark pool, sodden and streaming.

The Serpent and Timeus stood above her, on the stone bridge.

The god still wore Nilos's face. He bent to seize one of her hands, helping her climb out of the water. "Welcome, Sister Sephre."

"She said not to call her that," warned Timeus. "She's not an ashdancer anymore."

"No," said the Serpent, his green gaze holding hers. "She belongs to the House of Dusk now."

CHAPTER 35

YENERIS

Yeneris had always thought that Sinoe was attractive. Even when she'd been convinced that the princess was a frivolous bit of thistledown, there had been no denying the merry brilliance of her fine hazel eyes, the coy sweetness of her smiles. A kitten used to being petted and primped, to winning her admirers with silky softness.

Now, she saw the claws. Now she saw not a kitten, but a lioness.

Sinoe stood in the center of her dressing chamber, the morning light turning her into a pillar of flame, caught by the gold threads of her gown, the gold ornaments in her hair. Her face was a mask, painted white as marble, eyes ringed in kohl, with two blue tears marking her cheeks.

A lump filled Yeneris's throat, watching her. This woman who had snagged so deeply in her heart. Who made her believe that she could demand more of the world. That she could be more than a blade to sink into her enemy's heart.

Was this Sinoe? Or was this some goddess, something rare and strange and *surely* beyond her reach?

"What's wrong, Yen? Don't tell me the tears are uneven. This is my first public scrying. I want to look impressive."

Yeneris swallowed the lump. "You are."

Sinoe tilted her head, giving a sly smile. "That's it? No 'yes, my love, you are as fine and fair as the summer dew?'" She tsked. "You'll have to work on your love-talk if you're going to be sticking around."

She smiled, but her eyes dropped as she spoke, as she fiddled with the sleeve of her gown unnecessarily.

Yeneris didn't know what to say. She wanted to stick around. Wanted to stand beside this glimmering creature to the end of her days. *Careful what you wish for,* she told herself. That end might well come today, if they failed.

"You're just spoiled by all that poetry." That was better. If they were teasing each other, if she could make Sinoe smile, she could pretend that there would be another day, and another, and another. That today was not so fraught with danger and disaster. That it might not radically alter everything in her life.

"Give it a chance, Yen. It might grow on you. Like me." The trailing hem of her gown whispered across the floor as she padded over to take Yeneris's hand, twining their fingers together. "Are you worried what your people will say? When you bring them the kore, but not me?"

"No."

Sinoe squeezed her hand. "Will you be safe?"

"I doubt they'll attack me. They'll want to get the kore's bones to safety."

"But they'll be angry."

Yeneris shrugged. "I'll tell them there were too many guards, that it wasn't possible."

Sinoe frowned, creasing the heavy white face paint. Yeneris smoothed her thumb across the crack without even thinking. Because it was only natural, now. "You're going to ruin your makeup," she said.

Sinoe huffed. "And wouldn't that be a shame? The Fates don't care what I look like. This is all for Father's sake." She shook her head. "I used to love getting dressed up, you know. Before—before my visions started. I used to sneak into my mother's dressing room when she was preparing for feasts and watch her do her braids. She had the most beautiful hair. Red-gold, like copper."

Her somber gaze had shifted to the window. Now it swung back to Yeneris. "Come here." She tugged her toward the dressing table that was still littered with pots of face paint and brushes. "Turn round."

Yeneris turned. Then sat, as Sinoe's small hands pressed her down onto the stool. Fingers ran through her hair, pulling free the cord she used to tie it back into a neat ponytail.

"No, don't move." Sinoe slapped her lightly on the shoulder when she started to turn, to ask what she was doing. "Or I'll have to start over. I'm not sure I remember the trick. Ah! There."

Soft fingers bumped against Yeneris's scalp as Sinoe separated out sections of hair, then began weaving them together. "Scarthians have all sorts of braids, you know. They mean different things. There's one pattern you only ever use *once* in your life, on the day you ride your first horse. They braid the horse's tails and manes, too. Something to do with the endless cycle of life and death, I think. I'm not exactly sure. I wish . . . I wish I'd asked."

Yeneris closed her eyes, and for one brief moment she was six again, Mother's hands guiding her own, showing her how to weave the hyacinth stems into a garland to offer the kore. *Just as your grandma taught me, Ris. And maybe one day you'll teach your own daughter.*

"You'll see her again," said Yeneris, and felt the echoes of those words. Would there be a daughter, someday? Yeneris could almost see her: a fierce little girl who would learn to ride horses and braid hair and swim in the azure sea and weave garlands of hyacinth. Fates. It was too dear a dream even to whisper.

Sinoe worked silently for a moment. Then she cleared her throat. "I hope so. And . . . and I hope that you'll meet her too. Someday."

A lump filled Yeneris's throat. "Someday," she agreed. "Everything will be different, after today."

Sinoe's fingers stilled. "Yes," she breathed, like a prayer. "One way or another. Fates, you really do have lovely hair, Yen. I'm not sure why you insist on keeping it tied back all the time."

"That would be because of the palace regulations."

"Pff. Well, this is much better. See? Not bad, if I do say so myself."

Yeneris stood, patted her head gingerly to feel Sinoe's work. The princess had interwoven a dozen smaller braids into an intricate knot at the back of her skull, the tail ends hanging loose down her spine.

"Wait!" Sinoe cried, spinning away to root through one of the baskets of trinkets nearby. "One last touch. Aha!"

She turned back, something glimmering gold in her hand. It was the hair ornament her mother had sent. She bounced up onto the balls of her feet, sliding it into the knot. "There! Perfect."

Yeneris coiled her fingers through the loose braids. "What does it mean?" she asked. "You said the braids meant different things. What do these mean?"

Sinoe cleared her throat. "It's . . . a sort of blessing. Or an invocation to the spirits of the winds. To keep a loved one safe." She fussed at a loose tendril. Yeneris reached for her hand, stilling it, and wished that she would never need to let go.

But it was time. They had a holy relict to save, and an apocalypse to avert.

———

Everything was going according to plan. It made Yeneris nervous. True, they had the voice of the Fates on their side, but still. It was too easy.

Eight soldiers had accompanied the royal palanquin from the palace, with Sinoe tucked inside, accompanying the corpse bride, now decked in gilt finery, her veil spangled thickly with golden disks. Yeneris wondered if it was deliberate, an acknowledgment by Hierax that his people might find the sight of a skeleton bride unwholesome, for all that they believed the myth of the Faithful Maiden.

No matter now. The moment they reached the prearranged location, Hura and his people had sprung their trap. Yeneris had barely needed to help, serving mostly to keep the palanquin from tipping over as the soldiers collapsed, struck by Scarthian sleeping darts.

"Right, stick them in the warehouse for now," Hura ordered four of his people, who were already busily stripping the unconscious palanquin-bearers of their ceremonial costumes. "We don't have long before they come searching." He looked to Yeneris.

She nodded, making her way toward the palanquin. "Sinoe?" She drew back the curtain.

The princess was already crouched in the narrow base, tugging a large cedar box from beneath the seat. Yeneris joined her, and together they pulled the thing free. It had been Hura's idea, and Hura who had provided the chest. The original reliquary box had been cedar, too, carved from the wood of an ancient tree that was said to have been over a thousand years old when it fell during the cataclysm.

This cedar was from a different tree, of course. But it had been a thoughtful touch. Yeneris liked the idea of the kore being once more surrounded by the familiar sweet scent. Safe. No longer on display, no longer a prize to secure a king's glory.

It made it easier to confront the corpse in its current state. *Don't worry. You'll be home soon. I won't let them use you.*

She realized Sinoe was watching her. Waiting, her painted face ghostly and serious. "It's time to set her free, Yen."

Yeneris nodded, chest tight. Gingerly, she reached out, carefully tugging off the spangled veil, the golden circlet.

The kore's dark, empty eyes held her. Filled her with a sensation she couldn't name, too dark for joy, too bright for sorrow. Next came the gown, and the gloves, and the slippers. Beneath, the bones had been bound in fine linen, with golden wires wrapped around the joints to hold them in this mockery of life.

Sinoe had made no move to help. Had perhaps understood that this was not a task for her hands. But Yeneris was glad she was there, to bear witness.

"I wonder what happened to the actual Faithful Maiden," Sinoe said, as Yeneris began to unwind the first strips of linen. "Given everything else Lacheron has lied about, I can only assume that she's nothing like the woman in the stories. I wonder if she knew your kore. They both witnessed the cataclysm. Maybe they were friends."

Yeneris shrugged, continuing to unspool the linen bindings. "I don't know. There are stories of the kore having a sister. But—" She broke off, hissing, as a sudden jolt of pain rippled up her arm.

"Yen? Are you all right?"

Yeneris shook her hand, her fingers still stinging. "I must have poked a sharp edge of the wire when I was trying to . . ."

Her throat closed, as she saw what lay beneath the linen. She had already uncovered the lower limbs, had been working on the left arm when she'd touched the wire.

But it wasn't a wire. It was a gold bangle. Identical to the one that bound Sinoe's wrist.

No. Surely it was jewelry, nothing more. She reached out again, to slide the bracelet from the kore's bones.

This time she could not stifle her shriek. Pain roared up her arm the moment she tried to free the bangle. Even so, she might've tried again, except for Sinoe's hands, gripping hers. Stilling them.

"It won't work," she said, with chill certainty. "I've tried. With mine."

And the hope that Yeneris had gathered so tight in her chest shattered into a hundred tiny, painful shards. What could she do now? Simply take the kore's bones to Mikat as they were? But then what? Lacheron had said the other bangle would let him hunt Sinoe down. This one almost certainly served the same purpose. And maybe more. For all she knew, he might be able to work some power on the bones through the bracelet. Simply taking the kore from the city might not be enough to prevent them from committing sacrilege. A long, painful sigh slipped from Yeneris, and she stared into her empty, useless hands. "Curse the man."

"I'm sorry," said Sinoe.

Yeneris shook her head. "It's not your fault. I should have expected this. Maybe I could have—"

Crack!

She jerked her chin up to see Sinoe holding two pieces of broken red clay in her hands. The amulet. The one they'd stolen from Lacheron. The one that was meant to unlock Sinoe. To save *Sinoe*.

But the gold bangle on Sinoe's wrist remained as sleek and unbroken as ever.

It was the kore's bracelet that clattered to the floor. With a whisper, the golden wires binding the bones began to unspool like snipped threads, releasing the skeleton to patter softly onto the padded seat of the palanquin.

"Now she's free," Sinoe said, softly. "Now you can take her home."

"Sinoe," Yeneris croaked her name, reaching for the princess's arm. For the golden band that had not fallen. She thought of the second clay token, the one she had not taken. Because Sinoe told her to take the one on the right. "You knew," she accused.

"I suspected," said Sinoe, giving her a sad, wry smile. "*Only the right key can set the future free.* I'm not the future, Yen. She is. The future of your people. It was my choice. We couldn't risk the kore's freedom for mine. Now help me put things right. She deserves some peace, I think."

Silently, she began to gather the bones, placing them gently into the cedar chest. After a moment, Yeneris forced herself to do the same.

"What about the plan?"

"Plans change. I'm still going to confront my father. I don't need the Fates to speak. I'll use my own voice. And I'll make him listen. I'll make them all listen. No matter the cost."

Yeneris's fingers froze against the smooth knob of a femur. The cost? What did that mean? She searched Sinoe's face, but found only calm resignation. "You once told me you'd seen your own death. It wasn't a joke, was it?"

Sinoe's lips tightened. "No."

HOUSE OF DUSK 389

Something inside her cracked. "What did you see?"

Sinoe cupped a tiny fingerbone in her palm, staring at the fragile thing. "I was wearing a veil. There was . . . fire. And a dagger."

A dagger like Lacheron's god-killing blade? Yeneris was no sibyl, but her brain was more than capable of casting up terrible visions of the future. Sinoe, all her golden glory spilled across cold stones, a pool of dark blood leaching away that vivid, precious life.

A boulder clogged her throat as she watched Sinoe tuck the fingerbone carefully into the box. "There. She's ready for you to take her to your people. Goodbye, Yen. Please don't try to stop me."

She could, though. Easy enough to sweep Sinoe into her arms then and there. Carry her off to the stables and bundle her onto the swiftest horse and get her as far away from this doom as possible. Safe as a caged ailouron. Yeneris swallowed the boulder, and her own fear. "I won't stop you. But I'm not letting you walk into some Fates-damned future alone. I'm coming with you. Hura can take the kore to Mikat."

"No need for that," said a cool voice from outside.

The palanquin's curtained door was flung open, revealing Mikat, sword in hand, a look of cold determination on her face. "We'll take things from here, Yeneris."

CHAPTER 36

YENERIS

Things did not look good. There were at least six other Bassaran agents spread around the street. They had pressed Hura and his people back against one of the nearby walls.

"Yeneris, you'll take the sibyl," Mikat ordered crisply. "We don't have much time."

That was true. So the sooner they finished this, the better. Yeneris took a breath, then drew her sword. She stepped carefully and deliberately out from the palanquin, setting the bare blade between herself and Mikat.

The other woman backed away slowly. A she-wolf challenged for her prey. "What are you doing?" Mikat narrowed her eyes, looking past Yeneris.

Sinoe had followed her. She stood on the palanquin steps holding the reliquary. Yeneris licked her lips, making her voice firm. "You can take the kore, Mikat. But not the princess."

"And how exactly do you plan to stop me?"

"I don't need to stop you. That gold bangle on the princess's wrist will."

Mikat's lips pursed. "You have the key. Open it."

"I can't," Yeneris said. "There was another ward on the kore's bones. We used the key on that."

"How unfortunate." Mikat shook her head regretfully. "A true sibyl would be invaluable in restoring Bassara."

A thread of relief began to unspool in Yeneris. Mikat believed her. Maybe this wouldn't all go to the abyss. Maybe—

"But if we can't have the sibyl, we will not let Hierax continue to wield her power." Mikat lifted one hand, gesturing toward Sinoe.

Instinct threw Yeneris into motion, sword swinging even before she was aware of the distant *twang!*

Her blade caught the arrow, slashing it out of the sky. The reliquary clattered to the stones as Sinoe jerked back. "Go!" Yeneris shouted at her. "Get inside!"

She turned, holding her position before the door, heart thudding, body fizzing with tension, every nerve on fire now. The cedar chest lay abandoned on the street before her.

"Think very carefully, Yeneris." Mikat's voice was harsh, but not cold. "Remember who you are."

Even now, she did not want to disappoint Mikat. The woman had saved her life. Saved her spirit. Given her something to hold fast to, when everything else in her world had crumbled. Emotion gripped her throat as she remembered a warm blanket, tucked around her skinny shoulders. The few, precious smiles. The feeling of belonging to something—to someone—again.

Yeneris dragged in a steadying breath. Yes. That was who she had been. And perhaps a part of her would always be that ragged, hungry, lonely girl. But she did not belong to Mikat. And not to Sinoe, either. She belonged to herself.

"I'm the person who's going to stick a sharp blade somewhere very painful if you touch a hair on Sinoe's head."

Now, the chill. Mikat narrowed her eyes. "Best take care." She reached—slowly—into a fold of her robe. Drew out something small and metallic: a dagger barely as long as her palm. "By my reckoning you've only got five left."

It was her own blade. The one she'd planted on the supposed Bassaran spy. The boy. Right before she killed him. Nausea roiled her belly. For a moment she smelled the hot tang of his blood. Felt the sticky squelch of it between her fingers.

"He was a brave lad," said Mikat. "Almost as good as you. His name was Cirrus."

Cirrus. Yeneris chiseled the name into her memory. How had

Mikat recovered the weapon? She thought of the boy's body, dumped into some pit. She hoped Mikat had at least given him a proper blessing.

"I didn't want to do it."

Mikat shook her head. "Of course not. I know that. Everyone here knows it. You did what you had to do. Because you're strong. Because I trained you to do hard things." The dagger winked in the sunlight as Mikat spun it between her fingers. "You care about the girl. I see that. I understand what I'm asking of you."

"Then *don't*," Yeneris burst out. "Don't ask me to choose. Listen to me when I tell you there is a greater enemy than Hierax. One that threatens all the world, not just Bassara."

"Let them burn. We have the kore now. She will keep us safe." Mikat snapped shut, tight as an ironclam.

"The way she kept us safe ten years ago?" demanded Yeneris. A pain burst in her chest, to speak the words. But they were true. They were a thorn dug deep in her soul. She honored the kore. The bones were a sacred trust, and she would still do everything she could to ensure Hierax had no chance to abuse them further. But they were not some panacea that would heal every wound. "We need to do more, Mikat. If we truly honor the kore, we need to do what she did. Give everything to protect this world. The Ember King is trying to kill the god-beasts. We need to stop him before he unleashes a second cataclysm."

Mikat's lip curled. "We owe this world nothing."

Maybe Yeneris could reach her, if she had a week. A month. A year. But there was no more time.

A dull pain had begun to beat against her temples. "Then take the kore and go." With one foot, she nudged the reliquary forward. "But Sinoe is under my protection."

"I trained you, girl," scoffed Mikat. "You really think you can best me?"

That was it, then. Yeneris released the last of her hope. It was almost a relief, to let it go. To come back to what she knew best.

Her body, honed to a weapon. She crouched, falling into the familiar stance, her muscles tense and ready. "Yes."

Mikat's attack was sudden and brutal, a quick punch of blades that sent Yeneris leaping to the side. One slash caught her sleeve. Mikat gave a bark of laughter. "You're out of practice. Spending too much time making eyes at the princess. Not enough remembering to watch your left flank."

Another feint and stab, but Yeneris blocked the blow this time, then followed up with a slash of her own.

Mikat evaded it easily, though she gave a nod of concession. "Better. Maybe you haven't forgotten everything I taught you."

"I know who I am," Yeneris panted. "You're the one who's lost her way, Mikat. Take the kore and go."

Mikat's only answer was a sweeping kick. Yeneris dodged, only to find a blade arcing into her face. She wrenched her own sword to block it, but the blow shuddered through her arm, rattling her bones.

"You know, I once thought you could be another Akoret," said Mikat. "That was the girl I saved. That was the girl I trained. A true Bassaran, willing to sacrifice anything for her people."

They traded blows, circling, weaving. Every time Yeneris thought she might have a window of attack, Mikat closed it. Despair began to chew at the edges of her mind. Mikat was quick and strong, and had twenty years more experience. Yeneris could match her speed and strength, but was that enough?

Every trick she knew, Mikat had taught her. There was no way to surprise her, no way to catch her off guard. And the longer this fight ground on, the greater the risk of discovery. "The Helissoni will come looking for us," she warned.

Mikat drew back so abruptly she thought her warning had worked. Then she caught the furtive movement, a quick snatch to seize a hidden blade and send it streaking at Yeneris.

She blocked it, but the move left her open, and suddenly Mikat was there, pressing close with a flurry of blows that battered her faltering defenses.

Then one final twist, and Yeneris lost her grip, her sword skittering away. She coiled herself, ready to fight back with fist and foot.

But Mikat had spun away, making for the palanquin. For Sinoe.

Yeneris pulled two of her hidden daggers free and flung them at Mikat. One missed entirely. The other whistled past her cheek. Enough to send her ducking to the side. There was no time for relief.

She had her last two blades in hand by the time Mikat recovered. Blood oozed down the woman's cheek, but she was grinning, triumphant. She hefted her sword and took a pace closer.

Yeneris flung one of the daggers. Mikat blocked it, moving confidently. She knew how this would end. Knew everything about Yeneris. Because she had shaped her, honed her, trained her, turned her into a living weapon to slice the heart out of their enemies.

Yeneris weighed her last blade in her hand. She knew what she had to do. She flung it straight at Mikat's face.

The woman batted the blade aside as if it were a fly, laughing. "You're out of weapons, girl."

Yeneris held her ground as Mikat stalked closer. "Look at what she's done to you." Her lip curled. "Did she have her handmaidens give you those ridiculous braids?"

A faint squawk of protest came from the pavilion. Yeneris breathed in, one hand lifting to touch the braids, sweeping over them as if they were a talisman. Her fingers brushed the amber hairpin. *To keep a loved one safe. Let's hope the wind-spirits are paying attention.*

"I'll give you one last chance," said Mikat. For all the bitterness in her voice, her brown eyes held something softer. "Prove that you still hold true and I'll spare you. You'll be a hero, instead of a traitor."

"No. I'd be a traitor to the kos," said Yeneris. "If there is a world soul, then Sinoe is part of it. She's part of my heart. I will not cut that out just to please you. I'm not your blade anymore."

Mikat took a long, slow breath in. Then let it out, sharp and quick, as if she were blowing out a lamp. Her sword slid under Yeneris's chin. "Then you will both die."

"You're wrong about another thing too," said Yeneris.

Mikat frowned. "What?"

"I still have one weapon left," she said, and jabbed the amber hairpin into Mikat's arm.

The woman shrieked, stumbling back, but Yeneris had already seized the hilt of her sword, twisting it away.

A heartbeat later their positions were reversed. Now Mikat was the one with a sword tip resting gently against her throat. Yeneris held her gaze coolly. "You have a choice, Mikat. You can swear by the kore that you will not harm Sinoe, or you can die."

Mikat looked as if she were chewing a mouthful of thorns. She glanced toward the palanquin, then to the cedar reliquary lying a few paces away. Finally she swallowed, and nodded. "I swear by the kore that I will not harm the princess, nor will any other here. She's free to go. Stand down," she called to her people.

The Bassaran agents lowered their weapons, retreating slowly, releasing Hura and his people. Yeneris paced back a step, nodding to the cedar chest. Mikat went to claim it.

As she hefted it into her arms, her gaze found Yeneris again. "I will keep my word, Yeneris. But you will regret this choice. I will see that everyone knows what you've done. We will restore Bassara, but there will be no place for you there."

Then she turned and stalked away, accompanied by the others. A few glanced back at her. Some with that same outrage and disgust, but others less certain.

"Yeneris?"

She barely had time to lower Mikat's sword before Sinoe slammed into her, arms wrapped tight. "Fates. I thought . . ." The princess dragged in a long, shaking breath.

"You thought I was extremely competent and talented," Yeneris suggested. But she gripped Sinoe's shoulders as if daring the world to tear her away, and the words were rough.

"Yes," Sinoe's voice was a strangled mixture of laughter and relief. "That's it exactly."

A darker thought occurred to Yeneris. She pulled back, searching Sinoe's bone-pale face, finding her hazel eyes in the dark rings of kohl. "You didn't think I would do it, did you?"

"No. Never." Sinoe slid her hands up, lacing her fingers into Yeneris's tightly. "But I'm sorry. I didn't want you to have to make that choice."

"I'd do it all over again," said Yeneris, steadily, clearly, so that Sinoe would see the truth of it. "A thousand times over."

Sinoe's lips parted around a soft sigh. Lifting Yeneris's hand, she pressed a single kiss into her palm, then winked. "I'd thank you more properly, but you really don't want to be covered in face paint. It's horrible stuff."

Yeneris was entirely willing to take that risk, but she was also keenly aware that this wasn't over. The kore was free, but Sinoe was not. Which was going to make challenging Hierax and Lacheron even more dangerous.

CHAPTER 37

SEPHRE

The water shimmered under Sephre's fingertips. Not the bright leap of flame, but a silvery gleam, like starlight. Beautiful. And deadly.

But not to her.

She sat cross-legged at the edge of the pool, one hand drifting just above the surface. Reveling in the cool shiver that echoed in her own flesh. It was quiet here now, in the center of the labyrinth. No doubt there were other spirits, wandering the maze of their own past sorrows. And other skotoi, lurking in wait for them. Maybe that was where the Serpent had gone. Sephre had only a dim memory of him leaving, promising to return shortly from whatever serpent-godly business called him away. She supposed he had three centuries to catch up on. For his sake, she hoped very much that there were no account ledgers in the underworld.

She could see Timeus, over across the bridge, standing beside the flame. He was attempting to send a firespeaking to Stara Bron. What would Beroe think, she wondered, hearing Timeus's voice speaking from the heart of the flame, warning her that Lacheron was going to try to kill the Phoenix? Would she believe him? Or would she dismiss it as more corruption?

And what about the rest of them? Abas. Dolon. Vasil. She hoped they would understand her choice. That they would still love her. She thought of Dolon, telling her about how it was before the cataclysm. *A balewalker, stopping by to take tea.* She'd like that. Very much.

When she first stepped out from the waters of the Lyrikon, she'd braced herself for Timeus's disappointment. That he would look at her, and see her failure, her broken vows. Or worse, think that she was abandoning him, turning her back on the ashdancers.

But instead he surged forward—actually *pushed past* the Serpent to embrace her and congratulate her—and something broke inside Sephre. A wall she hadn't even realized was still there. She had hugged him back, all the gangly, living, joyful bulk of him, and wept. There was no judgment, no censure. Timeus was simply happy for her.

She would never regret her time as an ashdancer. Her garden was a joy, a sanctuary that had guarded her in her most fragile hours. She loved her siblings. And siblings they would remain. Her chosen family, whether or not her veins burned with flame.

Sephre tapped her forefinger to the water. Watched the ripples spreading. Like the sureness of her own choice, rippling through her flesh. But much as she loved the people of Stara Bron—well, most of them—the faith had never quite suited her. Or maybe *she* hadn't suited the faith. It turned her inward. Focused her on her own flaws, her shames, her past. Held her fixed in place, when she needed to grow and change.

Not that everything was suddenly sweet wine and roses, now she was a balewalker. Sephre doubted whether she would ever feel the sort of peace she once aspired to. But for the first time in a long while she felt . . . whole.

She heard his footsteps approaching. No doubt he meant her to. He was a god, after all. He could probably float, if he wanted. She uncoiled her legs, wincing at the prick of invisible needles along her skin. Stood, drew a bracing breath, then turned to face him.

It wasn't enough. Her world spun at the sight of the man who stood there in his slippery dark robes and his stolen human face. Maybe he thought it would be less frightening for her. She would almost have preferred the fangs. Then, perhaps, she could forget the kiss. *Fates, get your head turned straight.*

She wondered if she should salute. Or kiss his hand? No,

definitely not. But she had to do something more than stand there, staring at him like a stubborn goat. She was his priestess. Or something like that. *She belongs to the House of Dusk now.* That's what he had said, as he pulled her from the waters of death. She flexed her fingers, then tucked her hands behind her and settled on a simple bow.

"That's not necessary." His expression was exactly like the one Nilos had made when she'd insisted on cooking breakfast, their final morning before reaching Stara Sidea.

"You're a god," she told him. "I don't want to get smited for a lack of proper respect."

He looked pained. "There are things you should know," he said, apparently deciding to ignore the topic entirely.

Many things. But not all of them as urgent as others. "Like what exactly Lacheron is planning?" she suggested. "And how we're going to stop it?"

"Yes. But first, these are for you." He produced a folded pile of cloth, as if from thin air, and held it out to her.

Sephre regarded the bundle warily. It looked like clothing. On top lay a pair of dark blue gloves. "You have a wardrobe in the underworld?"

"You'd be surprised." He flashed her Nilos's quick smile, and her heart gave a foolish wobble. "The balewalkers kept a number of outposts within the labyrinth. I found this in one of them. It's . . ."

"A balewalker habit," she finished, understanding. It was very like the robes she'd worn at Stara Bron. But more blue than gray, with rippling green lines embroidered along the hem and sleeves. She arched her brows at the gloves, though. "Is it . . . especially cold at Stara Sidea?"

Another stolen smile. "No. The gloves serve a different purpose. You carry the waters of the Lyrikon in your flesh now. My waters." He hesitated a moment, and she thought there might have been a faint flush darkening his cheeks. "Venom. Deadly to the living. And to the skotoi as well."

"You're saying I'm poisonous?" Sephre lifted her hands, turning them, taking note of the shimmer she'd been admiring earlier.

"You can learn to control it," he said. "As you did your flames. But for now . . ." He held out the bundle, as if to press it into her hands.

She started to flinch away. Then caught herself, remembering who he was. "I can't harm you."

He regarded her for a long moment. "The poison won't affect me. Nor any other mortal sworn to one of my siblings."

Thank the Fates for small mercies. She thought of Timeus, surging into her with that warm embrace. Still, it would take some getting used to. "What about plants?" she asked, with a flare of panic. "Can I still garden?"

"Yes." He sounded amused. "Your prized hibiscus is safe."

She cut her gaze to him, startled. He remembered? Was it only that he had Nilos's memories? Or was the mortal man still there, somewhere?

She had the distinct impression he had surprised himself as much as her. And for a moment his eyes were the eyes of a man, eyes that watched the world fade, that valued each sunrise.

"Nilos?" The word came out a whisper, afraid of startling this hope, sending it galloping away with her heart.

Then a quick drum of footsteps turned them both toward the bridge. Brother Timeus was jogging back toward the shore, his expression animated.

"I reached Brother Dolon!" he proclaimed triumphantly. "He said it was good luck that he happened to trade duty for the dusk vigil with Sister Polia, because Sister Polia always falls asleep, and so she never would have heard the firespeaking. But he heard me and he came and I told him everything that's happened. He wishes you well, sister, in your new office, and, er—" the boy ducked his head shyly to the Serpent"—he congratulates you on your return, Lord Serpent. And then he told *me* all the news from Stara Bron!"

"Which is?" Sephre prompted, as the boy finally paused to take a breath.

"Agia Beroe left the temple four days ago," said Timeus. "She's agreed to perform the Blue Summons for the king. To call on the Phoenix to restore the Faithful Maiden to life."

"It isn't her," said Sephre. "The bones, they belong to someone else."

"Oh," Timeus blinked at her. "How do you know?"

"I had . . . a vision." Sephre could feel the Serpent watching her. It made her skin prickle, and a part of her wanted to ask if he had already known that. "When will Beroe do it?" she asked Timeus, instead.

"Tomorrow. She'll likely be at the palace by now."

Sephre rocked back on her heels, cast her eyes up to the iron gray sky, and muttered a curse. "There's no way we'll reach them in time. Even if we go back to Stara Sidea, it's still at least a day's travel to Helissa City. If we steal horses, and ride them bloody."

She turned on the Serpent. "But we have to stop him. Lacheron has the god-killing blade, and now he has Beroe, and an excuse to summon the Phoenix. Everything he needs to slay a second god."

"Yes." His green eyes searched the middle distance for a long moment. "And break the second seal that binds my eldest brother."

Timeus blinked. "The Sphinx?"

"No, the Sphinx is my sibling, not my brother. And while they've caused their fair share of trouble, they have no cause to destroy this world." The Serpent smiled briefly, then began to pace. "Unlike our eldest brother, who has no name. My siblings and I took it from him, when we cast him into the abyss."

He halted beside the glimmering pool, staring across the still waters. "Each of us gave a piece of our own power to seal him there. But mine was broken, when I died. And if my sister dies, hers will shatter as well."

"Leaving just two," said Sephre. "Is that enough to keep the First Power bound?"

"I don't know. But with every broken seal his power will grow. When the first seal broke, he tore down mountains and sank islands. Shattered the old empire. With the second . . ." He shook his head. "There will be . . . many dead spirits."

She sucked in a breath of dismay. "And no Phoenix to grant them new life."

"You came back, Lord Serpent," said Timeus. "She might, too."

Sephre shook her head. "We don't have three centuries."

"And she would not be the same," said the Serpent. Sephre frowned at him. What did that mean? Was he speaking from experience? How was he not the same?

He blatantly avoided her questioning look. "There is no other option. You must stop it."

"*Us?* What about you?" Sephre demanded. "You're the god of death."

"I am," he said. "And my place is here now. I can't leave it."

"You left it to woo the Maiden," Sephre said, knowing even as she spoke it that she was being unfair. *Get over it, woman,* she told herself sternly. *More important things to worry about. The fate of the world and all.* "There must be something you can do."

"There is. This is the realm of the dead. It touches the world of the living in many places, not just at the shrine in Stara Sidea. I will see that you reach the city by tomorrow morning."

=====

Sephre had considered insisting—as reverently as possible—that the Serpent open the path to Helissa City right then and there. The sooner they reached Lacheron, the better. Or Beroe. She doubted she could convince the agia not to go through with the invocation, but she *was* fairly confident she could knock the woman silly.

Then she'd noticed the dark circles under Timeus's eyes. The hollowness of his cheeks. After the firespeaking and war council, he'd inhaled the last stale bread and rinds of cheese she dug from Nilos's pack, then fell almost instantly asleep, curled against the base of plinth that held the holy flame. He likely hadn't slept properly in days.

It was probably the safest spot for the lad in the entire labyrinth, but there were still skotoi skittering about, and Sephre had not come this far to lose him again. She settled herself wearily against the base of one of the dead trees that lined the shore, prepared to keep watch. Though as she leaned back against the gnarled bark, she saw that the tree was not so withered and wasted as she'd first thought. There were tiny, dark-green leaves beginning to sprout along several of the branches. She gazed at them, wonderingly, until she felt a presence behind her. Even then, she did not turn.

"You can sleep too, if you like," said the Serpent. "Nothing will hurt you here."

A blatant lie. The bittersweet ache in her heart was proof of that. She shook her head. "I'm not tired."

"Hungry, then?"

"I gave Timeus the last of the food."

Dark robes fluttered at the edge of her vision as he folded himself onto the stones beside her. He held something. A bowl heaped with figs. Dark purple, with a paler bloom, looking ripe as if he'd just plucked them.

"Those can't be from the balewalker outpost. Are you growing fig trees down here as well?" She nodded up to the tree. The leaves looked even larger now, and more vivid. She still couldn't identify them, though. Maybe this was the fabled duskbloom. Whatever it was, clearly it appreciated having its proper master back in charge of the underworld.

"No." He looked slightly sheepish. "The figs are . . . grave goods. Left by a woman mourning her son. They were his favorite."

She arched a brow. "That sounds like sacrilege."

"He won't miss them. His spirit is . . . gone." He dipped his chin, jaw tight.

"The skotoi?"

"Yes. They caused considerable harm. I have a great deal of work to do."

He set the bowl of figs beside her knee. She peeled off her new gloves, but waited until he drew back before she took one. She tried to eat it neatly, but failed utterly. The juice spilled down her chin like sticky tears. "Shouldn't you be off doing it, then?"

He winced. Was that possible? Could a god wince? He had fallen in love with a mortal once, so perhaps.

Sephre took another fig. This time she drew her dagger—Nilos's dagger—to section it more neatly. She paid close attention to her work. "Do you remember?"

"Remember what?"

Her courage failed her. "The Maiden. Who she really was. The truth behind all the stories."

She thought of the gray-eyed woman conjuring Lacheron's face in that strange, watery vision. Staring at it, haunted by it. "You said she was a novice in the House of Dusk. That the Ember King somehow convinced her to destroy you. But there's more to it, isn't there?"

"Well, yes. Gamales of Tarkent spends twenty full stanzas going on about the Ember King's preparations for battle, but honestly, no one needs to know that he wore a breechclout embroidered with flames."

Evasion again. But she would not be turned aside. "Who was she, really? The Ember King's bride?"

"No. The queen died in the first year of the plague. The Maiden was Heraklion's daughter." Nilos gave a rueful laugh. "Bards try to make every story a romance."

"It sounds like there was already a romance in this one."

He said nothing.

"He sent her to seduce you, but it didn't work. I mean, yes, she did destroy you. But she also . . . cared for you."

She wasn't certain it was true until the words slipped free from her tongue and burned scarlet into his high amber cheeks. Fates, had she actually made the god of death blush?

"Well? Do you remember?"

A sigh. She couldn't tell if it was relief, or regret. Or impatience with her mortal curiosity.

HOUSE OF DUSK 405

"More than before."

Her hand slipped, the blade nicking her finger. She hissed, then stuck the cut into her mouth, tasting blood and figs. *More than before?* Meaning, more than when he was Nilos?

"Here," he said, pulling her hand from her lips. His thumb pressed the base of her wrist, and she could feel every throb of her pulse. He leaned over the wound, and for one terrifying and uncomfortably exciting moment, she thought he meant to kiss it.

Instead, he exhaled, the warm flush of his breath tickling her skin. A hum filled her, as if she'd swallowed a hive of bees. When he released her, the wound was gone.

He regarded her evenly, green eyes inscrutable.

She crossed her arms, tucking her still-buzzing hand away. "Impressive. But party tricks aren't going to distract me. You remembered my hibiscus. What else do you remember?"

"I remember her name."

Sephre sat very still, waiting.

"Martigone."

He stood abruptly, a smooth uncoiling, graceful and just slightly inhuman. The long hem of his dark robe whispered over the stones, brushing her thigh. "Use it well."

"That's it?" she demanded. "That's all?"

"All for now," he said. "Come back to Stara Sidea after this is done. I'll wait for you at the undying shore. And ask me again."

Then he turned and left her with the figs and all her unanswered questions.

=====

"Are you sure you can do this?" Sephre asked Timeus. The Serpent's divine portal had brought them as far as the Helissa City necropolis, and they had spent the past hour making their way across the city to the Temple of the Fourfold Gods. Now, they lurked just outside the main entrance. Bright banners had been strung from the walls, decorated with Hierax's chosen emblem, a flaming crown of laurels. He had added something new: a stylized dagger in the center. A celebration of the Ember King's long-awaited union with his Faithful Maiden.

Timeus gave her an injured look. "I thought you said I could do anything. You sent me to destroy a wall of skotoi and free the spirits of the labyrinth."

"I know you're brave and wise and strong," she told him. "But can you lie to the royal guard?"

He sniffed. "I'm a better liar than you."

"What have I lied about?"

"After Nilos opened the portal into the city necropolis, and he said 'Farewell, Sephre, don't be long,' and I asked if you were sad and you said 'No, of course not, what a ridiculous notion.'"

"I'm not sad," she told him, peevishly. "But I will be if we're too late to stop the Ember King from destroying the world."

He said nothing more, but there was an infuriating quirk to his lips as he stepped out and began pacing serenely toward the gate.

It was open, as it usually was during the day, presided over by the inevitable great bronze statue of Breseus. Sephre recalled hearing that Hierax had brought in artisans to alter the features of the hero, to make it resemble his own. Not hard to believe that such a man had been all too eager to believe that he was the Ember King reborn.

How had Lacheron done it? Clever manipulation of prophecy. Whispers and nudges. A thousand drops to form a sea of conviction. But why? Because he preferred a figurehead? She might never know.

There were four soldiers. Two standing a few paces beyond the threshold, beneath the portico, and two others further back. Timeus led the way toward the nearer pair of guards, his expression calm and serene, a proper ashdancer.

Sephre followed, keeping her eyes downcast slightly, bowing her head as she calculated how to take the soldiers down if things went sideways. Fates, she hoped this worked. A coolness bloomed in her palms. The water of death, waiting beneath the thin veil of her gloves. But these soldiers were not her enemy.

"Hello," Timeus greeted the guards cheerily. "Could you please tell us where to find Agia Beroe and the others?"

The soldier studied him, her gaze scanning Timeus up and down, lingering on the crimson flames embroidered along his sleeves. "My name is Brother Timeus," he offered amiably. "Of Stara Bron. We're not late, are we? I did my best, but we had to go all the way to the south market to find the incense the agia needs for the invocation. You do still have it, don't you, novice?"

Sephre dutifully lifted the small sack containing a handful of olibanum that they'd borrowed from the necropolis earlier that morning, after emerging from the underworld. The soldier flicked a bored eye over Sephre, then frowned.

Sephre tensed, but the woman only glanced back to Timeus. "She's a *novice*? She's old enough to be your mother."

"I came to my calling late," said Sephre, keeping her expression scrupulously serene. She noticed that Timeus had suddenly been afflicted by a coughing fit that caused him to cover the lower half of his face.

"Oh?" The soldier seemed more curious than scornful now. "What did you do before?"

"I was a soldier."

"Huh." The woman looked thoughtful. She nudged her fellow in the side. "What do you think, Crisus? Should I put down my spear and take up prayers?" Then she laughed, and Crisus laughed, and they waved for Timeus and Sephre to pass inside. "Turn left, and take the wide blue stairs. That will take you to the atrium."

Timeus gave Sephre an arch look. "Come along, then. We shouldn't keep the agia waiting."

CHAPTER 38

YENERIS

Yeneris crept along the rear of the crowd inside the temple, making her way slowly toward her target. The central atrium was packed with richly garbed celebrants expecting to witness the restoration of the Faithful Maiden and her marriage to the Ember King. And they were growing restless. The royal palanquin was late.

Yeneris herself had only arrived at the temple a few moments ago, and she had run. It had been a wrench to leave Sinoe, but she needed to get into position. As close to the king and Lacheron as she could. It might be vital, if things went wrong.

Or rather, if things went even *more* wrong. Bad enough that Mikat's attack had delayed them. That Sinoe had freed the kore, rather than herself.

At least the kore's bones were surely well beyond the city walls by now. For all their differences, Yeneris trusted Mikat to guard the reliquary. To deliver the kore safely to one of their southern outposts, where she would no doubt seek to rally more of their people to her cause. Supplies, timber, weapons. Eventually, they would sail away across the sea.

So there would be no wedding. And Hierax would fall. He ruled on the power of his claim to be the Ember King reborn, not because he was a wise or beloved man. And it was Sinoe's prophecy—twisted by Lacheron's self-interested interpretation—that had given Hierax that power. Once it was stripped away, he would be merely a man.

That still left Lacheron, though. The true Ember King. A

sorcerer with uncanny powers gifted by the first spawn of Chaos. Yeneris tapped her blades, all six now back to their proper places, and the golden hairpin tucked into her braids. Would any of them pierce the flesh of such a man? She would find out soon enough. She breathed in, feeling the tug in her chest, the memory of Sinoe's crooked smile as she wished her luck. It hurt, to not be with her. To be unable to count on her own body and blades to keep the princess safe.

Yeneris swallowed the ache, then continued on, ducking beneath the bright banners that hung from the pillars of the large hall. Some bore images of the Phoenix, others the circlet and dagger of the supposed Ember King. The air was thick with the perfume of roses, rising from the carpet of petals scattered across the marble floor, now crushed under the sandals of a hundred of the most notable folk in the city. Judging by the rustling whispers, the guests were growing restless. She caught their muttered questions as she edged through the crowd. *Where is she? Why hasn't she come?*

Yeneris skulked around the back of one of the pillars. She had nearly reached the raised dais at the eastern end of the hall where Hierax awaited his bride. Across from him stood Agia Beroe and her ashdancers.

The crowds were thinner here, fenced back from the dais by ivory-inlaid screens and a row of armed soldiers offering a less symbolic deterrent. Yeneris continued to weave through the crowd, keeping her movements slow, casual, unremarkable. Meanwhile, the king summoned one of the soldiers, snapping a question she couldn't make out. Whatever the answer, Hierax clearly didn't find it satisfying. He spun toward Lacheron, a dull shadow amid the brightness, and gestured impatiently. The Heron frowned, one hand moving to a gleam of red tucked into his waist sash.

He pulled it free, staring at it. A tight wedge filled Yeneris's throat. Which was it? The true amulet, that still bound Sinoe's bracelet? Or the decoy that had allowed her to steal away the key to release the kore?

A ripple of some dark emotion passed over Lacheron's face. His fingers clenched tight, snapping the clay. He let the shards fall. The decoy, then. She thought of soldiers, riding swiftly from the city, chasing after Mikat and the kore.

Yet he made no move to raise any alarm. Why? Surely he needed the kore for this spectacle. Without a Faithful Maiden to raise from the dead, why summon the Phoenix?

She watched him, the faint flicker of his eyes. The press of his lips. Her heart fell as he tugged free the second amulet. Studied it. Then gave the faintest and most terrible of smiles.

Only one will go free if the divided heart remains.

No. She had heeded that warning. It was time to stop worrying about the damn prophecy and focus on stopping the apocalypse. Even the Fates could only do so much. And what had Sinoe said? *The Fates reveal patterns. They don't tell us what to do. They shine a light, and we decide which path to take.*

Yeneris had chosen her path, and it led to the dais. If Lacheron suspected them, she would be close. She would be ready. She edged along the line of pillars that flanked the north side of the hall, slipping silently past attendants.

Lacheron slid the amulet away, speaking to Hierax, his unruffled calm chewing at Yeneris. The king took no apparent comfort from his advisor's words. He spun on Ichos, who had been doing his best to fade into one of the ivory screens. Hierax jabbed a finger into the prince's chest, face gone ruddy with displeasure.

Then a stir rippled through the crowd. All eyes turned to the far end of the temple as the ornate royal palanquin processed into the atrium. The onlookers drew back, some cheering, others calling out prayers and invocations. The silken panels fluttered, revealing only a dim shadow of someone seated inside.

Yeneris's heart stumbled, but she took strength from the sight of Hura, bowed under one of the supports. The bearers carried the palanquin across the atrium, up to the base of the dais, then they finally set it down, in a bright circle of sunlight that streamed down from the open oculus above.

HOUSE OF DUSK 411

A flutter. A small hand pushed open the curtained door. Then Sinoe stepped out into brightness. Not a girl, not a woman, not a princess, but the Sibyl of Tears in all her terrible glory.

Her face white as bone, her eyes wide and dark enough to drink in the night, her small figure sword straight, so that the circlet of golden feathers in her hair blazed like a crown of flames. It was enough to wrench Yeneris's heart out of her chest, to leave her breathless with awe.

And she was not the only one. All around the temple, people were whispering, gasping, murmuring, making invocations to the Fates.

Enough goggling. Take advantage of the distraction.

Yeneris continued her advance toward the dais, even as Sinoe began to speak.

"People of Helisson," she proclaimed, her voice resonant, not quite the unearthly tones of prophecy, but close enough to send shivers down Yeneris's spine. "I am the Sibyl of Tears, and I speak for the Fates. There will be no wedding today. There will be no rebirth of the Faithful Maiden."

More mutters, and shouts as well. Hierax was frowning furiously.

But Sinoe was implacable, the words rolling on, echoing from the marble walls. "The Faithful Maiden was a lie. The war was a lie. All of it meant to bring power to my father. Power he has misused."

A swell of pride filled Yeneris as she edged past a slack-jawed soldier and slid behind one of the ivory screens. She was right beside the dais now. She could see Hierax—furious—and Lacheron—inscrutable—as well as Ichos, who was trying vainly to hide a triumphant smile. And beyond, the gray blur of the ashdancers, with the agia a bright note in her white habit, frowning in apparent confusion. And . . . who was that?

It was the way the woman moved that caught Yeneris's attention. A familiar furtive creeping, twin to her own. She was clad in a simple blue robe, and at first Yeneris thought she was one of the ashdancers, perhaps a novice, though if so, she had come to it late. She must be close to Mikat's age.

Well, whoever the mysterious woman was, Yeneris hoped that she was on their side. Her movements were compact, not especially graceful, but they held the sureness of someone who knew how to use her body to commit violence.

"Silence," Hierax's bellow rippled over the crowd, stilling the mutters and hum of questions. "Daughter, you are overwrought." He gestured to the soldiers at the base of the dais. "See to the princess. Take her back to the palace."

"Why, Father?" Ichos called out, his tone mocking, but his expression deadly serious. "You've always been more than happy to have the Sibyl of Tears at your beck and call, to have her voice at your command. Maybe you should listen to her now, when she offers you guidance once again."

Good. She was glad the prince had finally found his spine. But his father was less pleased.

"I will not have my authority questioned by ingrates," growled Hierax.

"What exactly should I be grateful for, Father?" asked Sinoe, pacing toward the dais as she spoke. The crowds peeled back from her like waves, yielding her the bright, open shore.

"For being locked in the palace for half my life? For being summoned only when you need your pet prophet, and never to be simply your daughter? For having the visions the Fates granted me twisted by that lying, treasonous wretch you call your advisor?"

With every accusation, the rumble from the crowd grew louder, and more and more eyes turned toward the dais. Toward Hierax. A fine hum of danger bristled in the air, but it was a spectacle, too. Like a public execution. No one would look away from this.

"My prophecies were meant to be a gift," proclaimed Sinoe. "A glimpse of the great patterns of the world. A chance to see the dangers that threaten our people, and make choices that would serve all humanity."

It wasn't true prophecy. Yeneris knew that. Lacheron's bangle bound Sinoe's gift. And yet even so her voice held a strange and numinous power, the cadence of the immortal, the unknowable, the divine.

"Instead, they were twisted to serve another purpose. Misinterpreted by a man who seeks only his own vicious ends. That man convinced you to give up your wife. My mother." Sinoe's godlike voice snagged slightly, becoming briefly, heartbreakingly mortal. "To wage a war and slaughter thousands for a lie. A *lie*."

Silence washed over the temple. It felt as if the entire world was waiting for the Sibyl's next words.

"But you can end it now. There is no Faithful Maiden to restore. The only looming evil is the one standing beside you. Lord Lacheron isn't your ally, Father. He's used you. Used all of us. But you can end it now. Cast him down. Imprison him. End this."

Hierax regarded his daughter in silence for a long and terrible moment. His face was flushed crimson, his features twisted with outrage.

"I will do nothing of the sort," he bellowed. "Your lies mean nothing. I am the Ember King, reborn to save this world! You will accept this, or you will be silenced."

"I will not be silenced," cried Sinoe. "I am not yours to command. I am the voice of the Fates, the Sibyl of Tears, and I say this here and now. You are not the Ember King!"

CHAPTER 39

SEPHRE

Sephre had managed to work her way through the crowd of soldiers and servants, all the way to the dais while the princess spoke. She might not be a giant serpent, but the Sibyl of Tears was still an excellent distraction.

Now Sephre skulked in the shadow of one of the pillars, leaning out to measure to distance between herself and Beroe. The agia stood beneath the bright sun, her gold ornaments glinting and shimmering, turning her into a living pillar of light. Sephre risked a glance toward Timeus. She'd sent him to the far side of the Stara Bron delegation, to try his best to spread a warning through the rest of the ashdancers. She hoped they would listen.

Sephre doubted anything she said would sway Beroe. But maybe the Sibyl of Tears would have more luck. Beroe was frowning, listening to the girl speak. Then came the final passionate accusation.

You are not the Ember King!

The temple fell utterly silent. It seemed as if the thick hot sunlight turned to amber, prisoning them in the moment. Except for one tiny flicker of movement behind the king. Someone creeping toward Hierax, almost a mirror to Sephre herself. A tall, brownskinned girl barely older than Timeus, moving with an admirably compact grace. She looked fierce and wary and infinitely capable. *Fates, I hope she's on our side.*

Hierax's thunder shattered the silence. "Enough. My daughter claims to speak for the Fates. Let us see what the Phoenix has to say. Agia Beroe, invoke the Blue Summons!"

Beroe hesitated. Sephre saw it, the tiny crease between her brows. Her wary glance toward the sibyl. Sephre clenched her fists, her body bent as if she could will the woman to reject the command. *Don't do it.*

The crease faded, swept beneath a mask of resolve. Beroe lifted her hands. Blue flames leapt to her fingers. She began to speak. "Daughter of dawn, mother of flame, child of chaos and bringer of life, I call to you, as agia of the House of Dawn. I bear the—*oof!*"

Sephre caught her around the waist, carrying them both to the ground in a tangle. She shifted, grappling Beroe's arms, keeping her weight on the other woman's legs to stop her thrashing. "Don't do it! If you care anything for the Phoenix, you can't bring her here!"

Beroe spat blue fire into her face. *That* was a trick Sephre hadn't seen Halimede use. She jerked back, her memory spinning to the last time she'd faced Beroe's flames. The scorching heat of them, blistering her skin. The scent of her own hair burning.

A spasm of old pain rippled through her shoulder. A dim voice pleaded for her mercy. A baby wailed. But she did not turn aside. She accepted who she was. Who she had been. It was part of her, but not all of her. The flames sizzled against her skin, but they did not burn. Coolness welled from her own flesh to meet them. Quenching them. Beroe gave a huff of surprise as her flames found no purchase.

"I'm not yours to burn," Sephre growled. "I belong to the House of Dusk now." She dug her fingers into Beroe's wrists, prisoning her there. Making her listen. "Lacheron means to kill the Phoenix. That's why he wanted the blade of oblivion. He's working for—"

Pain cracked sharp and sudden across the bridge of her nose. Stars shattered her vision. She tried to shake her head to clear it, which only set off a cascade of further agony. Furies' tits, she'd forgotten how much a head-butt *hurt.*

She scrabbled to right herself, to grapple Beroe again, only to find herself surrounded by a hedge of spears. Beyond the soldiers, Beroe clambered to her feet. Lips open, eyes blazing, hands entreating the sky.

"I bear the holy flame!" she cried. "I stand anointed and ready to receive you. Come, Holy One, and honor your ancient vow!"

If the world had a heartbeat, those words halted it. Sent out a ripple that surely must have been felt by every living creature, ants to elephants. Sephre felt it hum over her skin, itch at her gums, drag tears from her eyes. *Don't listen,* she screamed silently. *Don't come!*

If Sephre had still belonged to the Phoenix, maybe the god might have listened. Could she refuse the summons? Or did it bind her, that old ancient promise, even if it meant her own doom?

A brightness fell through the open oculus above, harsh and clear, trailing sparks of gold and crimson. An ache caught Sephre, a memory of flame. Not burning, but warming her, keeping her safe, driving back the nightmares. Then her vision paled, and she had to throw a hand over her eyes. The last thing she saw was Beroe, arms lifted, face turned up to welcome the brilliance, her expression rapturous.

Then a gasp of—shock? Surprise? Indignation? Sephre lowered her arm, wondering what it meant. Beroe still stood, arms spread in supplication, but her eyes were no longer on the sky. She was staring down at a fragile figure swathed in gold who stood below the dais. Princess Sinoe, the Sibyl of Tears, wreathed in a bright corona of flame that spread from her shoulders in a rippling cloak.

No. Not a cloak. *Wings.* Sephre watched, her mouth dry with wonder, as the flaming wings beat inward, into the princess, infusing her with their brightness. The girl gave the smallest sigh, like a child slipping into sleep after a restless night. Her eyes blazed with a pure white light, utterly consumed by what she carried. She lifted them to Beroe.

I have come, daughter. I honor the old promise.

Her lips moved, but the words came from elsewhere, from the sky, from the earth, from the pulse of Sephre's heart. Before her, the entire world trembled. Beroe had gone ashen, her fingers twisting into her sleeves. Sephre almost felt sorry for her. She could not have expected this. For the Phoenix to claim the princess as her vessel, rather than Beroe herself.

But for all her flaws, Beroe had never been one to quail under pressure. She gathered herself. Straightened her robes, then dipped in obeisance. "Holy One, we beg your aid. The old enemy seeks to return."

Sephre staggered to her feet, every movement leaden. The Phoenix tugged at the fabric of the world, at the flow of time. Not unlike the awe she had felt in the presence of the Serpent. Though not, she realized with an uncomfortable lurch, when he took human form. When he was Nilos. Maybe that was what he meant, when he warned that a god reforged would not be the same. The Phoenix was still wholly a god, even if she had claimed Sinoe's voice.

Yes, said the Phoenix incarnate, her eyes shimmering. *My eldest brother stirs, deep within the abyss. And he has found one of you to serve him.*

Beroe jabbed an accusing finger at Sephre. "Her! She's his creature. She's given herself to the Serpent! His poison is in her skin. She can't deny it."

Sephre stood taller. "I don't want to deny it! The Serpent is the god of death. The spirits in the labyrinth need him. The *world* needs him. Unless you'd rather let the First One rise up from the abyss and destroy us all."

Beroe blanched. Shook her head. "That's not—"

Yes. The Phoenix spoke, her flaming eyes shifting away. To Hierax. *You carry his weapon.*

"No. That's the Ember King," protested Beroe. "Your champion. Please, grant him your blessing, so he can cast down the Serpent and prevent a second cataclysm."

It is there. In his grasp.

Hierax set his hand on the hilt of the dagger.

An evil thing. Crafted by a power that would unmake this world.

"Letheko is my holy weapon," said Hierax. "I'm going to use it to save the world. I am the Ember King reborn!"

He spoke strongly, defiantly, but he was a lion roaring thistle-down. The words had no power beyond his lips. They floated, wisps of false glory, then blew away to seed themselves elsewhere.

Slowly, terribly, the Phoenix began to advance upon him. *It does not belong in this world. It must be cast back into the abyss. And all marked by its taint shall be burned away.* Her arms began to rise, crackling with white-blue flames.

The king took a step back, skin flushed bright as his mantle. His heavy eyes were wide, on the edge of panic. "Lacheron! Tell her who I am!"

Sephre had lost track of the Heron, her brain full to brimming with the Phoenix's presence. It was a mistake. He was the true enemy. Beroe was only his tool. The agia had played her part, despite all Sephre's efforts to stop her. Her only hope now was to prevent Lacheron from carrying out the rest of his plan.

But he was already moving, pulling something from his belt. She could not make out what it was. A bit of clay? Lacheron touched the thing, and the Phoenix suddenly howled, her voice mortal and immortal all at once, both of them agonized. Ribbons of darkness clawed up beneath her feet, clutching at her, prisoning her.

Furies take the man. What had he done?

Wails and protests spiraled up from the crowd. They must feel it too. A queasy lurch, as if the world had tipped just slightly askew. The terrible certainty that those ribbons of gleaming darkness were something else: the sharp talons of a vast and perilous beast, reaching up from the abyss.

Only Lacheron seemed unmoved, unaffected. "Of course, my king." He regarded the Phoenix, trapped within the cage of dark claws. She made no effort to escape. Only stood, blazing and defiant.

"This man," said Lacheron, sweeping a grand gesture to the king, "is no one."

HOUSE OF DUSK 419

Sephre wished she could take pleasure in the look on Hierax's face. The slow crumbling of those arrogant walls, the ones he'd held so fast around him all this time. But she did not dare take her eyes off the Heron, as he stalked closer and closer to the sputtering king.

"No great leader. No hero reborn. Only a fool of a man. And soon, not even that."

He moved faster than her eyes could follow, snatching Letheko from the king. Hierax gaped, only managing to draw a single shocked breath before Lacheron stabbed the blade neatly into his chest.

It was the opportunity Sephre needed. Two of the soldiers let their spears lower, watching in horror as their king toppled, as blood spurted.

She kicked out the knee of one man, grabbing his spear. Then swung it in a sharp, solid arc, slamming the other soldier across the side of his helm. The blow shuddered up into her arms. She leapt past them.

Lacheron had turned away from the dying king. Now, he pointed the bloody tip of the dagger toward the imprisoned Phoenix.

"A shame," he said. "I would have spared the girl, if I could. Her visions have been most helpful. But you claimed her, as I knew you would. You could not resist one touched as she."

The Phoenix regarded him steadily from within her prison. *You can still choose another path, Ember King. My eldest brother makes sweet promises, but he cares nothing for you. Nothing for this world. He will devour it all.*

"Good," snarled Lacheron, a sudden fury twisting his lips, darkening his eyes. "This world was broken long before the cataclysm. When the plague came it took half my people. Do you know why they called me the Ember King? Because that was what I ruled. A dying empire. A world turning to ash before my eyes. And I did everything I could to stop it. I cast myself down at your shrines. I begged you to burn away the illness. I begged the Beetle to give succor, for the Sphinx to bless our physicians with the knowledge of a cure, for the Serpent not to take any more innocents. But you did not answer. None of you." He spat. "You don't deserve this world."

Hierax had stopped moving. He had been a large man, but his body looked strangely small now, curled against the stones, a dark pool spreading beneath him. Ichos knelt beside his father, looking ill. But at Lacheron's words he stood and drew his sword. He leapt from the dais, placing himself between the man and his sister.

"You'll have to go through me first," he growled, knuckles pale on the grip.

Lacheron gave a bitter laugh. "This is far beyond you, boy. Learn from your father's mistakes."

"I have," said Ichos. "I learned not to trust you, you traitorous scum-licking pissmouth."

Oh, well done. If she lived through this, she'd have to remember some of those.

Lacheron, on the other hand, was unimpressed. He merely arched a colorless brow. "I am no traitor. I am humanity's savior. I will set us free from the callous cruelty of the fickle, so-called gods who rule our lives."

"And give us over to their brother, instead?" Ichos scoffed. "That's not freedom. That's not salvation."

The prince moved so quickly she barely had time to gasp. A single vicious slash of his sword across Lacheron's throat. A killing blow.

And yet the man did not fall. Only grimaced, lifting one hand to the bloody wound. Crimson dripped between his fingers. "It will take more than that, boy," he croaked. He lowered his hand. "Witness what the First One can offer."

Ichos swore. A stir of startled mutters spun through the uneasy crowd. The gaping slit of raw flesh shivered, knitting itself together. A heartbeat and even the blood was fading.

Lacheron went on, his voice growing stronger with every word. "Knowledge beyond any common alchemy. Life beyond the limits of our flesh. Yes, this world will fall. But it will be remade. Better. Stronger." He spread his arms wide, triumphant. "I have walked this earth for three centuries, thanks to my lord's gifts."

"Ah," said Ichos. "You know, if he'd let you keep your hair, I might actually be impressed."

Good. Keep him talking. Sephre was edging sideways, inch by inch, trying to work her way into position to strike. She would have one chance. The blade of oblivion could end her life as easily as it had Hierax's. And yet according to the Maiden—Martigone— it was also the only thing that could kill Lacheron. Which made it worth the risk.

That was when she noticed the girl again. The capable one, who had been creeping toward Hierax earlier. She had coiled herself tight, perfectly positioned so that Lacheron would not see her.

Sephre eyed Lacheron's dagger. That blade had already destroyed one god and one king. The girl might take Lacheron by surprise, but would she be quick enough to avoid that merciless blade?

The girl seemed to be harboring similar doubts. Then her gaze skimmed past Lacheron, onto Sephre. Brown eyes, deep and warm. Such young eyes, full of fury, and something else. Dedication, devotion, passion. Had her own eyes ever looked so brave and hopeful? Maybe once. Maybe still.

Sephre knew what she had to do. She straightened, abandoning her efforts to sneak up on the Heron. She'd always preferred a face-to-face battle. Today was no different.

"Ember King," she called out. "Your daughter has a message for you."

Lacheron jerked toward her, skin paling around the lips. "*You. You remember?*"

The girl made her move, swift as a serpent. Between one blink and the next she was upon Lacheron, knocking aside the dagger of oblivion, sending the weapon skittering away across the stones. She did not go after it. Instead she tore at the man, pulling something from his other hand: the red amulet he had used earlier to trap the Phoenix.

With a cry of triumph, the girl cracked the thing in two.

A pulse of light burst from the split clay. The dark claws holding Sinoe abruptly shuddered, then splintered, releasing the princess. She straightened slowly, sheathed in pale flame. With a delicate shake of her shoulders, the Phoenix spread her flaming wings once more.

Her eyes blazed silver-blue, pitiless as the noon sun. Sephre quivered as they settled upon her, feeling all the heaviness of her former vows. The ones she had turned from. She knew, in the depths of her bones, that it would be no more than a cosmic wink for this terrible, bright creature to smite her then and there.

Thank you. The words resonated in her head, in her chest. The Phoenix dipped her head, speaking to all of them. *You have done me a great service. This trial is past.*

"You're very welcome," said Ichos, with enviable poise. He cleared his throat. "In that case, may we please have my sister back?"

But there will be others.

The uncanny silver-blue eyes of the Phoenix returned to Sephre for one more heartbeat. *Be ready.* Then she flared so brightly that it bled all color and shape from the world. The beat of flaming wings filled Sephre's ears. A breath of hot, sweet air washed over her. And below the dais, the slim, golden princess crumpled to the ground as a great rush of brightness leapt from her into the sky.

Sephre was aware of the other girl, the quick, clever one, crying out. And more voices. Ichos. Beroe. Soldiers and ashdancers. But the roar dimmed, because her own work was not yet done.

The Fates had made that clear enough. She didn't even need to take a single step. Letheko was right there, at her feet. Waiting for her.

All she had to do was take it. Then she could end this. End Lacheron. She closed her eyes briefly, a lump clotting her throat.

Seph. Please, whispered Zander. Swallowing the bitterness, she bent and reached for the dagger.

It seemed to ripple beneath her fingers, jittery, not quite a part of this world. Her flesh recoiled from it. This was a dagger that could shatter souls. She didn't want to touch it.

Good. This doesn't make you a hero any more than the last time you snatched up a sword. It's just what needs to be done. So do it. She forced her fingers to tighten. It was suddenly too hard to breathe.

Lacheron lay another five paces further. He was only just shoving himself upright when she knelt beside him and pressed the tip of the blade to his throat. He froze, searching her face. Briefly, she caught something vulnerable in his expression. A yearning that she ached to look upon, no matter how she despised the man.

Then it fled. He laughed, long and bitter. "No. You hate me as much as she did. But *she* still loved me, even when she discovered how I'd used her. I could see it in her eyes, even as she cursed me and swore she would stop me." His throat bobbed as he drew in a long breath. "My daughter is gone. She burned herself out of this world. Which means that dagger is useless to you."

A chill rippled through her. She fought to keep her grip on the weapon. "You're lying. Letheko can kill a god."

"*Letheko,*" he scoffed. "I thought as much. Only someone who can name that dagger truly can wield it. And that is not her name."

She wanted to protest. And yet his words woke an echo. The vision in the waters. She had said something similar. *It had a different name, once. So much has been forgotten. Cast into the flames and burned away.*

"You see?" Lacheron's lips twisted into a wry smile. "You cannot stop me, captain. Even if it takes another three centuries."

No. Not again. *Never* again. She did not accept this. Not everything was lost to the flames. The Maiden might have burned her own memory to ash, her story might be warped and woven into other tales, but something had endured. *Remember.* Halimede's dying words. But was she talking about Sephre?

Because there was someone else who now remembered things long lost.

I remember her name. Martigone. Use it well.

"Martigone," she said, and watched the arrogance bleed out of him, as if the word were itself a blade. Which, she realized, shivering, it was. Letheko, the blade of oblivion, the forgotten dagger, had been named for the woman who wielded it. A woman who had burned herself out of the world in penance, and left only echoes.

Sephre felt those echoes, rippling through her own life. Through this moment, staring into the eyes of a man who had used her, too. Sent her to kill, never mind the cost to her own soul.

His gaze flicked to the blade in her hand, then back to her face. All she saw in him now was grim resignation. "Go on, then," he said. "Better oblivion than endless pain and suffering."

Yes. He had suffered. Like so many others. Timeus. Dolon. Vyria. Ichos. Sinoe. Even Sephre herself.

And it had twisted him. In all his three centuries, he had learned nothing but how to make others suffer. It had made him cruel and rapacious and merciless.

What had he said, just before he stabbed the dagger into Hierax?

No great leader. No hero reborn. Only a fool of a man. And soon, not even that.

She plunged the dagger of oblivion into the Ember King's throat, and he was no more.

CHAPTER 40

YENERIS

Yeneris had no memory of crossing the dais. One moment she was snapping the clay key, and the next she was beside Sinoe's crumpled form, scooping the princess into her arms. "Sinoe? Fates, Sinoe, say something!"

She pressed shaking fingers to Sinoe's throat, feeling for a pulse, then nearly collapsed when she felt the faint flicker. A slight groan wheezed from Sinoe's lips, followed by something unintelligible.

"What was that?" She leaned closer, trying to catch the words.

"I said, 'Being a god is surprisingly painful.'" Sinoe moaned, lifting a hand to pinch the bridge of her nose. "I know it sounds wonderful, all that power and glory, but honestly, it's worse than the morning after Ichos and I stole a pot of milk-wine. Ugh. Yen, do you think you could possibly carve my brain out from my skull? Just for a little while?"

"No," Yeneris said, with a choked laugh. "That would be a fairly serious dereliction of duty for a royal bodyguard."

"All right, then." Sinoe closed her eyes, drawing in a long-suffering breath. "You're fired."

Yeneris huffed. "That's the reward I get for saving your life?"

"Mmm. Yes. You'll be much happier, I promise."

"You really want me to go?" Yeneris started to pull back. Surely Sinoe was joking. She couldn't seriously mean to send her away, after . . . well, after *everything*.

"No, you ridiculous fool." Sinoe clung to her collar, pulling her close again. "I want you here. I just don't want you distracted all the time, keeping watch for assassins and firebombs and sharks."

"I don't think you need to worry about sharks in the city, princess," said Yeneris.

Sinoe rolled her eyes. "That's not the point."

"What is the point, then?"

"I want to be able to distract you myself." Sinoe arched her brows meaningfully.

Yeneris choked, feeling a hot flush rising up her cheeks.

"Don't worry," Sinoe said cheerfully. "We averted the apocalypse. We can flirt all we like now."

Yeneris dragged in a breath. "What if I want more than flirting?"

Sinoe's teasing smile melted into something sweeter and more serious. Her fingers still clutched the collar of Yeneris's tunic. "Like what? What do you want?"

Yeneris didn't answer with words. But she knew, in the sweetness that followed, that Sinoe understood. And that she had the same answer.

You. Always you.

=====

Yeneris paced along the edge of the terrace, keeping watch over the tomb. She knew it wasn't necessary. From what the balewalker, Sister Sephre, had told them, things were well again in the world of the dead. The Serpent restored, the skotoi contained within the labyrinth of the dead. And on top of that, there were at least a dozen royal guards along the perimeter of the necropolis, to ensure that Ichos and Sinoe could have their privacy at the tomb.

But old habits were hard to break. Yeneris tapped the hilt of her sword, considering the best options if she needed to whisk Sinoe away from this place.

King Hierax has been interred quietly a few days earlier. There had been no grand funeral procession, no bards singing his deeds. They had hung mourning banners from the palace, but even those had been simple indigo cloth, with no sigil, and Yeneris suspected that most folk who did bow their heads to them were mourning something else—something more. The loss of identity. The loss of certainty.

And what did Sinoe and her brother mourn, Yeneris wondered, watching the pair of them standing in front of the stone niche. Ichos had one arm around his sister's shoulders, and she leaned into him, united in whatever it was they felt.

Sorrow. There must be some of that. He was their father. They had loved him. Some parts of him, at least. Even if those parts had dwindled over time, replaced by the brutal, greedy man whose thirst for glory had murdered thousands. And now he was gone. His spirit shattered by the blade of oblivion.

Perhaps he deserved it. Lacheron might have been the secret master, but Hierax wasn't simply a tool. Sinoe had given her father a chance to free himself, to do the right thing, and he'd rejected it. He couldn't accept losing the false vision he had of himself, even after all the terrible things that vision had caused. The thousands of dead, both Helissoni and Bassaran. The destruction of Yeneris's home.

Because it was, still, her home. A part of her would always yearn for it. Would be looking for blue doors, for smooth white domes against an island sky. Would ache for the scent of her mother's hair, sweet with lily oil, for the thrum of goldwings at dawn. For a life that had been stolen. She thought of her mother's words. *Sometimes the world is like that, love. We can't always get what we want. We have to choose one path, and give up another.* For now, this was her place. Ensuring that the victory they'd won remained.

Ichos and Sinoe turned away from the tomb, and began making their way back toward Yeneris. She considered the prince, now soon-to-be king. He hadn't wanted it. In fact, when Hura had told him he had to claim the title, his reply involved stuffing the crown into a very rude and frankly physically impossible location.

But they had all agreed. As Hura said, an empty throne was an invitation to war. And that was the last thing the world needed just now. It could not be Sinoe; her gift bound her too tightly to the Fates for her to be accepted as queen. Still, Ichos would soon have the assistance of another queen. The dowager, Kizare, was already on her way from Scarthia to rejoin her children and help ease the transition. And she had promised to return Tami, as well.

"Keeping the sharks away, I see?" Sinoe greeted Yeneris, her smile bright in the dusky gloom. It was nearing sunset, rosy streaks staining the light that streamed narrow windows. Sinoe's hair caught the glints, the ruddy waves brighter now that she no longer needed to dye it.

Ichos gave Yeneris a polite if slightly skeptical nod, continuing on, leaving her alone with Sinoe.

"I still don't think he trusts me," Yeneris said.

"He doesn't trust anyone, not even himself," said Sinoe. "But that's his problem." She seized Yeneris's hand, tugging her away from the tomb. "I've had enough of this place."

They exited the necropolis through a heavy wooden gate. Freshly carved, Yeneris thought, frowning as something tickled her memory. They were halfway down the steps into the plaza beyond when she remembered. She stopped, dragging Sinoe to halt beside her.

"This is where it started," she said, her gaze tracing the stones, the four faded statues of the god-beasts. There were no fire spinners, no crowds, and thankfully no skotoi, but this was where they had been standing. If not the exact spot, then no more than a foot from it.

"Where what started?" Sinoe's lips quirked in a way that suggested she knew exactly what Yeneris was talking about.

"Where I first realized you were . . ." Yeneris floundered.

"The love of your life? The flower of your destiny?" suggested Sinoe.

"That you weren't the person I thought you were."

Sinoe laughed, a clear whoop that set several pigeons winging away in protest. "That's fair. So you never expected we'd be back here? Like this?" She swung their linked hands, squeezing.

"No," answered Yeneris, truthfully. But the spark in Sinoe's eyes made her frown. "Did you?"

Sinoe shrugged, looking away.

"Did you?" Yeneris asked again. "Did you see all this? Did you know?"

"Of course I knew," said Sinoe, turning back again. "But not because of any vision." Her gaze held Yeneris, wide and deep and glittering.

"Careful." Yeneris lifted a hand to brush at the corner of Sinoe's eye. "The bangle's gone. If you weep—"

"I'm not afraid of what I might see," said Sinoe fiercely. "I know you're going to leave someday. Bassara still needs you."

A shiver rippled up Yeneris's spine. The words had the tinge of prophecy. The ache of homesickness she'd thrust deep surged up suddenly, leaving her breathless. Could it be true? Possibilities spun out, like fireflies in a summer twilight. *Someday.*

"Someday," she repeated, her throat tight, hand still pressed to Sinoe's cheek. "But not today. Today I'm exactly where I want to be. Where I need to be."

"Where's that?" whispered Sinoe.

"With you."

CHAPTER 41

SEPHRE

It was strange, being back in Stara Bron. Sephre would have preferred to go straight to the garden, to spend the afternoon with Timeus, to collect seeds and roots, and to make sure he remembered to trim back the gauzebloom now that it was going past. Then maybe a stop in the infirmary, to share a cup of medicinal wine with Abas and make sure they had plenty of tonic. She wasn't sure when she might next return.

That was partly up to the agia. Which was the main reason Sephre was not in the garden or the infirmary, but here, in the small office with sunlight streaming in to gild the agia's mantle, making the pale cloth shimmer.

No doubt Beroe had positioned herself intending just such an effect.

"Agia," said Sephre, dipping her head slightly.

"Sister Sephre." Beroe's politeness was frosty, though that was understandable, given the circumstances. "Please. Sit." She gestured to the couch beside the window. It was new, and she had moved Halimede's desk into the other corner.

Sephre sat, smoothing the hem of her blue habit. She noticed Beroe eyeing the green ripples along her sleeves. "Thank you for inviting me."

The corners of Beroe's mouth pinched. "Of course," she said. "We're in your debt. You saved the Phoenix."

Sephre hadn't expected that. But then, she hadn't expected Beroe to head-butt her either. She narrowed her eyes. "You don't need to play games with me. Tell me what you want."

HOUSE OF DUSK 431

Beroe rolled her eyes. "You're going to have to learn to play games if you're to be the agia of the House of Dusk."

"There is no House of Dusk," said Sephre.

"Maybe not yet. But there will be. King Ichos has recognized you. And the stories are already spreading. About the wicked Ember King and the Faithful Maiden's return."

Now it was Sephre's turn to roll her eyes. "I'm not the Faithful Maiden." Not in the way Beroe meant it, at least.

Beroe gave her a weary look. "Stories matter, Sephre. What people believe can be as important as what truly is."

"You mean like when they believe that the Serpent was an evil death god and that they need to summon the Phoenix incarnate to stop him?"

"Yes," said Beroe, frostily. "Exactly like that. I was wrong, Sephre. I understand that now. I believed the wrong stories. Which is why we need to work together now. To make certain it doesn't happen again."

Sephre chewed the inside of her cheek. She thought of the last words Sinoe had spoken, infused with the god of flame. *This trial is past. But there will be others.*

She had unmade Lacheron, the Ember King. But he had been only a man, in service to a greater power. One she still did not entirely comprehend. The First One. An ancient god, bound within the abyss by his siblings, the four other children of Chaos. Except that one of the seals had already been broken. And no doubt the First One would continue to try to break the rest.

"We of the House of Dawn will continue our work in this world," said Beroe. "But there are other worlds. Other dangers. And you are . . . only one woman."

Sephre shook her head. "Speak plainly."

"I will send some of the ashdancers to help you," said Beroe. "Until your own numbers grow larger. We will . . . work together. An alliance. As we did in the days before the cataclysm. Maybe in time we can even reach out to the others. The Houses of Noon and Midnight."

She knew she should accept the offer. There were still many skotoi loose within the labyrinth, and while the Serpent was no doubt hunting them, best to ensure they were dealt with quickly. And . . . and it would be nice to have some company.

"Can you spare them?" she asked.

"Our numbers are small, yes." Beroe looked away, frowning at the small shrine, the golden Phoenix glimmering there. "Especially since . . . since the attack."

Her jaw worked. "I didn't know it was Lacheron who summoned them. That he killed Agia Halimede. I never would have—" She caught herself, cutting her gaze back to Sephre. "You probably don't believe me, but I truly didn't know."

"I believe you." Sephre breathed deep. Released the breath. Then she stood. "I accept your offer, Agia Beroe."

Then she turned, and set off for the gardens.

===

It was another week before she made her way back to Stara Sidea. She arrived midmorning, and spent several hours planting the bits of root and tubers she'd brought with her from the garden at Stara Bron. She had discovered a small cloister within the canyon, walled by stone but open to the sky. Overgrown, disused, but with rich soil beneath the weeds. There was even a well. She imagined it blooming, tangled with vines. Maybe even an apprentice, carefully sorting through last season's bindweed.

When that work was done, she washed, and changed into a clean habit, and combed her hair. It meant nothing, except that she didn't want to present herself a dusty, disheveled mess to the god of death. Assuming that he would be there.

I'll wait for you at the undying shore.

By then it was nearly dusk. She lit a lamp and took it with her, descending the same winding stair. She had not come this way since Nilos had first brought her here. Her heart thudded loud, echoing each step at first, then quickening, drumming faster as she emerged into the cavern.

He stood at the edge of the water. The barge was there as well, drawn up onto the sand, the pole laid neatly across the keel. She thought of the last time they had stood here, together, and heat bloomed up her throat. But that had been Nilos. The man.

This was the Serpent.

She paced up to him. Hesitated, still uncertain what sort of greeting was appropriate.

Strangely, he looked just as uncertain. "Sephre." The word was a sigh, a release. "I'm glad . . . you came."

Had he been going to say something else? She was still debating how to respond when he spoke again. "I've been waiting."

Another flush of heat. She could have come sooner. But there had been business. Accounts to give, scribes to record her words, a meeting with the new king, who had fortunately forgiven her for throwing a sword at his head the last time they'd met. Royal advisors insisting that she be properly attired for various public events to reassure the people of Helisson that there was no looming cataclysm, that the danger of the skotoi and the Ember King was past. Or at least, under control. And then Stara Bron, Beroe and Timeus and Dolon and Abas. And another visit, strange and awkward and beautiful, to see an old man and an old woman and a little girl who was full of stories about her uncle. And a dog who had earned her name because she had a trick of pulling a blanket over herself during thunderstorms.

"I . . . I'm sorry. I've been busy."

"Ah. Yes. Busy saving the world." The corners of his eyes crinkled. He wasn't angry.

But the words plucked at the wound, the one she'd been carrying since that day. She touched a hand to the hilt of the dark blade that hung from her waist in a plain leather scabbard. Sephre had not taken it off. Even when she slept or bathed it was in her sight, within her grasp.

"I shattered the Ember King's spirit," she said. "Will he come back? Like you did?"

"I don't know," said the Serpent. "He was a mortal. But he had been given power from the First One. Only time will tell."

She nodded, chewing the inside of her cheek.

"He was dangerous," said the Serpent. "He had the chance to be something better, but he became something terrible. You removed that danger from the world. But . . . it wasn't a decision you should have had to make."

It wasn't a decision she ever wanted to make again. "I can't keep this," she said, starting to unbuckle the dagger. "You should—"

He jerked back from her, heels splashing into the water, setting free a lacy web of ripples. "No. I can't."

"Why?"

"It holds too much power."

"You're a god."

A strange mix of humor and sadness crossed his face. "Mostly."

"Mostly?" She rocked back on her heels. "What does that mean?"

"I . . ."

"Nilos?"

She hadn't meant to say his name. But the seed had been planted, and had grown, for all the lack of sun.

"Sometimes, yes."

She stepped closer, watching his face like a sailor watched the skies, hoping for the wind to send her home, but fearing the storm.

"It's never happened before," he said. "A god, bound for so long in mortal form."

"You took mortal form long enough to get stabbed and scattered into bits."

He glanced away. "That was different. And . . . painful. Being Nilos was . . . not painful."

"Not painful," she repeated, wryly. "Just what every girl wants to hear."

His lips curved. His smile broke open a tight knot in her chest.

"Come with me," he said then, reaching for her hand, pulling her toward the barge. "I want to show you something."

She let him draw her closer. The boat creaked as she stepped into it. "What?"

He took up the pole, sliding it into the silt, shoving them out into the waters. His grin gleamed wickedly. "I've started to make some changes to the labyrinth. I was hoping you might approve. I know you have strong aesthetic opinions about the netherworld."

She settled herself into the prow. "Bloody waterfalls and towers of skulls?"

"All in good time. For now, I thought I'd start with the guard dog."

Sephre cast her mind back, scouring for the conversation. "With three heads and horns?"

"Oh, something much better than that. He's just a pup now, but I think he shows great promise. So. Would you like to meet him?"

"Yes," she told the god of death. "I would."

ACKNOWLEDGMENTS

I had to be brave to write this book. Firstly, to believe that I could write it, especially after I'd spent twenty years trying and failing, producing a half-dozen trunked manuscripts. Secondly, to allow myself to take the time to work on it with no promise it would sell. And thirdly, to let these characters truly get into my heart and be as messy and complicated as they needed to be.

The reason I could do all that is that I had, and have, an amazing group of human beings (and one dog!) supporting me:

My amazing agent, Pam Gruber, who helped me navigate some very stressful and confusing publishing waters, and has been a fierce champion for my books and my career.

My brilliant editor, Navah Wolfe, who saw into the heart of this story and knew exactly how to make it even stronger, whose edits continually challenge and inspire me.

Assistant editor Madeline Goldberg, who works incredibly hard to keep everything organized behind-the-scenes; art director Katie Anderson, who guided my gorgeous cover to life; production supervisor Liz Koehler, who ensured this book actually became a real, physical object; Laura Fitzgerald, the mastermind behind publicity and marketing; superhuman managing editor Joshua Starr; and last but certainly not least, DAW publisher Betsy Wollheim.

Serena Malyon, who is responsible for the glorious cover art.

A number of talented colleagues who provided vital critical feedback and encouragement at various stages in this book's development: Rebecca Anderson, Stephanie Burgis, Melissa Caruso, Megan Crewe, Hilary Harwell, Anne Nesbet, and Jenn Reese.

438. ACKNOWLEDGMENTS

I will be forever grateful to everyone who supported me during some particularly anxious and uncertain publishing times, especially Kate Testerman, Hannah Fergesen, Paul and Cynthia Van Der Werf, David Van Der Werf, Maureen Drouin, Tracy Banghart, and all my friends in the Memory & Reason community. And to my good boy Titan, who I made sure took plenty of belly-rub and walking breaks.

Lastly, always, and ever, thank you to my beloved Bob, who I would trust at my side no matter where the journey takes us, even into the Labyrinth of Souls itself.